BY LLOYD R. PRENTICE

Freein' Pancho
Aya Takeo Vol I-III - a manga

Lloyd R. Prentice

The Gospel of Ashes

A Thriller

WRITERS GLEN
PUBLICATIONS

Marshfield, MA

Writers Glen Publications

Marshfield, MA

Published 2012

Printed in the United States of America

ISBN: 978-0-9825892-2-9

Library of Congress Control Number: 2011940433

cover design: Pinkham Advertising & Design - www.pinkhamadvertising.com

To Jay and the Writing Group — Andrea, Wiesy, Barbara P, Jenny, Brian M, Lynn, Barbara W. Thanks all.

Visit Lloyd's blog: *lloydrprentice.com*

I am come to send fire on the earth

Luke 12:49

...my greatest fear is that domestic extremists in this country will somehow become emboldened to the point of carrying out a mass-casualty attack.... That is what keeps me up at night.

Daryl Johnson
former senior domestic terrorist analyst
Department of Homeland Security

It doesn't seem like much of a stretch to foresee a day when a 'secessionist' group... will use their U.S. passports, white skins, and solid-citizen standing as a cover for importing a weapon of mass destruction to 'liberate' the rest of us from our federal government's 'tyranny' and/or to 'punish' some city like New York, known as the U.S. 'abortion capital' or San Francisco as the place that 'those gays have taken over.'

Frank Schaeffer
author
Sex, Mom, and God: How the Bible's Take on Sex Led to Crazy Politics and How I learned to Love Woman (and Jesus) Anyway

Strategic attacks are possible with a network of less than 70 people.

John Robb
http://globalguerrillas

Prologue

"WHY CAN'T I just say no?" the young park ranger mutters. He leans into the familiar turns, pumps up the rise.

Usually he would be more alert to the subtle changes of the passing season, but today his sensibilities are shadowed by his brother's all-too-familiar supplication.

"Sucks totally, bro. I put that company on the map. Made the boss man look bad so he knifed me. So, just a couple thou or whatever, little bro— you know until this new gig comes through."

Three years on the job and the young ranger knows every grade and easy glide along these park trails.

A lifetime of promises and disappointment and he knows every missed hurdle, slip, and descent of his big brother's life.

On drizzly days, icy like today, few hardy souls venture out on bikes. Few souls venture out at all. On days like today, usually, the ranger would find joy with the wet cold and swish of his tires.

But today his mind is locked in painful mind loops that inevitably end in— "Why?"

But now all thought ends.

Topping the rise he glances down the rain-slicked slope toward the river— sees a beige Audi mired in ice-crusted mud where it hadn't been when he'd passed just hours ago.

He peddles hard, then grips his hand brakes as he slaloms down the slope. He jumps off, nearly tumbles into the riverside slush— eyes fixed on the red-splattered spider-web that mars the driver-side glass.

He unsnaps his Motorola to call it in. Presses the talk button. Nothing. He flicks the power switch. Nothing. He'd grabbed it out of the charging bin just this morning. He turns the unit over in his hand, sees

1

the small swatch of tape— *defective.*

"Wonderful," he thinks. But no matter. The dispatcher would just ask more questions than he can answer.

The front wheels of the Audi are sunk axle deep in mud.

He walks his bike around behind the Audi, noting deep tire tracks weaving down the grassy slope, uncomfortably aware of the dark shape hulking in the driver's seat.

Against all training he opens the front passenger door— studies the figure slumped over the steering wheel. Tall, thin, wispy blond hair. The suit quality but, now, forever blood splattered.

The young ranger is beyond thought and feeling. He leans across the passenger seat, draws back, revolted by the rusty smell of blood, faint note of feces. Then he notices the envelope on the passenger seat, unsealed, creamy paper with expensive texture— discreet K Street return address.

Inside he finds two pages, crisply typed:

```
Sealy, Marchesni, and Devine
1279 K Street N.W.
Washington, D.C. 20005

Why?

As a young buck, heady with the conceits of Boalt Hall,
facts for me were hard-- gleaming-- so many black and white
marbles to be dropped through the calculus of logic to reveal
indisputable truth.

Then, as a counselor to our much reviled Chief, I was all
too willingly, indeed, eagerly, seduced by the singular
truth of power:  loyalty to power is the only truth.

I learned to adjust the lighting-- shift point of view--
transform white marbles into black; black to white.
```

Holy crap, he thinks, a hitter.

He takes a second look at the address, glances at the contorted face, tries to ignore the smudged entry wound just below the faintly stubbled chin. The eyes, shocked, open wide, bring the situation home. He suppresses the need to vomit, takes a deep breath, gags.

In the years since, I have lifted the veil of conceit to
reveal hard realities. I have toured the places without
names.

I have sought out and inhaled the toxic emanations-- the
direct and indirect human consequences of my artful opinions.

I have confronted the hollowed faces-- witnessed the broken
minds and bodies, vicariously succored the scars of bruised,
burned, and shredded skin, ill-healed limbs-- I've heard
in life and dreams the screams, pleas, moans, cries, and
whimpers.

I can no longer bear the gaze of family, friends-- seeing
in their eyes, real or not, questions and accusations.

By my acts I have remanded all that commends me as human
to the black dungeons of guilt and remorse. And the stench
fills my mouth with bile.

So why this?

Faint pain knifes the young ranger's lower back. His hand shakes un-
controllably. He backs out, straightens, looks across the brown turbulence of river, scans the stark line of trees on the far shore. He sees
nothing, no one, but feels somehow observed, eyes, omniscient eyes
watching his very move. He turns, looks up toward the path. Misty
drizzle against a gray patch of sky.

I've come to understand that facts are progeny of method.

Compromise method and facts become indeterminate, truth
subordinate to power.

Method, then, is key. Know a man's methods and you know
his heart.

As a young buck, heady with the conceits of Boalt Hall,
I pledged allegiance to the Constitution of the United States
of America.

But in the seat of power I conveniently filed this sacred
oath "For Times of Peace Only." These were Times of War--

National Security at stake. Ruthless Realism rules. War
trumps all. If the Commander wills, anything goes.

To put it bluntly, I swore loyalty to the Constitution of
the United States of America and then-- I betrayed it.

And now they're back, presuming on the old loyalties.

The ranger stares again at the river— watches a twisted branch roll in
the current, sink, surface further downstream. A bloated plastic bag
filled with who knows what bobs in the muddy water. Blood pulses in
his ears.

Now they're back demanding that I turn dubious facts into
bullets for their unholy war. They were good men, patriotic
all. But fear and power corrupted their souls-- as ambition
did mine.

To their minds the illusion of the Ticking Bomb justifies
all. But now the ticking bomb is no longer the infernal
device of the terrorist's perverted world view but, rather,
the harsh judgment of history.

I've come to to accept this stern verdict. They haven't.
I've looked into my soul and found it irredeemably corrupted.
They haven't.

The course they've set is the ultimate perversion of power
and I in my craven weakness know not how to stop them. I
know not even whom to trust. So there's only-- this.

I pray that the right people listen-- listen, heed, and
act. They must be stopped.

Ruth-- Please forgive a husband and father who has faced
hard choices and chosen wrong. I make this one last choice
for the sake of our children.

Please accept this choice as, I pray, the correct one. I
love you and the children so so much. I just don't know
what else to do.

Donald F. Devine, (former and unworthy) Esq.

The young ranger shudders. But now he senses a presence. He starts to turn but feels hard steel behind his ear.

"The letter, please."

"What—"

"Don't talk. Just hand back the letter. Don't look! The envelope too—"

"Who—"

"Don't look! Now, I want you all the way in the car, sit."

"But—"

"He won't hurt you. Keep your eyes on the steering wheel."

"But—"

"Don't look! Just sit. That's good."

"I—"

"Shush. Now, pick up the pistol on the floor under Mr. Devine's feet."

"But I—"

"Look, I'm sure you're a bright enough young man. I'm sure you know by now that you are going to die. The question is, do you die with honor? Or do you die slowly, in excruciating pain?"

"Why?"

"Wrong place. Wrong time."

A hand clasps the back of the young ranger's neck. He feels a thick thumb press mercilessly under his ear into the back of his jaw, pushing his head down between his knees. Meanwhile, the cold metal, unmistakably the muzzle of a gun, is pressing with unbearable force into his temple.

He screams.

"Pick up the pistol now. If you even think of turning my way, you'll be dead before your muscles respond."

The young ranger slumps, picks up the pistol, shaking. It drops, earning a sharp jab to his temple. He picks it up again.

The young ranger senses the dark presence shift position, feels the muzzle pressed hard now into the back of his neck.

"That's good. Let me help."

The young man feels the hand, strong, gloved in latex, cover his; feels the thumb snaking into the trigger guard. He feels the press of a body against the back of his shoulder, the heat of another's flesh behind his ear. He hears even breath roar across his ear, smells cinnamon.

Now he begins to shut down with fear. He feels the muzzle of Devine's pistol press up under his chin.

"Why?"

He can barely get it out, his teeth clenched so tight. And there's too little time until—

"Come Reunion," the missionary says.

He takes time for artful rearrangement. When he's done the scene looks like a homosexual tryst gone bad— even better than the original scenario.

"Rest in peace, little lads," he says. "May the Lord take your souls."

The missionary closes the car door gently, looks down. Nice bike, he thinks. He worries about his footprints in the mud. But not much. His liaison in the park police will take care of it.

I

Kimberly

THE LAST thing Kimberly expected when she stepped into Temple's office was termination.

Now, she smells the funky testosterone of the two security guards standing behind her chair.

"These two gentlemen will escort you off premises."

"But I need my purse— coat—"

"Sorry. Your office is sealed. Your personal belongings will be delivered by courier when we've finished our investigation—"

"Investigation?"

"Oh yes. Serious issues here."

"But you haven't told me anything except— except— you're fired thank you very much."

"Sorry."

"So what have I done?"

Temple shrugs.

"I need my car keys."

"Sorry, your car is impounded."

"But you— can't do this."

"We can."

"I'll sue big time, mister man!"

"I have a copy here of the agreement you signed when you accepted your position. I can assure you that it covers this situation thoroughly. You have a copy in your termination packet."

"Don't think the media won't hear about this—"

"And here's the confidentiality statement you signed. You'll find a copy in your termination packet."

"Temple, what's going on here? I thought we were friends."

"Sorry, Kimberly. Think I like this?"

"Then why are you doing it?"

"I do what I'm told."

"Always the good German."

"You stepped on the wrong toes,"

"Well, *Seig Heil!* and screw you too. You haven't heard the end of this, you shit. You're not the only one with friends in high places."

"Kimberly, I'd strongly advise you to go quietly. You're lucky we're not pursuing criminal charges— yet."

Kimberly stands. Each guard grips an upper arm. She struggles, but they grip harder, almost to the point of pain. One guard has a shaved head, purple veins and razor nicks. The other a Fu Man Chu mustache over an ax-thin face.

"Let's make this easy, ma'am," shaved head says.

The guards shove Kimberly through the door. Last thing, she sees Temple pick up his phone, hears him mumble softly.

They near frog march her through the cubical bays. People stare— avoid eye contact— people she's known around the office. All she can think about are the cut flowers she'd brought in that morning to freshen up her desk, golden irises.

Suddenly she feels feverish, sticky with cold perspiration.

They frog march her to the elevators. Fu Man Chu presses LL. Now she feels fear.

"Where are you taking me?"

The guards are silent.

"Where?"

"You'll find out soon enough."

In the lower level, an area Kimberly has never seen, they frog march her to a white security pickup. White Toyota. Like the Taliban, she thinks.

"In—"

They drive up the ramp and out bay doors into glaring sun. The two fat bodies press in on her. Rank masculinity. She tries to shrink into herself. They drive past the shift-workers' parking lot and up to a secondary plant exit that Kimberly never knew existed. The security hut is unattended. They stop.

Kimberly notes the steel teeth rising out of the exit ramp. A skeletal sphere of tumbleweed, caught on a tooth, quivers in the desert wind.

Kimberly releases her breath, feels violated by foul breath and body odor, stale cigarette smoke. Fu Man Chu presses hard against her, removes his wallet, swipes his ID. Kimberly watches the yellow arm rise, the steel teeth sink between two steel strips.

They drive through the gate, creep onto the frontage road and brake; no cars to be seen.

"Out, Miss," baldy says. "And have a nice day."

Kimberly watches the white truck creep back through the gate.

Unseasonably sharp winter wind knifes through her thin ivory silk blouse. Her fingers, moist with perspiration, pucker the surface of the termination packet, raise tiny rolls of fibrous cruft. She turns 360 degrees. Stares back toward the plant.

Razor wire, rising beyond a dry sandy ditch, stretches in both directions, an SVS Aerospace sign, aggressive logo, wired to the chain link every hundred yards.

Tumbleweed clogs the ditch, is banked up against the fence. Beyond the wire the four-story administration building now seems so far, so alien. Her eyes sweep the vast sea of cars. The assembly plant, low and dark, stretches beyond sight.

Kimberly follows the razor wire for a quarter of a mile, stops to stare through the wire at the small landing strip, the concrete control tower, just beyond Facility C.

She sees a corporate Gulfstream powering up on the apron, red navigation lights flashing, three black Ford Expeditions moving in formation toward the hanger bays.

Kimberly chokes back tears.

"I've failed you," she says.

Now Kimberly turns toward the highway that flanks the frontage road, becomes aware of semis swishing past, trailing swirls of sand.

Across the two lanes south, the sand and cactus median, the two lanes north, she sees the silvery arc of irrigation spray, alfalfa, and cows, some grazing. One cow seems to stare at her, but she knows it's too far to know for sure.

Heat mirages ripple off the far desert. Purple mesas rise above the horizon.

Kimberly walks, pauses, looks down at her week-old Via Spigas.

Scrimped two pay periods to buy them. Her comfortable shoes, the Reeboks she wears into work, are in her office, under her desk.

Already her feet hurt— hot and swelling from the seering blacktop.

A white F-150 panel van whips around her on the frontage road, brakes, backs up. The driver leans across the passenger seat, opens the door.

"Ya'll look like a lady could use a ride."

Kimberly starts to thank the driver, climb in, but takes a second look.

"No— No thank you," she says. "Someone's on the way."

"Suit yourself, bitch," the driver says, slamming the door, peeling away with the sound and smell of burning rubber.

Six miles. Six miles to a phone. She can do it— even if her feet are killing her. She walks.

Now a Saab approaches from behind, passes and stops. The driver door opens.

"Kimberly? My God—"

"Mika?"

"I saw those thugs drag you through the office. What's going on, Sweetie?"

Kimberly starts to cry, but holds back.

"Get in, Sweetie. You look like a girl could use a drink."

The Shadow Lounge is nearly deserted this time of day, too late for the last of the lunch crowd, too early for happy hour.

"How can they do this to you?" Mika asks, a whisper over the distant drone of a vacuum cleaner.

Mika has an exotic look. Pale blue eyes. Kimberly envies her sleek near-white hair, flawless pampered complexion. Her white tailored suit, accessories, are worth a month of Kimberly's salary— former salary.

"You didn't really do anything— wrong— did you Sweetie?

"I mean—"

Kimberly so wants to confide, but holds back.

Mika's office is on the top floor, three doors down from the CEO. Something to do with strategic planning.

Kimberly hears a soft musical note. "Sorry," Mika says, "My cell—

"Yes," she says into the phone, smiling at Kimberly as she slips the tiny smart phone back into her purse.

"You're very talented, Kimberly," Mika says. "I know you'll land on your feet. It's so pleasant here, out of the office, just us girls. Would you like a refill?"

It's near dark when Mika drops Kimberly off in front of her small faux adobe home. Kimberly steps out of the car, glances back, sees Mika lift her smart phone.

Kimberly feels warm and woozy from the drinks, a hollow pit in her stomach as she thinks about her lost job, her daughter's tuition—mortgage payments.

She opens her front door, feels suddenly stricken.

Her home is trashed. Floor to ceiling— holes punched in the Sheetrock, lamps broken, mantle pieces smashed on the flagstone hearth.

She sobs. Enters her daughters bedroom. Even her daughter's Coldplay posters have been ripped from the walls. She grips her termination packet in both hands, nearly tears it in two. Thank God her daughter is in a dorm this year.

Her daughter— My God!

She turns for her iPhone, but it's in her purse— locked in her office. She steps across books with broken spines, pried up floor tiles. Her kitchen cabinets— swept clean; china and glass shattered on the yellow vinyl. Cabinet drawers are strewn haphazardly, contents scattered. Her refrigerator door stands open, light still on, box emptied, the floor a hazard of shredded cartons and shards of glass among broken egg yolks and splatters of Aunt Jemima maple syrup.

She finds her kitchen phone coated in raspberry yogurt; wipes the worst with a dish towel. Thankfully, hears a dial tone.

She dials the number he'd made her memorize.

"They've fired me," she says. "How did they find out so soon?"

Carmichael

"I EXPLORE realms where words fail," the young poet says.
"Yeah?" Carmichael clenches his fist, juts his chin, thumbs peanuts into his mouth one-by-one.

"I mean words— There are vast realms beyond words."

"Like what?" Carmichael asks.

"I mean like let's say we're down in Marshfield there— Brant Rock. Ever go down to Brant Rock to watch the sunrise— sunset?"

"Sure," Carmichael says.

"So let's say it's sunrise. We're standing shoulder-to-shoulder watching the sun rise out of the sea. Maybe it's been a long night. Lifted a few. We watch the day unfurl in mauves and reds— seagulls skimming up from the icy rocks down where the cold waters cut the shore."

"Yeah?" says Carmichael.

"How many poets— novelists— have truly captured the essence of the sea? And how many have failed?"

"How many?"

"Every man jack."

"Meaning what?"

"Exactly! How many so-called writers have captured the true meaning of sunrise at the beach?"

"Still don't get you, kid—"

"I mean we're standing there shoulder-to-shoulder— you with your thoughts, me with mine. Our minds all a swirl with colors and waves and chill— the shrill cry of waking seagulls— lurking fears, broken dreams, distant memories.

"Our minds are vast aquariums. Little fish, minnows, darting here and there. Predator fish under dark ledges.

"Now I believe that somehow— can't exactly point to pipes and valves here— but somehow subterranean plumbing connects our minds. Currents in your mind ripple through the pipes to mine. Fish dart across my mind— stir water in yours."

"Kid—" Carmichael says.

"You know what I'm getting at here?"

"No— Kid, listen to me. Look. All I know is this. You're a nice enough kid. But you're so full of bull it's no wonder you can't hold down a steady job."

"But—"

"But nothing. Listen to me now. I've listened to you. I only sit here because it's been one of those days. But now you listen to me.

"I know this— I work for this guy and you owe this guy money and this guy wants his money. You said you'd have this guy's money now, here, today. This money— you got this guy's money?"

"No. I—"

"No nothing. No. Not good enough. No next month— next week— tomorrow. Now! No pay— there's a way these things are done."

"But—"

"Nothing personal here, kid. No pay— we walk outside. That's the way these things are done."

"You know me Carmichael. Please— another week— couple days. I'm really strapped here."

"So— There we are then. Drink up kid. And don't make a fuss. I've got a long night ahead."

Carmichael

FACT is, Carmichael hates his job.

Can't say why. But it's been coming on.

Pay's good. One thing about Stanley— takes good care of the help. Just don't cross him.

How else could a guy like Carmichael afford a baby like this Lexus LS? Carmichael sinks into the smooth throb of open road; opens his hands to better enjoy the silken feel of the wheel.

Carmichael loves driving. Loves these early hours. Not many cars on the road. Feels he could drive forever.

He loves the flicker of images in his headlights; dancing red tail-lights; approaching pin-points growing ever brighter, diverging, then vanishing in the on-coming lanes.

Who are these people? Why are they on the road? Bars long closed. Shift workers? Night people? Hospital? Cops?

These are the real people, he thinks— the people who keep the machinery running while the civilians sleep.

But what about me, he thinks. What am I doing here? Who wonders about me?

Carmichael wonders what his old man thought on the long stretches of night highway.

Carmichael sees his dad high up in his cab. His dad drove big rigs across country for Ferris Freight Lines. Gone two weeks at a time. Come home so whacked all he can do is sit on the Barcalounger, drink Rolling Rock. Stare at the tube.

Carmichael remembers the days of yearning, waiting for his dad. What would his dad bring him from the exotic, far away places along the routes he drove— Denver, Moline? But his dad never brought a thing. Just a sweaty hug and "Hey, bub."

Carmichael's dad was paid by the mile. Enough miles and the family could just make ends meet. But more often his dad spent hours, days, sitting in a terminal along some interstate in the middle of nowhere waiting for a load.

Carmichael hums to himself.

Carmichael's dad always said, "Got a ten spot, bub— Never spend more than nine."

"Smart, smart—" Carmichael whispers. "Never gave you much credit, old man—"

Carmichael's mother designed, cut, and stitched custom wedding gowns in the family's cramped back porch. Never charged enough. Sometimes she switched in extra fine materials out of her own pocket. This Carmichael heard from a teary neighbor during his mother's wake.

During his teens, Carmichael was car crazy. Souped-up hot cars all he could think about. Driving far and fast. Getting away.

But when Carmichael reached legal age, his dad refused to take him down to motor vehicles.

"Seen too many stupid teeny boppers smeared across two lanes," he'd said.

So Carmichael had left home. Lied about his age. Joined the Army.

He loved the Army— more than the Army loved him. Gave him something to measure himself against.

Basic was nothing. The rest a blur. He pushed the limits at every chance. But he was good. Never gave it a thought. He was a loner and not much for rules and that rubbed the fass time servers the wrong way. But he was good so the long-stare combat vets saw something in him— put up with him— kept pushing him.

One bird colonel said, "You weren't such a hot-shot, Corporal, I'd have you out of this man's Army in a heartbeat. But I'm recommending you for ranger school instead. They know how to turn know-it-all nitwits into war fighting machines."

Next thing, Carmichael found himself leading a long range reconnaissance patrol in 'Stan. Killed a bunch of Taliban. No big thing. Why else had Uncle fronted his ticket?

He remembers mostly the sand. Sand in his eyes. Sand in his nostrils and sand between his teeth. Sand in his ears and gritty sand in the crack of his ass. This wasn't the beach sand he knew at home. This was ancient sand that knew how to wear a man down, bury him.

And he remembers the flies. Small little buggers with bite of fire. And the screaming camel spiders, big as your hand, could jump four feet in the air.

Carmichael remembers one dead Taliban— just a kid. Face smeared with blood, covered with flies. Carmichael felt bad about that.

So what's going on, son, Carmichael wonders. What's with the job? Who else would hire a guy like you?

Carmichael doesn't mind the rough stuff. There are limits in this life. Pukes got to learn that.

Fact, he takes pride in the job— deliver maximum pain short of incapacitation. Takes skill, discipline. Where to hit. How hard.

"Incapacitate one of my marks," Stanley says, "And I'll kill you myself.

"We've got big bucks invested in these crumb bums."

Carmichael takes the off-ramp. High halogens illuminate the first three blocks. But nothing open. Except the Dunkin' Donuts.

Orange and brown. A light in the night.

"Morning to you honey," Sharlee says. "The usual?"

"Yeah, the usual," Carmichael says. "And one more of those chocolate glazed."

Carmichael sits, stares at the second chocolate glazed.

"What's this, son?" he thinks. Now he'll have to run extra miles— do a few hundred extra bench presses.

Carmichael watches Sharlee serve the few predawn customers. Same with everybody. Always bright, open, friendly. Where does that come from?

Carmichael feels like there's a thick pane of glass between him and people like Sharlee. Like they know something. Like they're going somewhere.

Jesus, Carmichael thinks, there must be a better way to make a living.

Carmichael

IT'S ONE of those bone-chilling January days in Greater Boston. Eleven degrees. Minus seven wind chill. Sky blue as a starlet's eyes.

Here's Carmichael in his Lexus LS, idling at the curb.

He's shaking. Can't get warm enough even in his brand-new camel hair overcoat, cashmere muffler, mink-lined lambskin driving gloves, so weak he can barely lift his arms.

Flu. In bed two days with it. Where's this coming from, he wonders. Never sick a day in his life. Then again, some of the joints he's been in lately, it's no wonder. Should still be in bed. But that damned Stanley calls every other minute.

"Come on, kid. You're young, healthy as an ox. Low hanging fruit out there. Time's a wasting."

"I'm 102," Carmichael says.

"102's nothing. Cold out there will do you good. Exercise. That's all you need," Stanley says.

Finally, today, Carmichael gives in.

"Just one collection," Stanley says. "Take you twenty minutes— Less. Jimmy Phan. Peach of a guy. Always on the dot. Always smiling."

So here's Carmichael idling at the curb in front of the All Bright Laundromat.

God what he wouldn't give for a cup of hot chocolate.

The air in the laundromat is warm, moist. An older woman, baggy white man's dress shirt, skinny as a stick, is pulling a heavy green shag rug out of a large industrial dryer, hoisting it onto a rolling laundry cart.

"I'm looking for Mr. Phan," Carmichael says.

The woman stares at Carmichael. She strips off orange rubber gloves, stretching each finger one at a time, wipes a wisp of gray hair from her

21

forehead.

"Mr. Phan. He's supposed to meet me here."

"Mr. Phan. Not here."

"And who are you?"

"I Mrs. Phan. Mr. Phan not here. Who you?"

"I'm Mr. Carmichael. I was told Mr. Phan would be here."

"You man come every week? Collect money?"

"That's not me. But, yes, I'm here to collect money."

The woman's eyes move down to Carmichael's shoes. Then slowly back up, catching and holding his eyes. He sees deep wrinkles, tuft of black hair below her lower lip, eyes so deep he can't make them out.

"OK. I get money. But—"

"What?" Carmichael asks.

"You big man. Strong. Dryer have loose screw."

"I don't know about dryers, ma'am," Carmichael says. "Call a service man."

"Easy fix. But I can't reach. Too short."

"Then get a tall service man."

"Service man come today, maybe. Maybe next month. You want money next week— fix dryer today. Easy fix."

Carmichael looks around the laundromat. He needs something to lean against.

"Okay," he says.

She leads him to the dryer.

"In back. Way in back— Here screwdriver."

Carmichael leans into the dryer. It's hot. Hotter than his fever.

"Need a flashlight," he says.

"No flashlight."

Carmichael pushes up on his toes to lean further in.

Suddenly he feels his feet pulled out from under him. His forehead hits hot metal. He drops the screwdriver, grabs for something, anything, but the tub is slick and too hot to hold.

Strong hands jerk him back. His face scrapes the lip of the dryer and then he falls too fast to catch himself. He turns his head, hits the floor, ear ringing.

Now he feels clinging fabric, clothes, dirty from the smell, all enveloping. The clothes, his heavy overcoat, make it impossible to maneuver. He kicks out, turns, but heavy metal, the laundry cart maybe, slams into his shins, pinning his legs.

He lashes out with his arms, hears something scrape across the floor, a chair maybe pins his right arm. He can't see. Can't breathe.

"You—" he mumbles.

Now he feels wire lashing his ankles to the laundry cart, must be. A heavy weight, a knee, pins his right arm. He feels his wrist lashed to more metal, a chair leg— he can feel it.

He tries to strike with his left arm. But the knee falls again. Pain radiates. He feels the cold chair leg, the wire biting into his wrist.

"Ms'a Ca'michael. You in there?"

Now Carmichael feels hands pull the smothering shirts, pants, underwear away from his face. He's glad for air, breathes hard to clear the stink of dirty socks.

He glances down. Sweet Jesus. Coat hangers. He's bound up with wire coat hangers.

Mrs. Phan leans into his face, focusing a camera.

"Smile, Ms'a Ca'michael."

The flash blinds him momentarily.

"Now— wallet."

Mrs. Phan gropes through his pockets. He feels his wallet slide out of his inside breast pocket.

"Fucking bitch!" he yells. "I'll rip your head off."

"Oooh, potty mouth," the old woman says. "I fix potty mouth."

Carmichael feels the sharp edge of a plastic nipple forced between his teeth. Squirt. Jesus! Liquid laundry detergent! He gags, spits, tastes the slimy bite of detergent, feels it foam.

Mrs. Phan smiles. "Had brush, do betta job. But no brush.

"Now—" Mrs. Phan holds Carmichael's driver's license, squinting.

"You Ms'a Landry S. Ca'michael? 1732 Washington Street?

"What S stand for? Must be Sucka. Yes, Sucka. Mr. Landry Sucka Ca'michael."

Carmichael lifts his hips, tries to kick, struggle. But with each thrust the coat hangers bite more deeply into his ankles, wrists.

Mrs. Phan leans away, then back; holds something over his head. He looks up. Tries to see what she's doing above his head. Oh dear God, no! Laundry bleach.

"Say here— No good for eyes."

She shakes a few drops loose. He feels the cool drops on his forehead, then a stabbing, burning in his left eye. He shakes his head, squeezes his eye shut, moans.

"Now, Ms'a Sucka Ca'michael. I tol' you. Mr. Phan not here. Mr. Phan has the cancer. Never sick. All life— Healthy. 'Til you suckas. Now Mr. Phan has the cancer. You understand me?"

She shakes the bleach bottle. He nods.

"Now I have picture. Know where you live. I know people. I from Vietnam. I know Viet Cong. I know CIA. You understand me, Mr. Sucka Ca'michael?

"You touch my Jimmy— hair on his head— You touch single gray hair on my head— You ha'm this All Bright Laundry— any way— Viet Cong— CIA— They find you. Maybe middle of night. Maybe in bed. They find you. Then you hurt. Oooh you hurt very very bad very long time. Maybe never walk again. You understand me, Ms'a Ca'michael?

"Now, I know— You just messenger boy. Right, Ms'a Ca'michael? You messenger boy for big boss."

Carmichael looks away. More cold bleach lands on his forehead, burns into his eyes.

"You answer me!"

Carmichael may have answered. He can't be sure. Time may have passed. He can't be sure.

He remembers a heavy snip snip as the grip of wire around his ankles fell free.

"Now— you go, Ms'a Ca'michael. You tell Big Boss Stanley what I say."

Somehow Carmichael manages to rise, two blue stacking chairs wired to his wrists. The weight of the chairs, the wires, dig into his flesh. He feels blood running down his fingers.

"Keep chairs, Ms'a Ca'michael. Final payment."

A customer enters as Carmichael struggles to the door— a woman, young, hair in curlers, arms around a laundry basket. But to Carmichael, she's a blur. Her hip hits the chair hanging from his left wrist. He draws breath, groans in pain.

"Ah, Mrs. Lipski. No worry. Ms'a Ca'michael here, magician. Doing disappearing act."

Carmichael struggles through the door, unaware of the pair of pink panties, 42 waist, clinging to the back of his new camel hair overcoat.

"Jesus," Carmichael thinks. "What the FUCK am I going to tell Stanley?"

Kimberly

"WHERE are you?" he asks.

"Home— What's left of it."

"What do you mean?"

"They've trashed it—"

"Kimberly— I want you out of there— now!"

"Why?"

"If they haven't found it they'll be back. They're ruthless. Paranoid. Desperate. Do you have a place to go?"

"No— I—"

"OK. OK. We've got to get off the phone. You remember that place— where we had the argument?"

"Yes—"

"Meet me there. In front. One hour."

"But my car— I don't have a car."

"Well, whatever, don't call a cab."

"But how—"

"Kimberly, look— We're out of time. You'll figure it out."

Now Kimberly is more than frightened. Maybe it's better if they had found it. Maybe it would be over. No— They would never stop at that.

She runs into her bedroom, stumbles— toe snagged in scattered clothing, bedding. Her night table is kindling. Her reading lamp smashed. Her clock radio— circuits, twisted wires, and jagged shards.

Kimberly throws aside terrycloth slippers; her latest Harpers, cover torn; a Barbara Kingsolver paperback. She hopes to God they haven't found it. It's her only insurance.

Now she sees it under a fluff of pillow down— her vibrator— well, her daughter's— confiscated. She flicks the latch on the battery

27

compartment. Thank God! She tips the computer thumb drive into her palm.

Kimberly is finding it hard to breathe. Just wants to lie down and sleep. Maybe it will all go away. What should she take? Can't take much. She slips out of her work clothes. Finds soiled Levi's, a flannel shirt, her jogging shoes.

She can buy what she needs. But, wait, her purse is locked in her office. Her cash, her credit cards.

Kimberly picks through the scatter of paid and unpaid bills, discount coupons, letters from her daughter that some creep has read and tossed aside, now buried under smashed drawers and shattered legs of her antique secretary. She'd inherited the secretary from her late husband's mother. She'd loved her late husband's mother.

If only she can find her checkbook. But she can't.

She hears a heavy car door slam. And another. She finds a canceled check. It'll have to do.

By habit Kimberly starts toward the front door, catches herself, turns toward the kitchen door. Had she locked the front door? Yes. She hears glass shatter as she slips out through the kitchen.

The sun is down now behind her neighbor's pool house. She creeps low, sticking to flag stones, then through a rose hedge. It hurts to breathe. She tries to calm herself, knocks on Mrs. Blanchard's back door.

"Why Kimberly dear—"

"Sorry," Kimberly says, pushing herself through the door.

"Are you all right, dear?"

Mrs. Blanchard is dressed in her usual lime-green pant suit, white blouse. Kimberly has never seen her without her pearls.

"A little car trouble— and a crisis at work. I'm wondering—"

"Yes, dear?"

"May I borrow your car?"

"Why, of course, dear. But I'd be glad to drive you wherever—"

"No! No— I don't want to trouble you—"

"No trouble. It gets so lonely here. It would give me a good reason to get out."

"No— No—"

As Kimberly backs out of the spacious two-car garage she sees the two black Ford Expeditions parked in front of her house.

She backs Mrs. Blanchard's big Chrysler New Yorker out of the garage, eases onto the street, and away. She looks at the gas gauge. Near empty. Just what she needs! Twenty-five miles. She'll have to make it on fumes.

Traffic is light so she makes good time. But she's still late. A delivery truck holds her up. Stalled in traffic, three car lengths from the parking garage, she spots Tim on the sidewalk, near the hotel entrance, pacing back and forth, looking into the stream of traffic. Tim— the one who'd promised to protect her. She tries to wave, but he's looking in the wrong direction.

Traffic clears. She turns into the parking garage, eases behind a BMW and up the spiral ramp. But now, half way up the ramp, Mrs. Blanchard's New Yorker chokes, dies, gas gauge well below E.

"Come on— Come on—" Kimberly says, cranking the key. The driver in the Town Car behind her honks. She pulls the emergency brake, steps out of the car, raises her hands. "Out of gas," she yells.

Kimberly

THE GARAGE attendant, stubbled grey facial hair, exacerbated middle Eastern accent, helps clear the spiral, directs Kimberly as she backs down the ramp. Her hands are shaky on the wheel. The wheel turns hard. She's afraid of scraping the curved concrete walls.

"No! No, left left. No. Right. More, more— No. Left."

A chorus of impatient horns echo up the spiral ramp as cars try to back down behind her. On the level the big car is too much for the small attendant. He yells into his portable intercom. A skinny assistant, scraggly beard, greasy cowboy hat, saunters over from the ticket booth, winks at Kimberly as they push the big Chrysler into a service slot.

"Got Triple A?" the attendant asks.

"No," Kimberly says. "It's my neighbor's car. May I leave it here?"

"Few minutes. Leave long, we tow."

"May I call? My neighbor—?"

"Sure. Sure. Be guest—"

"But I don't have a cell phone."

The garage attendant looks at her, then across the vast parking garage.

"Pay phone in hotel."

"But I don't have change."

"OK. OK. Phone in office."

Kimberly dials information, then Mrs. Blanchard's number three times. Her finger keeps missing the right sequence.

"Mrs. Blanchard—"

"Yes—"

"It's Kimberly—"

"Oh, Kimberly, dear— Thank goodness— I'm so sorry—"

"Sorry?"

31

"The fire—"

"Fire?

"Your home— Just after you left."

"My home?"

"Terrible blaze. Smoke all over the neighborhood. Four fire trucks! Those darned firemen crushed my roses!"

"My home— On fire?"

"Yes, I'm telling you. You didn't leave something on the stove, did you? I always worry—"

"No— No— I— Look, Mrs. Blanchard, I've got to go. But your car— it's—"

"My car?"

"It's out of gas."

"Oh, my. I meant to fill the tank."

"It's in a garage downtown. 1000 Adams St. You'll have to pick it up."

"Downtown? Kimberly, dear, can't you just call triple A?"

"I— I don't have my purse. They'll tow it away if you don't pick it up."

"Your purse? What's going on, dear? You must have your driver's license?"

"No— No—"

"Well, I must say, you're being very irresponsible, dear. How am I supposed to get downtown?"

"I'm sorry," Kimberly says.

"Well I just can't imagine—"

"You can't possibly imagine, Mrs. Blanchard. Please— I've got to go."

The attendant calls after Kimberly as she exits the garage. She ignores him. She starts toward the hotel. Starts to run. But now she sees them, slides to a stop.

She sees two men, one half bald, one in black, walk casually up behind Tim. He takes on a look of surprise as they grab him by the upper arms. A black Expedition swings into the curb. She sees a brief struggle, Tim folded into the van. Then, they're gone.

Kimberly turns back to the garage. She stands in the large bay door, looking up and down the street. The garage attendant sees her, yells.

She hurries down the block, away from the hotel. Her head is light. She feels dizzy, finds a concrete trash receptacle to lean against.

"Are you all right, Miss?" an elderly woman asks.

"Yes. Yes," Kimberly says. "A little light headed."

Kimberly realizes that she hasn't had a bite in nearly twelve hours. Food. How can she even think about food after— after everything. But she's ravenous. She has no money. Shelter. Be night soon.

Her home. Everything she owns! Fire. They must have started it. But why?

Think, Kimberly. She starts walking. If she can only make it through until the banks open. She reaches into her hip pocket to make sure she still has her canceled check. Will they watch the banks? Do they have that many people? That much power?

Then it hits her. She can't go to the bank. She can't make a withdrawal. She has no identification.

There must be someone she can call. But who? Her daughter? But, no. They'll know about her daughter, will be watching, maybe tapping her phone. And how can she call— no cell phone— no money?

Friends? Kimberly thinks. What friends— a few girls at the plant. That's a laugh. Who has time to make friends?

Are they really so all-powerful?

Yes. Kimberly knows her father— C. Norbert Stone, Chairman of SVS Aerospace. Big time investor in half a dozen other strategic defense conglomerates. She knows what he's capable of. Knows what he'd tried to mold her into. Most certainly he's behind this; known from the beginning what Kimberly was trying to do.

Would he really hurt her? Only if he hates her as much as she hates him. Does he really hate her? Maybe. But he would certainly hurt her if she stood in his way. She is certain of that. And she has sworn to stand in his way. Has taken the first steps.

A siren, swinging around the corner, startles her. An ambulance. Kimberly's eyes follow the blinking red light as it dodges traffic.

Yes. Yes. Maybe, she thinks. First things first, she says under her breath. Food— shelter— She picks up her pace.

It's just the beginning of evening visiting hours. The lobby is busy with streams of people entering, leaving. What better place to spend a night without money?

Kimberly studies the directory. Chapel. Maybe. Surgery. Don't they have waiting rooms? Cafeteria. Maybe she can find leftover food on the tables.

Kimberly wanders through several floors, checking out spaces, looking through open doors. She spots a tray of food on a rolling cart, glances over her shoulder. No one looking. She steps behind the cart and pushes it down the hall, keeps pushing. No one pays attention.

Yes, she thinks. I can make it through the night here.

Carmichael

SOMEONE, somewhere, had told Carmichael that reality is a turbulent sea of energy raging across multiple dimensions.

In Carmichael's experience, reality is hard as a hammer.

But what about dreams? Neither hard nor soft. But some clutch at the heart like a frozen hand.

For three days Carmichael has been in and out of fever dreams—hauntingly real, but no places Carmichael has ever been. Vivid colors—every shade of green, dapple of green light through high canopy. Smells—stench of swamp water, cordite, rotting corpses. Sounds— weeping, the rhythmic thud of approaching ordnance.

One image recurs in Carmichael's waking moments. A water buffalo seen at a distance, wallowing haunch deep in a rice paddy. Then, dream-cut, Carmichael is inside the skin, looking out through glassy eyes— waiting, waiting.

Vietnam? The closest he's been is the History Channel.

Now Lonnie and George are at Carmichael's door. Lonnie six-foot-six, black as an abandoned mine shaft, pink-tinted glasses. George fat and bald, temperament of a cobra.

"My man," Lonnie says, "You lookin' like cat turd."

"I'm feelin' like cat turd," Carmichael says. "Why do I have the feeling this ain't a social call?"

"Why, you know we love ya, babe! And why you lights out? And why you squintin' at me the way you do?"

"The light. I'm seeing halos."

"Halos?"

"Halos around everything— you know, like those religious pictures."

"Well don't look at me, my man," Lonnie grins. "Angel I ain't."

35

Georgie says nothing.

"So," Carmichael says.

"So the Stanley man been askin' 'bout you."

"Yeah—?"

"You know, not good when the Stanley man start askin'."

"Been sick," Carmichael says. "Stanley knows that."

"Well the Stanley man wants to see you."

"And I want to climb back in bed—"

"No can do," Lonnie says. "You know how it works."

"Yeah," Carmichael says. "Let me get some clothes."

They're stalled in traffic now on Storrow Drive, Lonnie's cherry-red Hummer straddling two lanes.

"Lonnie," Carmichael says, "Tell me what you think about this shit?"

"What shit's that, my man?"

"Civilian wants to take a step up the ladder. Gets into Stanley— can't spend a nickel to feed his kids. We get the nickel or we whack him."

Lonnie laughs.

"Man, folks been stealin' food out of my mouth for 300 years. Just feels like I'm gettin' back my own.

"And the whackin' part," Lonnie glances up at Carmichael's reflection in the rear-view mirror. "Most times— the whackin' part just feels sooo good!"

Lonnie punches George in the shoulder, "What say, Georgie Porgie, my man?"

Tone flat, "Unbridled capitalism at it's finest," the bald man replies.

In the beginning Stanley held forth from a small alcove at the back of a strip club in the Combat Zone— unfinished door on beer crates for a desk, rickety round bar table cluttered with liquor bottles shoved against the wall.

Now you take an elevator to visit Stanley— walk into a reception area like a State Street law office. You see the big brass letters on the walnut paneling behind the receptionist's desk— S&S Financial Services. And you see Selma, the receptionist. Big tits.

"He's expecting you," Selma says.

Light glaring through the large plate-glass window blinds Carmichael. He sees halos. Then he sees a blurry shadow— Stanley.

Carmichael looks away, focuses on the rosewood sideboard cluttered with golf trophies, not a one, Carmichael knows, won in fair competition.

"Hey, kid! Christ on a stick, you look like death warmed over."

"My man been sick," Lonnie says.

"Yeah, yeah," Stanley says. "But tell me about the collection, the Jimmy Phan pick-up."

So Carmichael tells him. And Stanley laughs.

"It's not funny," Carmichael says.

"No— No—" Stanley laughs. "But tell me this part again— This old lady twice your age, half your size, has you wired down on the floor with— coat hangers?"

Stanley laughs again, looks at Lonnie, George.

"What's this? Some hinky sex thing?"

"It wasn't funny," Carmichael says again.

Now Stanley is dead serious.

"No, what's not funny is I send you out on a simple collection— hanging fruit. And you don't collect. There's a matter of honor here."

"What could I do?" Carmichael asks.

"It's not what you COULD do— It's what you CAN do. And what you CAN do is take Lonnie here, and George, and go out and collect what you were supposed to collect with vig on the vig.

"Got me, kid?" Stanley leans across his desk, "Matter of honor here."

"Not sure that's a good idea—"

Stanley's face steams up. "Not sure—"

At that moment Selma steps into the office, interrupts.

"I'm in a meeting here!" Stanley bellows.

"The boy said to give you this—"

"What boy?"

"Messenger boy— oriental."

"What messenger boy?"

Stanley stares at the FedEx envelope like it's crawling with spiders.

"The boy says to open it now. Matter of life and death—"

"Life and death?" Stanley takes the envelope, lays it on his desktop, probes it with his fingers.

Stanley stares at Selma, then slips a pen under the flap, shakes out a yellow CVS photo envelope.

Stanley smiles. "Must be from the wife, Harmony. A real practical joker."

Stanley shakes a deck of four-by-eight photo prints onto his desk.

"Look, here's my Jimmy!" Stanley says. "Must be at school. And Jennifer. Jesus, what a sweetie. Ain't she a heart breaker? And wait— wait a minute— that's Harmony. And— that's me! I know that place That's the 10th hole out at the Brookline Country Club there."

Stanley's silent for a long beat. He looks up at Carmichael.

"What was that the old lady told you?" Stanley asks. "Viet Cong— CIA?"

"Viet Cong—" Carmichael says, "CIA."

"Mother of God," Stanley says.

Carmichael

STANLEY stands. Walks to the plate glass window. View's not much. Beige slab of office building. Sliver of Boston Harbor.

Stanley is proud of that sliver. Points it out every chance he gets.

Stanley returns to his desk. Looks down at the four-by-five print of himself on the golf course.

"OK— OK— We got a situation here. We need ideas— ideas—"

"Nuke the bitch," George says.

"Yeah— Yeah— Wish we could."

Stanley looks at Carmichael. "You got us into this mess, kid. So how do we turn it around?"

"Walk away—" Carmichael says.

Stanley turns some kind of red.

"Walk away? Walk away? You some kind of stupid? Give a putz an even break— next day it's all over town that we're easy marks— suckers. I'm lookin' for ideas here!"

"Maybe what we be needin'," Lonnie says, "Is intel. Catch the cred on this ho's posse. They be as bad as we be thinkin'? Maybe we can cut a deal— Get them to co-sign."

"Yeah— yeah—" Stanley's voice is so tight now, he's almost whistling.

"Wait a minute— wait a minute—" Stanley says. "Got an idea here. We pick up the old man, hold him hostage like. Get him to tell us if the lady has real juice— who the old lady knows."

Carmichael wants to speak up, but holds his tongue.

Lonnie says it for him, "What then?"

"Yeah— yeah—" Stanley says. "What then? That's the bitch of it."

Now there's silence, Stanley staring down at the photographs.

"OK— OK—" he says at last. "Here's what we do. I send the wife and kids on a long vacation. Lonnie— You and George move into the house with me. Watch my back—"

"I'd rather do the vacation gig," Lonnie says.

"Kid— you find Jimmy Phan. Collect what he owes. Then, get the book on this bitch."

"Book?"

"You know— Who's her rabbi. How's she connected—"

"She's an operator—" Carmichael says.

"Operator? What's that mean?"

"Trained."

"Trained in what?"

"Interrogation. Unarmed combat."

"And she's what? A hundred years old?"

"Yeah," Carmichael says.

"And you're what? Tweety Bird?"

George laughs.

"That's it then," Stanley says. "That's the plan."

"One thing—" Lonnie says.

"Yeah?"

"My man Carmichael's got the fever. How he be gettin' back to his crib? MBTA?"

Now, in the confines of the elevator, Lonnie throws a few shadow punches.

"I tell you, that cracker Stanley man, he losin' it."

"Maybe," Carmichael says.

"You goin' do what the man say?"

Carmichael shrugs.

"Why we need his skinny white ass anyway? We do all the work. Cracker just sits in his jive office."

"We need him," Carmichael says.

"What's he got we don't? Jive office. That's it."

"Capital— protection. That's what he's got."

"So, we take him down. Make him like a— silent partner."

The air in the stairwell has an unfamiliar tinge. Carmichael senses it the instant he unlocks and opens his front door.

He steps inside— carefully— quietly—

Then he sees it. Placed precisely on the floor just beyond the door where he can't fail to see it. His wallet.

"Why am I not surprised," he mutters.

Kimberly

"Miss— Miss— Wake up, honey bun. Please—"
Kimberly opens her eyes, feels stiff and cramped in the unforgiving pew. The dim chapel light is disorienting. Her mouth is dry, her tongue sticks to the back of her teeth.

"Didn't want to wake you, hon, but we have a private service at nine. Here— Brought you hot coffee. Thought you might need it."

"Oh—" Kimberly says.

"Mostly they stay in the rooms. But sometimes they come down here to pray. You must have fallen asleep. You look so exhausted, hon, I really didn't want to wake you. I do hope it all turns out well."

Kimberly looks up at the heavy-set woman, wonders how she moves her massive weight, pushing the aluminum walker while carrying a cup of hot coffee.

"Oh, you're an angel," Kimberly says.

Kimberly finds a ladies room, looks in the mirror. What a fright! She washes her face, runs her fingers through her hair, rubs her teeth with a paper towel. If you expect people to help, it won't do to look like a bag lady, she thinks.

Kimberly walks back out into the wide hallway. The hospital is all business at this hour— chimes ringing, nurses scurrying in and out of rooms, aides pushing gurneys. She falls in behind a group in white coats— a doctor and interns doing rounds. A nurse behind a desk gives Kimberly a sharp look. Kimberly realizes that her jeans and flannel shirt aren't suitable camouflage for this time of day. She snaps a salute and walks on.

My house! Kimberly remembers. Job— Feels the emptiness.

OK, first thing, Kimberly thinks, is ID. With ID, I can get money.

With money, I can get anything— well, almost. Kimberly fights tears, feels hopelessness creep in but, No! It's not going to get her anywhere.

It's a twenty minute walk to the city library. Kimberly arrives early. It's not open until ten. The day is already hot with morning sun beating on parched white concrete. Kimberly finds a patch of shade, sits. She's hungry now, but her stomach will have to wait.

Now, inside, the librarian is one of those women who can't make eye contact. She fingers a rubber band, glances over Kimberly's shoulder, down at her worn oak desk. Kimberly wants to shake her, maybe slap her upside the face.

"I told you. I lost it all in the fire," Kimberly says. "Every bit of ID."

"Well we can't issue a card without ID."

"But how can— My dissertation is due tomorrow. I need to check references. I'll miss graduation."

"Policy." The woman smirks like she's just played a trump card.

"Well, maybe I can talk with the head librarian," Kimberly says.

"Not here," the woman says, darting a quick glance at Kimberly's eyes, then over her shoulder.

Kimberly stands. Unwilling to move.

"On this floor, I mean—"

"Then where is she?"

"In her office."

"And her office—?"

"Up the stairs, turn left."

The cramped office is cluttered with books on carts, shelves on every wall, no windows. A tiny desk is brightened by a single yellow flower. The woman behind the desk has tight silver curls, glasses with rhinestone frames hanging on chains over her slight bosom.

Kimberly repeats her story about the fire.

"Do you have anything at all, my dear? Any kind of identification?"

"Well, yes," Kimberly says. "I have this."

She pulls out her canceled check.

"And this is your signature?"

"Yes—"

"And your address?"

"Yes—"

"Then I don't see a problem. Come with me, we'll fix you up."

"You're a savior," Kimberly says.

"It will just be a pass, you understand. Good for today. A card will be mailed to your home."

A pass— Kimberly feels uneasy.

As they walk down the stairs, suddenly, the librarian stops.

"Wait," she says, "May I see that check again?"

Kimberly's heart stops.

"This is made out to Gold's Department Store."

"Yes," Kimberly says.

"Was this a purchase or payment against a credit card?"

"Credit card," Kimberly says. "I seldom pay by check."

"Well then, when you leave, my dear, take this check to Gold's. I'm sure they'll replace your credit card."

"Oh, why didn't I think of that! I'm forever grateful," Kimberly says.

And Gold's does just that— Almost. The black lady in blue business suit behind the service desk, all smiles, hears Kimberly's tale; doesn't give it a second thought.

"Here's your temp card," she says. "Your card will be in the mail."

First thing Kimberly buys a comfortable pant suit suitable for travel, a large shoulder bag, and three changes of underwear. She wonders if she can buy more and return it for cash.

Don't push your luck, she thinks.

Instead she buys an expensive gold bracelet inlaid with small cut diamonds. Maxes out her credit limit. Pure impulse. But maybe not so dumb she thinks. The stores give you "stuff" on credit, stuff cut and sewn in sweatshops and low-wage factories around the world. She's seen them. Worked in one. But department stores are not in the business of giving out cash. The bracelet, maybe, she can turn into cash.

Should she change here or later? Here, she thinks. She must look her best for the bank.

The sun is grueling now. Kimberly feels sticky sweat under her light linen suit, wishes she'd been able to shower. Hunger hits her again. She passes a Starbucks, thinks how easy it's always been when she's had cash in her purse— had a purse for that matter. And now she worries. Will they watch her bank? They know she's strapped for funds. Can they watch every branch? Or just her neighborhood branch? But they knew she was headed downtown. They knew about Tim. Quite likely they'll watch the downtown branches as well.

She passes demonstrators, cops ringing them in. Maybe she should join them. But they scare her. The cops even more than the demonstators. There has been violence.

Kimberly walks eighteen blocks to a commercial strip. Mattresses For Less. El Sol Dentista de la Familia Painless Extractions. Pappy's Liquors. More stores dark with For Lease signs and, across the wide arterial, a branch bank with a familiar logo. Traffic is relentless; the black asphalt almost too hot for her swollen feet. By now she's drenched in sweat, wishing for a place to just sit— sit out of the sun. Rest.

The teller listens to her story, suggests that she consult an officer. She sits in a small alcove reading home equity loan brochures until the small man with a chicken neck, patches of eczema, invites her into his cubicle.

"Miss— Miss—" he says, appraising her up and down.

"Ms. Bolton," she says.

"And you say you lost your ID when your home burned down? I'm so sorry," he says. "You don't have any form of identification at all?"

"Just this temp credit card and receipt from Golds and— this library pass," she passes them across the desk. "And this canceled check."

The bank officer scans the documents carefully.

"But these were issued today. And how did you happen to come to this branch— so far from your residence? Why didn't you go to your local branch where they know you?"

"I— I had an appointment in the neighborhood with— with my attorney."

"Oh, very good. Someone we might know?"

"Maybe— a ah— John Ferrenzi?"

"No, sorry. I thought I knew most of the professionals in the neighborhood. But there has been turnover. This terrible economy. Let me check your account."

Working from the canceled check the bank officer keys Kimberly's account number into his workstation, then frowns.

"This account, Mrs. Bolton, was emptied this morning. Closed out. May I ask what you are trying to do here?"

"No! It can't be. I never authorized that. I should have more than twelve thousand dollars in my account."

"Shows here, zeroed out."

"But how can someone do that without my signature?"

"I'm sure my colleagues confirmed the signature when they closed out the account. May I ask you again what you're trying to do?"

"I'm trying to get my goddamn money!"

The officer stares at Kimberly, starts to pick up the phone. "Well—"

"Wait— Wait—" Kimberly says. "Look, here's my signature on this canceled check. And here, let me write out my signature again with you as witness. Then you can check my signature against the document that closed out my account."

"That will take some time, I'm afraid."

"Well if your bank closed out my account illegally, then you best get on it before— before I sick Mr. Ferrenzi on you!"

"Very well," the officer looks at her suspiciously. How can we reach you? Shall we use this address on the check?"

"No— No—" Kimberly says.

"Well we'll need an address. And a telephone number."

Kimberly stares across the desk. Feels fear, rage. It's all she can do to hold back tears until— she can't.

Carmichael

IT's TWO days before Carmichael is up to driving. Stanley calls, cajoling, threatening. Halos still haunt Carmichael's vision. The ophthalmologist says he may need surgery; advises against driving at night.

Jimmy Phan's is a small white ranch with red shutters in a transitional Weymouth neighborhood redolent of unrewarded aspirations— dirty snow packed up under wilted rhododendrons— heaped up like dead pandas.

Carmichael tries the bell, then knocks.

"Yes— Yes." The door opens. The tiny man holding the door is unmistakably Jimmy Phan— stubbles of black hair, hollow cheeks, hospital pallor. But Carmichael is struck by the smile— wide, innocent, child-like.

"Jimmy Phan?"

"Yes— Yes."

"We have things to discuss. May I come in?"

Jimmy Phan, still smiling, cocks his head.

"Name's Carmichael."

"Stanley's man?" Jimmy asks.

"Yes."

"Here to hurt me?"

"No. I won't hurt you," Carmichael says.

"OK. Come in."

Inside, Jimmy Phan stops in the foyer. The medicinal smell assaults Carmichael— a yellow-greenish smell of flesh beyond redemption.

"OK, hurt me now," Jimmy says. "It's OK."

Carmichael steps back a step.

"Can't hurt me more than this tiger demon—" Jimmy Phan taps his chest.

"Why would you want me to hurt you?"

"Gamble. Lose. Can't pay. That's the way—"

"Why can't you pay?" Carmichael asks.

"Dragon Lady."

"Dragon Lady?"

"Mrs. Phan. You know Mrs. Phan?" The sparkle in Phan's eyes suggests he knows the story.

"Oh yes," Carmichael says. "Had the pleasure."

"Mrs. Phan— That lady— Something. Am I right?"

"Oh yes. She's something," Carmichael says. "But what does she have to do with the money you owe Stanley?"

"Everything. Get sick. Dragon Lady say, 'No gambling!' Dragon Lady take my money. Hide my money!"

They step down two steps into a living room barren of furniture but for two director's chairs, a folding card table, and a small Buddhist shrine neatly arranged in a corner.

Now Carmichael picks up the smell of incense.

"Where's your furniture?"

"Oh, doctors— hospitals— blood suckers. Worse than Stanley," Jimmy shows his teeth. "You play cards?"

"No," Carmichael says.

"No cards? What, horses? Sports? Don't tell me— Lottery? Tell me no lottery, please—"

"Don't gamble," Carmichael says.

"Don't gamble! Life a gamble. Life insurance? Big gamble— Every morning— wake up— heads you live. Tails—"

Jimmy Phan snorts.

"Big payoff! Only trouble— you dead."

"Let's talk about Stanley," Carmichael says. "So how much do you owe Stanley?"

"Thirsty? Drink? Have San Miguel. From Philippines. Number one beer."

"So how much?"

Jimmy Phan steps into the kitchen, returns with a tray, on it a glass of water, three pill bottles, and a bottle of San Miguel.

"For pain," Jimmy says, shaking pills into his hand.

"You in pain?"

Jimmy shrugs. "Sometimes more. Sometimes less."

"So come on, Mr. Phan. I need to know. How much are you into Stanley?"

"More—"

"More?" Carmichael asks.

"Every day— more. Here, I show you card game. Very simple. Fun." He extracts a deck of blue Bicycle playing cards from his black robe.

"So how much?"

"Twenty, maybe—"

"Twenty what?"

"Big ones."

"Twenty grand?"

"Yes. But, that not so much. Sometimes more. Sometimes less. Always pay. Sometimes win. Stanley pay me!"

"So why can't you pay this time around?"

"Dragon Lady. Told you. So pick a card."

"I don't gamble. I told you."

"OK. OK. No gamble. Fun. Pick a card. Soon I walk down the long black road— greet ancestors. Bow. Blue noses. Father, 'You gamble? Lose money?' Father hate gambling. Father say, "You not my son! I disown you!' So do me favor."

Carmichael picks a card.

"Jack of spades. Good card. Now I pick. Oh— Three of diamonds. You win! You lucky! Easy, eh?"

Jimmy Phan's delight gets to Carmichael.

"But more fun with something to lose. We need big stakes." Jimmy Phan ducks into the kitchen. Returns with a box of Diamond tooth picks, starts counting them out.

"Mr. Phan—" Carmichael says.

"Put two in pot—"

"I don't gamble—"

"No gamble. Just tooth picks."

After four rounds they're still even.

"OK," Jimmy Phan says. "Now, make more interesting. Don't show me your card. Bet. Bet that you have highest card. How much you want to bet?"

"Tell me about Mrs. Phan?" Carmichael asks. "The money you owe Stanley— She good for it?"

"Dragon Lady— Oh, very stubborn. Never pay."

"Somebody's going to get hurt here," Carmichael says. "Somebody has to pay. You understand that, don't you?"

"Take card— take card—"

"Mr. Phan–"

"Hurt me," Mr. Phan says. "Not Dragon Lady."

"Look, Mr. Phan. Look at me— I don't want to hurt you. Don't want to hurt anybody. But Stanley— Stanley wants his money. And what Stanley wants, Stanley gets. You have a nice house here. A business."

"House— Dragon Lady. Business— Dragon Lady. Look— Come tomorrow. We talk money. Today— play cards. Have fun. Maybe tomorrow— tomorrow I walk down long black road— greet ancestors. Bow before blue noses. All eternity— never play. Sad. Sad. So sad."

"OK. OK. Tell me about Mrs. Phan."

"Mrs. Phan, Dragon Lady— Wait—"

Jimmy returns with a red photo album, gold dragons embossed on the cover. The first print, faded, shows a circle of Vietnamese hunkered around a small cook fire.

Jimmy Phan points to a small figure. "Dragon Lady." Now he sweeps his finger around the circle. "Viet Cong. Big shots," he says.

"She was with the Viet Cong?" Carmichael asks.

"Jimmy taps his finger on the next photo. A bare-chested figure with bull shoulders, dark glasses, campaign hat fills most of the frame. His beefy arm is draped around a small woman with long black hair. Carmichael can just make out her great beauty in the faded gray pixels.

Jimmy Phan runs his finger around the small face, lovingly. "Dragon Lady."

"So who's this?" Carmichael asks, pointing out the bull elephant.

"Bad man. Very bad. CIA."

"So which side was she on?" Carmichael asks.

"No side. Her side. Vietminh kill father, mother. French soldiers kill grandmother, sister, brother. She just baby girl. Tiny girl. Lose whole family. Everyone in village— Dead. She just baby girl hiding in basket. Walk barefoot to Saigon."

"So what did she do? Why is she in both pictures?"

"Never say. Only smile. But I not want to be Vietminh— French either— who kill her family. So, pick a card."

"Look, Mr. Phan. Jimmy. There's got to be a way. You don't want Stanley to hurt her. Maybe kill her."

"Oh Stanley never touch Dragon Lady. Stanley try— too bad for Stanley. Let me show you."

Phan steps out of the room again. He returns with a black box. He pulls out a red bandana. Then, a sinuously curved blade. A kris.

"U.S. pull out of Vietnam. You know Vietnam?"

"Heard of it."

"U.S. pull out of Vietnam— leave Dragon Lady. But she hate communists. Find man with boat. Communists want to kill her!"

"She became a boat person?"

"Yes. She find man with boat. Small boat. They leave Vietnam in boat. Twenty people— old men, women, babies— all in small boat. Third night, pirates board boat. Pirates kill every man. Brrrrr. Machine guns. Kill them. Throw them overboard. Feed sharks. Every one. Start to rape women."

"Jesus," Carmichael says.

"That bandana— that blade— belong to pirate big shot— captain."

"What happened?"

"Don't know. Mrs. Chee, on same boat, say total dark. No moon. She hear screaming. Screaming and fucking. She not say. But I know. They rape Mrs. Chee. Then morning. Blood everywhere. Throats cut— Every pirate. Mrs. Phan's hair— red with blood. Mrs. Chee— she say Mrs. Phan wash hair in ocean. Ocean red. All I know."

With the dry heat in Jimmy Phan's living room, and the remnants of fever, it's all Carmichael can do to stay awake. He counts three empties on his side of the folding coffee table. He's lost the last of his tooth picks.

"Mr. Phan, look—" he says. "I've got to go."

"Yes— yes," Jimmy Phan says. "You good man. Not so good card player. Tell Stanley— now Stanley owe me three hundred tooth picks!"

Carmichael

WIND-DRIVEN snow slashes Stanley's plate-glass window. Carmichael wonders about the civilians working at the flickering monitors in the building across the way, scurrying around under fluorescents.

"You listening to me kid?"

Carmichael nods.

"So where is my money?"

"There is no money."

"What do you mean— no money?"

"Man's dying. Has no money."

"Then get it from the bitch."

"You get it from the bitch," Carmichael says.

George, sitting in the side chair shelling pistachios, looks up.

"Say what, kid?" Stanley whispers.

"I say walk away before someone gets hurt."

"Yeah, starting with Jimmy Phan, then the bitch, then you— give me more lip."

"Look, Stanley, no disrespect here. But you're dealing with something you don't understand."

"Understand! Kid, I've been doing this business since I was fourteen years old. You were still floating around between your daddy's legs. Just what is it I don't understand?"

"This is something else."

"They don't pay, hurt 'em. Still don't pay, hurt their old lady— hurt their kids. They always pay. What's to understand?"

"You can't hurt Jimmy Phan more than he's hurting now. He's a dying man. May be dead already. Mrs. Phan is a force of nature. Push her and she'll come down on you like my Lexus dropped from the top of that building over there."

Stanley drops his head, raises it slowly.

"Look, kid," he says. "Phan don't pay, I take it out of your end."

"Take it out of my end and you'll have something worse than Mrs. Phan come down on you."

Now Stanley is red with rage.

"Threaten me? God damn! Threaten me? I want my money!" Stanley stands, pounds the desk. "I want my money! I want my money!"

Carmichael stands, turns.

"Your funeral."

"You putz! Just where do you think you're going? You can't walk out on me—"

"You want your money, go get your own damn money."

"God damn it! You can't— can't— George— George, now where in the hell are you going? George—"

George raises the frothy beer to his lips, sips delicately, sighs.

"Look, kid," he says. "What's this about?"

"What's what about?"

"This thing with Stanley?"

"What with Stanley? I've got nothing against Stanley."

"But Stanley's starting to wonder, you know?"

"Stanley's losing it. We all know it."

"But knowing and doing are different things. You with me?"

"So what are you telling me, George?"

"I like you kid. You got potential."

"Potential for what?"

"Could go places—"

"You shining me, George? Or what?"

"No. Look— Nothing to me. I played my last card years ago."

"And?"

"Go along to get along. Get me? But you—"

"Me— what?"

"You're young, smart, things to look forward to."

"And you're saying?"

"An observation."

"Tell me—"

"You don't belong in this business."

"Yeah? So just where do I belong?"

"You're a decent kid. Good mind. Could go places."

"I've heard all this before, my man."

"Yeah?"

"Somebody always wants something from me— until they don't."

"Look— I heard about your bum deal. Old news. So what? You going to swim around in the cesspool the rest of your life?"

"Like I have options."

"You always have options—"

"Stanley took me in."

"Stanley's out for Stanley."

"Stanley's been a good friend."

"Open your eyes, kid. Stanley does what's good for Stanley."

"Think so?"

"Know so."

"Think it's getting out of control? This thing he has for blow?"

"Yeah, maybe, and that makes him a dangerous man."

"Think I'm afraid of Stanley?"

"You'd be stupid not to be afraid of Stanley. And there's one thing I know—"

"What?"

"Stupid you're not."

"So what are you telling me here, George?"

"The problem with Stanley— he's lost perspective."

"The problem with Stanley— he's a greedy puke," Carmichael says.

"I worked for his old man, did you know that?"

"Yeah, guess I did. Maybe you told me."

"His old man, Marco— now there was a man. He had perspective."

"How so?" Carmichael asks.

"Know what he'd do? The old man— this situation— this Phan business?"

"What's that?"

"He'd say, 'Man's dying. Forget the money. Dying man deserves respect.' He'd cancel the debt. Pay for the funeral. Make the old lady an ally."

"Smart man," Carmichael says.

"Yeah, smart man. Make her an ally. Then he would pick her clean and crush her."

Stanley calls first thing. Carmichael is just out of the shower. Feeling like himself— first time in weeks. Sun fills his small kitchen with light.

"Look, kid, we can't end it like this— hard feelings. You've done good by me. Maybe I went too far."

"And you've done good by me too, Stanley. And I appreciate it," Carmichael says. "But it's time to move on."

"Yeah, yeah. Guess it's come to that. You're still a kid. Lots to look forward to. But look, one more collection. Forget Jimmy Phan. Just one more collection and we'll call it even."

"One more?"

"Yeah, one. Red Mantico. Easy mark."

"Then we're done?"

"Yeah, then we're done. I'll even kick in a— what do you call it— a severance bonus."

"Yeah. OK. Tell me where to find this puke."

Most times, when Carmichael walks into a crowded joint, people give him room. Sense his armed perimeter.

But tonight they crowd him. He's jostled as he makes his way to the bar— a trendy sports place with a 50-inch plasma flickering silently above the bar.

He sees his man.

"Hey, Red—" he says.

Red turns, stares, his eyes rheumy.

"Let me buy you one?"

"You some kind of faggot?"

"No. Friend of Stanley's."

"Stanley— Oh, shit!" Red says, seems to sit straighter on the stool.

"Fact," Carmichael says, "I'm here to collect Stanley's money."

"Collect— Collect— Yeah, sure. Just got paid."

Red reaches back for his wallet.

Suddenly Carmichael sees a flash of blade, feels a cool wind enter his stomach.

He reaches down with his right hand, grips Red's wrist before he can do more damage, sweeps a bottle off the bar with his left, feels the shock of broken glass and bone, then, tumbles to the floor.

D'Mello

D'MELLO is in a pissy mood and has been since Klegg offed the federal agent.

FUBAR, no lie.

A taste of honey and vinegar and the bozo would have spilled. No question.

Dude was hooded. No way he could have recognized the dynamic duo. They could have wrung him dry and dumped him out on a country road. No penalty.

But Klegg has the patience of a two-year-old. Especially when he's half in the bag— which is most of the time.

Shoots the guy in the knee. Misses. Hits the femoral artery instead. Then, runs around like a headless chicken as the schmuck bleeds out.

So what are you going to do? Call 911?

D'Mello has showered three times since, but still can't rid himself of the smell of blood.

Then the body.

Where do you dump a body in a strange city?

Klegg wants to dump it in a dumpster. A federal agent. Stupid shit.

Might as well call in a flight of F-16s packing smart bombs— call 'em right in on their GPS coordinates. X marks the spot.

D'Mello put his foot down on that.

So they drive out into the desert and what do they find? People. People everywhere they turn. Old folks in RVs. Families on mountain bikes. Indians on horses. Kids screwing in pimped up pick-ups. Backpackers, rock hounds, cactus fiends.

Where do you dump a body that you don't want found?

Time they'd figured it out they'd missed the target. Third time.

Signal came down that she'd triggered the flag on her account. Branch bank out in the sticks. Time the dynamic duo makes it across town the lady is long gone.

The old man was really pissed about that. Gave D'Mello the distinct feeling that his new career was headed for the crapper.

Now they're checking out homeless shelters. And Klegg is into telling him how to drive.

"Right! Right! I told you to turn right, you retard."

D'Mello slams on the brakes.

"Yeaoohhh!" Klegg screams.

D'Mello looks over. Klegg is shaking his hand, squirming in his seat.

"Made me spill my coffee, you pudwhacker."

Klegg pours two fingers from his silver flask into his half-empty cup.

"Serves you right."

"For what?"

For what?

At the time D'Mello had thought that three times Army pay for the same work was a no brainer. So he'd quit the Army and joined the outfit. Height of the Iraq war. Pentagon outsourcing everything. Private security. Next big thing. He'd be protecting diplomats. Fighting terrorists. Big bennies. Big pay check and a 20-year Army pension—

PRET-TY Sweet!

Besides, the old man himself had looked him up down at Fort Bliss. Taken him up in that pimped-out corporate jet, fed him French food and fine wine. Made him feel like a prince. Made him see how little the Army really appreciated him.

"We only recruit the cream of the crop," Stone had said. "And you're it."

Never expected that he'd be dismantling some poor civilian's life piece by piece— hunting her down like a wounded rabbit.

And never expected that he'd serve his hitch under cowboy psychopaths like Klegg.

And now he's an accessory to murder.

Army pension's not much. But gotta be better than this.

D'Mello's still chewing over the phone call. Good news or bad— he can't decide.

He'd blown big with Klegg over the federal agent. Big time. Klegg had threatened to fire his ass. No need he'd told Klegg. He'd just walk.

Klegg had called HQ on the secure sat phone, was put through to the old man himself. He'd heard Klegg say that D'Mello was a screw-up, wanted him out. Wanted someone who knew how to take orders. Smiled when he handed the phone over to D'Mello.

"So what's your side of this fairy tale, sonny boy?" the raspy voice had asked.

"This mission is totally FUBAR. Fire me. Reassign me anywhere. But I want out."

"You want out— Why?"

"Truth?"

"Klegg listening?"

"Yeah—"

"Tell Klegg to take a walk—"

D'Mello walked down the road out of hearing range.

"This guy you've got running this op, this Klegg, is certifiably nuts— Judgment of a squirrel. I don't give a squat if he is a major."

"Tell me again about the fed."

D'Mello went over it again. Felt good to get it out.

"This comes out, sir, I'm up for murder of a federal agent and SVS Security is hanging by the short hairs. I'm saying, Major Klegg is a psychopath— a strategic and tactical liability."

"Came well qualified."

"Well I don't care if he is a ring knocker or how many ribbons he's got stuffed in his goodie drawer. He's a lush and a liability."

The response surprised him.

"My conclusion exactly. Klegg wasn't my choice. I have partners— Klegg was their man— Insisted I put him in charge of the operation. Never was sure about the man myself. So now I'm putting you in charge."

"What about Klegg?"

"History. But, look, for now, don't tell Klegg. Suck it up 'til I can deal with it."

"Look, this op is going down the tube. We need more feet on the ground— Experienced operators."

"Look, read the papers. Every hot spot on the globe— you name it,

SVS is ground zero. Secretaries, Ministers, CEOs tracking me down—
begging me for protection. Can't take a crap here without someone
knocking on the stall door—"

"But, sir—"

"I'm telling you, Sergeant, I'm scraping the bottom of the barrel as
is. Klegg was the last and only name on the list. Had my doubts from
the beginning."

"Guy's trouble—"

"So charm him along, Sergeant. This isn't the Army any more. SVS
rewards initiative. Why do you think you get the big bucks?"

"Had my way I'd frag him."

"Maybe later. But, hey, this is private enterprise."

"Private enterprise?"

"Got to treat the help right— motivate them."

"I'll motivate him—"

"Well keep our little talk between us for now."

"Tell you one thing— I'm not going to take any more of Klegg's shit."

"Well don't. Just don't disappoint me."

"This op, sir— it's jinxed."

"Why? Should have been a walk in the park. Temple fires the girl.
Mika detains her while you search her house and Temple searches her
office and car. You pick her up at the house when Mika drops her off,
bring her to me. Why was that too much for you clowns?"

"Klegg," DMello said.

"And whose idea was it to torch her house?"

"Klegg."

"Should have guess. Klegg. My bad. Should have listened to my
gut. But you'll fix it. If anyone can bring her in, you're the man."

"Maybe—"

"Maybe?"

"Yes, sir. We'll get her sir— It's just—"

"She's a willful little minx and I'm telling you now, a national
security risk."

"Yes, sir."

"Well, damn it all— Bring her in. Unharmed! Understand?"

Klegg was smirking when D'Mello handed back the phone.

"Take it he ripped you a new asshole." Klegg said.

"Something like that."

"So when are you shipping out?"

"I'm not."

Klegg gave him this pig-face stare.

"Well then, Sergeant, I expect you to get with the program."

Now Klegg is playing with his Kershaw.

"You and that toad sticker trying to make some kind of statement?" D'Mello says.

Klegg looks over— trying for a hard-on.

"Come on, say it to my face— man-to-man. Forget the oak leaf. Serves me right for what?"

"Call me retard or pudwhacker again and I'll take that blade of yours and turn you into dog meat."

"Contain yourself, Sergeant!"

"Count on it!"

"Look Sergeant! Who's packing rank here? Don't care if you are the old man's golden boy."

"Maybe— and maybe not."

"So, tell me, man-to-man, what's got your drawers in a twist?"

"You hadn't screwed up I'd be home soaking in my pool right now."

"Screwed up when?"

"Back at the lady's house."

"Couldn't help it if I had the runs."

"Could have used the lady's toilet."

"Yeah— lady comes home— I'm sitting on her pot. Get real."

"Least we could have grabbed her instead of dorking around looking for a gas station, you trying to hold it in."

"Well you're the one talked us into eating in that beaner joint— salmonella city."

"And you were the one downing margaritas and straight shots. Doing thirds on the chips and queso dip—"

"That it?"

"And torching her house— what was that about? No one ordered that."

"Bitch hears about the fire— what's she going to do?"

"You tell me—"

"Come running— stand in the street and cry. She comes, we snatch her."

"Nice theory."

"Look, bro, last thing we need is bimbo babe sneakin' home— hiding in the broom closet while we're spread thin as it is across the city— This way, one less hidey hole to cover. This way, she can run but she can't hide. We've got her money, ID. She's in this butt-hole city without a crutch to lean on— We'll find her. Simple psychology."

"Big city."

"Got to sleep somewhere. Where's she going to hole up?"

"Maybe she's caught a ride out of town."

"Think she's that smart?"

"Better hope not— for both our sakes."

"There you go again. So what's the old man going to do? Dock our pay?"

"You really don't want to know."

"Well, you've met the man. What's he like?"

"Eats screw-ups for breakfast, tell you that."

"You calling me a screw-up?"

"Shoe fits—"

Klegg tosses his coffee cup out the window. Makes his voice low and hard.

"I'm getting fed up with your insubordination, soldier. I ask a civil question— expect a civil answer. What's he like?"

"Charming. Makes you feel like a prince—"

"Yeah?"

"And would rip your tongue and shove it where the sun don't shine."

"So what if we find her—"

"Yeah?"

"What if we find her and she don't have the documents?"

"Major Klegg, sir, you'd best be advised to buff up on sign-language."

Carmichael

NOW THE water buffalo is mired in sand. Carmichael hears the beast, lowing. He is the beast, lowing. The wind, keening, drives sand over the dunes. Wicked grains, knife sharp. Carmichael knows that something is wrong. Something approaching. He wants to shout it out. His mouth moves, but sand fills his mouth, fills his lungs.

Now he's aware of an angelic face.

"There," he hears. "That should make you more comfortable."

Later, he's aware of the needle taped to the crook of his elbow, and the white plastic ID bracelet riveted around his wrist.

"These wounds on your wrists, Mr. Carmichael, why don't I believe you're the suicidal type?"

Suicidal.

"Mr. Carmichael—"

"What?" he says.

"These wounds. Look recent."

Carmichael focuses. The wrist wounds are angry red. The face is young, angelic.

"Why don't I believe you're old enough to be a real doctor?" he says.

"I was old enough to head an ER unit in South Los Angeles. And I was old enough to pull you through from critical to stable."

"Then you've seen combat," Carmichael says.

"I've seen combat, and judging from your scars, so have you."

"Occupational hazards."

"Well, that knife wound— two inches higher— would have been the end of your occupation."

"That's what the medic said about the wound on my throat."

"So you like living on the edge?"

"No, the edge kind of seeks me out."
"Well, tell me about the chemical burns around your eyes."

Carmichael sleeps.
Now, two faces fill his vision.
"How you feelin', dude?" the older face says.
"Like, flying, know what I mean?"
"Don't doubt it. Thank the Lord for those opiates. I was gut shot once. Wouldn't want to do that again."
"And why do I have a feeling you're carrying a badge?"
"We try to hide it, but what can we do?"
"And you want to ask me questions."
"If you're up for it. By the way, I'm Detective Brenner, Boston Police Department."
"Then fire away, Detective."
Most of the questions are about the stabbing.
"But here's the bitch of it," Brenner says. "We have six witnesses. Three say you hit this Mr—"
Brenner checks his notes.
"Mantico— with the bottle for no reason. So he pulled his knife and stabbed you in self-defense. The other three say he stabbed you first."
"So how is the gentleman?"
"Fractured skull, concussion. May lose his right eye."
"Case closed," Carmichael says.
"Meaning what?" Brenner says.
"Meaning that kind of damage, how's he going to be stabbing me?"
Brenner stares, looks back at his partner. The partner nods.
"Yeah," Brenner says. "That's the way we figure it too. But then there's this other matter—"
"And that is?"
"You work for Stanley Polito, am I right?"
"Wrong. What day is this?"
"Wednesday, why?"
"Gave the man notice three days ago."
"That right? Well, this morning Polito was found in the basement of his building— two .22 caliber shorts in his head— one through his heart."

"Jesus—" Carmichael says.

"You don't happen to know anything about this, do you?"

"Jesus, no—" Carmichael says. "Ask around. Been kind of busy here."

"The man had a roll of benjamins stuffed in his mouth."

Now the sounds of the hospital are clattering in Carmichael's head—chimes, voices, wheels on hard flooring.

"Ms'a Ca'michael—"

Carmichael opens his eyes.

It's Mrs. Phan.

"Just shoot me and get it over with," he says. "You here to finish the job?"

Mrs. Phan is standing at the foot of his bed, sheathed in black.

"You OK, Ms'a Ca'michael?"

"Fit as a fiddle," Carmichael says. "Can't say as much for Stanley."

"Stanley? Whaa—"

"You haven't heard?"

"Whaa Stanley?"

"Then why are you here?"

"Need help."

"Help? Near kill me— then come to my hospital bed asking for help?"

"Mr. Phan— With ancestors."

"Mr. Phan— When?"

"Two days ago— Took pills."

Mrs. Phan looks toward the ceiling, holding tight.

"I'm sorry. Mr. Phan was a good man."

"Good man. Now, no one help."

"So you're asking me? Help? Why me— with what?"

"Please—"

Now he sees her grief.

"Yes. Please, Ms'a Ca'michael— You only one. I need you— help find my daughter."

Carmichael

"DAUGHTER?" Carmichael say.

Mrs. Phan looks away, too choked to speak.

"Sit—" Carmichael says.

Carmichael is groggy, stiff with his own pain, but feels her pain, palpable, radiating out from the slim dark body. He's taken by her composure— the dignity with which she sits, her hands flat on her knees. He focuses on her hands, red and chapped, nails down to the quick.

"Your daughter—" he says. "You want me to help you. Help find your daughter. Why me?"

"I watch you—"

"When?"

"Long time—"

"Today?"

"You sleeping."

"Doped up—"

"You look— so sad."

"Sad?"

"Ms'a Ca'michael— Let me ask you—"

"What's that?"

"When last time you— happy?"

"Happy?"

"Really happy—"

"Happy? What kind of question is that?"

"Just asking—"

"What a question— When was the last time YOU were happy?"

"Last time happy— really happy— I with Kim Le."

71

"Your daughter—"

"Vietnam— Long time ago."

"Vietnam?"

"I was sixteen— fifteen maybe. Living with this man— CIA. Bad man. Very bad. But we have daughter."

"And you were happy—"

"You remember Tet— Tet offensive?"

"Before my time."

"Well, Vietnamese People's Army, you know, from north— VPA and NLF, you call Viet Cong— attack Saigon during Tet. Tet like Thanksgiving. No one expect attack. But VPA— NLF— attack. Kill many all over Saigon. Very bad for U.S. Show Communists strong. U.S. weak. Take eight more years, but VPA and NLF throw U.S. out of Vietnam.

"But— I know attack coming— Tet— Was briefed. I was cadre, see— in movement. Told to do some things. I know they plan to kill the father. Him, I don't care. Just want my baby safe. So I tell the father— attack coming. Tet. He call me crazy lady. Saigon safe. Gooks never attack. Americans slaughter them.

"But attack come. Tet. NLF almost kill the father. Now, Saigon not safe. Bombings— Shootings— Every day. For Americans— very bad. He ask me— 'How you know attack coming? Tet.'"

"I say, 'I know—'"

"He say, 'How you know, bitch! Tell me that!' He knock me down— call me slopey whore— gook spy. Pull gun. Point. Say he shoot me.

"He keep shouting— 'How did you know?' Beat me— with gun. Then, he pick up baby. Walk out door. Baby crying. 'Mama! Mama!' Last I see my baby— my Kim Le."

"And you've looked?"

"I look. Vietnam. I look. Spend money. Every dolla'. Ask around. 'My baby? My baby?' In America I ask people I know from CIA— people I know from movement."

"And you never found her—"

"One day, two men— big men— come to my door, push me inside. 'Your daughter's dead, bitch. Keep poking your nose where it don't belong and— we kill you too.'"

"Don't care—" I say. 'Where my baby?'

"They knock me down. 'Where Kim Le?' I scream.

"They— They— rape me!"

"Jesus," Carmichael says.

"Vietnam— last time— happy."

Carmichael looks over, sees the patient in the bed beyond the open drape staring. Eyes big. He looks back at Mrs. Phan. Is silent.

"You help? My Mr. Phan— with ancestors. My Kim Le— now— only family."

"Why me?" Carmichael asks. "The laundromat— You beat me silly. That's all you know about me."

"No— I know more. Find out. You good man."

"How can you say that?"

"Mr. Phan say so."

"Don't get me wrong. But Mr. Phan was one of life's innocents."

"Mr. Phan good gambler— good judge of people. But I know more— Find out."

"What do you know?"

"I know— what you do over there— Afghanistan—"

"How do you know about Afghanistan? That's— classified."

"Have friends. You brave— very brave— Afghanistan."

"Afghanistan— I was stupid."

"No— Brave. You hero."

"Anyway— Your daughter. That was more than forty years ago."

"Yes. But I have information."

"Information—"

"Friends call me— Killers— father's men— looking for my Kim Le— looking for my daughter. The father, I think, want her dead."

D'Mello

THE DESSSAULT Falcon 10 passes low and fast down the short asphalt runway, dematerializes in heat shimmers, climbs sharply, circles, and floats back in for a perfect landing.

Klegg follows through his binoculars, then, bringing them down to his chest, grins at D'Mello, "Your ass is grass now, partner."

D'Mello eases the Expedition out of the hanger's cool shadows and into the bright glare of the concrete apron, braking just beyond the descending ramp.

Stone ducks out of the sleek white fuselage, stands for a moment at the top of the ramp as though taking in sun while D'Mello and Klegg exit the SUV to greet him.

"The man himself," Klegg whispers.

Papa Hemingway, D'Mello thinks. Or maybe a muscular Hunter S. Thompson.

But as Stone descends the ramp D'Mello notes again, surprised that he hadn't remembered, the fat in Stone's face, fat under his jowls, a hard body suffering the indulgences of age and privilege. Stone's dark glasses are too small for his face.

"You I know— D'Mello, isn't it?" Stone says, nods, turns to Klegg, "So you must be Major Klegg."

"Honor, sir," Klegg says. Klegg, standing at full attention as Stone stares down on him, starts to say more but falls silent under Stone's gaze.

"Well, time is money. Let's get on with it."

Stone is already moving past the Expedition and across the apron, D'Mello and Klegg double-stepping to catch up.

"The car, sir—" Klegg says.

"Don't need it. I'll walk," Stone responds. "Need the exercise."

Now they're assembled in the dark hanger heavy with the kerosene smell of Jet A-1 aviation fuel— D'Mello, Klegg, the two muscle-bound Ukrainians, the electronic techs. Stone is looking like a four-star who has just stepped in a cow pie.

"No need to tell you gentlemen that this op has been a cluster fuck," Stone says.

Klegg throws a hard glance at D'Mello, then turns back to Stone.

"But I'm not here to bust your chops. We all know that ca-ca happens in the heat of battle. Major Klegg, here, I'm sure is doing his best in a challenging field of fire. Am I right, Major?"

Klegg salutes. D'Mello fights to keep a straight face.

"Indeed, I'm sure Sergeant D'Mello will confirm that the Major has shown admirable initiative."

D'Mello, tracing the whirls of an oil stain under Stone's feet, looks up.

Klegg starts to speak, but Stone raises his hand, pats the air. For the first time D'Mello notices the gaudy ruby ring. It looks out of place on the weathered finger.

"No, I'm here to give you a little incentive and a chance to redeem your stellar reputations."

The techs stand a little straighter.

"I can't begin to tell you how much rides on the success of this operation. This woman has stolen something vital to our national security. Vital, I say. And we can't stand for that."

"Sir," Klegg says.

"Yes, major—"

"Are we talking executive sanction here?"

"Executive sanction?"

"You know— I mean, I just want to reconfirm—"

"Of course I know. Listen to me, Major. If you so much as ruffle a hair on that woman's head, I'll ship you out so fast it will take two weeks for your sorry ass to catch up with your torso— That clear?"

"Clear, sir."

"And another thing, one word leaks out about this operation— I don't have to tell you. It will be dealt with most severely."

Stone is leaning forward, head nodding, eyes sweeping the team.

"So this is just— apprehend?" Klegg asks.

"Now you're talking—

"So here's the incentive— You bring this woman in unharmed, re- cover the documents she's stolen, and every one of you will see $10,000 tax-free in your pocket."

"Very generous, Sir—" Klegg starts to say.

"And here's your chance to redeem yourselves. We thought we'd cut this woman off from all sources of funds. Thought it would make it easier to pick her off the street. But it's just come to our attention that she's been able to obtain credit— Gold's Department Store."

"That means—"

"I know what it means, Major. Bought herself new clothes and an expensive gold bracelet. Maxed out her limit."

"A bracelet?" one of the techs asks.

"Of course," the other replies.

"What?"

"She can't get cash, but she can hawk the bracelet, pick up enough cash to skip town."

Stone nods at the tech, "Good thinking, son.

Stone steps close to Klegg, and slaps him hard on the back. "Major— You've got your work cut out for you—"

D'Mello sees Klegg wince, wonders. Then he sees Stone remove the ruby ring and slip it into his pocket.

A fluid move. A magician's move. And now Stone pats his other pockets, removes a document from one, and hands it over to Klegg.

"Here's a catalog photograph of the very item. You keep an eye on the places where she can turn that bracelet into cash and you'll find our good Mrs. Bolton."

Klegg drops the photograph, bends to pick it up.

"Now you've asked for more manpower on this op, Major. So here's someone I want you to meet. And she's bringing the ready cash you'll need to buy the eyes of every jeweler and pawn shop operator in town.

"Mika—"

D'Mello turns, sees one of the most beautiful women of memory or dreams step out of the shadows, hears her high-heels click on the hard hanger floor. But before she can fully register, he hears Klegg gasp.

"Major— you're not looking well," Stone says, face full of concern.

Klegg grasps out with his right hand, starts to fall, his face contorted, fighting for breath.

D'Mello kneels, feels for a pulse, then looks up at Stone in alarm— alarm morphing into horror. D'Mello has seen his share of people die, but never in cold blood— never— like this.

"Dear, dear!" Stone says. "Our poor Major seems to be having some kind of stroke. Heart maybe. Too much heat. Someone, please, call 911—"

But nobody moves, all staring down at the Major.

"Mika, see to it."

The team is still stunned in silence as Mika pulls out her cell phone. Klegg is now a twisted rag doll on the oil-stained concrete, mouth open.

Stone reaches down and grabs D'Mello by the upper arm, "Sergeant, a word, please—"

D'Mello follows Stone back into the shadows.

"Terrible, terrible thing," Stone says when he turns. "And terribly inconvenient. We can't let inquiries interfere with our mission."

D'Mello is still speechless.

"Yes— Yes— Flawed man, Klegg— but to see one fall in the full of life— simply terrible."

D'Mello tries to stare into Stone's eyes, but all he sees is reflected light off small dark lenses.

"I can't tell you how heavily this job weighs on a man, Sergeant. Sometimes I just want to give it up— Chuck it. I've got the ready. Plenty. But I can't up and retire. Know why?"

D'Mello shrugs.

"Patriotism."

"Patriotism?" D'Mello says.

"I walk the halls of power, Sergeant— highest reaches of power. Know what I hear?"

"No, sir."

"Hollow echoes, sir. Nothing but hollow echoes.

"Know what I see?"

"What, sir?"

"Empty gestures. Nothing but empty gestures—

"Where once leaders stood fast before every challenge, guiding our ship of state through the most perilous waters, we now have misguided ideologues at the helm, blind to true facts. We have cowering bureaucratic time-servers in the Pentagon and throughout the executive. And Congress, whores— whores with their hands out.

"Know what the biggest threat to our nation is today, Sergeant? Our world?"

"Terrorism?"

"Terrorism?" Stone laughs. "Fleas on an elephants back—"

"But 9/11—"

"9/11— Yes, sometimes even terrorists knock one out of the ball park. But we're a great and vast nation, Sergeant. A military-industrial power. Terrorists only win when we lose our courage, vigilance, and resolve. No, sir."

"So— what, sir?"

"The biggest threat is our own greedy appetites— living beyond our means. Procreating without thought for tomorrow. The result— debt out of sight, greenhouse gases, climate change— global warming."

"I'm not following you, sir?"

"I'm telling you, son, storms coming that will make Katrina look like a summer drizzle— Rising seas driving millions out of their home lands— hungry refugees pouring across our borders. Crops failures. Famine. Tropical diseases sweeping hideous death across our northernmost cities. Looting. Rape."

"I thought that was a liberal thing. Some kind of hoax."

"That's the story— way to buy time. But here's what I want you to know, son—"

D'Mello is silent, seeking something in Stone's face beyond madness.

"A few of us are preparing to grab the rudder— exert leadership— maintain order before the worst unfolds. Opportunities here. Big."

"How's that, sir?"

"Takes just a few men of resolve, Sergeant. True patriots. Can't tell you more. But I can tell you this— This mission that I'm handing over to you is crucial— Crucial!"

D'Mello doesn't know what to say. He hears the siren approaching. He hears the siren resound in the hanger, then abruptly stop.

"Now I know you're worried about this murder thing— This federal agent—"

D'Mello starts to speak, but Stone hushes him, batting down air with his hand.

"The murder of a federal agent— they'll never rest. Most they could convict you on is accessory, of course. Reach for more, no doubt. But I can promise you this, son. Won't happen. My word. An oath. This is something that will never go beyond the two of us. That tape I have will never see the light of day. Understand?"

"Tape?" D'Mello says. ˙

Stone removes his dark glasses, touches D'Mello on the shoulder.

"Some things should never be spoken— even across secure lines."

D'Mello is silent. He was proud to be a soldier— serve his country. But this?

"Understand?"

Now Stone's eyes penetrate.

D'Mello nods.

"Now, I need to know this, son. Are you with the program?"

D'Mello has many thoughts but still doesn't know what to say. But he sees something in Stone's eyes, fleeting, some struggle. Looks down. Sees Stone's right fist clenched, shaking. Wonders.

"Son?"

"Yes, sir."

"Son?"

"Yes, sir!"

Carmichael

SHE STAYS with him to the end of visiting hours, in silence mostly, Carmichael drifting in and out. The nurse asks her to leave.

She returns the next day with a gift. A ceramic water buffalo.

"Bring luck," she says.

Carmichael fingers the smooth ceramic. The tiny figure reminds him of— something. He feels a different kind of pain in his stomach.

"This search for your daughter," he says, "It could cost you big time— a lot of money."

"No worry. I pay," Mrs. Phan says. "Money no problem."

"But you had to sell off your furniture to pay the hospital."

"Who say?"

"Mr. Phan."

"Mr. Phan? Ha!" Her laugh is short and explosive. "Mr. Phan tell you that?"

"Yes," Carmichael says.

"I tell Mr. Phan no more gambling. Hide money," she says. "So Mr. Phan sell furniture."

Carmichael grins.

"Don't laugh. That Stanley. He take furniture money— take it all!"

"Well, no worry about Stanley," Carmichael says. "Stanley will never bother you again."

"No," Mrs. Phan says softly. "Stanley no bother—"

On the third day the hospital needs the bed— Or they've milked the insurance dry. They don't say.

Carmichael knows he still feels wrong inside.

"You're a tough one," the doctor says. "I don't see danger of infection— Just try to avoid knife fights— at least until the bandages come off."

Mrs. Phan is with him. He's grown used to her. Her dignity. Her silences.

Nights following her first visit, groggy with medication but restless in the dim glow of hospital light, he'd looked forward to seeing her again, hoped she'd come, mind turning   questions to ask— things to say.

And each morning she came and he was pleased.

Carmichael wants to walk, but the nurse insists on a wheelchair— regulations. Mrs. Phan insists on pushing the wheelchair.

"I feel ridiculous," Carmichael says.

"Tough one. That you," Mrs. Phan says.

Lonnie's cherry red Hummer glides through the portico just as Carmichael wheels through the hospital door. Lonnie had called. They'd arranged a time. But Lonnie had failed to show.

Now here he is— late.

The Hummer stops.

"Nearly missed me," Carmichael says.

"My man! Dig you fly ride. Just comin' to see you sorry ass!"

"Hey, Lonnie. Minute more I be long gone."

"Been busy, man! Busy busy. And you—" Lonnie looks up at Mrs. Phan, "Whoa, you must be—"

"Mrs. Phan," Carmichael says. "And you— you lookin' for work or what?"

"Work, man! The man you lookin' at, Mr. Lonnie, me, is takin' on Stanley's book. Hopin' you join my posse."

"They gave you Stanley's book? How's that work?"

"Well— They didn't 'xactly give it to me. Got to work my sorry black ass off to make their end. Even before I get a taste, you understand? But it's a start, you know? Start small— work up to the big time. American way."

"And what about George?"

"Georgie Porgie? The man thinkin' retirement. Florida maybe."

"So who did Stanley?"

"Don't look at me, man!"

"Yeah—" Carmichael says. "Wouldn't think of it."

"But when the Stanley man put the mark on you, you know—"

"Stanley put the mark on me?"

Lonnie lowers his chin and stares over the top of his dark glasses, "I may have said some things to some people about some things."

"Thoughtful of you—"

"Well, you know— So you want to join my posse, man? Cut you in big."

"No, Lonnie," Carmichael says. "You're the man and all. But I got this new gig."

"Chance of a lifetime, man!"

"Yeah, so they say. But, you know, one life to live' and all that."

Lonnie nods toward Mrs. Phan, "Well maybe the mama here. Hear she got some bad chops."

"Bad chops?" Mrs. Phan says.

"Like I say, Lonnie, we got this thing—"

"OK, tha's cool, man. But maybe you help me out once in awhile? Like I need someone to watch my back?"

"You got it," Carmichael says.

"Don't like that man," Mrs. Phan says as they watch the red Hummer glide into the glare of the street. "Bad chops—"

"Lonnie? Lonnie just got more ambition than brains."

"So you help me?"

"Well, I don't know what you're getting me into, but sure bet it'll beat riding shotgun for Lonnie."

Kimberly

KIMBERLY has changed back into her dirty jeans. She walks into Auntie's Breakfast Shack, has had her eye on it since dawn. She threads her way through the tables, slips behind the counter, picks up a pot of hot coffee, and steps around to a table of truck drivers.

"What's yours, gentlemen?"

Kimberly calls to the heavy woman across the counter, "Three eggs over easy with hash browns, a full stack with country links, one Spanish omelet, and the Rancher's special— scrambled."

Mattie Flores, the woman at the grill, looks over her shoulder, steps away and into Kimberly's face. She looks Kimberly up and down.

"Just what do you think you doing, girl?"

"You need help. I need a job. And here I am."

"What makes you think I need help? And why should I hire you?"

Customers are turning in their seats.

"Mr. Courtney at the bank told me you need help. And you won't find better than me."

"Hire her, Auntie," one of the customers says. "She's a looker."

Mattie looks across the crowded tables. "Mr. Courtney, huh?"

"Look, I'm down on my luck. Maybe we can help each other."

"Well, business ain't been so great."

"I've been watching you trying to do three jobs at once."

"Well, can't pay much."

"Breakfast and tips. All I ask."

"You're not running from the police or nothin' are you, Sweet Cakes? I mean way you talk and those hands, you could get a job up town."

"No— No— Nothing like that. But I'd rather— rather— well, my husband's trying to find me and—" Kimberly lets tears flood her eyes.

With stress, fatigue, and hunger, it's easy.

"Say no more, child" Mattie says, "We got a pack of hungry mouths to feed here. Apron behind the counter there. Just call me Auntie."

Auntie's closes at 2:30, but it's 3:15 before the last of the lunch crowd walks out the door.

"Whoo wee," Mattie says. "Sit, Sweetie. I like to make myself a big salad about this time. How about you? Chef's special—"

"I'd die for a salad," Kimberly says. "Let me help."

"No— no— You sit. I know where everything is."

"These customers of yours. You'd think this was a strip club. My bottom is going to be black-and-blue all over."

"They're mostly good boys, here. But don't you put up with that sass. Next time one of those randies gets fresh, you just pour a pot of hot coffee down his jeans. Got me, Sweetie? He'll get the picture. Word'll get around."

Kimberly laughs.

"So how'd you make out?"

"What do you mean?"

"Tip wise—"

"Don't know. Couldn't keep count. Put it all in that big bowl behind the counter."

Maude leans down.

"Did right good looks to me— But here's another somethin' to put in that bowl. Never got your breakfast this morning."

"Auntie!"

"Got a place to stay?"

Kimberly is silent.

"What— Been sleepin' on the street?"

Kimberly turns her head toward the sun-drenched window.

"Well I got an extra room. You, know. 'Til you get your feet under yourself."

"I can't—" Kimberly is trembling.

"Hush, Sweetie. Been there. You just listen to your Auntie ."

"Thank you," Kimberly says. "You're such a dear. I don't want to be trouble."

"Sweetie," Mattie says, "I don't see you bein' no trouble at all."

Carmichael

TRANSLUCENT lips, flecked with scarlet, suck the pellet from General Vo's fingers, then sink back under the roiling surface.

"Grand Champion. Three international competitions," General Vo says. "Yesterday— turn down one hundred twelve thousand dollar."

"One hundred twelve—" Carmichael chokes. Mrs. Phan smiles.

"Yes, see body— perfect shape. Skin vibrant, youthful. But this fellow— old-timer," the General shows yellow teeth. "Like me."

Seen from behind, the General looks like a ten-year-old with wiry white hair sticking out from under his Red Sox cap. From the front his face is reddish brown from decades of sun, heavily scared. His right eye is sightless.

"Handsome, I'll give you that— But one hundred twelve—"

"Notice brilliant color, interesting pattern, perfect balance. Edges razor sharp. White is clean, creamy, lustrous. See how he swims— Like emperor— proud personality, but generous. See— he backs away— gives others chance to eat."

"So you going to sell?"

"Still thinking. Yes, this one, maybe sell— maybe not. Maybe we retire together!"

Smiling, the General's sun-battered face breaks into a Mondrian surface of fine lines.

"Retire— you—" Mrs. Phan shakes her head.

"So who buys these things?" Carmichael asks, "I mean, no offense, but who has that kind of dough to spend on fish?"

"Oh, we sell all around world. True koi lovers? What's word— besotted. Money no object. We sell rare water plants too. Won't tell you price. Shocking!

"And we formulate own brand of fish food. Our secret. Wipe out competition. Best koi farms in Japan buy from us now. Nothing too good for them."

The General drops his voice to a whisper, "But they don't like to buy from Vietnamese. So catalog in Japanese. Japanese brand name."

Carmichael looks out through the open doors toward the acres of ponds and greenhouses. The greenhouses are silver with condensation; the near ponds shifting swirls of red, orange, white, and silver.

"Are all these fish in these ponds worth that kind of dough? I mean one hundred twelve—"

"No— no. But that one, the Showa, worth maybe eighty thousand— eighty five. But most— in this pond— twenty-five hundred— three thousand. That pond out there— by tractor— dollar eighty five."

Carmichael shakes his head. "Dollar eighty five— That I can afford."

"I ring it up," the General smiles, leads them from one humid greenhouse into another and toward the front of the farm.

"But, enough tour. You not here for fish tour."

"Mrs. Tho call me—" Mrs. Phan says, "About Kim Le— say you have big news."

"News, maybe—"

"Maybe?"

"My friend, An Duc Tran own flower shop— Four men walk in— My friend Tran know these men. Bad men. Killers—"

Mrs. Phan looks down, stares at the wet wooden slats under her feet, then looks up at the General.

"Killers?"

"Men wave this photo around. Woman— Vietnamese, maybe. Maybe not. Can't tell. One man, not leader, say 'Big Fish offer big reward.' Leader hit him, say, 'Shut the f up!' pardon language."

"Photo— Kim Le?"

The General shrugs.

"Kim Le— Must be! We must find her!"

"How?" Carmichael asks.

"Catch Big Fish," the General says.

"And what makes you think the old man is behind all this?" Carmichael asks.

"During war— father big shot. CIA. Code name— Big Fish."

"And what makes you think this mystery woman is Kim Le?"

"An Duc Tran say woman— what you call— Eurasian. Right age."

"Kim Le— Why? What this about?" Mrs. Phan says, "Why that *lo dit* want to hurt her?"

"Maybe Kim Le have something Big Fish want," the General says.

"What could that be?" Carmichael ask. "Money?"

Mrs. Phan snorts.

"An Duc Tran think woman in big trouble. These men— Killers."

"Just doesn't add up," Carmichael says.

"Other people call me— frightened. 'Bad men,' they say. Searching for this woman. Everywhere. Threaten people. Hurt people."

Mrs. Phan's face hardens.

"So the only way to find the daughter," Carmichael says, "Is to hook into this Big Fish— let him lead us to her."

The General smiles.

"No—" Mrs. Phan says.

"Only way.

"Too dangerous!"

"So what can you tell me about this father?" Carmichael asks.

"Big shot. C. Norbert Stone. Slippery fish. Very dangerous— Shark."

"Big shot," Carmichael says, "So how can we get close to this C. Norbert Stone?"

The General turns, his sighted eye bright, shining, "In war— my orders— kill this Big Fish aka Conrad aka C. Norbert Stone. Very clever man. Almost kill me. Not easy. Yes, come—"

Carmichael is glad to escape the greenhouse humidity into the air-conditioned quonset hut. They move through the sales area, then a discreet door.

"My office—" the General says.

The office is more laboratory than executive space— a binocular microscope on a long bench, petri dishes and dissection tools, bottles of reagents, small tanks with colorful fish. The General moves to a battered desk cluttered with sales brochures, technical journals; dominated by a flat-screen computer monitor.

Moving from humidity of the greenhouses to the cool of Vo's office, and lulled by the soft burble of aerators, Carmichael begins to feel fatigue. He touches his stomach, feels sharp pain.

The General hands him two thick notebooks.

"For you. Everything we know about our Conrad aka C. Norbert Stone."

Carmichael sets the notebooks on the bench, starts thumbing through.

"Jesus!" he says. "This stuff— You didn't get this from press clippings."

"Network—" the General smiles.

"Network? You some kind of spy?"

"No— no— Think gossip. We Vietnamese village people— we stay in touch. Especially those of us from North."

"But how? This stuff—"

"Vietnamese people hard workers. Little job. Big job. This country— all around world— just gooks. People pay no attention."

"But how do you pull all this stuff together— this information? I mean, this is professional work— the work of a professional analyst."

"Some I bring from Vietnam. But now we have IRC— Internet Relay Chat. Private channel. For Vietnamese only. Our private Google. Go through Freenet. All encrypted. Much easier than Vietnam days."

"And the analyst, I suppose, is you."

The General bows.

"Are these your only copies?"

"Computer copies. I print for you."

"Then you—?"

"Knew you were coming?"

Carmichael nods.

"Oh, yes. I knew."

"General Vo know before I know," Mrs. Phan says.

"Christ, says here— back in Vietnam days— you traded personally with this guy Stone— heroin for arms."

"Not me— Comrades. Movement poor. Needed arms. Besides, good strategy— weaken enemy."

"Was this a CIA thing? Or just Conrad?"

"Oh, just Conrad— Maybe few others. Probably others."

"But he tried to make an end run— hook up with your suppliers while double-crossing your cell."

"Why they send me in to kill."

"And you failed—'

"Three months re-education. Failure no option."

"So how much shit was this low-life moving?"

"Shit?"

"Heroin."

"Oh big operation. Went on long time."

"This Conrad guy must have made a fortune."

"Conrad return to US. Become C. Norbert Stone. Invest in private prisons in Texas. Big state contracts. Take over company. Expand into security field. Make more money. Right off, big supplier of security guards in Iraq— play golf with Pentagon big-shots. Buy up defense companies."

Carmichael continues thumbing through the notebooks.

"I can't believe this," he says, "You've got a copy of next week's appointment schedule, the name of his barber, last week's golf score, here's— here's, Jesus! His favorite sex games?

"Why so much interest in this C. Norbert Stone?"

"Keep enemies close. You know that one, Mr. Carmichael?"

"And he's still your enemy."

"Oh yes."

"You've lived a long life. So how many enemies do you have?"

"Too many—" The General looks tired now. "Too many. But now, want you to meet my good friend, Nuygen."

Carmichael hears a cough, turns, looks down, startled. The old man with the eager smile is even smaller than the General.

"I didn't hear him come in," Carmichael says.

"Nuygen very quiet, can't speak. During war Big Fish cut his tongue. After war, find him. Say sorry. Hire him. We call him Not There."

Nuygen beams.

"Nuygen expert in surveillance— and what you call bag jobs. Now house boy for C. Norbert Stone. But report to me. What I know I pass to you."

Carmichael shakes Nuygen's hand, turns back toward General Vo.

"If he works for Stone, why is he here?"

"Sister sick— visiting sister. Everything I know I send to you. Here's e-mail address, password. Log in. Read. Don't save. Don't reply. Best I can do for you."

"General, you big help," Mrs. Phan says.

"One more thing—" the General opens a locked cabinet under the laboratory bench. Pulls out two pistols.

"Glock 17. Receiver, grip, mostly plastic. Take special training to see in airport X-Ray machines. These— no serial numbers. Untraceable."

"And you think we'll need these?" Carmichael asks.

"Oh yes," the General says. "I think so."

The Missionaries

"SPEAK of the devil!"

Speaking into the mirror, Senator Robert Macintyre raises his hand in a back-handed wave.

Dexter Blaine flashes his gold-plated smile.

"What's say, parishioners?"

Blaine edges into the cramped make-up studio off the guest lounge, shadowed by his young Georgetown intern.

"Hi there, Senator," Elaine says. "With you in a jif."

Elaine readjusts the towel covering Macintyre's shoulders, sponges the final touches of face powder onto his puffy cheeks.

"Just need a touch of foundation on my sweetie's forehead here."

"Always feel like a damn fool in this chair," Macintyre says.

And act like one in many another, Blaine thinks, but says, "You're looking fit for battle, Bob."

"Ten minutes, gentlemen," the floor producer says, poking his head through the door.

"Honey cakes, get me a diet Coke," Senator Blaine asks the intern.

Elaine flips off the towel, flicks a brush over Macintyre's powder blue shirt and signature red suspenders.

"That's going to have to do, my good sir."

She turns to Blair.

"And now let's see what we can do with you handsome."

The first few questions are soft-ball— Sharon Sawtelle softening them up.

Blaine knows that her aim is to provoke a dog fight. He also knows that Macintyre is too self-righteous to duck and dodge.

"So Senator Blaine, this bill you've just released from committee, won't it open up old partisan divisions? I mean your own President—"

"I should hope not, Sharon," Blaine responds. "I'd say it's about hands across the divide."

"Hands across the divide—" Sawtelle says. "Really?"

"We all know that our country has lost standing around the world, Sharon. Our bill shows the world that we're a law-abiding nation. While individuals may step over the line in times of threat, there's ultimate accountability— rule of law."

"Accountability!" Macintyre sputters. "Your bill throws good men— patriotic men— to the wolves!"

"Bob— Bob— You know that S. 6703 does nothing of the sort."

"The wolves! You remember what it was like after the attack. Who knew when the next one was coming? Could be a nuke— Anthrax— We needed intel.

"Patriotic men and women throughout our military and security services went the last mile to keep us safe."

"And some of those patriotic men and women stepped over the line— broke the law, Senator— Our law. International law. S. 6703 simply aims to get to the bottom of who did what to whom and what laws apply."

"It was war, Dexter. We have a right to defend ourselves. Our national security was at stake. Still is. Our Commander in Chief has a sworn duty to protect us. Jefferson said so. Lincoln said so. FDR said so. And you know it."

"Even if I take your point, Bob, the world has moved on. Yet unchecked power persists. Look, you have grandchildren, am I right?"

Macintyre flashes a smile at the camera. "Two lovely towheads I'm proud to say—"

"And when you think about the future, Bob— don't you worry about your grandchildren?"

"Worry—?"

"Your lovely grandchildren living with the awesome weapons we have today— living on the edge of annihilation?"

"Of course, but—"

"Doesn't it concern you whose finger is on the button?"

"Of course— But you know damn well—"

"Then why aren't you just as worried about unchecked domestic surveillance, secret detention centers, even U.S. citizens subject to indefinite military detention, torture?"

"Look, this is America! We don't—"

"Exactly! This is America. Then you must certainly agree that all centers of power must be accountable. Even the President of the United States. There's no place for Dirty Harry in the White House."

Macintyre is now red with rage.

"Dirty Harry! You're talking about true patriots here."

"We're talking about the rule of law."

"Tell that to your damn terrorists!"

"Gentlemen," Sawtelle says, "Let's move on to a different topic—"

Blaine holds the heavy glass door, waves the young intern out into the pale D.C. sun.

The intern, reflecting on the interview, wonders what it would be like to sleep with a United States Senator.

"You were wonderful, Senator!" she says.

Blaine wonders whether to buy his wife pearls or silk for their third anniversary. Jumping the gun by a few years, his secretary warned him, but leather just doesn't convey the depths of his feelings.

The shooters watch, wait until the senator and the student step into the guest parking lot before moving in.

Then, when they move, they move in fast. They deploy into a classic L, fire six silenced shots, four shattering heart, two brain.

The shooters are in separate cars and moving before the young Georgetown intern fully realizes that Senator Dexter Blaine is no longer at her side but is, rather, lifeless in a pool of blood at her feet.

The intern is still screaming, hysterical, when the responding officers arrive.

"They were old guys," she screams. "In suits! They were old guys. In suits!"

Later, in the stark interrogation room, sedated, she remembers the only words spoken.

"Come Reunion—" the detective repeats.

He raises his eyebrows.

"What in hell is that supposed to mean?"

Carmichael

THEY WALK two miles into the state park. Carmichael is breathing hard, out of shape— worries about the stitches in his belly.

The late winter landscape is bleak, snow gone, ground soggy, but still too early for spring buds. The trail is deserted.

"Why here?" Mrs. Phan asks. "He expecting us. We late."

"Won't take long."

"Why not go to pistol range?" Mrs. Phan asks.

Carmichael drops the shoulder pack, unravels the nylon tie, and pulls out the Glocks wrapped in red flannel.

"With these weapons?" he says. "No serial numbers?"

"I see, yes," she says.

"OK, this weapon has three safeties— an external trigger safety, a firing pin safety, and a drop safety.

"You engage and disengage the external trigger safety with this small lever. The other two safeties disengage automatically when you pull the trigger. That makes them sort of dangerous. So keep your fingers away from the trigger until you're ready to shoot.

"You know safety, yes?"

Mrs. Phan looks on with interest. "Yes. I know safety."

"This weapon has a double box magazine that holds 17 rounds— 18 if there's a round in the chamber. Here's how you remove the magazine, rack the slide, and clear the chamber. Best not to keep a round in the chamber unless you know you need to fire on a moment's notice."

"Life in danger," she says.

"Yes, life in danger. But, otherwise, I wouldn't count on the safeties alone to keep you safe. Now here's how you load the magazine and snap it into place. You want to try?"

"No. No."

"Won't bite," Carmichael holds out the pistol, grip first.

Mrs. Phan backs away. "You do it. I can do when time come."

Carmichael pulls an empty Coke can from the bottom of the day pack, paces off thirty paces, sets up the can, and strides back.

"Now hold the pistol in two hands, like this— squeeze through smoothly like you're stroking a baby's cheek. Whatever, don't jerk the trigger."

Carmichael slowly squeezes off the trigger. Misses the can by inches.

"Now, I try," Mrs. Phan says.

"Yeah. Yeah. OK—" Carmichael drops the magazine, and empties the chamber.

"Load magazine— Safety off—" Mrs. Phan says.

"It'll kick," Carmichael says. "Don't be surprised. Don't fight it."

Mrs. Phan takes the position, slowly squeezes off three rounds, sends the Coke can flying, third round hitting the can on the fly.

"Why am I not surprised," Carmichael says. "You've done this before."

"Yes. Yes. I do this before."

"Well I would have done better if you hadn't half blinded me with laundry bleach."

"Oh, big baby. More practice. You do better."

Walking back down the trail they're intercepted by a park ranger on an ATV.

"Heard shots down this way," he says. "You folks hear anything?"

"Yes. Yes—" Mrs. Phan says, looking distressed. "Back that way. We scared. You escort us out?"

"No. No. Just stay on this trail and you'll be all right. I've got to check this out. Probably just some knucklehead."

They listen to the ATV roar down the trail.

"You some knucklehead," Mrs. Phan giggles.

"Speak for yourself, Madam," Carmichael says, holding back a grin.

"Hurry now," Mrs. Phan says. "He expecting us—"

"Who's expecting us?" Carmichael asks, but Mrs. Phan has retreated into silence.

Carmichael

CARMICHAEL slows, edges to the side of the road. All he can see is the billowy back-glare of his driving lights.

"Why stop?" Mrs. Phan asks.

"Fog. Can't see a damned thing."

"We late. Must hurry."

"We're alive. Want to keep it that way."

Carmichael dims his lights. Then tries his parking lights. Now he can see faint gray-on-gray shapes through the swirling fog. He checks his Magellan GPS. One mile to the turn-off. Wild Turkey Lane.

He feels like a turkey chasing a wild goose. Mrs. Phan has been silent ever since they'd crossed into Maine. She refuses to give him a name— tell him who they're going to see.

"Must hurry, Ca'michael. We late."

"Please, let me drive," Carmichael says.

It's the only house on the lane. Set back. A single porch light illuminates cedar shakes black with condensation. Carmichael can smell the beach roses overgrowing the cobblestone walkway. Mrs. Phan rings the brass ship's bell hanging beside the door.

For a moment the dog barking between the man's legs distracts Carmichael. Then he's aware of the familiar looming shape— curly black hair, black eye patch, heavy shoulders, slight hunch.

"Thought you'd never see this sorry-ass face again, did you soldier?"

For a moment Carmichael wants to panic. He looks at Mrs. Phan.

"So come in. Come in. Milly, you lookin' fine, girl. Sorry about your troubles, beautiful thing."

"Milly?" Carmichael looks again at Mrs. Phan.

"Mei Li," she says. "Vietnamese name."

"Come get warm by the fire. And don't worry about me, son. I don't bite anymore."

Inside they smell the fire and the sweet smell of raw wood. The space is large, two rooms opened into one, but half taken up with two saw horses holding the ribs and chines of an unfinished skiff.

The dog, a yellow lab, is still sniffing out Carmichael, his hands and crotch. But when Carmichael reaches out it backs away with a snarl.

"That's Pirate. Only bites strange white men."

The dog looks at the man for reassurance.

"Big pussy cat, aren't you, Pirate. Tear your throat out if he takes a disliking."

"What's going on?" Carmichael says. He wants to leave.

"Sit down, son. Here by the fire. And let me get you a cold one. Must have been hell driving up through this fog."

"How do you know this man?" Carmichael asks.

"Vietnam," Mrs. Phan says. "Good friend."

"Yes, we both worked for our good friend Conrad," the man says returning to the fire with three Heineken's. "Milly here was our best asset."

"Last time I saw you," Carmichael says, "You were trying to nail my ass to the barn door. You treated me like scum of the earth."

"No soldier, that's where you're wrong."

"Wrong, how? And what am I supposed to call you now? Sir—? Major—? Ass Wipe—?"

"Ned will do. Ned— Boswick— or Ass Wipe if you prefer."

"Well— Ass Wipe— last time you were pointing your finger at me. I can still see your face all full of righteous indignation. What were the charges? Failure to obey orders—? Dereliction of duty—? Insubordination in the face of the enemy—?"

"Last time, we were actors in a Kabuki play, had our roles to perform."

"And you the Lord High Executioner."

"Well, yes. But there's something you didn't know."

"And that is?"

"I was on your side."

"My side? You were going for dishonorable discharge and twenty years hard time in federal prison."

"Yes, there's that. But what you didn't know is that the high command wanted you wrapped up in foil and tied to a Fourth-of-July rocket. Wanted you to blaze a bright and sparkling path across the sky— an object lesson for all to see. Don't fuck with power."

"Oh, that I knew. You made that plain as day."

"But what you didn't know is that I thought you'd done the right thing."

"Didn't show it at the court marshal."

"No. Not my role. But what you didn't know is that young buck defending you didn't know his tender white ass from a soccer ball."

"Knew enough to get me a general discharge."

"And what you didn't know is that I fed him the evidence and the arguments that enabled him to win the day."

"Jesus," Carmichael says.

"Son, I'll go to my grave believing you did the right thing saving those young girls.

"See–" Ned turns to Mrs. Phan, "Carmichael was leading a long-range reconnaissance patrol. Tasked to keep an eye on this village that was being terrorized by the Taliban. But not, under any circumstances, to engage. See, they were expecting Omar himself to show up. But there was this secret school for girls in the village. You know— teach 'em basic reading and writing. The Taliban discovered it and— decided to burn it to the ground— girls inside.

"Our boy here decided to save the day. Orders one of his men to follow him in, the four to provide cover. A total of six men against thirty-two battle-hardened Taliban warriors."

"I knew it," Mrs. Phan says. "Ca'michael hero. Should have medal."

"Yes, ma'am, routed the Taliban and saved the girls. But— lost three of the Army's finest. And one of those boys just happened to be the favored son of a United States Senator. And that's not enough, he blew an operation that went right up to the highest command. So you see, this kabuki play was a show trial, politics pure and simple— power seeking revenge."

Carmichael is looking into the fire. Remembering.

"Son, let me tell you something. I was a fair-haired boy until your trial came along. And then I had to do something against every rule in the book. Against my oath. I had to throw your trial. Just had to."

"Why?" Carmichael asks.

"Why? Because it was the right goddamn thing to do! Then, the day that court marshal ended, I filed papers for retirement. So, you see, we're not so different you and me. Now, why are you here, son?"

"Mrs. Phan's daughter."

"Right. Why?"

"Well— because—" He looks at Mrs. Phan.

"Money's good."

"Money— that's it?"

"What else?"

"You tell me, soldier."

Long silence.

"So what do you want me to say?"

"Tell me what's in here—" Boswick thumps Carmichael hard on the chest.

"What the fuck do I know? I'm here, OK?"

"You're here. Guess that counts for something."

"I can leave."

"No. There's one thing I know about you, Carmichael—"

"And what's that?"

"Know you better than you know yourself."

"Tell me—"

"You'll see it through to the end."

"Think so?"

"Know so."

"Why?"

"Because it's the right goddamn thing to do."

"We'll see— maybe."

"See! I told Milly that. Some people are bred in the bone. You can't imagine my surprise when Milly sent me a copy of your driver's license. I took one look at that photo and saw a face I'll never forget."

"Why would she do that? Send you a copy of my driver's license?"

"Long story, but look, I need help with this beauty over here. You know how to sand don't you? That's a classic New England Banks Dory. When I finish her, be my fifth one. Hopin' to get this one right. You sand. I'll keep the cold ones coming."

Carmichael is itching to know where Ned fits in. But it seems to be a kind of initiation— or meditation— the three of them, silently sanding the soft white pine. Ned scribbles graphite onto a pattern, lays it in place, points out the marks— the high spots that require more sanding.

"You see, son," Ned says out of nowhere, "I work for this group— just a dot in the organizational chart, really. And a certain person keeps lighting up our radar—"

"You're working for the government, you mean," Carmichael says.

"Yes, in a manner of speaking."

"And this person is C. Norbert Stone I take it—"

"See, Milly," Ned says, "I told you this young buck is a clever one."

"This person keeps coming up on your radar— what does that mean?"

"Well back aways you know the zeolots in power were hell-bent on privatizing everything— up to and including the White House chef—"

"Read something about it."

"Well this man that Milly and I used to work for in Vietnam— fine man we once both loved, in fact— asshole who betrayed us— has built himself a private empire that's a one-to-one parallel with our national security infrastructure— army, navy, air force, intelligence. Winning billions of dollars in federal contracts along the way."

"Where's the crime?"

"We think he's playing both sides of the fence. He's taken pains to set up several deep-cover off-shore companies and has been hiring unsavory characters from South Africa, Chile, the 'Stans in Central Asia. And we hear he's been playing footsie with the Russians, Iranians, North Koreans, and Chinese."

"So what do we have to do with it? Why don't you just bring him down?"

"For one— insufficient resources. Our agency has been hollowed out— functions outsourced to private contractors."

"So— light a fire under the contractors."

"Who do you think we're investigating?"

"For one, you said. What else?"

"Guy's titanium. Biggest political contributor in the country. Member of the ex-President's prayer circle. Pols love him. I raise a finger and I'm flat out on my ass and blacklisted in the private sector— unquote."

"And you think we can penetrate his defenses? You've got to be crazy."

"Carmichael— I had a long talk with your commanding officer. He told me that you had the best tactical mind of any young recruit he'd ever had the privilege to command."

"But why us?"

"Well, Milly here knows the man better than anyone. This lady has all the incentive in the world to bring him down. And when she sent that copy of your driver's license up to me, and I recognized you, I thanked the good Lord. Deliverance at last."

"But surely—"

"Carmichael— you're it. You and Milly. I had a man, but he's gone off-line. Don't know where he is. Fear for him. And they've cut my budget. Keeping me on a short stick."

"No." Carmichael says. "I told Mrs. Phan that I'd help her. But this thing— this is waaay too big."

"Ca'michael—" Mrs. Phan says.

"Totally nuts."

"Well look, this fog— it's too late to go anywhere tonight. Stay the night here. I've got a guest room with twin beds. We'll take another squint at this thing in the morning."

"Time to go, Mrs—" Carmichael starts.

"Ca'michael— Please," Mrs. Phan says. "Stay."

"Yes," Ned says, "A good night of sleep. We'll all feel better."

Mrs. Phan

SOMETIMES the layers of grief weigh so heavily on Mei Li's heart that she can barely breathe. It's worse in the dark of nights like this when she wakes, her heart pounding.

She sees her mother, father, kneeling in silent acceptance. Sees blood seeping through the woven bamboo.

She sees shadows— shadows that run a bayonet through her sister, then violate her corpse. She hears them laughing.

She sees shadows in the doorway— shadows in the alley— shadows retreating with her baby, hears her baby's cry.

She sees shadows from that night of horror, and now the horror-stricken eyes of the boat women as she frantically scrubs blood out of her hair with sea water.

She sees shadows between the pill bottles lined up on the night table, her husband, Jimmy, dead in their bed.

Mei Li has used her body.

Used it as a girl to survive in Saigon.

Used it for the Viet Cong, for information, betrayal.

Mei Li has used her body for the CIA, a whore in a shadow war.

Boom boom. Fuck fuck. The dirty.

She thought she had burned all womanly honor and instinct out of her body, felt nothing, until the baby came. Kim Le. Small miracle. Some kind of grace, redemption.

The baby had changed everything. Then the shadows— the shadows devoured her baby.

Mei Li has killed. They trained Mei Li how to kill with stealth. Kill with knives, guns, forks, chopsticks. Kill with fingers, fists, elbows, feet. First the Viet Cong, then the CIA. She has killed for the Viet Cong.

Killed for the CIA. Killed for survival. But the shadows defy her— she tries with all wit and strength, but the shadows refuse to die.

Mei Li remembers the deaths. Counts the deaths. Grieves for every one. Prays for their souls, knowing only the futility of her prayers.

Ghosts haunt Mei Li on nights like this.

Mei Li thinks of Ca'michael. Stupid ghost. She smiles, sees in her mind the sad way he walks, his sad ghost face. So strong. So innocent. But she needs Ca'michael, even knowing that he's a ghost. Knowing that he's bound to die.

For how can this Ca'michael possibly survive? How can even an army defeat these shadows baring down— the shadows that devoured her family— her baby— her life?

Mei Li wants to cry. But she's a ghost too. Her cheeks are dry. Ghosts shed ghost tears.

"Mrs. Phan," Carmichael says, a soft voice across the dark room.

Mei Li bites her hand.

"Mei Li, I can tell you're not sleeping."

"Ca'michael— why you not sleeping?"

"Same reason you're not. How can this thing be done?"

"We can do it, Ca'michael."

"How?"

"Don't know. But we can."

II

El Diablo Negro

THE FISSILE material, sufficient for a 12 kiloton device, was re-purposed from a 203 mm tactical nuclear artillery shell.

The projectile was originally intended for the 2S7 Pion self-propelled artillery gun, one of the most formidable weapons in the old Soviet armory.

Little Boy, the device that leveled Hiroshima, had an explosive yield nearing 15 kilotons. By Little Boy standard, 12 kilotons is more than sufficient for the task at hand.

The Pion has a range of nearly 43 miles, laughably insufficient for the task at hand.

The shell had long rested on a paint-chipped cradle in an underground bunker in a Belarus weapons depot, unmolested but not forgotten. The tip of the shell was painted red. The cradle was olive-green.

Sale of the shell was brokered in Brest, Belarus, within easy driving distance of the eastern Polish border.

The buyer was an older man, thin, formal in manner, dressed in a dated black suit.

The broker was Lieutenant General Valentin Siderov (Ret.) The General was known in the arms trade for the disconcerting limp earned in Afghanistan when rocket grenade fragments seared muscle to bone down the length of his left leg.

The Pion shell was wrapped in lead shielding and smuggled via truck, fishing boat, and air across eight national borders, delivered at precisely 1:10 am to the north end of an abandoned airstrip 23 miles south of Herat, Afghanistan.

The 240-pound package was delivered by a 43-year-old Antonov cargo plane flying dark.

At 1:29 am, not three minutes into its return flight, the Antonov lit up the night sky, brought down by a single Stinger missile.

Eight hours and forty two minutes later General Siderov was found dead in his widower's bed, apparent heart attack.

Boswick

BOSWICK is awake, aware of pale dawn stepping through his window, creeping down his wall, but the cell on his handcrafted cherry night stand brings him to full alert.

"Yeah? Yeah— My God! How'd they find him? Accident maybe? Yeah, of course. Look— Keep this contained. Don't break it to Caroline just yet. Yeah, until we're sure. Keep me posted. I'll fly out. Confirm it's him. See if you can work out a schedule— for three. Yeah. Today. Commercial. Yes three. No more rides on the agency jet. Budget reasons they tell me."

Boswick shuffles into his cramped bathroom, stares into the mirror, not seeing. He places hands on each side of the mirror, braces himself, drops his head. Whispers a lengthy prayer.

Now he steps out of his sweat pants and into the shower. He dries, shaves, and clothes himself in fresh sweats.

The house is silent, just the usual morning settling, tick of the furnace. Pirate, Boswick's yellow lab, presses against his thigh. Boswick absently squeezes the dog's long muzzle, feels the wet of lips and cold nose. He pauses by his skiff, knocks the gunwale with his knuckles. He stoops to run his hand along a pine strake, rolls the fine sawdust between thumb and middle finger, brings his dusty fingers to his nose.

Shuffling into the kitchen he turns the cold water tap to fill Pirate's bowl, glances up through his window and sees a figure down near the bottom of his land— Carmichael— hulking dark figure standing in the mist at the steep rock edge that plunges into the sea.

Boswick walks barefoot down through the wet grass. The ground is cold, but he doesn't feel up to retracing his steps for sneakers. The Atlantic is morning gray, long ground swells roll beneath the glass-smooth surface. Three black cormorants stand like death down on the black rocks.

"Hey," he says.

Carmichael is silent, staring out to sea.

Boswick, now silent too, stands beside him.

"We can't split our forces," Carmichael says finally.

"Meaning what?"

"You've handed me two objectives. We can't take 'em both on at the same time."

"Two objectives?"

"Find Kim Le— Take down this clown— C. Norbert Stone."

"Maybe it's really one objective."

"How so?"

"We could track down Kim Le. But then we'd have to keep her safe. Stone's a powerful man, and determined, so safe might not be an option. Besides, we don't know where she is— where to begin."

"So you're telling me we have to neutralize Stone first. That's the prime objective."

"Way I see it."

"And what about Mrs. Phan? How will she see it?"

"Let's walk."

"Where're your shoes?"

"Easy path here along the cliff. No sweat."

They walk in silence, mist swirling, dripping off trees. Boswick feels soft mud ooze up between his toes; breaks off a shriveled beach rose, rubs the petals between fingers and thumb, brings the scent to his nose.

"Looks like they've murdered my man Tim Valentine," Boswick says.

"Murdered—"

"Couple of mining engineers found a body in an abandoned silver mine."

"His?"

"'pears as though."

Carmichael stops. "Where?"

"Arizona. Scratch on the map called Martinez Canyon some 40 miles east of Phoenix— Four-wheel drive country."

"Stone has an aerospace plant near Phoenix."

"Thought has occurred to me."

"How'd he die? Your man—"

"At first they thought he'd accidentally fallen into the pit. But then they found a bullet wound through his inner thigh."

"Inner thigh?"

"Medical examiner says the bullet severed his femoral artery. Says he bled out."

"Shot himself maybe? Accident?"

"Never carried a gun— That was Tim. Fancied himself a better negotiator than shooter. Besides, not enough blood at the site. He'd been shot and bled elsewhere, then transported to the mine— thrown into the pit."

"Someone erasing their tracks?"

"Maybe."

"Look, Major—"

"Ned—"

"Ned. Was your man in contact with Mrs. Phan's daughter, Kim Le?"

"Don't know. Maybe. Said he was working on something. Had a line on hard evidence."

"Hard evidence?"

"Something we could use to bring charges against Stone."

"OK, Stone's beating the bushes for his daughter. Suggests that Kim Le may have information the man wants— information that could hurt him. Stone finds out your man is sniffing around— wants to find out what he knows."

"Valentine was tough— stubborn. Doubt he'd give up much without a fight."

"Maybe that's the story— and your man lost."

"We need to get back," Boswick says. "I'm waiting for a call."

Mrs. Phan is on the back lawn, dressed in white tee, loose white pants, black canvas shoes. She's moving slowly, smoothly, through postures— knees bent, her hands part like pulling taffy, roll. Each move blends into the next, seems to take an eon. Her face is blank, meditative. She sinks, touches her right toe, rises, suddenly strikes, then kicks so fast that Boswick hardly catches it.

"God, she's beautiful," Boswick says.

Carmichael nods. "Moves like a 16-years-old."

"Man o' man if you could have seen Mei Li at 16— Spectacular. Full
of fire. I found her first— wanted her so badly I could hardly breathe.
But Conrad took her. Privileges of rank. Conrad took her, then— corrupted her."

"Boswick, Carmichael says, "Tell me something—"

"Yeah—"

"What did you know about the heroin?"

"Heroin?"

"Your buddy Conrad was trading with the Viet Cong— arms for
heroin."

"And you know this how?"

"Straight from the horse's mouth. North Vietnamese General. Friend
of Mrs. Phan's."

"Swear to God, no," Boswick says. "I didn't know about heroin. All
I know is that the bastard betrayed us."

"Betrayed you how?"

"Leaked names of our best agents. Last three months in 'Nam our
unit had a sixty percent loss rate."

"What makes you think betrayal?"

"Had to be. Two years without a loss. Then seven good men wiped
out in seven actions. Just like they knew we were coming."

"Why do you think it was Stone?"

"He tasked them. He was the only one who knew where they would
be when."

"Ever think that it might have been Mrs. Phan?"

"Mrs. Phan?"

"She was working with the Viet Cong— Knew about the Tet offensive before it happened."

"And this you know how?"

"Told me herself—"

"Christ." Boswick turns, stares at the sea, turns back.

"No. If Milly was working with Charlie, Conrad was running her."

"Maybe—" Carmichael says. "She's a deep lady, our Mrs. Phan."

"So what are you going to do?"

"Help her."

"Why?"

"Wish I knew."

C. Norbert Stone

SEAGULLS swoop and dive in the wake of the forty-foot Catalina. S. P. Stewart Graham inexpertly tacks into the gusty mid-winter wind. He fills the cockpit in his bulky Navy pea coat. The former Deputy Director of NSA, once known as No Such Agency, has fleshy hands, more suited to glad-handing than weather.

Stone wipes salt from his glasses, leans in to better hear General Lyman R. Baxter (Ret.).

The General's sibilant voice and face express defiant discomfort. He's hunkered up against the cabin bulkhead to avoid the icy spray, hands holding his coat tight to his thin body, shivering.

Mika, on the opposite bench, unclasps the latches securing an elongated clam-shell case.

"This antic, Stone— We're not going to see our project smeared across the front page of the *Washington Post* are we?"

"It's contained, General."

"That's not what my radar tells me—"

"You suggesting, sir, that your sources are better than mine?"

"Count on it."

"Well— then you know we're copacetic."

"What I want to know, Connie Boy," Graham yells over the wind, "Is how did this woman become employed by SVS in the first place?"

"Yes, tell us," the General says.

"Husband was a test pilot employed by SVS before the takeover."

"Wait—" Graham says. "Don't tell us that her husband was that joker who crashed and burned in that screwed-up Impaler test—?"

"Unfortunately. Mrs. Bolton, Kimberly, applied six months later— Outstanding recommendations."

"Looking to avenge her husband no doubt," the General says. The General's face hardens. "And you didn't recognize the name— the face? How is it she slipped through your pickets?"

Stone is silent, eyes on the unsteady horizon.

"We're talking about your daughter here, Connie Boy," Graham says.

"Look, I was stationed in ten countries during the first twelve years of her life— Saving the world from Godless Communism. Last I saw her she was an angry punk wannabe with white make-up and purple hair. Wasn't invited to the wedding. Never knew her married name. It's been years."

"Exemplary family values—" Graham mutters.

"Look— I gave that girl everything— best private schools— top tutors— foreign travel— anything and everything her heart desired."

"May be the trouble right there," the General says, teeth tight, eyes following the seagulls hovering over Stone's shoulder.

"She threw it all away on sex, booze, and drugs—"

The General's gaze snaps back.

"Drugs? She's a junkie?"

"No. Recreational only. Years ago."

"Well she's got to be stopped," the General says.

"Understood."

"Terminated ask me," P. Stewart Graham says.

"No!" says Stone.

"Rendered inoperative—" Graham says. "We can't risk a single leak."

"Look— I know about security risks. Wasn't for me that dipso major you forced down my throat would still be spewing our secrets to every barfly in Phoenix."

"According to you—"

"Damned right, according to me! I was there. Where were you?"

"So?"

"So— I did your shit work. Done it for years. But my daughter stays out of it. Touch her and there will be consequences."

All eyes are on Stone. The General breaks the tension.

"What have we here, Missy? A little show-and-tell?"

"The Impaler II, sir. Number two off the production line."

Mika screws two short tubes together, loads a finned projectile, and cradles the five-foot launcher in her arms.

"Remind me."

"An order of magnitude more deadly than any other shoulder-fired anti-aircraft system on the planet."

"How so?" Graham asks, "But, hold on— Coming about here."

The Catalina heels. The trio brace. Stone catches the empty camo case with his foot as it slides across the wet deck.

"Yes, more deadly how?" the General asks, shaking spray, hunching up against the wind.

"Smarter, faster, stealthier."

"Smarter? Meaning what?"

"Passive multi-spectral sensors feeding a giga-node neural net."

"In English—"

"Sucks every signal out of the environment from audio through gamma rays. Processes them to identify and track the threat."

"And speed?"

"Faster by ten percent than any combat aircraft in the sky."

"So with all that, why stealth?"

"Pilot doesn't see it coming, what's he going to do?"

"So you're saying, Missy— with enough of these on the ground, we can totally neutralize enemy air power—"

"Checkmate, sir. Just what you ordered."

The General turns to Stone. "Well, Stone, it's good to see that some folks on your team are using their God-given noggins."

He turns back to Mika.

"So where do we stand, young lady— production-wise?"

"As you know, sir, SVS is developing two models— The Series I Impalers that the government ordered seem to be jinxed with design glitches that are holding up production."

"Praise the Lord. And the Impaler IIs?"

"Our private stock. Components in manufacturing in six countries and ten factories here in the U.S as we speak. Two shifts assembling units in Facility C at SVS. Four hundred seven in inventory and combat ready as of 8:10 am this morning."

"Excellent. But we'll need four thousand."

"So you giving us a demo?" Graham asks.

Mika looks at her watch, waves her hand across the sky. Sun and sky are nearly the same color but for a thin band of blue just above the western horizon.

"At some random time within the next hour an autonomous drone will be launched from a location unknown to me. The launch team is programming it with a randomly selected altitude and flight path. The drone's flight characteristics have been entered into the Impaler's target queue. Doubt we'll be able to see or hear the drone from here."

"So how will we know that the Impaler has hit the target?" Graham asks.

"You'll know. The drone is packed with explosives."

"So when you activate that thing it will detect, and when you fire, kill?"

"Correct General. But it's already activated and listening."

"Listening? It can hear us talk?"

"Of course. But it's mind is on other things."

"Well, while we're waiting, what's progress on the IT front, Stu?"

"You read about the Internet going down in China last week?"

"That was us?"

"That was us. Mutating worms. Brought down their military command and control system too. Down for three minutes."

"Why three minutes?"

"Didn't want them to catch our hand in the cookie jar."

"And how about our taps into domestic traffic?"

"The Stardus people have been most accommodating. Their STA technology is astounding."

"STA?"

"Semantic Traffic Analysis. You feed Internet trunk lines in one end, program whatever patterns you're looking for— names, keywords— traffic patterns— and you get transcripts and network cluster diagrams out the other. "

"Network cluster diagrams?"

"Who's talking with whom."

"E-mail and all that?"

"E-mail, IRC, Skype, Google queries, Facebook— If it's online and digital, STA will dig it out. And, today, it's all online and all digital."

"Why are these Stardus people so accommodating?"

"They'd sell to Satan himself if he flashed sufficient green. North

Korea is one of their biggest customers."

"Didn't think North Korea had much of an Internet."

"Who knows where North Korea is installing these things."

"So how do you deal with encryption?"

Graham laughs.

"You forget where I once worked and who invented their best encryption and decryption algorithms."

The General turns back to Stone.

"So, Conrad, your daughter seems to be the only stink in the outhouse. Clearly planning to push our reset button."

"Maybe—"

"Maybe nothing. Most certainly."

"Look— It's contained, sir."

"Not good enough, Stone. That daughter of yours is threat number one. That makes her enemy number one. I want to hear that she's been neutralized. Hear me?"

"Hold it," Mika says.

"—or we'll turn the matter over to the Missionaries," the General says. "Should have done it a week ago."

Mika lifts the narrow tube to her shoulder, scans the sky, and fires. The back-blast is slight, but jarring. Moments later there's a faint streak in the sky and, six seconds later, the sky is illuminated with a brilliant flash.

"Bingo," Mika says.

The General nods, brings his palms together and lowers his head.

"Let us pray," he says.

"Dear Lord you've given us the stone to smite our enemies—stone such one with stones and such one must die."

General Lyman R. Baxter

"I'D SAY that's why we need accountability," the radio guest says.

"Who gives a rat's ass what you say!" General Lyman R. Baxter (Ret.) yells at the softly glowing dial.

Cruising up I-64 in his reliable old '87 Buick Electra, half-way home from Graham's cursed boat, the General has picked this misguided liberal trash out of the spectrum— smearing the fine name of the CIA— Secret Forces.

Normally he would have pushed the station selector, but the words "Phoenix Program" have caught his ear.

"The Phoenix Program was based on South Vietnamese law— breaking U.S. and international law," the commentator continues.

"Bullll pucky," the General says.

"It was an assassination program plain and simple—"

"You lying leftist pig!"

"Thousands of innocents slaughtered in their huts in the dead of night. Who knows how many innocents murdered in front of their children on hearsay alone— Ears cut off for trophies. Who knows how many innocents were brutally raped and tortured."

Counter arguments rage through the General's head like searing lava. He imagines himself in the studio. Full uniform. Full out fruit salad displayed proudly on his chest.

"That program was work of the Lord," he'd tell them, iron control. "We were rolling back Godless Communism while hippie pinkos like you were smoking pot and screwing like brain dead rabbits— Without patriots like us you and your sort would be long buried in a Commie gulag. And good riddance."

The annoying voice drones on.

"The Phoenix Program gave hundreds of CIA operators and U.S. Special Forces a four-year graduate course in brutality— The curriculum of assassination and torture perfected in Vietnam spread around the world— it was taught in official institutions like the United States Army School of the Americas.

"Guantanamo, Abu Ghraib, extraordinary renditions— these are post-grad brush-up courses— training the killers and torturers of tomorrow. And it will go on— maybe even come to a prison or police station near you— unless and until we bring the people behind these programs to account."

"No, sir!" the General responds. "The Phoenix Program was a glorious victory for the Lord. Neutralized eighty-two thousand commies; terminated more than twenty-six thousand. We were rolling them back. I personally did my share until that Bouncing Betty vaporized my best buddy— blew out half my intestines. Spent six months in Walter Reed just so lefties like you can procreate and spout pig crap."

The General turns up the heat. He can never get warm enough.

"The Phoenix Program—"

The General slams his palm down on the off button. He's heard enough. Now he hears the hum of tires and sizzling anger deep in his inner ears.

No wonder this country is going to the goddamned jackals, he thinks, what with the airwaves spewing vicious leftist propaganda. Secular humanist poison. Well, the time is near at hand—

"You, sir, are spouting treasonous nonsense—" he mutters toward his now silent radio. "You, sir, should be thrown up against the wall," he yells.

The General takes a deep breath, counts under his breath to subdue his rage.

Anger has always been his curse. Anger at a father who demanded so much but was never satisfied. Anger at a mother who spent more time playing bridge at the country club than looking after her own children. Anger at the politicos who blocked every path to victory in Vietnam. Anger at the gooks who planted the mine that took out his best friend and the better half of his innards. Anger at the hippies who spit on him and his brothers just home from the hell of war. Anger at the liberal leftest death-spiral that's sucking his beloved country down the path to Hell.

Pastor Cecil helped him get a handle on his rage. He remembers the pastor's words, years ago, remembers his comforting whisper cutting under the restless noise of ward 303 at the Walter Reed. Remembers every syllable.

"Anger is a fine emotion, lieutenant," the pastor said. "But you need to gather it up into a ball. Shape it like clay. Shape it into a glorious vision— a vision you can see, hear, smell, touch, and taste. Tuck it away next to your heart. Take it out and breathe fire into it. Take it out every time you feel anger coming on.

"This is your personal vision. The power vision of a true warrior. Your vision of a world cleansed by fire— cleansed of evil, ignorance, and apostasy. This is Reunion. A world under Holy Writ where all men bow their heads and submit to the Lord. The Lord gave you wounds to refine and forge your strength. You are now a true warrior. A warrior in service of the Lord. Use your anger to purge and cleanse wickedness with fire."

The Army made moves to muster him out. Disability discharge. But the pastor pulled strings. The pastor was good at that. So the Army kept him on— behind a desk, true. But behind a desk he found far more power than he'd ever had with cold steel. With Pastor Cecil's guidance he had gathered in and used that power— deceptively— with stealth— just as the pastor taught. And together they built a formidable covert Army for the Lord.

It started small.

They needed funds so they recruited Stone. They appealed to patriotism but soon learned that Stone was in for the money. But Stone never evolved. Never saw the light. Never felt the enfolding glow of the Lord Almighty.

Still, over the years, Stone has had his uses— a cats paw— a secular mask to conceal their true visage.

But now, moment at hand— Stone is wobbling like a weak sister. Would Stone cave with all he knows and all they have on him?

Could be Stone is no longer so useful? Have to think about that. Stone and his goddamned hippie whore daughter. Yes indeed. Have to think that one through.

But the day is at hand and there's so much left to do.

Baxter's cell warbles.
"Yeah?"
"Been thinking—"
It's P. Stewart Graham.
"About?"
"That pebble in our shoe—"
"Stone?"
"Careful—"
"So, thinking what?"
"Feel a blister coming on."
"Yeah, been thinking along similar lines."
"So?"
"Maybe we should talk to Pastor."
"Maybe, but we still need the man."
"The bitch could blow us out of the water."
"Got that right."
"So you trust the man? Think our boy can contain her?"
"Hasn't shown us much—"
"The Missionaries. Were you serious?"
"Thinking about it."
"Well, count me in."
"Yeah, well, let me think about it— talk to Pastor."

Baxter swerves around an Exxon tanker truck doing thirty in the slow lane.

Problems like Stone, he thinks, precisely why they created the Missionaries.

They combed the rolls for talented psychopaths— men exquisitely trained by the services for black operations. They sought out men who were disillusioned, burned out, walking time-bombs. Pastor knew how to bring them to the Lord— anoint their lives with reverence, meaning, and mission.

Baxter is ever amazed at how many men cloak their lives in hatred and violence; how deftly Pastor turns such men into servants of the Lord.

They were few in the beginning— Pastor's security team. But now they are more numerous— now shadow troops, hunter killers, deep penetration forces— ninjas for the Lord. Even Baxter knows little of their operations.

Pastor holds up his left fist. "In the left hand behold the Lord's love—" he'd say. Then he pounds his right fist on the pulpit. "And in the right? His wrath!"

And the Inner Core knows— Fear the wrath of the Lord. And damned well fear the Missionaries.

"Love is fear," Pastor says. "Fear is love."

The road is clear now, dark highway, just his headlights and now-and-again lights beside the road. But Baxter holds it at fifty. He takes a deep breath to tamp down his anger. It's been a long road, he thinks, but not long now.

The Inner Core was forged over time— forged with ruthless discrimination, patience, and discretion.

The Inner Core is their general staff— their strategic thinkers— the men who know how to get things done.

Some of the best they recruited during the Church hearings on intelligence abuses— Fine warriors raked over the coals by politico pinkos.

True patriots vilified.

Pastor Cecil tapped church funds for legal defense. Pastor Cecil invested thousands of hours counseling the lost and the confused, bringing them in through the outer rings— testing them— slowly bringing those who responded to his light into the inner circles— bringing only the best of the best to the sacred gospel shared by the elect.

And they recruited even more true believers when Iran-Contra hit the front pages and the Congressional hearings started grinding up and spitting out selfless men of courage and distinction.

The Pastor's growing Army forged alliances. Promoted careers. Co-opted the weak. They took on the dirty jobs of politics— insinuated their Warriors up through the capillaries of international power.

They built front organizations and mighty global corporations.

They let themselves be recruited into the greedy power plays of the world's wealthiest families and corporations. The General shudders at the arrogance and corruption. Grubby tactical alliances, but necessary.

Their time is soon. He thinks about the filthy beds they've shared. Yes, he thinks. Their time is soon— Come Reunion.

If only that little bitch doesn't bring them down.

The General shivers. He's bundled up in layers. Heater full on. But he still can't get warm enough.

That damned Graham and his infernal plastic bucket. Out in the damned wind. Rain. Soaked to the skin with icy spray. The lengths they go in the name of security.

The General moans, "Dear Lord!"

The General prays that he'll never again have to go out on the water.

But eyes and ears are everywhere. This, if anyone, Graham should know. And this the General knows since he gets a fair share of the take through this channel and that.

If there's one thing the General is proud of it's the network he's so patiently constructed— eyes, ears, and willing hands in every branch of the executive— the military— the civilian security services— and down through the states and municipalities— some witting— most not. The witting all Brothers in the Service of the Lord. Fine warriors all.

Three blocks from his home the General pulls into the convenience store. Needs Campbell's tomato soup.

This store is a perfect symbol of America's decline. Once owned by a hard-working Christian family. Then a Jew. Then a chink. Now a fat Indian, sitting back behind the register, working his family like slaves.

"Thank you, sir," the fat Indian says. "Come again, sir."

Now, turning into his block the General slows, checks out the cars parked up and down his street. Satisfied, he pushes his garage remote, pulls into the garage under a dim 40-watt bulb, pushes the remote to close the garage door.

He sits, engine ticking. Home. Not much. A cookie cutter tract house in Arlington Heights within easy walking distance of the Arlington National Cemetery. He's given most everything he's earned to Pastor Cecil and the Mission. He stares down at the bag of soup cans sitting on the car seat beside him.

Campbell's Tomato Soup. About all he can stomach these days.

Kimberly

S HE'D SPENT six hard days on her feet in the noisy diner, so Kimberly is enjoying the patch of morning sun on Auntie's tiny patio.

Auntie looks out, sees Kimberly flopped out on her old sun-baked lounge with a book in hand.

Auntie steps out, dressed to kill, The screen door slams behind her.

Birds flit up and down between earth and eaves in search of breakfast among the thorns in Auntie's tiny cactus garden. Auntie shades her eyes with her hand, watches the birds with a smile.

She turns to Kimberly.

"Whatcha doin', Sweetie?"

"Just sittin', listenin' to the birds."

"Like to come to church with me?"

"No thanks," Kimberly says. "I've got stuff to do."

"What's that, sit there reading that book? Had your nose in that book for days."

Auntie sits down on the edge of a rustic patio chair.

"I'd do more around the house here, Auntie, but you're always telling me to sit and relax."

"That's not it, Sugar. You do plenty around here. Old place never looked so spic and shiny. It's just that—"

Kimberly flips the last few pages of the book.

"Well I'm almost done. I'd like to finish it."

"So how many pages in that book? Looks a bunch—"

Kimberly flips to the last page.

"Nearly 900—"

"Lordy. And you've read all that? What's that book anyway?"

"*2666*. South American writer— Roberto Bolano. Snuck it out of the library."

"Snuck it out of the library?"

"I'll bring it back."

"2666— What kind of name is that?"

"I'm still trying to figure that out."

"So what's it about?"

"Ooo— That's a hard one— life, death, sex, love, loss?"

"Sounds like the Holy Bible."

Kimberly laughs. "I wouldn't go that far. But Belano does devote a bunch of chapters to evil."

"What do you know about evil, child?"

Kimberly is silent. Her eyes tear up.

"More than you'd ever want to know," she says fiercely.

It hits Auntie like a blow. She's silent for a moment, thinking her way around Kimberly's sensitivities.

"I'm sorry—" she says.

Kimberly closes her eyes, stretches her face to the sun.

"You read your Bible?" Auntie asks.

"Not much—"

"You have something against religion?"

"No— not really."

"That's good. Religion can be a comfort."

"Well if you must know—" Kimberly turns her face toward Auntie. "I think religion is a scam— a power trip for the preachers and an easy way to extort money from incredulous folks."

Auntie is indignant.

"That's not my church! And my preacher is poor as a church mouse."

Kimberly's voice softens.

"Was this preacher used to come around when my father was out of country. Pastor Cecil was his name. Claimed to be looking after my spiritual development. Would shoo my nana out of the room, then start telling me how many ways I was going to hell— An eleven-year-old girl! Tried to touch me. I could tell he just wanted to get into my pink panties. Slime ball!"

"Goodness!"

"Tell me about your church—"

"We sing, we pray, we have a grand old time."

"Sounds nice."

"And we help one another in time of need."

"Does your pastor talk about good and evil?"

"He does—"

"And what does he say?"

"Evil is the doing of an uninformed heart. That's what he says."

"Makes sense— if it were only true. Does he talk about God?"

"Sure he talks about God. Some of us believe. Some don't. Some just come for the box social."

"Does he talk about burning in hell and all that stuff?"

"Not that you'd notice."

"Sounds like my kind of church— if I were into it. Religion, I mean."

Auntie stands.

"They's all kinds of preachers, Honey. And all kinds of churches. Why not just come along with me. We won't try to make you believe nothin' you don't want to believe. Just want to get you out— get you a little fresh air."

"No, thanks, Auntie. I'd just like to enjoy the sun here— finish my book."

"Well if you want to read the real thing, Sugar, just go in there and you'll find it on my night table."

Kimberly smiles.

"Thank you, Auntie."

"By the way, Mr. Courtney called. Says some folks come into the bank the other day— askin' about you. Says he didn't like the look of them— not one bit."

Kimberly tenses. Looks across the small yard.

"Say anything about my money?"

"He's workin' on it, Sweetie. Promised he's doin' best he can."

"Tell them where I am?"

"That's our secret, Honey Child. He knows that. Don't nobody else need to know."

El Diablo Negro

POWER CONTROL, timing, and navigation circuit layout, board manufacture, assembly, and wave soldering were all done under one roof by Chiyoku Technologies, a one-man custom fabrication shop in Amagasaki, four miles northwest of Osaka, Japan.

Chiyoku was known in specialized circles for meticulous precision and innovative ultra-miniaturized packaging.

Chief Engineer Koichiro Sato could only guess at the ultimate application of the four diminutive circuit boards. He recognized 17 analog-to-digital converters, precision timing circuits, GPS navigation functionality, two satellite radios, four servo drivers, and a micro controller programmed to do who knows what.

It was a significant contract for Chiyoku. Two each of four circuit boards. It meant that Chief Engineer Sato could finally propose marriage to Akiko, who had lately given him an ultimatum.

Chiyoku beat the contractual deadline by two days. The assembled and tested boards were picked up by private courier at 6:55 pm on November 17.

The Chiyoku plant was destroyed in a tragic fire during the early hours of November 18.

Chief Engineer Sato's remains were confirmed through dental records.

Carmichael

THE MOVIE was gutter wash the first time around. But without sound it makes Carmichael want to throw his cell phone through the nearest glass tube.

Carmichael tries to ignore the insistent images, dancing in repetitive synchronization like toy Rockettes down the narrow beige arches between the overhead storage compartments. But the jerky colors seduce his eyes.

Maybe not so wise, son, he thinks, jetting off into battle so soon. The pain in his stomach is wrong. There's right pain and wrong pain, he's learned. But what's right with a stomach wound?

He wishes he'd asked the doc, foxy little thing.

This pain is a kind of twisted thing, gnawing— slicing— like digesting rabid gophers and glass. Three hours before his next pain killer.

Maybe it's just from sitting so long.

At one time Carmichael loved flying. The adventure. But now, it's pure claustrophobia— bruised knees, twisted ankles, fat hips knocking his elbow off the arm rest.

He's come to hate it. Wonders why more people don't go flippin' berserk.

And he wonders what he's getting himself into this time.

Seems like every fresh start lands him deeper in shit.

Leave home to suck up four years of Army bullshit. Crawl through mud, eat snakes, blow stuff up.

Ship over to 'Stan. Eat sand for six months. Shoot a few Taliban. Try to do good. Lose good men. Freeze his balls in the cargo hold of a C130. Fourteen hours trussed up in Zip Ties like a serial killer.

Three months in an Army stockade fighting off genuine psychos.

Three days in a hard varnished military courtroom breathing stink of disinfectant and furniture wax. Told he's a disgrace to the Army. General discharge.

Six months of rejected job applications. Three months of drinking alone in a cockroach-infected motel room.

Three glorious weeks of drinking and whoring with Stanley. Three years as a bone breaker for Stanley. Watching Stanley go from prince of the streets to cocaine-addled corpse with two slugs of lead the size of pencil erasers in his skull.

Some resume.

Well, maybe this time he really can do good.

But this spook stuff with Stone—

He's met more than his share of intelligence pukes. Every one running a game.

Boswick must be out of his freakin' mind. If Boswick and the government can't do it, how can a guy like Landry Carmichael and a dear old lady like Mrs. Phan bring down a bull elephant like Stone?

Carmichael shifts in his confining seat. Winces. Mrs. Phan is hunkered in her window seat, dressed in black, more formal than other passengers. She's staring at a wallet photo of Mr. Phan, the grainy print cupped lovingly in her hands.

"You all right?" Carmichael asks.

"All he ever wanted was— stay on family farm— be farmer like father."

"Farmer—" Carmichael says.

"But they burn village. Agent Orange kill crops."

"He was a good man, Mr. Phan," Carmichael says.

"Yes— good man."

"Was that your dream? To be a farmer's wife? Raise a big farm family?"

"Oh no. Wanted to be big shot. See world."

"So where did you meet him? Mr. Phan—"

"America. CC school."

"CC school?"

"George Washington— Bill of Rights."

"Ah— You were studying for citizenship—"

"Yes. Day we raise hands— pledge allegiance to flag— big day. Mr.

Phan all smiles. So proud— That moment—"

Mrs. Phan's smile is inward, pained.

"That moment I look at Mr. Phan. That moment I fall in love. First time."

"And you— were you proud?"

"Oh yes. Why not proud? Big honor. We citizens now. Can vote."

"But in Vietnam—"

"No. Don't say—"

"What?"

"U.S. terrible. Not true."

"Way I heard, the U.S. did terrible things in Vietnam—"

"U.S. big baby. Throw tantrums. Hands— feet— flop here— flop there. Break things. But in heart— sweet."

"Sweet? That's one way of putting it."

"U.S. take us in! We nothing! U.S. give us hope. Give us business— give us home!"

"Was it difficult?"

"Difficult?"

"Hard. Coming to a new land? Starting from scratch?"

"Hard? Of course hard! Yes hard. But life hard—"

They hear a ping. The stewardess interrupts.

"We're experiencing slight turbulence. The captain has turned on the seat belt sign. Please return to your seats and fasten your seat belts."

"—but you— what about?"

"Me?"

Carmichael struggles— squirms to find his buckles.

"You have girl frien'? Or what?"

"Girl friend— No. Not now."

"What, you han'some man. Why no girlfrien'?"

"Had my share—"

"Share?"

"Women. But guys like me—"

"Mean what— guys like you?"

"My dream was to be a NASCAR driver. Tony Stewart, Dale Erenhardt— Guys like that. Then— after 'Stan— the court marshal— I mean— women— Don't get me wrong. I love women—"

"But what?"

"Well— women get their hooks in. Next thing, they try to tame you. Change you. Reel you down into their nests."

"What so bad?"

"Well—"

"What so great now, Ca'michael? No NASCAR. Last job, you break bones for Stanley."

"Point there, Mrs. Phan. But—"

"But what?"

"Look. In 'Stan I tried to do something right— something great— once."

"And?"

"My country called me unfit— Failure to obey command. Dereliction of duty. Unfit to lead. Unfit for my chosen profession. Unfit to do what I did better than ninety-nine percent of the U.S. Army. A misfit they called me. Threw me out on the street. Like so much trash."

"But you heard what Ned say—"

"Ned what?"

"They cowards. In hearts. They know you do right thing— afraid maybe they not so brave. And— girls you save. They know you very brave man."

"Look— I learned one thing—"

"What thing?"

"Forget about right and wrong. Go with the flow."

"No! You know right. Time come, you do right."

"Know what I see when I look in the mirror?"

"Han'some face?"

"No. I see a thug. Hired muscle. Good pay. No sweat. No worries."

"Know what I see— you' face?"

"Can't imagine."

"Big baby. Sweet heart."

D'Mello

D'MELLO backs the Expedition into the narrow slot behind his motel, no lights in the parking lot, cars on either side crowding his space. It takes two tries.

"Pigs," he says, not sure he has space to open his door.

He switches off the ignition; sits for a moment in the quiet dark wondering why he's the one hitting all the pawn shops, flop houses, used-car lots.

If he's learned one thing— twenty years service in the U.S. Army— it's the difference between appearance and reality. Lift the surface of things and you find ugly shit.

Best to maintain appearances and do things your own way. Create your own reality.

But what's the reality here?

Stone has him by the short-hairs. Reality one.

So here he is doing Stone's thing. Who knows to what evil purpose. Reality two.

Stone's put him in command of this op. Supposedly. But the reality of reality two is— this new babe, Mika, comes and goes as she pleases, treats him like a doorman— gives him the willies.

The Ukrainians—Marko Dolinski and Vitali Shapko—are non-stop sharing secret jokes, whispering together in their gobbledygook language, worse than useless for the kind of canvassing this op entails. Their English— tonalities and intonations enough to scare old ladies and horses. Vocabularies most likely learned in third-world cat houses.

And the techs— What're the names? Jeremy French and Martin— Martin McKenna. The techs haven't shown him much either, plugged into their iPods, pecking non-stop on their Mac Powerbooks, situational awareness restricted to bits in cyberspace. Hope to God they're never on the downside of in-coming.

"Think, soldier," D'Mello mutters. Where's the third— fourth— fifth way here? The way out.

Now D'Mello reaches under his left shirt pocket flap for his Droid X, punches out the number.

"Inez—"

"Oh, Si, *Señor. Buenas Noches.*"

"Hope I'm not calling too late."

"*No, no, Señor.* Just watching the TV— *la pelicula.*"

"So what's on?"

"*Señor Ben Stiller y Jennifer Aniston. Es stupido.*"

"Boy sleeping?"

"*Sí.*"

"And how was his day today? Better?"

"*Mas o menos, Señor.*"

"Still losing hair?"

"*Sí— Oh, uno momento—*" D'Mello hears mumbling.

"Da?"

D'Mello feels the knots in his stomach.

Between one mission and another, he's never learned how to talk with his son. Which is maybe why he hadn't called earlier.

Never learned how to talk with the ex either, which is probably why he'd dragged himself into his non-com housing unit one sleety morning after an all-night training march to find the ex absent, closet and dresser cleared out, no note, and his two-year-old son eating Cheerios off the kitchen floor.

"Hey, champ. Why aren't you sleeping?"

"You said you'd call."

"Well, I'm here now. Sorry it's so late."

"I waited up."

"It's this op. Told you about it—"

"So why can't you tell me where you are?"

"Operational security. Told you that. Would if I could."

"You far far away?"

"Not so far. Sometimes hard to get to the phone, though."

"You said a few days— you promised you'd be gone for just a few days—"

"I'm really sorry about that, champ. Nothing I could do. You know I'd be home with you if I could."

"OK."

"So how was your day?"

"Da—"

"Yeah, champ?"

"Inez says I have to take this new medicine."

"It's real important, big guy."

"It makes me feel—"

"Like what?"

"Don't know."

"Bad?"

"Sort of—"

"Sort of, how?"

"Just sort of— Tastes icky."

"Well, you know what the docs say—"

"Yeah—"

"You sound pretty beat, champ. It's way past your bedtime."

"Da—"

"Yeah?"

"When you coming home?"

"Soon, hitter. Real soon. But, hey—"

"Yeah?"

"You know I love you more than anything in the world."

"Yeah, me too, da—"

"Get some sleep now, will you?"

"Yeah—"

His son. A whole separate reality.

D'Mello snags his Heckler & Koch USP from the glove compartment, squeezes out of the SUV, slams the door with his shoulder, and wriggles out sideways into the parking lot.

He beeps the key fob remote, slips his pistol into the half holster at the small of his back, adjusts his shirt.

D'Mello feels a blast of cool as he opens the heavy metal side door into the motel.

He smells disinfectant and fainter odors that soon fade. The compressor on the ice machine kicks in. He hears muffled sounds and empty silences as he walks past the identical doors toward his room.

He's dog tired but knows something is wrong the instant he opens his door, catches a glint of reflection.

He drops to a roll and has his pistol combat ready, steady in two hands.

Stone flips on the desk lamp.

"Steady there, killer," Stone says. "Don't want to spill my drink."

Stone is sitting in the desk chair, eyes red, bottle on the desk, tumbler half full and held loosely on his knee.

"Had me going there, sir," D'Mello says.

"A drink then, soldier. Quiet the heart."

Stone waves vaguely toward the bathroom.

"Glass in there somewhere. If not, drink from the bottle. Fine single malt but screw the formalities."

"So— why—?"

"Why am I here, sir?"

Stone lifts his glass, takes a deep swallow, then touches his lip primly. With glasses off, Stone's eyes are too close together, buried in flaccidity, impossible to read.

"Secrets. You have secrets, D'Mello? Course you do. Fact, let's drink to secrets. Where's your glass, soldier?"

D'Mello enters the bathroom, snaps on the light. The fluorescents over the mirror flicker then kick on. Too bright. D'Mello squints, stares at his face in the mirror, studies the lines of exhaustion.

"What's keeping you, soldier?"

D'Mello steps back into the small room— anonymous like so many— his room, but Stone dominating the space. He holds out his glass as Stone fills it. Stone taps it with his own.

"To secrets— You know, D'Mello, some secrets weigh a thousand pounds. Know that, soldier? A million pounds. More."

"Not exactly following, sir."

"Sure you are, bet you're carrying more than your share of secrets."

"Some, I guess—"

"Well I'm here to give you one more secret to stuff into your ditty-bag. Can you keep a secret, soldier?"

"Good as the next guy, I guess," D'Mello says.

"Not good enough."

"Well, maybe, yeah—"

"I know you can."

"Yes, guess I can."

"Here it is, then. They're sending in another team."

"Another team?"

"They're sending in another team to track her down. Call 'em the Missionaries. Hunter-killers really. Track her down and kill her."

"Track her down— who?"

"Who do you think?"

"The woman? The one we've been looking for?"

"My daughter."

"Your daughter? We've been tracking your daughter?"

D'Mello slumps.

"You have kids, D'Mello?"

"What about this big time security risk?"

"Oh yes. She's that too. But I asked about your kids, sir."

"A son."

"A son. Yes. Knew that. Kids. Never wanted kids. Me. James Bond wannabe. Man of the world. Jetting off here and there— Saving the world from the Big Red Bear. What the hell did I need with kids? But a kid I've got, sure enough. Love her even. And she broke my heart."

D'Mello is silent.

"Gave her everything. Didn't matter. Tossed me out of her life. Years ago. 'You're not to think for one minute that you're still my father,' she said. 'I forbid you to even think it.'

"Know what, Sergeant? I think of nothing else. How can you not think about your own daughter? Flesh and blood— I think about her— every day."

D'Mello thinks about his son.

"This team— who are they? Who's sending them?"

Stone raises his glass. Empties it.

"Who else?"

"A clue, sir."

"Containment, D'Mello. Wheels within wheels. Circles of trust."

Stone pushes his face toward D'Mello, his expression dangerous. D'Mello smells the sour liquor breath and something more. Anger. And more. Something rancid and offensive.

"So why are you telling me this, sir?"

"Obvious, wouldn't you think?"

"Not to this soldier, sir."

"Well I want you to intercept them."

"Intercept them?"

So here it comes, D'Mello thinks. Reality three— or is it four?

"Use the Ukrainians. Whatever you need. I'll send you more men. Intercept these hunter-killers and— neutralize them."

"Neutralize how?"

Stone is slurring now.

"Don't know. Don't give a good goddamn. Kill the fuckers for all I care. Make it messy. Do I have to think of everything?"

"Kill them? Just like that? Like Klegg?"

Stone stares at D'Mello— hard.

"Had to be done."

"You judge and jury?"

Stone's face softens. They sit, eye-to-eye— the only sound the soft whir of the air conditioner.

"Listen, son, I've killed for my country, yes. Didn't like it. Still don't. Don't think I don't think about it— the men— the women— what their lives would have been like. But sometimes duty is the higher call."

"And this time?"

"Would you kill for your son, Sergeant?"

D'Mello stiffens.

"That a rhetorical question, Mr. Stone? Or a threat?"

Stone runs his finger around the rim of his glass.

"I only disobeyed one order in my life, Sergeant. Glad I did. Do what has to be done."

"And that is?"

"Send a message."

"And your daughter?"

"Get her off the board. Somewhere safe."

Yes, D'Mello thinks. Reality three— four— whatever. Maybe the hardest reality of all.

El Diablo Negro

THE CORE was stripped and reassembled with mechanical components machined and assembled in a precision machine shop in Quetta, Pakistan.

The work, exacting and dangerous, was supervised by designer Raheem Khattak.

Khattak, educated at Caltech and MIT, had spent ten years working as a mechanical engineer at a Sony Electronics research facility in Hodogaya, near Yokohama, Japan. His specialty was mechanical miniaturization.

Returning to Pakistan, Khattak was recruited by Abdul Qadeer Khan, some say father of Pakistan's nuclear program.

A voracious reader, Khattak worked side-by-side with Khan for nearly a decade, learning the fine art and intricacies of destructive yield.

With this latest device, no doubt, Khattak felt he'd surpassed himself. It was truly a work of art.

"Thought it would be smaller," the client commented when he took delivery of the device on December 2.

"There's a minimum size to such devices imposed by the laws of physics," Khattak had said. "One must consider the application— desirable blast radius, fallout profile, and what not."

The client, a thin, older man in a black suit, was more than satisfied.

On the morning of December 3 Raheem Khattak, PhD, was struck and fatally crushed against the side of a building by a 1978 Mercedes Benz traveling at high speed.

Two hours later the machine shop and four adjacent buildings were totally destroyed in a horrific blast.

Six hours later a neighboring shopkeeper complained of nausea, then rushed to the outhouse behind his shop.

A second shopkeeper never made it to his outhouse.

Lost his lunch and breakfast over a new shipment of cotton T-shirts commemorating Osama bin Ladin.

Some thought it was an outbreak of stomach flu.

No one thought to monitor the blast site for radiation.

Carmichael

"MY DAUGHTER— Kim Le— you don't care!" Mrs. Phan screeches. Carmichael pulls the rented Chevy Cobalt off the wide airport exit road and into the Carl's Jr. parking lot, slumps behind the wheel, watches the stop and go of heavy traffic— red tail lights, harsh glints of early afternoon sun.

The pain has returned. Eleven hours of cramped confinement in cars, aircraft, and crowded terminals— his restricted diet— have left him sapped.

The argument between Mrs. Phan and Boswick has been simmering since Kennebunkport. Spun out of hand when Boswick directed Carmichael to drive straight through to the Maricopa County Forensic Science Center.

"Milly— Milly— Of course I care," Boswick says. "If I knew where to find Kim Le and how to keep her safe I'd do it in a minute. You know that. But I have no idea where to look."

"You government. Have information."

"But not enough to track her down. Don't you see that? She changed her name once to Kimberly. We caught that. But Kimberly Stone dropped out of the public record fifteen years ago. We have no idea what name she's using now. The father— C. Norbert Stone is our only link."

"You bring me here— this city— promise we find Kim Le. But all you talk is Stone Stone Stone."

"MAYBE we'll find your daughter here— my exact words. All I'm saying is that Stone can lead us to her."

"I know this *cho de*. You forget— I marry this *lo dit*. He tell you nothing. Slippery eel. Too dangerous."

"Look— You've told me yourself that Stone is desperate to find your

145

daughter— We suspect she has something that threatens him."

"That why! That why we must find her! Find her before that man ha'm her— kill maybe."

"He's her father. Why would he kill her?"

"He bad man. Killer. She know something."

"Just my point. Stone's more than dangerous. You can't imagine the resources he can bring to bear. Even if we find her he could still get to her and—"

"Talk talk talk. Lose time— Out, Ca'michael. Out now! We find own car!"

"Mrs. Phan," Carmichael says. "Maybe we should listen to what the man has to say. Can you calm down for a minute?"

"OK. OK. I listen. One minute."

"Look, there's more to this than Kim Le—"

"No. Kim Le only thing."

"No. You love this country, Milly. I know you do. This United States of America."

"What point?"

Boswick sweeps his hand, indicating the world outside the car. "I'm talking about them— all you see out there."

"What are you telling us?" Carmichael asks.

"Look, it's a long story— speculation mostly."

Carmichael gives Mrs. Phan a cautioning look.

"We're listening, Boswick— but the clock's ticking."

"Can't tell you everything. Classified some of it. But there's this bill locked up in Congress— calls for investigations into possible war crimes committed during the War on Terror."

"War crimes? Stone? You're investigating war crimes?"

"No. Not my bag. But we do know that Stone was heavily involved in the rendition program. And we suspect that he was a link between Fort Bragg and Guantanamo. We certainly know that he had big security contracts in Iraq."

"Fort Bragg—"

"You've heard of the SERE program— right?"

"You forget. I was a Ranger. They put me through that shit."

"How'd you do?"

"Another day and I would have been writing on the walls with my own feces."

"Then you know. They say that Stone's company, SVS Security, helped re-engineer SERE for use in aggressive interrogation in Guantanamo. Developed training courses."

"Christ. That was then. What about now? How does all this relate?"

"We don't know. But we know there's a heap of bitterness around that Senate bill. Think that's why that Senator was assassinated."

"Senator?"

"Blaine. Senator Dexter Blaine. They brought me into the investigation, briefly. Then there was that mysterious murder-suicide in Rock Creek Park— former White House attorney— Office of Legal Council."

"Are you telling us Stone is connected with this shit?"

"I'd be lying if I said yes for certain. But we do know that Stone's been up to something— something that involves Colombians, Pakistanis, Russian Mafiya— We've tracked his contacts and travels."

"What this have to do with Kim Le?" Mrs. Phan asks.

"Everything, we think," Boswick says, "In fact, Carmichael, you gave me the key—"

"Key to what?"

"Heroin— We wondered how Stone financed his way into the private prison industry on CIA pay. And you told me something else."

"What else?"

"That Stone has powerful backers."

"Backers?"

"Took a network, people with high access, to secure the arms he needed to trade for dope. Another network, or maybe the same, to distribute that dope. And big-time smarts to launder the dirty drug proceeds into a financial empire. Stone's a smart cookie. That we know. But Stone's not that smart. If Stone has backers, we think there's blow back between then and now."

"Blow back how?"

"There's the rub. We just don't know. Suspect maybe he's just a front man."

"You don't know—"

"Signs and portents. Smoke and shadows."

"Boswick," Carmichael says, "You're pissing me off!"

"All I'm saying is that something is in the wind that doesn't smell like down-home barbecue."

"This is WAY over my head."

"Mine too, maybe. But my job is to connect the dots."

"What dots? I still don't see dots."

"Well the dot we can see Is Stone. Stone is the connection to the dots we can't see— Kimberly. And maybe more."

"Maybe more than what, Boswick? Ask me, sounds like you're spinning some kind of liberal conspiracy theory."

"Maybe. All I'm saying is—"

"So how we save Kim Le?" Mrs. Phan asks.

Boswick slumps. "Look, if I knew another way I'd be on it."

"Time out," Carmichael says, looking longingly at Carl's Jr. "Blood sugar— Gets too low I get mean. And right now I'm ready to rip heads."

"You're not thinking about this place, I hope," Boswick says, following Carmichael's gaze.

"Why not? We're here. I need meat. A cheeseburger will do it. And quick."

"No cheeseburger for you," Mrs. Phan says. "Baby food."

"We're in Phoenix, dude. How about fajitas?"

"Fajitas— whaa fajitas?" Mrs. Phan says.

Boswick reaches back, grasps her hand.

"Milly, you know I love you, babe."

Mrs. Phan bats his hand away, gently.

"Shut up, you," she says. "You talk too much."

"Still love me?"

"We do your way. Fo' now."

Boswick checks his watch.

"Bear with me kids," he says. "Let's just make this one stop. Then we eat."

"Boswick, you're killing me," Carmichael says.

"Believe me, it's better to do this before lunch."

Mrs. Phan pats Carmichael's cheek.

"Big baby," she says. "You can wait."

Carmichael

"RIGHT TURN, next intersection—" Boswick says. Carmichael turns right off West Jefferson; follows a white van into the parking garage mid-block down S. 8th Ave. The van backs into a receiving dock marked "NO PARKING." Big block letters.

"Another day, another customer," Boswick says, gesturing toward the van.

"Meaning?" Carmichael asks.

"Some 300 homicides a year in Maricopa County— nearly one a day. Vics all go through that loading dock."

"So glad to know," Carmichael says.

Carmichael rolls further into the garage, parks the Cobalt between a sharply detailed red Alfa Romeo and a post-WWII pickup. The pickup is red with dust, golden stalks of straw in the bed. The parking space is the only open slot in visitor's parking, so tight that Carmichael sucks in and wiggles to slip out of the driver-side door.

Boswick tip-toes out of the narrow space between the Cobalt and the pickup, brushes red dust off his suit. He offers Mrs. Phan his arm.

"Shall we?" he says.

The reception area is stark white, high barrel ceiling, antiseptic smell. It's oddly empty. Their footsteps echo behind them.

Boswick steps up to the receptionist's window, shows ID.

"I'm here to identify remains brought in on Friday."

They wait in silence. A white door opens. A hunched woman, frizzled gray hair, smudged white lab coat, gestures.

"Coming?" Boswick asks.

Carmichael looks at Mrs. Phan.

"We'll wait here— just as soon," Carmichael says.

"Suit yourselves," Boswick says.

They sit on the padded bench in the reception area.

"This place gives me the willies," Carmichael says.

"Wha', dead people?" Mrs. Phan asks.

"No—"

"Wha', you afraid? Dead people? Ghosts?"

"No, but—"

"You ARE afraid! Ghosts!"

"No. Maybe it's just this space— so empty— like a tomb— the silence."

"That thing—" Mrs. Phan says.

"What?"

"Dead people—" Mrs. Phan says. "Lips sealed."

"So where do we go, Mrs. Phan?"

"Go?"

"After— You know, we die?"

"Dead don't say."

"But what do you think?

"I think—?"

"What?"

"I think here, there, everywhere."

"Heaven? Hell?"

"No heaven. Here. Now."

"Ah— YOU believe in ghosts."

"Not way you think."

"What way?"

"We live. We talk. Do things."

"So?"

"Change people— change world."

"Not following—"

"Mr. Phan still here. In my heart. Mr. Phan good man."

"The good lives on after us?"

"Good not only thing—" Mrs. Phan stares down the long, stark reception area.

Carmichael is silent.

"You know, Ca'michael, in Vietnam— I do things—" she says. "Many things. Bad things. Bad things live on too— here." Mrs. Phan pats her heart.

"What things?

"Evil things."

"Evil?"

"You know story of Vietnam?" Mrs. Phan asks without hearing him.

"Which story?"

"Mother told me. Long ago, man hungry. Steal chicken from village. Villagers angry. Catch man. Poke out eye. Man's elder son catch villager. Poke out two eyes. Villagers rise up. Kill elder son. Elder son's cousins, middle of night, burn down village. Soon, whole country at war. Thousand years. War. Sticks, stones, swords, guns, cannons, bombs. Many dead. Much pain. Men, women, babies hungry. Many scream. More war!"

"Revenge. That's the root of evil?"

"Revenge— ignorance, what's word— arrogance, greed—"

"How so?"

"First man ignorant. Don't know how to grow food or trade so steal chicken. Villagers arrogant. Kill hungry man. That stop stealing. Cousins greedy. Think burn village— think more land make rich."

"One way of seeing it, I guess."

"So how you see it?"

"Beats me. What's the answer?"

"Mr. Phan say lady with scale—"

"Lady with scale—" Carmichael frowns, puzzled. "Ah— justice?"

"Justice."

"How so?"

"Lady weigh right— wrong. Punish bad— help people forgive— life more fair. More peace. People grow food. Fight less. Less need to steal chicken— less need to kill neighbor."

"But justice leads to punishment. What's the difference between punishment and revenge?"

"Different."

"Suppose lady justice fails?"

"More revenge, more killing, more war. Vietnam."

They sit in silence.

"What you think, Ca'michael?"

"About what?"

"Where we go— when die."

"Way I see it? Life and death? The difference? Seven grams of lead."

"No! No! Don't you see? Difference between life and death is way you live! Way you treat people!"

Carmichael shakes his head.

"You know, the Taliban I killed in 'Stan? First time I felt more alive than ever before in my life. Every time it was a high."

"Ah—"

"That's something I never told anyone."

Mrs. Phan is silent.

"We are born killers, Mrs. Phan. Can't deny it."

"And now? How you feel now about killing Taliban?"

Carmichael thinks.

"Don't know. I think about it."

Mrs. Phan shifts on the bench, catches Carmichael's eyes. Carmichael is struck by her sadness.

"Someday Ca'michael— Someday ghosts come for you too."

Now Ned Boswick emerges from the white door. A tall man, face red and wrinkled from long sun, follows.

"And?" Carmichael asks.

Boswick exhales, closes his eyes for a long moment.

"It's Tim."

"I'm sorry."

"This is Detective Antonio Martinez. He's in charge of the case— looking for the people who did Tim."

They shake. Martinez is chewing gum, shifts the gum from one side of his mouth to the other.

"So you're looking for your daughter—"

"Yes," Mrs. Phan says. "Look— Don't know where."

"Detective Martinez found a note in Tim's shoe, Boswick says. "I made a copy."

Carmichael studies the Xerox.

The letter K with an arrow pointing toward the phrase Impaler II. The II is circled.

"So? Shoe size?"

"Impaler is a super high-tech ground-to-air missile," Boswick says. "Highly classified. But the program is in big trouble. Delays— cost overruns— guess who has the contract—"

"Don't tell me—" Carmichael says, "SVS—"

"Bingo. But here's the stumper—"

"Yeah?"

"Tim's note says Impaler II. And Tim circled the II."

"So?"

"Tim was a careful man. Impaler is state-of-the-art— advanced weapon. Still in R&D. In trouble at that. I'd think that Impaler II would be some-where down the pike."

"And 'K?' Suppose that's Kim Le?"

"Your guess good as mine. But if Tim hid this note in his shoe, it must be important."

"Detective," Mrs. Phan says, "Kim Le— How we find?"

Martinez stops chewing. Looks hard into Mrs. Phan's eyes.

"Your daughter?"

"My daughter."

Martinez's jaw starts up again.

"Good question. Pushing on 3.8 million people in Maricopa County, Mrs. Phan. I suppose you could check all the usual places."

"You help?"

"Sorry, Ma'am. Can't. Not until you file a report. Missing person."

"How file?"

"Milly," Boswick says. "We don't have enough information to file a missing persons report. No name. No previous address."

"Then what good!" Mrs. Phan says. "You no good. This stupid! We waste time!"

"Look," Martinez says, "What proof do you have that your daughter is even in Maricopa County? You don't have a name— prior address. You haven't seen her for how many years?"

Mrs. Phan stares at the floor.

"I'm sorry," Martinez says. "If you can connect your daughter to this Tim Valentine thing, maybe I can put resources on it."

Mrs. Phan shakes her head, turns toward the exit.

"What about SVS?" Boswick asks.

"Good a lead as any," the Detective says, looking toward Mrs. Phan, now standing near the exit door, head down. "But you'll have a hell of a time getting past the front gate."

"Love to get my hands on their personnel records."

Martinez takes an empty gum wrapper out of his jacket pocket, spits his gum, wraps it tight. He looks around for an ashtray, seeing none, slips the rumpled package into his jacket pocket.

"Well I know this guy—" Martinez says. "Avery Greene."

"Yes?"

"If anyone can get you in—"

"Can you set up a meet?"

"Maybe. But you never heard it from me."

"Can we eat first?" Carmichael says. "Cheeseburger, remember?"

"Fajitas," Boswick says. "Join us, Detective?"

"Wish I could, pards," Detective Martinez says. "But the wife, expecting me—"

"Here's my cell," Boswick says, handing over a card. "This guy, Greene–"

"Yeah," Martinez says, "See what I can do."

Carmichael

THEY ARGUE. Cheeseburgers or fajitas.

They compromise.

Mrs. Phan and Boswick have Mexican. Carmichael has four jars of Gerber's pureed Apples and Chicken, topped off with a jar of Apples and Bananas.

Mrs. Phan carries the sheet of dietary recommendations for stomach surgery patients in her shoulder bag. She also carries jars of baby food.

"Just in case," she says.

Carmichael knows that the only way he'll be able to transgress is well out of her sight.

Carmichael wonders what's with babies and apples. The fajitas smell sooo fine.

"Really think Tim Valentine knew Kim Le?" Carmichael asks.

"Tim was onto something— evidence against Stone. He was meeting someone here in Phoenix. We know that Stone is turning Phoenix up-side-down trying to find Kim Le. The note they found in Tim's shoe suggests that she had evidence that both Tim and Stone were after."

"Evidence? Where she get evidence?"

"Stone owns SVS Aerospace. SVS has the Impaler contract. It's possible that Kim Le worked at SVS."

"Possible— maybe— we think—" Mrs. Phan says in disgust.

"So what would you suggest, Milly? Where would you start?"

Mrs. Phan lowers her head, shakes it.

"Don't know," she says. "Just don't know."

"Go on," Carmichael says. "Suppose SVS is a dead end?"

"I have Valentine's credit card records. He had a room,"

"Slim— slim. Probably cleaned ten times since then."

"And he had a rental car. Never turned in. Find the car, we might be able to backtrack— maybe get closer to Kim Le."

Carmichael shakes his head.

"You don't agree?"

"I think you were right the first time—"

"First time?"

"Stone," Carmichael says. "Stone has the resources to find Kim Le. All we have is us."

"Meaning?"

"Find Stone. Find what he's after— what he knows."

"Now you're talkin'. But tall order still—"

"We've got Not There."

"Not there?"

"Stone's house boy."

Boswick raises his eyebrows.

"Long story. But, this SERE shit— maybe we can use it against him."

"You're not thinking—"

"Just let me and Mrs. Phan hassle details. You follow the Valentine trail."

"And you?"

"We'll need a panel van— nothing fancy. And a secluded space— old barn— ranch house or something."

"Carmichael— you're not thinking—"

"Boswick— what you don't know won't hurt you."

"Not sure I like this. Not sure I like it at all!"

"Like you said, Boswick— What's the choice?"

"Well SVS for a start. Just bear with me. If we could just get a look at their pay records."

"What good would that do?"

"We look for a Kimberly or a woman her age who hasn't been showing up for work."

"Can't you get that information from government records?"

"Maybe before 9/11. But these days government records are locked down tighter than a drum."

"But you're with the government— an investigator."

"These days— records are locked away ESPECIALLY from guys like me."

"Why's that?"

"War on Terror. Too many skeletons in the closet. Too many contracts at stake."

Just now Boswick's cell vibrates.

"Yeah?"

"Martinez here. Got a pen?"

Avery Greene

THE WHEELCHAIR surprises them.

"Come in. Come in."

Avery Greene's upper body is too big for the chair, spills over. His pepper-colored mustache droops over the corners of his mouth. His legs, clad in faded jeans, are stick thin.

The floor is littered with toys.

"Don't mind the mess. My granddaughter. She's three."

"Thanks for seeing us," Boswick says.

"You're interested in SVS Tony tells me."

"More specifically, personnel records."

"Hope you're prepared—"

"For?'

"Consequences."

"Of getting caught?"

"Getting caught. They do black stuff in that plant. Highest classification. Get caught they'll classify you as an enemy combatant or some shit. Send you off to a black hole in Syria. No trial."

"Never happen—"

"Oh, yeah?"

"You're scaring me," Carmichael says.

"My intention."

"But they've shut down the rendition programs, right?" Carmichael asks.

"They say. But on that point the latest NDAA is rather ambigous. And who knows what pranks the so-called national security contractors pull in the dark of night."

"You think?"

"Weird stuff going down."

"Now you're really scaring me."

"Either way, you'd still be looking at a heap of time."

"So how can it be done?"

"Glad you asked."

Avery Greene leads them through the house into a back bedroom that's no longer a bedroom. No bed.

"Wow!" Boswick says.

A 42-inch rack stuffed with 1- and 2U servers, routers, and network attached storage dominates one wall. LEDs blinking.

Three wide-screen computer monitors sit on a room-wide bench against another.

Opposite the bench is a glass trophy case filled with gold trophies— marksmanship and karate.

The monitors are cycling through screen savers— Walt Disney cartoon figures.

"Tony was a little vague," Greene says. "This agency you claim to work for— tell me more."

Boswick flips out his ID.

"Ah, yes," Greene says. "Worked with you guys once— years ago. Impressive bunch."

"Today— Just a shadow of our former glory—"

"So I hear."

"Well?"

Greene rolls over to his desk, opens a folder. "Took the liberty—"

"What's this?"

"Blueprints."

"Of?"

"SVS Aerospace."

"No way—," Boswick says.

"Way. Had my doubts about that place for some time."

"Why's that?"

"Follow the stock market?"

"No."

"Well, follow SVS you'd know there's fishy stuff going on in that company. And if you dig as deep into company filings and open-source defense documents as I do, you know that more than a little fishy stuff is going on in that plant just outside town."

"So what's your interest? Investor?"

"No. Used to be SWAT commander for the Phoenix Police Department until—" Greene pats his legs.

"Now I help out various law enforcement agencies. Keeps the mind sharp."

"So who you working for now?"

Greene smiles.

"OK. So what's the best way in?"

Greene opens a drawer under his desk, pulls out a small, flat electronic pad. At first Carmichael thinks iPhone.

"Think you can get this device within a few inches of an SVS ID badge?"

"Don't know— where would we find an SVS ID badge?"

"Wallet or purse?"

"You mean you just want us to walk up to some SVS employee and ask kindly if we can borrow their SVS ID card?"

"No— just need to maneuver this device within a few inches of the card. It'll work through fabric or leather."

"Yeah, we can probably manage that."

"SVS is using embedded RFID tags in their badges. They have readers at the employee entrances and around the plant. Pass the ID badge over a reader and, computer confirms your status, you get access."

"You make these RFID tags sound easy to defeat."

"Yeah. Told their security chief just that. RFID is a stupid way to go. But he's an arrogant prick."

"What's RFID?" Carmichael asks.

"Radio Frequency Identification. Something like those anti-theft scanners at the big box bookstores."

Greene rests the electronic pad on his knee.

"This device can make duplicate ID cards. I'll show you how when the time comes."

"So now we're in," Carmichael says, "What next?"

"The hard part. You need to break into their computer system."

Carmichael looks at Boswick.

"I don't know diddly about computers, you?"

"No need," Greene says. He opens a drawer, shuffles around, holds up a thin round disk.

"I'll point you toward the right office on the blueprint. All you need do is get in, peel off this strip and attach this disk to the underside of a computer keyboard. I can take it from there."

"And you'll be where?"

"Right here, waiting for someone to log in. They do— I get their user name and password. Given that, I download the personnel files you need."

"Amazing."

"One other thing. You may need this," Greene hands Carmichael a can of instant foam.

"What's this?"

"SVS has these Takeo Mark III security robots roaming the halls. Nasty bastards."

"So what's with the foam?"

"Blind 'em. What else."

"Think you can pull this off, Carmichael?" Boswick asks.

"Why me? Why not you?"

"Look— I'm an agent of the United States government. You wouldn't want me to break the law would you?"

Carmichael

"THE MAN'S certifiable," Carmichael says, dropping the binoculars, rubbing his eyes.

"Vibration sensors on the wire, video cameras every twenty poles, guards in white Toyotas cruising the perimeter every twenty minutes— This place is buttoned up tighter than the White House under threat-level red. What makes this guy think we can just copy a badge and walk in?"

"Mis'a Greene— You not trust?" Mrs. Phan says.

"Always like to do my own recon."

They've circled the vast SVS Aerospace campus three times, mostly on little-trafficked county roads. They've trudged across sparse desert to check the back fences. They've checked and double-checked the blueprints.

Now, sitting on the side road, they're studying the employee entrance and the parking lot beyond, watching the yellow gate arm go up and down as vehicles come and go.

"But maybe the man is right. Employee's swipe their ID cards both entering and leaving," Carmichael says. "Guards never check the cards. What time is it?"

"Nea'ly four," Mrs. Phan says.

"Traffic's building. Must be coming on to shift change."

Now a white Toyota pickup exits the gate, rolls down the side road toward them, stops grill-to-grill, sun glinting off the windshield. Two bulky forms sit motionless, stare across the space.

"Big Green Meanies—" Carmichael says. "We just might get lucky."

"Wha' mean?" Mrs. Phan asks.

"Two-to-one these bozos carry their IDs in their wallets and their

163

wallets in their hip pockets."

"Ah," Mrs. Phan says.

"I get one of these clowns bent over looking in the engine compartment, you know what to do, right?"

"Think so—"

"Well— show time."

The Toyota's passenger door opens. A guard, khaki-clad, steps out, adjusts his patrol belt hung with holstered pistol, ammunition pouches, baton, flashlight, keys.

He steps up to Mrs. Phan's window. She sees herself reflected, distorted, in his dark glasses.

"You're in a no-parking zone," he says. "You'll have to move along."

"Wha' this place?" Mrs. Phan asks.

"No-parking zone. Can't park here."

Carmichael leans across the seat.

"Sir, do you know about cars?"

The man scrunches down— studies Carmichael. Looks confused.

"This funny light came on? Then we heard this terrible noise under the hood?"

"Well, can't leave your vehicle here—"

"I'm afraid to move the car, officer. Could you just take a look. Maybe you can see some loose-wire dohicky or something?"

The guard hitches his belt, looks back toward his car.

"We late fo' funeral," Mrs. Phan says.

"OK," he says. "Let's take a look."

Carmichael unlatches the hood, steps out.

The guard leans over the fender. Mrs. Phan opens her door, steps out behind the guard.

Carmichael flashes the partner his dumbest smile, shrugs, then steps between the vehicles to block the view.

"Looks OK," the guard says. "Start her up."

Mrs. Phan passes the RFID reader past the guard's hip pocket.

"Yes, sir," Carmichael says.

The car starts.

"What do you know about that!" Carmichael says. "Genius!"

"You folks move along now."

"Yes, sir! Thank you, sir!"

Carmichael laughs.

"Get it?" he asks.

"Think so," Mrs. Phan says.

"Well that was easy. But I still think Boswick is a fruitcake if he thinks we're going to find anything in this place worth the effort."

"We make two cards," Mrs. Phan says.

"Why, you're not going in."

"You need back-up," Mrs. Phan says.

Carmichael gives Mrs. Phan a look.

"Look, Mrs. Phan," he says. "This kind of work, I do best on my own."

"Yes," Mrs. Phan says. "I remember— laundromat. Mis'a James Bond— superspy."

"Whatever," Carmichael says, embarrassment rising. "Let's get back. They're waiting for us."

"Superspy James Bond, you— for sure."

Avery Greene

"Oooo— Good work!" Avery Greene says. "Glenn Petrovsky, Security guard. This I like."

Greene has plugged the RFID scanner into his computer. Petrovsky's data is displayed on the screen.

"Let's see what else we can find out about our young prince."

"Look," Carmichael says, "Can't we just make the ID card and get on with it?"

Greene swivels in his chair, casts Carmichael a look over the top of his glasses.

"Then what?"

"I go in— plant the bug— you get the data and we get on with it."

Greene swivels further. Looks at Boswick.

"Ah impatience. The indulgence of youth."

Boswick puts his hand on Carmichael's shoulder.

"What he's saying, my young buck, is we can't go in half cocked."

"But we're wasting time— We've already got Petrovsky's ID."

Greene snorts.

"Screw this up, my friend— you'll be doing plenty of time."

"Don't intend to screw it up."

"You show up, let's say— flash your spanking new duplicate ID card—"

"OK—"

"Now Petrovsky shows up. Flashes his ID card."

"Oh—"

"Yeah. Big red flag pops up on the computer— You'll have security crawling all over your ass."

"OK. I'll shut up."

No. Don't shut up. Just help us work the kinks out of this caper."

The planning is meticulous. Even Carmichael is impressed.

"Should he wear the uniform of an SVS security guard?" Boswick asks.

"Absolutely. It'll give him an edge."

"Petrovsky has a mustache."

"That's easy—"

"Should he carry a gun?"

"Yeah. Same model as Petrovsky be best."

"How do we know what model that would be?"

"I can check it out," Greene says.

"If cornered, should he draw down?"

"Definitely a bad idea— Shouldn't even have bullets."

"How do we keep Petrovsky out of work on D day?"

"Good question— let's work on that."

"What kind of car should Carmichael drive into SVS?"

"Why not Petrovsky's car?"

"Now you're talking—"

"But how do we borrow Petrovsky's car without his knowledge?"

"I've heard about these drugs," Boswick says. "They make people forget things."

"Yeah, propranolol— U0126— forget about it. Still experimental."

"OK," Carmichael says, "How about acid— good old LSD?"

"Send him on a trip— I like that!" Greene says.

"Keep him out of our hair for a few hours, for sure," Boswick says.

"A few days, maybe—" Greene says. "And it'll blow holes through his credibility."

"Where do we get LSD?"

"*No problemo*," Avery Greene says.

"This guy Petrovsky have immediate family?" Carmichael asks.

"I'll check it out—"

Greene turns to the computer. Starts typing search terms.

Boswick turns to Mrs. Phan.

"You OK with this, Milly?"

"I go in— with Ca'michael" she says.

"Why?"

"Ca'michael need back-up."

"I can handle it," Carmichael says.

"No. No. I go in."

Greene turns to Mrs. Phan.

"Mrs. Phan— We need you. To call in the bomb threat."

"Bomb threat?" Carmichael and Boswick ask together.

"Mrs. Phan, you'll be outside the plant with binoculars. You'll watch Carmichael enter the gate, park, and enter the administration building. You'll give him ten minutes to get to the personnel floor, then you'll call in a bomb threat on this phone. Tell them the whole plant's wired to go."

"Someone else can do—"

"No, your accent— They'll take you more seriously."

Greene hands her a cell phone.

"That phone?" Boswick asks. "Why?"

"Prepaid minutes. Untraceable."

"I like it," Carmichael says.

"One more edge."

Greene turns back. "So just how do we get our young prince to ingest LSD?"

"Hold him at gun point and invite him to imbibe," Boswick says.

"And you an officer of the law," Greene says.

"A desperate officer of the law."

"Not a bad idea," Carmichael says. "Who will believe him if he complains?"

Carmichael

CARMICHAEL sips the Starbucks latte with mild distaste. His preference is truck-stop hot-and-ready— black, strong and burnt. A second latte, still steaming, sits on the seat beside him. He scans the three-day-old front page of the *Phoenix Republic* that he'd found sitting on the greasy bench seat of Glenn Petrovsky's Ford F-150. He glances up now and again at Petrovsky's paint-peeled green front door.

The door opens. Petrovsky ducks out onto the make-shift cinder block porch, slice of toast sticking out of his mouth. He juggles a large thermos under his arm, turns, closes and locks the door.

Petrovsky starts across the packed earth, tufts of sun-dried grass, stops abruptly when he sees Carmichael sitting in his truck.

The toast drops out of his mouth.

"The fuck are you? And what the fuck you doing in my truck?"

Petrovsky fumbles the thermos, catches it, starts to draw.

"Easy, friend," Carmichael says, revealing his own weapon under the newspaper.

"Get in. Drive slowly. I'll tell you where."

"The fuck is this?"

Petrovsky's face is lined with red veins. He's shaking. Heavy drinker.

They drive out of the mobile park, Petrovsky looking left and right for help. They drive another block, desert cactus lining both sides of the road.

"Pull over, Mr. Petrovsky. Take a deep breath. You're looking kind of nervous."

"Don't like people pointing guns—"

"Look, this is just a drill. My company has been hired to test security vulnerabilities at SVS."

171

"Vulnerabilities? What?"

"That's what we're going to find out. You've been hand-picked to help."

"No shit? Say, haven't I seen you before?"

"I've been around. You like Starbucks?"

"Do I look gay? I'm a McD man."

"Well, here, I brought you a latte— show of good faith."

"Hey—Thanks. No offense man, really."

"OK, tell me about your routines—"

"This shit has sugar. I take it black—"

"Our files say sugar."

"Files?"

"Forget it."

"Files, shit."

"Anyway—"

They talk until Petrovsky is near incoherent. Still, Carmichael gets the outline of Petrovsky's day.

"Man—" Petrovsky stares at his latte cup, focuses in on the Star-buck's logo. "Oh man—"

"What?"

"I'm—" Petrovsky shakes his head, stares with wide-open eyes at Carmichael. "You— whoa—"

"Your pupils are dilated, Mr. Petrovsky. You on drugs or some-thing?"

Petrovsky shakes his head again, starts to cry.

"Must be a sugar high—"

Boswick knocks on the window.

"I can take him from here."

Carmichael turns Petrovsky's F-150 into the plant entrance, stops momentarily, third vehicle back from the barricade.

The F-150 has seen better days— muffler shot. Carmichael is slightly nauseous from exhaust fumes seeping up from God knows where. His head pounds from exhaust noise. Carbon monoxide poisoning, more likely. He's driven carefully for fifteen miles, worried about being pulled over. He'd searched the glove compartment for the truck's registra-tion just in case— scratched out lottery tickets, shriveled banana peel, shrink-wrapped Trojans, six McD's ketchup packs, but no registration.

Now at the gate Carmichael waves the ID card across the reader.

Nothing.

He waves it again. The car behind him honks.

Carmichael starts to worry. He waves the card a third time. The arm, yellow and black striped, starts to rise.

Carmichael parks the F-150 near the administration building, one row down from the executive spots. They'd argued several hours about the best approach, decided in the end on the most obvious— walk right in. The receptionist gives him a big smile.

"You must be new, handsome."

"Second day. Got a call— some problem on the third floor."

"Always something—"

Carmichael starts toward the elevators.

"Wait!" the receptionist says.

Carmichael turns.

She points toward a card reader on the corner of her desk.

"Oh, yeah—"

He passes his card over the reader. A red light flashes.

"Had trouble this morning too," he says.

"Let me see your card," she says.

"No—" He passes the card a second time. The light flashes green.

"Strange," she says.

Carmichael steps off the elevator— heads toward the men's room. Inside he prepares the stink bomb, opening two bottles, wrapping them together in a handkerchief— careful not to let them mix.

An executive, pin-striped suit, bald head, passes Carmichael in the corridor, gives him a strange look, but passes on. Carmichael finds an empty office, tips the bottles into a waste paper basket.

"Takes about five minutes," Greene had told him. Best make yourself invisible until people start to notice the smell.

"Invisible, sure—" Carmichael says. He drops down onto the floor, pretends to be looking for something under the desk. Soon the smell is overpowering.

And, on cue, the building evacuation bell sounds.

"Excellent timing, Mrs. Phan," Carmichael whispers. He stands, steps into the corridor.

"Attention folks— We have a security alert. Please move calmly to the stairwell and evacuate the building. Do not, I repeat, do not use the elevators."

People start pouring into the corridor.

"Don't panic folks, please— You must evacuate the building immediately," he repeats, moving among the cubicles. Some people are reluctant to leave their work.

"Bomb alert. Evacuate now!" Carmichael says more firmly.

The man in pin-stripes steps out of a corner office.

"Another brain-dead exercise?"

"Bomb alert, sir. Evacute now, please."

"Dear heavens!" the man says. "What's that ghastly smell?"

"We're working on it, sir. You best get moving."

Floor cleared, Carmichael makes a quick check around the corridors, then steps into the target cubicle.

It takes less than thirty seconds to attach the bug. Carmichael takes another 30 seconds to scan the cubicle for signs of his intrusion. He steps back into the corridor and is moving before he realizes that his exit is blocked.

The security robot is short and squat, rolling toward him at frightening speed.

"Halt!" it says.

"Crap," Carmichael says.

He evaluates, takes a deep breath, then takes off full speed toward the robot. Six feet out he launches and catches the robot solidly in the head with both feet. The robot tips on its treads, rocks. Still in flight, Carmichael grabs it and pulls it down, slamming the head on the floor, using it as leverage to flip back onto his feet.

"Halt yourself, tin man," he says, as he turns and moves down the stairwell.

El Diablo Negro

THE CORE assembly was shipped out of Karachi, Pakistan's busiest port.

The electronics were shipped out of Kobe, Japan, ranked thirty-eighth busiest container port in the world

Each package was hidden deep in a cargo container, the core assembly welded into a lead-lined iron box wedged among redundant mining equipment; the electronics package under the false bottom of a fermentation tank removed from a dismantled micro brewery.

As specified, the containers were hidden— three-down in four-deep stacks of superficially identical cargo boxes.

The core assembly found passage on the Panamanian freighter *Soledad Express*; the electronics on the Greek-owned ship, *Apollo Rising*.

The freighters were off-loaded within hours of one another in the port of Buenaventura, Colombia's most important Pacific port.

The containers were stacked in bonded warehouses two wharves apart awaiting customs inspection. There they sat for a day and into the next while the customs inspectors attended to other duties.

The discreetly marked containers were pulled from their respective stacks during the night shift, shunted aside, and opportunistically smuggled out of the port and into a run-down cotton warehouse owned by a Señor Fugio Willis, whose name is neither here nor there.

Sea transport and final transfer to the cotton warehouse were managed by the most sophisticated drug smugglers in the world, the Campania clan of the Italian Camorra,

The drug runners had no idea what they were transporting. They only knew that the fees were more than acceptable.

The containers were handed off at the cotton warehouse to Sergio

Fernandez, one-time work name for Hector Paz, logistics chief for the Magdalena drug cartel.

The electronics package arrived in the warehouse at 2:17 a.m,, January 17, the core assembly twenty seven minutes later.

Buenaventura is considered the deadliest urban center in Colombia population just shy of 200,000 souls. More than 42,000 residents are refugees from Colombia's long-running drug war; additional thousands are front-line soldiers in that war.

The murder rate in Buenaventura is 24 times that of New York City.

As instructed, Fernandez/Paz stole a GMC panel van, replaced the plates with another set, also stolen, and transported the two packages from Buenaventura to the Cuidad Bolívar settlement on the outskirt of Bogotá.

Fernandez/Paz was stopped at military road-blocks three times on highway 45 into Bogotá. But certain papers and sufficient *dinero* saw him through with little more than "*Hasta la vista, Señor.*"

The streets of Ciudad Bolívar are a maze. Even residents get turned around. This may account for Fernandez/Paz's tardy delivery. He pulled up to the one-story concrete block building twenty-four minutes late— honked three times as instructed.

Violent assault is the first cause of death for people aged between 15 and 44 in Ciudad Bolívar. It's second for people between 45 and 59. Ciudad Bolívar is known for the worst social conditions in Bogotá.

Few familiar with the ravine where the residents of Cuidad Bolívar discard their garbage were surprised to see black smoke billowing out of the hulk of a GMC panel van early on the morning of November 19.

Nor were they surprised when fragments of bone and teeth were found in the dying char.

Now and again, friends of Hector Paz wonder what has become of him. His family mourns.

D'Mello

D'MELLO has pulled more than one green-behind-the-ears first lieutenant through the hoops. No reason why he can't step into the starring role.

He's rented a warehouse as his base of operations. The Ukrainians and the techs are sitting on pallets watching how D'Mello handles the new guys sent down by Stone.

And here he is with the four new pukes standing at attention, each with shaved head and thick neck, three with sinuous tattoos covering their arms, necks, and who knows what other body parts, and one, the one he's now facing, with symmetrical scars decorating his face.

"Where you from, soldier?"

"Rwanda."

"Name?"

"Emmanuel, sir."

"Occupational specialties?"

"Occu— sir?"

"Skills? What are you good at?"

Emmanuel raises his arms, holds an imaginary rifle.

"Shoot, sir. Good shooter."

"Wonderful," D'Mello mutters.

He advances to the next man, this man barely reaching D'Mello's chest but solid as a stump.

"And your name, son?"

"Mickey Rourke."

"Like the actor?"

"Yes, sir. Ya'll know Mr. Rourke, sir?"

"No. You related?"

"Na. Wisht I was though. Shore like to meet the man. Shake his hand, like. Ya know— Rourke to Rourke.

"Would you now," D'Mello nods.

"Maybe he'd invite me out to that Hollywood—"

D'Mello shakes his head.

The young man continues, "That Mickey Rourke is a professional boxer, ya know! Man, would I love to go a round or two— just to say I done it!"

"You a boxer, Rourke?"

"Give as good as I get, sir."

"You're pretty short for a boxer. Says here you did four years in the U.S. Army. How is it the Army took you in?"

"Slipped under the door, sir."

D'Mello hears chuckles. Suppresses his own grin.

"So where you from, Mr. Rourke?"

"Flat Woods. Flat Woods, Tennessee."

"Can you read a map, Mr. Rourke?"

"Yes, sir. Sight a compass real good, too."

"This op— not much need."

Rourke stands taller.

"But I'm the best damn tracker in western Tennessee."

"Bet you are," D'Mello says.

"Just ask anybody. Bear, deer, cougar, I can track anything— They said you needed a real good tracker."

D'Mello shakes his head.

"Arnie Dingleman, sir," the next man says before D'Mello can finish his step sideways. "By way of Bosnia and Iraq."

"Funny name for a man from Bosnia," D'Mello says.

"No, sir. Served in Bosnia then Iraq. Born in the Bronx."

"And what are your skills, Mr. Dingleman?"

"You name it. I've done it."

"No specialties?"

"Yes, sir. That would be interrogation. Real good at that."

"So I take it you know all about SERE?"

"Oh yes, sir. Been through the training—"

"How long did you last?"

"No, sir. I mean the SERE folks come down to us in Iraq? Taught us all the techniques?"

"Torture, you mean?"

"Oh no, sir. Never called it that."

"So you called it what?"

"Stress techniques. Some call it extreme methods."

"I'll bet," D'Mello says.

"Worked," Dingleman says. "Say that for it."

The last man is six foot six at least. Three hundred pounds.

"And you'd be?"

"Duncan Boot."

"Got some muscle on you there, Mr. Boot."

"Bench press 400 pounds."

"Where have you served, soldier?"

"First time? French Foreign Legion."

"And after that?"

"Can't tell you, sir. Classified."

"Take it you're a competent man, Mr. Boot."

"Well—"

"'Spit it out, Mr. Boot. You're among friends here."

"Well let's just say— I'm the best of the best."

"Let's hope you are—" D'Mello say.

Now D'Mello steps back— snaps his fingers. The Ukrainians, Marko and Vitali, approach, each with two aluminum cases.

"How many of you are qualified in close-quarters urban assault?"

Duncan Boot's hand goes up.

"OK, Mr. Boot, you're going to teach these men everything you know about the subject."

"Where, sir? We need a training base."

"Set up those pallets over there. Make do. Live fire you'll have to head out to the desert."

"Yes, sir. How long do I have, sir?"

"Twenty-four hours."

"Twenty-four—"

"Mr. Dingleman—"

"Sir—"

"You assist Mr. Boot. Do what the man tells you."

D'Mello extracts a match-grade pistol from one of the aluminum cases, surface gleaming with the manufacturer's original grease.

"OK. How many of you gentlemen are familiar with the Heckler & Koch Mk23? The whole system— Knight suppressor— Tech Insight Technology laser aiming module?"

Only Boot's hand goes up.

"Mr. Boot— you're going to be one busy man."

"You want me to qualify these men on the Mk23. Am I right, sir?"

"That's correct."

"The whole damned system?"

"Right you are."

"In twenty-four hours—"

"You got it."

"But sir—"

"Damned glad to have you on my team, Mr. Boot. Always a pleasure to work with the best of the best."

Boot salutes.

"And the mission, sir?" he asks. "May I ask what we're up against?"

"Eyes on the prize. My kind of guy. You've got a lot more than muscle in that shiny head I see, Mr. Boot."

"Enough to keep me alive, sir— So far."

We're expecting a hostile team to arrive in town any day now."

"Hostile how, sir?"

"Remains to be seen. But they'll be looking for a young lady. We think they're looking to eliminate her. Your job is to intercept and neutralize before they find the lady."

"Neutralize? Like—"

"Another excellent question, Mr. Boot. I'd prefer to keep violence to the minimum. Best scenario would be something creative."

"Creative like deflect them from their target? Buy em off? Intimidate? Distract and confuse? Send 'em on a wild goose chase?"

"Mr. Boot— I like the way you think. Be assured I'll ask your input on this matter."

D'Mello snaps his fingers again and Jeremy, the tall tech, walks out, hands each recruit a map.

"On your map— standard automobile club issue— you'll find a set of clearly designated locations— Car rentals, motels, gun-shops, strip clubs— any and every place a hitter might show up to secure wheels, a bed, ammo, or R&R. Also, jewelry and pawnshops, known fences.

"Your mission is to systematically cruise your designated locations, see if you can get a fix on the bad guys."

"And just how do we separate sheep from goats here?" Boot asks.

"Good question, Mr. Boot. Frankly, on that matter, our intel sucks. But what can you do? We know they're trained special ops. So they're likely to look like you. We also know that they're a team of four. One hint— they'll be older guys."

"That narrows it down," Boot says.

"Don't I know it," D'Mello says. "But I can give you this— They're looking for a woman most likely homeless and on the streets. They'll be cruising— asking around."

"What's with the jewelry shops, sir?" Dingleman asks.

"Woman has a bracelet. Might try to pawn it. We assume the hunter-killer team has this intel."

D'Mello snaps his fingers yet again. Martin, the shorter tech, walks out with four fat beige envelopes.

"Now I'm entrusting to each of you God fearing gentlemen a fat wad of cash— five thousand in fresh-mint hundreds—"

Eyes widen.

"The purpose of this cash is to buy eyes— secure actionable intel. There's more if you need it."

D'Mello's face hardens as he scans the four recruits.

"But— if I find that so much as one dollar of your operational stash is used for any purpose other than specified— a pack of smokes, even— you'll find your liver hanging from a post. That clear?"

"Sir!" the four yell.

"Trust you don't want the local authorities in on this goose chase—" Boot says.

"Affirmative."

"Boss," Dingleman says, "If these dudes are trained special ops— they're dangerous cats."

"And you're what—" D'Mello snaps, "A pussy?"

Now Jeremy returns with four cell phones, hands them out.

"These cells are on a private sub-net— encrypted— interconnected only to the nine of us in this facility. Keep 'em charged. You get a sniff, call in immediately. I'll take it from there. Be prepared at all times to jump at my command. Jeremy French will read you in."

Micky Rourke speaks up.

"Sir, eye ballin' this map. This is one big honkin' town. How we supposed to get around?"

D'Mello nods.

"Thought you'd never ask, soldier— How many of you cowboys know how to ride a Hog?"

Four hands go up.

"Dandy. You'll each be requisitioned a brand new Harley-Davidson FXD Super Glide to make your rounds."

The men look at one another, clearly delighted.

"But don't ding 'em. They're just rented for the month."

"Sir—"

"Yes, Mr. Rourke—"

"What's this sar you all been talkin' about?"

"SERE. S.E.R.E. Survival. Evasion. Resistance. Escape."

"Mostly torture," Boot says. "Torture school. Don't let 'em kid you."

"Cool!"

Mickey Rourke

HE'S THE GREEN flag. Last in the convoy. Thirteen out of thirteen. Rolling hard through the night toward Baghdad, through dense desert fog, tensing his jaw, trying not to bite his tongue.

The convoy is pushing pedal down through a bad stretch. He's sailing over sand-filled pot holes, each carved to a different depth and pattern by IEDs, fractured metal, but sometimes he bottoms so hard his spine collapses like an accordion.

Sometimes when he accelerates, closes to minimum interval, he thinks he hears voices, mumbling and grumbling. But mostly he's deaf to Crissie Lou's throaty exhortations— the labored roar of his armored M923A2 gun truck.

His neck and shoulders ache from weight of his night vision system.

He squints, trying to keep his eyes on the green dots bouncing in the greenish fog. It's all he can do to keep his eyes open.

"Talk to me, Rusty," he says. "Ah'm fallin' asleep here."

But Rusty's dead. Long dead.

He twists his head toward the shotgun seat. No peripheral vision. He sees Rusty's ever smiling green face, Rusty popping amphetamines like M&Ms.

"Say there, Drink," Rusty asks. "Tell me 'bout the last time you got laid?"

He shakes his head, feels rising nausea.

Drink. Shorthand for short drink of water. Mustered in just a hair over minimum height. So short he can barely reach the pedals.

The contradiction tugs at the corner of his brain. Rusty. Can't bring it into focus. Just knows he can't lose the convoy to desert fog. Must keep the green dots in view. But orders are to hang back, maintain interval. But back here, mark on interval, the green dots fade in and out of desert fog.

Line haul. Iraq. Night. Pure tedium mostly. Pure butt pucker when not. No in between. Night after night. Riding shotgun for M915s, petrotankers, HETs, and HMMWVs.

And he's just so sleepy now. Never been so.

The fog is so thick he can no longer see the burned out pyres of M915s, tankers, HETs, and HMMWVs shoved up on the verge like so much scrap metal. But he knows they're there. Knows that every one harbors ghosts.

"Hajis always target the last vehicle in the convoy," Rusty says.

Who'd know better? He turns his head toward the shotgun seat.

He closes his eyes. Green fades to black. He pops them open— all green. Solid swirling green. No dots.

He's lost his convoy!

Now he feels something in his stomach rise and turn like an old wet dog smelling challenge, feels his heart race.

And he hears the POP POP and a BANG. Feels the jolt. IED! He's under attack. BANG!

"Rusty!" he cries. But Rusty's dead. Long dead.

"Up and at 'em, Daniel Boone," he hears. He starts. Damn! It's that ol' Duncan Boot banging on his motel room door.

Motel 6.

"Assembly in ten minutes."

Mickey Rourke sinks back into his pillow, rubs his eyes.

"Shut your yap, you ol' damn hard ass, he thinks.

"Never give you no permission to call me Daniel Boone."

He rolls to the edge of the hard mattress, mouth dry, drenched in sweat. He checks the clock radio, converts the time. Fifteen hundred hours. Hit the rack just five hours ago. Five hours!

That Duncan Boot kept them up twenty-six hours straight, first building a four-room toy house out of wooden pallets in the middle of the warehouse, then haul ass out to a griddle hot desert wash for pistol practice, shooting from every position and range, practicing quick draw over and over.

Say one thing, that ol' boy Boot is a pretty damn good shooter—

shot the head off a rattler at fifteen yards. But Emmanuel might be better. Quick draw. Clean shot the rattle off.

Then they field strip and clean their H&K M23s over and over until they can do it in the dark.

Fact— that Duncan Boot threw a nylon ditty sack over his head, kept it there until he could do a clean field strip in the dark.

Thought he'd suffocate.

Then, with no rest, back to the toy house for a straight ten hours of close-quarters combat drill— breaching doors, clearing rooms. Duncan Boot passes out Super Soakers. They trade off good-guy bad-guy. Any good guy gets wet Duncan Boot gives them a verbal boot up the backside then patiently shows them the error of their ways.

Last hour Duncan Boot is the bad guy. Fills his Super Soaker with his own urine. Says, "Any one of you pukes miss a beat you'll be wearing my cologne."

Dripping wet, Mickey Rourke now stands naked in front of the full-length mirror. The mirror is dappled down the left edge with black mirror rot. Dense swirls of matted hair, black, wrap his torso; vivid tattoos swirl around his arms. He stands five-foot-two. Built like a brick. But his eyes— no matter how long he stares he can never fathom who's looking back out at him. Judging him. His eyes— never feels like they're his own.

"But what the—?"

He sees a bright red smear under his chin, ear to ear.

He touches it, smells his finger.

Lipstick!

He rubs it but it just smears.

He hears another loud thump at the door.

"Two minutes, Boone."

He feels his temper rise. He's got some tall temper.

"Some donkey dick's going to get it now," he thinks. He wonders who's fooling with him now. Wouldn't be the first time.

Dwarf, Troll, Shrimp they called him in grade school. Chimp they called him in the showers back at Tipton High. Drink they called him in Iraq. From earliest days he took it all in silence, smiled even, knowing that his Pa would swat him a good one if he uttered a complaint.

"Give as good as you get," his Pa always told him.

And, once he took up boxing, learned a thing or two, he did.

Arnie Dingleman wipes his face with a motel towel, steps up to the foggy mirror, wipes the condensation.

"What the fuck!"

Lipstick. Ear to ear.

Someone pounds on his door.

"Assembly in two minutes," Duncan Boot yells.

Now they're assembled in the warehouse. Everyone except D'Mello and Boot are marked with lipstick. Ear to ear. Even the Ukrainians and the techs.

"I take it you ladies had trouble putting on your make-up this morning," D'Mello says.

He senses embarrassment, anger under the surface.

"Mr. Boot," D'Mello says. "How is it that you're the only one out of fashion?"

"Never went in for that sissy stuff," Boot says.

Now everyone is glaring at Boot.

"Why do I feel that you have some insight into this new fashion of adornment?"

"Just speculating, sir. But this soldier's thinking it might be some kind of field exercise— You know, penetration of unit security?"

"How so?"

"Well, whoever was out last night painting throats with lipstick could just as easily been wielding a well-honed blade— on a mission slitting throats."

Now there's silence. Eyes darting from face to face."

"And you have thoughts on the matter, I take it," D'Mello says.

"I do, sir."

"Well, then, why are we standing here? Looks like we have operational deficiencies to iron out."

Mickey Rourke

IT'S NOT RIGHT, Mickey Rourke thinks. It's been simmering through the day. One part he can understand. But sneakin' into a man's room at night— painting him up with lipstick like he was some kind of two dollar whore.

He'd asked Arnie Dingleman about it. But Dingleman had just shrugged— no big deal.

But to Mickey Rourke it is a big deal. Just doesn't sit right.

He finds himself staring at Duncan Boot. Duncan Boot doesn't seem to notice. Tall pork sticker. Hard ass.

Mickey Rourke thinks about that sweaty ditty sack over his head. Could hardly breathe.

"Drop that recoil spring in the sand one more time, Daniel Boone, and I'm going to break your fingers one by one."

Sweat is running down into his eyes, stinging bad. His mouth is filled with sand. He can hardly breathe. That sweaty rip-stop nylon closes off his nostrils and his mouth with every breath. And he's trying to juggle pistol parts in the dark.

Every time he drops a part he has to wipe it off with his shirt tail, finger every surface for grains of sand.

Hard Ass checks. One grain of sand and the pork sticker dumps all the parts back into the sand. Has to start all over.

"Get to know them pistol parts better than you know your own dick, Daniel Boone," Duncan Boot yells.

How can a man do a job with a man like that yelling in his ear?

"You know your own dick there, don't you Daniel Boone? Bet you play with it often enough."

Then they're back at the warehouse, that close quarters drill thing.

Barely given a chance to relieve his bladder. No chance to rest, cool off. And he's sweating like a pig. Duncan Boot yelling at him. Always him. Yelling at him. Spraying him with urine.

It's not right. Maybe he should up and quit.

But he's no quitter.

"Give as good as you get," his daddy always said.

Mickey Rourke goes through the motions of the day. He rides out, does his rounds. He rides back just as Duncan Boot is pulling his Harley into the warehouse. He stares at Duncan Boot, but Duncan Boot doesn't seem to notice.

It's supper time when the idea hits him. The perfect idea.

"We're headin' down to that Tex-Mex place," Dingleman says. "You ready?"

"Nah," Mickey Rourke says. "Got me some errands gotta do."

He fires up his Harley, rolls out into the street, weaves in and out until he hits Rte. 17. He merges into the commuter traffic, weaves in and out through the suburban sprawl. He rides out into the desert, picking up speed.

He exits onto an asphalt ranch road. It's dark now. A touch of cool in the air. He cruises the ranch roads, some narrow asphalt, some graded. He sees lights in the distance, but mostly the shadows of saguaros to his right and left. His headlight casts a jittery cone on the road ahead. He navigates by the stars. It takes him three hours to find what he's looking for.

It's two fifteen by the time Mickey Rourke climbs into bed. Duncan Boot pounds on his door at five. But Mickey Rourke is up and dressed.

They're gathering around D'Mello in the warehouse to hear the orders of the day. Mickey Rourke walks up to Duncan Boot, holds out a heavily laden pillow case, thrusts it out like Santa's sack.

"Brought you a present, sir," he says.

"What's this?" Duncan Boot says.

Duncan Boot takes the pillow case, looks inside.

He drops the pillow case and jumps back.

"*Merde!*" he says.

Two four-foot diamond back rattlesnakes spill out of the pillow case, coil on the floor, rattles working. Everyone except Rourke jumps back.

Before Duncan Boot can pull his pistol, Mickey Rourke dives down, grabs a snake and waves it over his head. The serpent stretches out like a staff. Mickey Rourke advances on Duncan Boot.

"The name is Mr. Rourke," he says. "Mr. Rourke. You got that Mr. Pork Sticker? You got no right to call me Daniel Boone!"

Duncan Boot looks surprised.

"Yes, sir!" he says.

"And you got no right sneakin' into my room and paintin' me up like some two dollar whore!"

By now the snake is wrapped around Mickey Rourke's arm.

Duncan Boot is trying to hold back a grin.

"Yes, sir, you're absolutely right about that."

"Just 'cause you're bigger than me don't make you better than me!"

"Yes, sir, you're the man," Duncan Boot says.

By now everyone's laughing.

Mickey Rourke looks around, eyes flashing.

"Rourke, you get those damn serpents out of here before I have to shoot you and your reptiles too," D'Mello says.

Rourke picks up the pillow case, drops the snake inside, grabs and bags the other, and twists a knot.

"Man, how'd you do that?" Arnie Dingleman asks.

"Third generation serpent handler," Mickey Rourke says.

"That's one stupid ass thing to do, ask me," Dingleman says.

"'They shall take up serpents and if they drink any deadly thing, it shall not hurt them,' that's in your Bible," Mickey Rourke says.

"You could have been bit bad."

"Oh, I've been bit ten or twelve times. Look at these here knuckles. Hurts like hell, but I'm still standin', praise the Lord. My daddy been bit more than a hundred times."

"Lucky he's still alive."

"Ain't," Mickey Rourke says. "Last one— killed him."

"Daniel Boone," Duncan Boot says, "You got more balls than I give you credit for, I'll say that for you."

"Damn!" Mickey Rourke stamps his foot. "I hate it when you call me that!"

So now here's Mickey Rourke tooling down West Camelback on his brand new Harley— more money in his pocket than his pa saw in a month of paydays. Slag-furnace sun blasts Mickey's face, but the roar of the Harley fills his ears with song.

First stop is Maricopa Jewelers. He boosts his bike up on the jiffy stand, steps into a wall of cold air. He's feeling tall until he sees her— most beautiful thing ever— just standing there behind the store-long glass counter, demure breasts wrapped in pink hanging over a case of gleaming diamonds.

"May I help, sir?" she asks.

"Ah'm— ah— looking—"

She smiles.

"Ah— ah'm—"

"Deep breath—" she says.

He closes his eyes, opens them, tries again.

"Ah'm lookin' for these ol' boys?"

She looks up and down the length of the store, shrugs, turns back, catches him staring at her breasts.

"Sorry, ma'am," he says. "Thing is, these 'ol boys are runnin' around lookin' for this here young lady—"

He smooths out a printed photo of Kimberly on the gleaming glass counter.

"And she has this here diamond bracelet?"

He smooths out a print of the bracelet.

"I think these are bad men set to do this young lady harm."

She takes in his blush, looks down at the images.

"One moment, sir—"

She rustles around in a drawer under the counter— pulls out an identical leaflet— smiles.

"My manager said there's this big— reward?"

"Your manager—" He looks up hopefully. "Speak to him?"

"Mr. Ortega," she says. "He's in Switzerland."

"Oh—" he says.

"You know, over there in Europe?"

"Europe—" he says.

"Left me here all by my lonesome—"

She pouts.

"—with all these bad boys around and all."

He shuffles, sees she's playing with him.

She pokes the print of the bracelet with her crimson nail.

"Pretty—" she says.

He starts to withdraw.

"Sure you wouldn't like to buy a diamond for your sweetie?"

"I ah just— Ah—"

He moves toward the door.

"Thank you, kindly, ma'am," he says as he bolts out the door.

And now on the road again next stop is Poochie T's, a not-much building, reminder of an older Phoenix.

He notes the scrum of bikes parked around the entrance— way bad Harleys and too many to count.

Inside screaming guitars, heavy bass, assault his ears. He'd heard his fill of this noise in Iraq. Prefers Waylon Jennings. Most of the crowd is pushed up against a small stage, bouncing to the degenerate beat. Others are crowding the bar, yelling above the music. He hears heavy curses, breaking glass, and the knock of pool balls.

The smell is stale beer, sweat, grease, cigarette smoke, and marijuana. And something that awakens the old wet dog in his stomach.

He sort of fits in. But he doesn't.

He notes that most of the men are wearing identical colors, big patches on sleeveless Levi jackets— Skorpions M.C.

He edges up to the bar, stands for ten minutes waiting for service. The bartender has yellow fingers, no front teeth. He serves to Mickey's left and to Mickey's right, pausing between serves to stare at the ceiling, inhale and exhale a crumpled roach. He shoves long cold beer bottles, four at a time, into anxious hands pushing through the bodies crowded up against the bar, some to the left of Mickey and some to the right.

Never once does the bartender look at Mickey.

"Say, friend, could ya'll get me a Diet Coke?" Mickey says at last, "If ya please sir."

Says it again.

Now the bartender looks at Mickey directly.

"What makes you think I'm yer friend?" he says.

For a moment Mickey is stuck for words.

"Ah'm just askin'," he says. "A Diet Coke."

Now Mickey's aware of others staring. The music seems to fade.

"For one thing, Little Toad," the bartender says. "We don't serve no diii et coke."

"A Bud, then, will do me kindly," Mickey says. "Just like everybody else here is drinkin'."

The bartender now leans in close. Mickey can smell a blend of cannabis and rotting teeth.

"For another, Little Toad, this is sort of like a private club and you ain't been invited."

Now Mickey feels a soft hand on the back of his head. He twists his head and sees two freckled breasts not two inches from his nose, one inked with a scorpion tattoo.

"Give the boy what he wants, Spookie," the woman says. "He's a cute little thing."

"Obliged, ma'am," the bartender says, "But—"

She leans down and kisses Mickey Rourke on the top of his head.

"Don't you like me?" she asks.

He looks up, sees wild red hair, jade green eyes, and freckled cheeks.

Now he feels a much larger presence pressing in on his other side, is stunned by a hard slap to the back of his head.

"You coming on to my woman?"

The man is six four easy, heavy weight, big as Duncan Boot.

Soft face, Mickey's Pa always said. Mickey does his best to keep a soft face. He steps back from the bar and turns. Now he's aware of others crowding in.

"Beg your pardon, Sir—" Mickey Rourke says, then steps left, pivots, and lashes out with a perfect front kick to the big man's right knee.

The man howls and drops to all fours.

The crowd goes silent and, before they can react, Mickey Rourke has his H&K 23 in a menacing pose.

Mickey sees the lady's face turn to fury, like she's ready to pounce. He shakes his head.

"That there knee'll heal up one of these days," he says. "But if I put one of these through his other knee he'll never walk again."

Mickey sees hands go up, leather and denim back away.

He dances to the exit, twirling once to protect his blind side. He's on his Harley and gone before all-out rage overcomes shock.

"Shoot," he thinks later. "Never got a chance to show 'em my pictures."

Dingleman

THE SNATCH goes down just outside Dennys.
Emmanuel loses the coin toss. Third morning in a row. He squeezes out of the booth laughing, shaking his head.

Arnie Dingleman chugs down a last swig of coffee, wipes his mouth, fingers three dollar bills out of his wallet and slaps them down beside his egg-and-syrup smeared plate.

Emmanuel steps to the register, pays with a crisp $20 bill. When he turns, pocketing pennies for change, he expects to see Dingleman by the exit. But no Dingleman. He looks back toward the booth— No Dingleman. He scans the restaurant. No Dingleman near the register nor anywhere in sight.

Men's room, must be, Emmanuel thinks.

Emmanuel steps outside, cars in the parking lot, but no people. He steps back in, waits, fascinated by the machine near the door— drop a quarter win a prize.

Emmanuel checks the men's room. He circles back through the restaurant, scans the booths. He steps outside again into the morning heat. A family of six, dressed for church, flows around him.

Dingleman's brand new Harley gleams in the sun. But still no Dingleman.

Emmanuel circles the building, checks behind the dumpster— scares a cat.

But no Dingleman.

Dingleman is gone.

Emmanuel calls in.

"You say Dingleman's bike is still parked in front of the restaurant?" D'Mello asks.

"Yes, Sir," Emmanuel says.

"Get back inside," D'Mello says. "Stay put. We'll be there in ten."

"No sign at the restaurant," D'Mello says when he returns to base, shuts down his Harley.

He turns to the techs, "Calls?"

The techs shake their heads.

Emmanuel coasts his bike in behind D'Mello, removes his helmet. He scans the faces, hoping. But no Dingleman.

"Maybe Mr. Dingleman up and walked?" Mickey Rourke says.

"And leave his bike?"

"Checked Dingleman's room," Duncan Boot says. "Ask me, no hint of cut-and-run."

"Passport?" D'Mello asks.

"Shirts, pants in the closet— skivvies, tees, socks in the dresser— toothbrush and razor still wet by the bathroom sink— passport and four bills under the mattress."

"Tell me, Emmanuel," D'Mello asks, "You guys eat at Denny's every morning?"

"Yes, sir, closest place. First run, then eat."

"Every day? Same time? Same route?"

"Yes, sir—"

"Today, at breakfast— Dingleman nervous? Acting strange?"

"No, suh. We joke. He there. I pay. Turn aroun'. Mr. Dingleman— he gone."

"Jesus," D'Mello says.

"Observe anything strange, Mr. Emmanuel?" Duncan Boot asks, "Anyone, like, taking an interest? Maybe like even before you sat down to eat?"

"No, sir."

"You're thinking?" D'Mello asks.

"Don't like it. Smells professional."

"Missionaries?"

"Two to one we're under surveillance."

"You think?" D'Mello asks.

"Snatch like that takes intel— planning."

"Big question—" D'Mello asks. "What's next?"

For a moment there's quiet in the warehouse.

"Sarge D'Mello, sir," Marko Dolinski breaks the silence—

"Could they— could we be next?"

D'Mello stares at the floor, looks up—

"Yeah," he says, "Assume it."

The Ukrainians stare at one another.

D'Mello catches it.

"What's on your mind, Mr. Dolinski?" D'Mello says. "Spit it out."

"This— This not what we sign up for."

"And what exactly did you sign up for?"

"Security work, sir—"

"And you think security work is a knitting circle? Sitting on your butt collecting pay?"

"Sir—"

"You afraid, Mr. Dolinski? Pissing your pants? That what you're telling me?"

D'Mello's face is hard, voice barely above a whisper.

"I— We—"

"Want to check out, Mr. Dolinski? That it? Be my guest. Door's that way."

D'Mello gestures toward the warehouse door.

"You and your *amigo* have been nothin' but dead wood, ask me."

"Sergeant— Please—"

"But hit that street, mister, you're on you're own. And if you're hopin' for a free pass— don't count on that bunch that grabbed Dingleman."

"That's what I'm wondering, sir," Mickey Rourke asks. "Who are these turkeys?"

D'Mello is silent.

"Sergeant D'Mello, sir," Duncan Boot says, "What aren't you telling us?"

D'Mello stares at Boot.

"We deserve to know."

D'Mello scans the dark corners of the warehouse.

"Level with us Sergeant— or maybe we're all out that door."

"Right. Yeah," D'Mello exhales. "Don't know. Just speculation."

"Speculate then."

"Stone's running scared—"

"Stone? The man's a legend."

"Few weeks ago— just before he sent you guys down here— the man was waiting for me in my motel room. Sloshed out of his gourd and— shaky as all get out."

"Shaky?"

"Shaky— scared."

"Stone? Scared? Of what?"

"Don't know. Wouldn't tell me. Evasive."

"Evasive?"

"Talked in riddles."

"About what?"

"Secrets."

"Secrets?"

"Talked in circles. Edgy. No— More than edgy. Panic. Brown streak panic."

"Man owns half the defense industry of the United States of America. Worth billions. You're telling me the man can't protect himself?"

"Said, 'They're sending in another team.'"

"Who's they?"

"Wouldn't say. Way above my pay grade made it sound— And maybe his."

"This other team— we're talking about these so-called missionaries here?"

"Check."

"And this woman, then— Who's she?"

"Stone's daughter."

"Stone's daughter?"

D'Mello nods.

"Shit!" Duncan Boot says.

"My feelings exactly," D'Mello says.

"And these missionaries? What'd he tell you?"

"Bad guys. Tasked to kill the woman."

"And take out anyone who stands in their way?"

"My impression."

"Take out Stone as well maybe?"

"Didn't say. But he ordered me to neutralize them."

"Neutralize them? Meaning?"

"Just what you think."'

"That's not what you told us when you briefed us. Told us you were looking to avoid violence—"

"My preference. I'm no two-bit hit man for Stone."

"So let's get this straight— C. Norbert Stone, *Forbes* front cover puke, CEO of SVS Aerospace, ordered you to intercept and kill these missionaries? Sent us down to aid and abet?"

D'Mello shakes his head. Yes.

"And you agreed?"

"Choice was not exactly on the table."

"You couldn't refuse?"

D'Mello shakes his head again. No.

"Why?"

"My business."

"But you figured you could finesse your way around Stone's order one way or another—"

"The man also ordered me to find and protect the daughter. 'Get her off the board. Keep her safe.' That I could swallow. Figured somebody has to do it."

"Somebody has to do it—"

"Yeah," D'Mello says.

Duncan Boot takes a long look at every man on the team.

"Let me ask you this, Sergeant D'Mello— Would you kill those missionary pukes if it came to that?"

"Like I say— didn't sign on as Stone's personal button man."

"That's not what I'm asking. Would you kill those pukes if it came to that?"

"If it came to that? Yeah, somebody has to keep that woman safe."

"Why? Because she's Stone's daughter?"

"Don't patronize me, Boot. Because she's some poor kid's mother."

Boot nods.

"You've got balls, Sergeant D'Mello. Give you that."

"Mr. Dolinkski," Boot says, "Those hours back there in the warehouse— Out there in the desert— Did I train you to prevail?"

"Yes, sir."

"So you willing to let this stand? Just waltz away with your pecker in your hand— Let some assholes kill an innocent young mother in cold blood— even if she is Stone's daughter?"

Dolinkski hesitates.

"Let's hear it."

"No sir," he says.

"Vitali—" Boot turns to Dolinski's partner. "What about you? You ready to cut and run?"

Vitali shrugs.

"Well?"

"Marko stay. I stay."

Duncan Boot turns to Martin McKenna, the short tech.

"Mr. McKenna— And where do you stand on this weighty matter?"

"In for a penny, I guess."

"Mr. French— Can we count on you?"

"Whatever—"

'Meaning?"

"Whatever. But I'd sure feel better if you'd issue me one of those H & Ks."

"And you, Mr. Emmanuel?"

"Mr. Dingleman was my frien', suh."

"Daniel Boone?"

"Stomp these false prophets!"

"There we are then, Sergeant D'Mello."

"OK— That's it," D'Mello says, "Let's take it to 'em."

The Missionaries

DINGLEMAN has dispensed pain. Seen pain dispensed. But never been on the receiving end. SERE training, sure. But nothing like—this.

Nothing like—

Jesus!

Cockbite!

Who— Sweet Jesus—

Oh!

Putz fucker!

What do they— want?

His mind is fuzzy with pain. World's black. Hood over his head.

He'd stepped outside Denny's. Closed his eyes to take in the sun. Blue Dodge camper van pulls up. Door opens. Older man steps out, points something and— Jesus! Muscles seize up. Teeth slam into his tongue. All he can do to breathe.

Now he's shackled, face down in a shag-pile carpet. The smell— Potato chips. Urine. Dog maybe. The voice— Can't make it out through the pain.

He can hear the roar of engine— stop and go of traffic. He can hear the roar of blood in his head.

A boot, must be, slams into his ribs.

"Christ killer!" he hears.

"Putz fucker—" Dingleman thinks. "That your best?"

The beating is remorseless. He tries to talk but— can't.

Oh, shit.

Shit!

He tries to breathe, but can't.

With every breath the heel slams into his face, ribs, solar plexus.
What do they— OH FUCK— want?
Stomach reflux burns his mouth and throat— gags him.
Fuck of fuck, if he could only get a breath!
The heel grinds into his throat.
Can't breathe!
I'll— I'll tell— anything— just— stop, he thinks, but can't form the words.
The pain in his chest is sudden, vice-like and vicious sharp, envelops his arm, more severe than anything so far.
"What's happening back there?"
"Seizures, looks like."
"Jumpin' Judas, Brother Michael— Why is it you always go too far?"
"He's a big one, Brother James. Just did what you told me."
"Didn't tell you to kill him."
"So what's wrong with him?"
"How should I know."
"What's he look like?"
"Gasping like a fish."
"Heart attack maybe. Now he's useless to us."
"Just kept saying 'Sara— Sara— Wrote the book.'"
"Sara? Maybe S.E.R.E? Survive Evade Resist Extract?"
"Beats me."
"Could be this guy's been through the program."
"Says he wrote the book."
"Doubt it. But still—"
"So what now?"
"Get him to an emergency room."
"We can't just walk into an emergency room!"
"We can't just let him die on us."
"We've killed plenty before."
"In the name of the Lord."
"So maybe it's the Lord's will."
"If so, Pastor would have told us. You heard Pastor— Wants intel not body count."
"Wants us to eliminate this Jezebel."
"That's different. She's a present threat to Dominion. You heard

Pastor."

"Pastor's been acting weird lately. You notice?"

"Reunion looming nigh. Plenty on his mind."

"Praise the Lord— Come Reunion. Can't wait."

"Yeah? Come Reunion. What then, Brother Michael?"

"Tell you this— I'm tired of runnin' around the country. Do this, do that. For Pastor, sure. But a man gets tired. I'll tell you that for sure."

"And?"

"Buy me a little place on a lake. Fish with unbaited hook. Cuddle with the Mrs. Take a long nap in the afternoon. You know—"

"What Mrs.?"

"I'll find me one—"

"And the Covenant?"

"Yeah— yeah, I know. What about you?"

"Me?"

"Come Reunion."

"Come Reunion I figure Pastor's going to need us more than ever."

"Need us? Why?"

"So many unbelievers—"

There's long silence in the van.

"Why won't they listen?" Brother Michael asks.

"Listen? Who?"

Brother Michael gestures toward the traffic outside the van.

"They drive around like zombies. Tend their little lives. If only they'd listen— take Pastor's Word into their hearts."

"Pastor can't reach them all. Lord knows he's tried."

"This Diablo thing— Think it'll make a difference?"

"Diablo?"

"Diablo Negro."

"Diablo Negro— Where'd you hear that?"

"Scuttlebutt. What is this thing, anyway?"

"Little something to get their attention— open their eyes. Shock and awe before they can react."

"Who?"

"Fornicators— Sodomites— Apostates— Filth of the world. All who refuse the Word—"

"So what's with this Jezebel?" Brother Michael says.

"Pastor told us— Find her. Secure all in her possession. Eliminate her. That's all I know— All you need to know."

"If Stone's people can't find her, how we supposed to?"

"Let them do the dirty work— lead us to her. That was Pastor's idea."

"So, we've got them covered with audio, video— GPS on their hikes, But we're no closer to the whore."

"Patience, I say. The Lord will provide."

Brother Michael gives Dingleman a gentle kick.

"Well this one didn't give us much."

"Yeah— I'm thinking we need a little *tête-à-tête* with that D'Mello. He may know more than he's telling the others."

"Then, let's dump this one— man sounds like he's breathing rocks."

"I've got a better use for him."

"Well, better be something before he stinks up this van more than he does now."

"So how do you catch a fly, Brother Michael?"

"Do tell, Brother James."

"Honey, Brother Michael. Think honey."

The jogger, a young intern catching a run out of St. Luke's Hospital, can't tell just what it is they've tossed out of the camper van. But it's something big, a pillow couch or something. He runs in place, watches the door slam, the camper van lumber around the corner.

The jogger resumes his pace, curious, but stops when the thing resolves into view.

"My God!," he says.

He fumbles in his belly pouch, pulls out his cell, and punches out 911.

Boswick

BOSWICK snaps his clamshell.

"A break," he says. "That was Detective Martinez— calling from St. Luke's emergency—"

Mrs. Phan looks up.

"They've pulled this guy in. Big guy with tattoos. Beaten to an inch— Might not make it. Had a picture of a Kimberly Bolton in his wallet."

"What mean?" Mrs. Phan asks.

"One of Stone's goons— could be."

"But beaten— Why?" Carmichael asks. "Who?"

"Pray the man can tell us," Boswick says.

At that same moment D'Mello gets a call from SVS Human Resources.

"You have a man in your unit?" the treacly voice asks. "A Mr. Arnold Dingleman?"

"Yes, ma'am."

"This call came in from St. Luke's Hospital in Phoenix?"

"St. Luke's—"

"Seems that Mr. Dingleman has been in some kind of accident? They called about his insurance?"

"Yes. He's been missing."

"Well I just called to let you know that he might not be reporting in any time soon? From what they tell us Mr. Dingleman's condition is like totally serious? We're trying to track down relatives."

"Jesus—" D'Mello says.

"Yes," she says, "We'll all pray for his swift recovery."

D'Mello

D′MELLO holds the door for the old man pushing the walker. The man nods his thanks, his eyes flat with little sheen. D'Mello watches the old man clump across the broad lobby, slowly, but with determination. He watches him pause unsteadily, then disappear into a cluster of patients and visitors, some old, some young.

D'Mello notes many faces inwardly focused with illness and pain, concern and fatigue. He can't help but think about his son as he makes his way to the information desk.

"Arnold Dingleman," he says. "Was sent over from emergency, I think."

The young Hispanic woman consults her computer.

"How's that spelled, sir?"

D'Mello spells it.

"Yes, we have a Mr. Dingleman in ICU," the woman says.

D'Mello moves through to the elevators. The familiar sour smell reminds him of how much he hates hospitals. Spends enough time in them.

A uniformed cop stops him just outside the intensive care unit.

"I'm here to see Mr. Dingleman,"

"Are you now?" the cop says. "Relative?"

"Employer."

The officer shakes his head.

"Don't know—" he says.

"Don't know what?"

"Man must have two jobs—"

"Why's that?"

"Last pilgrim claimed HE was the man's employer."

"Last pilgrim? When?"

"Ten— twenty minutes ago— And do tell— what's your name, sir?"

"D'Mello. Charles D'Mello."

"Wait here," the cop says.

The cop disappears through the swinging doors, then steps back out behind a lanky man in western shirt and cowboy boots.

"Mr. D'Mello," the man says. "Detective Antonio Martinez, Maricopa County Sheriff's office."

"What can I do for you, detective?"

"Let's step down here, sir— more comfortable."

They walk in silence to the small waiting room. A floor-to-ceiling window fills the waiting room with light.

"I take it you know Mr. Dingleman?"

"How's he doing?"

The detective rocks his hand equivocally.

"You're the employer, that correct, Mr. D'Mello?"

D'Mello nods.

"And, what's the nature of your business?"

"Security. Private security."

The detective gives D'Mello a long look.

"Any outfit I'm familiar with?"

D'Mello pulls out a business card.

"SVS Security— like the aerospace company?"

"Different division."

"I see."

The detective turns, looks out the window, fiddles absently in his shirt pocket, removes a pack of chewing gum. The view's not much. A parking lot. A line of palm trees. He unwraps a stick of gum, folds it into his mouth, starts to chew, drops the wrapper back into his pocket.

He turns back.

"Sorry," he says, offers D'Mello the pack of gum.

"I suppose you can't tell me what Mr. Dingleman is doing here in Phoenix?"

D'Mello shrugs.

"Then, I suppose you can't tell me who you're working for or what you're working on?"

D'Mello nods.

"Thought as much," the detective says.

"May I speak with Mr. Dingleman?" D'Mello asks.

"Not at this time," the detective says. "But don't go far. We'll have more questions. You can bet on it."

Stepping into the elevator, D'Mello glances back— sees a big man dressed in black.

And, just by chance, looking back from the hospital exit doors, he sees the man a second time, hard by the look of him. The man is stepping out of a second elevator, searching the lobby. He catches D'Mello's eye, looks away.

D'Mello steps out into the visitor's parking lot, but the heat off the black asphalt is so searing he sticks to the shade under the palms. It's a longer walk, but slightly cooler.

His black Expedition is parked near the helipad.

At the curb, just before crossing the exit lane toward the helipad side, he pauses, stoops to tie his shoe.

The big guy has kept pace, twenty paces back, following in the shade under the palms.

D'Mello unlocks his car, starts it, sits while he watches the big man backtrack two lanes over and fold himself into a beige compact.

D'Mello sits. The beige car sits.

D'Mello rolls out of the lot, pauses before turning left onto North 19th Street. He checks his rear view, sees the beige compact pull out of its parking row.

D'Mello punches redial on his cell.

"Speak," Duncan Boot says.

"Just leaving the hospital. Picked up a shadow. Beige car— recent model— one of those nondescripts—"

"Get the license?"

"Not from here."

"Hold a minute," Boot says. "Let me check a map."

"Back," Boot says. "Know your way to Phoenix Sky International?"

"Yeah," D'Mello says.

"Make your way slowly to the airport. Got luggage?"

"Sorry," D'Mello says.

"No problem. Just pull into the visitor's lot, park, then make your way into Terminal 4. But keep a sharp eye. Stick to crowds. When you enter the terminal, call me back.

D'Mello watches the beige compact through his rear view. It maintains a steady three to four cars back, too far to get a license. It turns when he turns.

"OK," Boot says when D'Mello calls back, "Find a place to sit. The bar maybe. Have a cool one. Keep your eye out for watchers. You'll need to waste thirty minutes while we set something up. When we're ready to rock and roll I'll ring you back on your cell."

Boot rings back thirty seven minutes later.

D'Mello has kept his eye out. Tried to look casual. But hasn't spotted eyes taking interest.

"OK, make your way back to your car. Move with the crowds. Call me when you're ready to roll."

"Got it," D'Mello says.

"You strapped?" Boot asks.

"Bet on it—" D'Mello says.

"Outstanding."

Now, back in the car, D'Mello redials. Boot recites more directions.

D'Mello drives slowly out of the terminal complex and onto East Sky Harbor Blvd. He slows down, confirms his shadow. He picks up the Sky Harbor Expressway, speeds up, turns right on E. Van Buren, keeps pace with the traffic.

"Bogey still on your tail?" Boot asks.

"Still there."

"OK, you'll be coming up to North 20th Street. Turn right. A long block down and you'll turn left onto East Monroe Street. Monroe's a dead end."

"And?" D'Mello asks.

"Turn onto Monroe. Drive slowly. You'll see a low industrial building on your left. Pull into the left lane. Just past the drive, make a sharp 90 degree right turn and stop so you're sitting in the middle of Monroe, passenger-side facing back down the way you came."

"And?"

"When you hear three horn blasts, step out of your car with your weapon ready, locked and loaded."

"So an ambush you're thinking?"

"I'm thinking we'll learn a thing or two by taking these *putains* alive."

D'Mello turns left onto East Monroe. His hands are shaking, but he knows they'll stop. Always happens in the moments before combat.

He slows, sees the drive, swings to his left then cuts a sharp right turn. Almost immediately he hears three blasts, followed by various accelerations.

By the time he's out of the car he sees the beige compact trapped, his team's black Expedition jammed up against it's back bumper, two Harleys with menacing shooters on it's passenger side, and Duncan Boot, H&K Mk23 aimed steady as a rock at its driver-side window, two-handed grip.

"Out of the car, please. Hands high in the air," Duncan Boot says.

No reaction.

"Out now!" Boot yells.

Slowly the car door opens.

Carmichael steps out.

Now the back door opens.

Mrs. Phan steps out.

"On your bellies, hands flat on the ground."

"Wha—" Mrs. Phan says. "You shoot old lady?"

Mrs. Phan starts advancing.

"Stop, now, lady," Duncan Boot says.

But Mrs. Phan keeps advancing.

"You big man? Shoot old lady?"

Who is this, D'Mello wonders. What is she, all of five two?

She advances until she's standing in Duncan Boot's face.

"You big bad man—"

"Lady—"

One minute Duncan Boot is staring down at Mrs. Phan, H&K Mk23 at the ready. The next, too fast to follow, professional sleight of hand, Duncan Boot is on the asphalt, clearly in pain. Mrs. Phan standing over him, pressing the muzzle of his H&K in his ear.

"Where my daughter?" she screams.

"Wait," D'Mello says. He motions for his team to stand down.

"Your daughter?" D'Mello says.

"Kim Le," Mrs. Phan says.

"Kimberly Bolton," D'Mello yells. "Is that who you're looking for?"

They fail to notice the blue camper van creeping down N. 20th.

"What's this, Brother James?" Brother Michael asks. "What's going on there?"

"Interference. Just what we need."

"What now?"

"Watch and wait," Brother Michael. "Watch and wait."

El Diablo Negro

E<small>L</small> A<small>RQUITECTO DEL</small> M<small>AR</small>, The Marine Architect, Sergei Tasarov knows as much about submersible vessels as any man alive.

He's served as crew and captain. He's designed them— built them. He's fought in them, gone down under raining depth charges, plunged to hull cracking depths breathing noxious gases.

Sergei Tasarov would have once imagined himself retired to a luxurious dacha with scores of adoring grandchildren— celebrated, revered. Retired Admiral of the Fleet. Hero of the Soviet Union. Kindly grandfather spinning tales of heroism under fire.

But now his beloved Soviet Union is history, his proud service a hollow shell, his family persecuted and impoverished, his name redflagged in mainframes of international agencies.

Once, as leader of men, he'd bravely confronted his nation's enemy with deadly nuclear missiles. Now he lives the cockroach life, a wanted man, hunted— DEA, the alphabet agencies of his adopted land— AFI, PJF, now PFM.

Now Sergei Tasarov is in the pay of narco *patrons*, closely watched by *secarios* with dead eyes— a pawn in the treacherous *plaza* wars, a chicken to be plucked by the ruthless and the corrupt.

Bottle in hand, Sergei Tasarov now presents himself as a *contratista*— "no, *prostituto* at your service, *dinero* in advance *por favor*."

Sergei Tasarov designs and builds submersibles to convey illegal contraband to the illicit markets of the world's leading superpower.

Tarasov's nights are third-world torpidity, heat and humidity, mosquitoes, bed bugs, faceless whores, and vodka.

His days are confrontations with cocaine-addled narco thugs.

But this assignment is different.

Pride in his work is the only thing that keeps Sergei Tarasov from putting the cold muzzle of his 9mm Tokarev into his mouth and pulling the trigger.

This assignment has given him new life, more interesting than all before. By far.

And now it's done, resting on cradles.

El Diablo Negro. His crowning masterpiece.

It's 365 cm long; 40 cm in diameter. Solid black.

It's not designed for beauty, speed, nor depth.

It's designed for stealth.

It's designed for relentless endurance.

It's a robot, designed to drift with prevailing currents at a depth just ten meters below the deepest draft of the world's most heavily laden ship.

It's designed to confuse sonar, elude active pursuit.

It carries a digital map of all known currents within its operational envelope.

It's designed to send up a discreet antenna at predetermined times, lock into Global Positioning Satellites, compute and execute course corrections, engage it's small, but powerful electric motor should circumstances require.

It's designed to deliver it's cargo some 1,200 miles to a precise location within an error of centimeters and a window of seconds.

Since power is drawn down from a small nuclear core, *El Diablo Negro* could conceivably cruise under power indefinitely.

But for ninety percent of its mission it's designed to simply drift with the currents, silent, deadly.

It's power, when needed, is drawn down from its payload.

It's payload is sufficient to destroy a city.

And *El Diablo Negro* is designed to do just that.

Kimberly

"Nooo!"

Mattie Flores drops the wooden spoon, dripping with chocolate, and rushes into the small bedroom.

"Kimberly— You all right, sugar?"

Kimberly is staring into a dresser drawer, her few underthings scattered.

"I had a bracelet here. Have you seen it?"

"Bracelet?"

"Gold. Inset with diamonds."

"Where?"

"Here— hidden in my underwear."

"Oh, sweetie— If I knew you had something like that—"

"It's all I have, Auntie! It's all I can count on."

Mattie looks stricken, eyes darting around the room.

"Lionel—" she says.

"Lionel?"

"A body can't keep a thing in this house. TV, radio, Mixmaster— nothing."

Kimberly scans the room she's been sleeping in, the small steel bed with the deeply slumped mattress, the battered dresser, the black velvet portrait of Christ on the wall above her skimpy pillow. She sees small touches— a daisy in a water glass, a hand-crocheted doily, white gauze curtains.

Mattie is in tears.

"I try, but I just can't keep nothin'. A gold bracelet— I knew you had something like that I would have told you to keep it out of this house and put it in a box down at the bank."

"Who is this Lionel?"

"My youngest boy."

"You never told me about a son."

"Oldest boy long gone. But that Lionel— just don't like to talk about him."

"You mean your son has been here? In my room? Pawing through my underwear?"

"That Lionel— He comes and goes as he pleases. Like a ghost. Sneaks around. That boy's got the habit. Real bad."

"Can't you lock him out? Keep him locked out?"

"Don't do no good! Lock him out— he breaks down the door— smashes the window. I got my restaurant to run. Can't be round here all the time to shoo him away."

"Can we find him?"

"Find him? I told you. That boy's a ghost. Here— there— never where you expect him."

"But I need that bracelet."

"Honey, I'm sorry. He take somethin' like that bracelet, it be long gone up his nose— in his arm."

Kimberly collapses on the bed.

"That bracelet— It's really that valuable? Gold and diamonds and all?"

Kimberly nods.

"I can try to pay you back, sugar. But you know that restaurant. A gold mine it ain't exactly. It'll take a spell."

Kimberly sits up, braces her head in her hands.

"Sugar, something I been meaning to ask you—"

"Yes?"

"This trouble you got— this ain't no man trouble is it."

Kimberly nods.

"Police?"

"No. I told you that. Nothing like that."

"Then what?"

"Auntie, these people—"

"What people?"

"These people who are looking for me— you don't want to know a thing about them."

"Know what?"

"They're dangerous men, Auntie. And I've got to get far far away."

"Well you ain't goin' nowhere!"

"What do you mean?"

"You wait here one second."

Mattie goes into the kitchen, returns with a twelve-inch frying pan."

"Anybody come into MY house lookin' for you, Missy— They goin' through me— Auntie!"

Kimberly stands, embraces her host.

"Oh, Auntie— If you only knew."

"These folks real bad?" she asks.

"The worst," Kimberly says.

Mattie Flores sits down on the bed.

"Listen," she says. "My late husband, Ignacio Flores, no angel he. But I loved that man and he loved me. Black and brown. That was us."

Kimberly stares at the floor.

"His people— What I'm saying is— his people are in the same kind of business that brought my Lionel to perdition."

Kimberly looks up.

"Narcotics?"

"They in the narcotics business. Yes they are. Narcos they call themselves."

"Why are you telling me this?"

"You need people to keep you safe—" Auntie takes on a hard look that Kimberly has never seen. "It would take all my pride to ask— But that Flores bunch— they know a think or two about keeping secrets."

Train

TRAIN chuggin' chuggin' now
 Chuggin' into town
Pickin' up a dime
For a real fine time
So here's Lionel "Train" Flores gliding down Eighth Street, signature pork pie low on his brow, over-sized black tee flapping around his skinny frame.
Got my pork pie
Lookin' right fly
Look me in the eye
Sugga's gonna die
One block. Two block. Easy block to go.
"Hey, Train, Wha's happenin'?"
"No time. No time. Lookin' for a rhyme."
Choo Choo Chugga Chugga
Can't catch me sugga
Diddle doodle dugga dugga
Train's a speedy motha fugga
"Damn!"
Choo Choo Chugga Chugga
Can't catch me sugga—
Now Lionel glides into the New York Authentic Pizzeria Best in Phoenix, high-fives Nestor, gives a nod to Gino, steps to the back, past the drinks machine and empty booths, and knocks on the grease-stained door.
"Mis ter Train!"
"Tha only and tha one— 'bout to board tha gra vy train."

217

Lionel slaps the gold bracelet on the grimy desk.

"What's this? What's this— costume? Told you no costume."

"Chill, bro o' mine. This be phat, my man— Original Coke. The Re
al Thing. Feel here— Heft that motha. Sol id gold— sol id gold with di
a monds."

"Solid, my ass. Plate maybe."

Gold chains, low-buttoned purple shirt, Frankie B. is new in Lionel's
life. His old connection was Bones— back when the pizzeria was called
Bones P. Pies. Back before, that is, Bones turned up in an irrigation ditch,
bloated and floating belly up in green scum .

"No, man. Jus' feel this weight. This be fatty boom blatty."

"Zircons. No way we're talkin' diamonds here."

Shortly after Bones' demise, Frankie B. gave Lionel a choice. Choose
door A and he could leave the newly named New York Authentic Pizzeria Best in Phoenix in a vertical condition. Then, again, he could choose
door B—

Naturally Lionel chose door A.

No matter to his skinny ass. Long as the— what they say— rate of
exchange is sweet.

Some say that Frankie B. is in the Witness Protection. Maybe. Maybe
not. But his influence is felt in ever wider circles— most definitely making some people nervous.

Well, truth, the rate of exchange ain't been that sweet since Frankie
B. on the scene. But what's a cholo-nigga to do? Make it up in volume.

"This be worth two three big ones— This be sol id gold!"

"Buck fifty, maybe."

"Buck fifty?"

"Could see, maybe, outside, buck seventy five—"

"Shee it!"

Frankie B. looks more closely at the bracelet. Turns it in his hand."

"No. No. Lose my shirt. Buck fifty."

"Man—"

"Then again— hardly worth the trouble. This piece of crap? Buck
forty— most definitely."

"This is broken, man. Confuckulated."

Frankie B. gives Lionel that look— look that reminds Train of doors
not taken.

"Don't like it, hitter— then get your skinny ass out of my face."

"Mannn—"

"So how you want it? Cash or product?"

"Half and half. If you don't mind, mas'a."

Ten minutes after counting out seven ten dollar bills and measuring out a small bag, Frankie B. is on the phone.

"Yeah. Yeah. Most definitely. Got the picture and the piece right here side by side. Most definitely the item you been looking for. But I've got to tell you—

"Wait. I've got to tell you. These other googs show up the other day? Funny coincidence— they're in the market for the exact same item. And their offer was— let's say— more generous. But since you come to me first— I'm thinkin'— I should at least give you—

"Yeah, yeah, I know it's a lot of— but these —

"Look— I'm doin' you a big favor here— just pickin' up the phone. We're talkin' free market here.

"Well, now, an offer like that just might put you right. But let me check it out—

"No! Now you wait! You gettin' tough with me? Get tough and you lose, gombah. Big time. Got me? Yeah, and a pleasant day to you too."

Frankie B. shuffles around in his desk drawer, pulls out a card, pokes out the number.

"Just calling to tell you this might be your lucky day—"

Carmichael

RUNNING shoes tumbling in the dryer remind Carmichael of distant artillery.

He shoves aside an empty laundry basket to make room for Boswick's netbook.

"That man," Mrs. Phan says, "I don't trust—"

"Which man?" Carmichael asks, poking keys, logging into the Not There e-mail account.

"That Ca'ton."

"Why?"

"He work for Stone!"

"Man's got a wide net. And so far, his info's golden."

"Stone. You don't know— Like magic man. How you say— sleight of hand."

"Damn!" Carmichael says. He's all thumbs, fingers too big for the keyboard. Fact is, he mistrusts computers. One more thing to weigh a man down.

"E-mail here from Not There," he says. "Looks like Stone is running scared."

Mrs. Phan, folding clothes, wipes perspiration from her brow.

"The man has hired on ten bodyguards. Four shadow him night and day."

"Ha!" Mrs. Phan laughs. "Demons and devils. Curse working!"

"Curse?"

"Ancient Vietnamese curse— secret. Ten thousand demons and devils eat his entrails. Bodyguards no help."

Now Boswick rushes in from the bright outside, waving his cell phone.

"D'Mello on the line. That bracelet has surfaced."

They meet at the warehouse with D'Mello's team.

"This guy is bad news," D'Mello says. "Frankie Benzoni alias Belagio alias Frankie B. His file— long as your arm. New in town. Moving in and up. Big-time dealer in stolen goods,"

"A fence," Boswick says.

"Thing is, the puke's running a game on us."

"How's that?" Carmichael asks.

"Thinks he's running some kind of auction here."

"So who are the other bidders?"

"Missionaries," D'Mello says. "Who else could it be?"

"Then we don't have much time," Boswick says.

"Wait," Mrs. Phan glares up at D'Mello. "Why we trust you?"

There's silence, looks all around.

"Meaning?" D'Mello asks.

"You Stone man."

"Look, Mrs. Phan," D'Mello says. "We went through all this. My paycheck comes from SVS Security, yes."

"So, you Stone man."

"But my mission is to find your daughter. Keep her safe."

"Look, Mrs. Phan," Carmichael says. "We don't have time for this. We have no choice but to take the man at his word."

Mrs. Phan stares hard.

"You lie," she pokes her finger into D'Mello's chest. "You die."

Duncan Boot folds his big arms around Mrs. Phan.

"Mother," he says. "Sergeant lies, I'll kill the lying puke myself."

She pushes Boot away.

"I mean it!" she says.

"Are we settled?" Boswick asks.

"This Berzoni guy hangs out where?" Duncan Boot asks, "We have an address?"

"Yeah," the tech Jeremy French says, "But it's way across town. Rush hour too."

D'Mello nods.

"So, Carmichael, what's your take?"

"You're on a roll."

"Boot?"

"Locked and loaded, Sergeant."

"Right, then. Daniel Boone— Hustle over to that address— reconnoiter while we work out deployment."

Jeremy French writes out the address.

Mickey Rourke looks at D'Mello.

"Go!" D'Mello says.

"Don't be a hero out there," Carmichael says. "Keep your distance. Eyeball only. Report in anything we should know."

"OK," D'Mello says, "How do we approach this guy?"

"Look," Boswick says, "I think Carmichael and Mrs. Phan should be the ones to negotiate."

"Dangerous," D'Mello says.

"We can handle it," Carmichael says.

"So our team— how do we deploy?" D'Mello asks.

"My thinking— an outer ring," Carmichael says, "Bring down the missionaries should they show their ugly heads."

D'Mello looks at Boot.

Boot nods.

Jeremy French has pulled up the New York Authentic Pizzeria on Google Maps.

D'Mello clicks satellite view, zooms in, studies it.

"Waste time!" Mrs. Phan says. "What waiting for?"

"Emmanuel," D'Mello says.

"Suh!"

"Bring your sniper rifle. You get into position here. If all goes to crap, you'll be our ace in the hole. Boot, you and I can deploy here and here."

"OK with you, Mr. Boswick?" D'Mello says.

Boswick looks at Carmichael. Carmichael nods.

"Then," D'Mello says. "We go."

By the time they pull into position two police cars are idling outside the Pizzeria. A small crowd has gathered.

"Where's that damned Rourke?" D'Mello asks.

Boswick pushes through the crowd, shows his credentials to the young officer stringing yellow crime tape.

He returns.

"The perps," he says, "Come and gone. Frankie B. dead. Two neat.

One in the heart— Two in the head. Office ransacked."

"The missionaries," Carmichael says. "Who else."

"That bracelet was our best bet—" D'Mello says.

"Tell me about it."

"Why kill him?" D'Mello asks.

"My bet— throw us off the trail," Carmichael says.

"Hope to Christ they haven't taken Rourke."

"Kid over there saw a bike peel out of the driveway."

Just now D'Mello's cell sounds. He flips it to his ear.

"Yeah?"

"Blue camper van— But I lost 'em."

"Who we talking about?"

"The pooch stompers— missionary dudes— idling in the parking lot when I pulled in. Blue camper van— Didn't pay 'em no mind. Just walked in— asked to see the boss man."

"As I recall, you were ordered to keep your distance—"

"I was starvin' man— Pizza smelled real good."

"Stupid move. You were off the reservation."

"Just gonna ask the boss man for a job— scope the place out for ya."

"And?"

"Thing was, I knock on the office door— no answer. Pizza man knocks. Still no answer. So the pizza man opens the door— faints. Man o' man, never seen nothin' like it— boss man is slumped over his desk— blood on the wall. Place trashed."

"Then what?"

"Ran outside. See this blue van truckin' down the block."

"So where you now?"

"Cruisin'— Lookin' for that van."

Boswick tugs on D'Mello's sleeve.

D'Mello cups his hand over the phone.

"We're looking for a young doper named Lionel Flores. Street name Train," Boswick says.

"Got an address?" D'Mello asks.

"Just so—" Boswick says. "His mother's house. The pizza man, Gino, says a young woman has been living there with this Train's mother. Eurasian. Kimberly most likely."

"Mr. Rourke," D'Mello says into his phone, "Get your ass back to the warehouse. We'll talk about this later."

They converge on Mattie's house.

They're greeted by a slim Hispanic sitting on the steps, black hair pulled back in a pony tail.

Two black low-riders idle across the street, hostile faces framed in the driver side windows.

"*Señores*," the young man says. "What is it I can do for you?"

El Diablo Negro

THE CALIFORNIA Current flows south along the western coast of North America, beginning off southern British Columbia and ending off the tip of Baja California.

The Costa Rican freighter *Marina Quezada* beats north against this vast river of the sea, its aging 10-cylinder engine throbbing against wind, waves, current, and neglect.

The freighter's journey has taken it north along the Mexican Riviera, northwest around Cabo San Lucas, and north again along the Baja coast, staying always well west of the cruise ship lanes. It has continued north along the California coast, and now it's thirty miles due east of Astoria, Oregon, mouth of the mighty Columbia River.

The small man, inappropriately dressed in a black suit, grips a hand-hold with tight knuckles, choking back nausea from the abrupt dips and rolls.

A modified CH-53E Sea Stallion had delivered this man through fog and drizzle to this God-forsaken vessel earlier in the afternoon. He had hated the roar of the Sea Stallion. Couldn't wait for it to end. But one look from the air at the *Marina Quezada* wallowing in the foam-topped rollers and he'd almost declined to board.

But he has a mission to perform. A mission for the Lord.

"You don't look well, my friend," Sergei Tarasov says.

They're standing on the bridge, the first mate half-asleep at the helm. The light on the bridge is red, better for night vision.

"How long before we reach the drop point?"

Tarasov checks his watch, then a green display, mumbles as he processes a GPS reading.

"Twenty six hours, maybe a few more. A taste of vodka, maybe?

227

Calm the stomach?"

The small man declines.

Tarasov turns, stares out into the night. Spindrift dapples the thick glass plate. All beyond is black, not a light to be seen.

The small man stares at the wily submariner.

He thinks about the stubby cylinder stored deep in the secret hold, deep in the hull where the air smells of rust and diesel oil— rust, diesel oil, and rats.

The small man says a silent prayer for the success of this mission.

One last objective and his work is complete.

It's been a stressful journey, the last of so many in His name. And he's tired, ready for others to take his place on the front line. Lord give me rest, he thinks.

Just one last objective.

He looks with compassion at Sergei Tarasov standing beside him on the bridge, unrequited Commie still.

The small man says a silent prayer for this complex, tormented, but vastly talented sinner without whom this magnificent work of the Lord would never have come to pass.

He imagines this man's formidable iron golem drifting back down the California Current, through the cold depths, silently converging on— Reunion.

He imagines this man's corporal body, lifeless, drifting beside it.

Pity— but must be done.

Over the months he's grown to respect this man— fond of him even.

He prays that the almighty Lord, when the moment comes, will forgive this man, wash away his sins, embrace his immortal soul.

III

Pastor Cecil

IT WAS breach birth. The infant lived. The mother died.

The doctor hung his head.

"Breach presentation happens four percent of the time," he said. "Did my best to save the poor woman. But not to be. God's will."

"Nooo!" the father wailed.

To the father the mother's death was not God's will, but the child's Satanic deed. Bulling its way buttocks first into this world— ripping, tearing its way— the child was born in mortal sin— murder of a sweet woman— sacrificing the mother's saintly life to satisfy its lusty greed for air.

And, so, the father took it upon himself to mete out punishment— long brooding silences punctuated with sheer brutality.

The father was a carpenter, a large man, seasonally unemployed, prone to bouts of alcoholic rage.

The boy was frail, effeminate, intelligent beyond the norm.

As the father saw it, the beatings were a sacred privilege, grace commanded by the Lord, meted out to bring the boy from Sin to Salvation.

The father beat the boy regularly with a two-inch leather trophy belt, awarded for a twenty-three second ride on a second-rate bull in a third-string rodeo.

Machine tooled with silver-plated buckle, the belt was the sole triumph of the father's life.

The belt the boy could endure.

But seven days before his seventeenth birthday the boy dared show meager resistance.

"Father—" he said, raising his hands in self-protection.

The father, blind drunk, put down the belt and chose a claw hammer

231

as the instrument of his rage.

And the father smote the boy down like a slaughter-house bull. The doctors feared, forever.

But, seven days on, his seventeenth year of birth, miraculously, the boy emerged from coma. He arose from timeless time with the sacred commandments complete and whole in mind.

These became and remain the secret doctrine, the inner core, the foundations and pillars of his fifty-three year ministry.

In every age the Lord anoints an elect band of Warriors to conquer and rule the earth in His name.
The infinite Lord rewards his Warriors with infinite abundance in this life and in the hereafter.
Warriors of the Lord must obey His Laws without question and to the letter.
Those who fail or refuse the gift of His Dominion must die.
Deception and stealth are the blessed paths to everlasting glory.

The boy, no longer a boy, emerged from coma with iron will and hypnotic demeanor. This new-born warrior the father no longer recognized. The father fought. Warrior strength prevailed. The father struggled. The Warrior subdued— physical strength no match for spiritual iron. The father was reborn as the warrior's first disciple, obedient to the son in all things, and groveling at the end for redemption.

This is the story as recorded in *Warriors of Everlasting Grace*, the secret and closely guarded history and scripture of Dr. Cecil B. Tidwell's Church of the New Dominion.

The belt may be seen today under glass in the inner sanctuary where only the elect, the sanctified inner core, may enter.

Now, seventy years on from first breath, fifty-three years on from enlightenment, they've come to him from near every capitol of the globe, traveling under assumed names— sub rosa— successful men. Leaders of commerce, culture, media, government, and military.

He looks out across the opulent assembly hall. He savors the silence, the attentive eyes, the tint of imported stained glass.

"We have witnessed," he says, "the signs and portents— Israel restored— Strife in the Middle East. Trials and tribulations world wide. Who with eyes cannot see? The time has come. Soon— Reunion."

"Come Reunion!" they respond.

"We have seen pornography, adultery, abortion, and rampant sexual inversion— the filth and grime of moral degeneration and spiritual rot tarnish our once great land. Who with eyes cannot see? The time has come. Soon— Reunion."

This is the Pastor's Leadership Council, his Warriors of Dominion. Seventy men. Obedient. Each, to a man, scrupulously hand-picked for a particular task— selected, indoctrinated, and tested.

These are the men with whom he has built his church brick by brick— this vast sacred campus.

These are the men who have wired and lit his network— fourteen hundred AM, FM, UHF, and cable outlets— two million three hundred thousand weekly listeners and viewers.

These are the men who maintain his supercomputing centers, world-wide network, his Ears on Power listening posts, and his vast DAU database— Deciples, Apostates, and Unbelievers.

These are the men who have organized his youth programs, home-schooling curricula, built six hundred and thirty two secondary schools and three accredited colleges, sent and supported eighty seven missions abroad.

These are the men who have guided his foundations and think-tanks to world-class prominence.

These are his publishers, publicists, and webmasters.

These are the strategic minds behind his aggressive campaigns to smite abortion, sodomy, gun laws, Darwinism, miscegenation, and secular government— all tactical battles in the War for Dominion.

These are his Patriot Pastors— his power brokers— the men who make, shape, and break the careers of influential people throughout government, military, and private spheres.

These are the many forged as one who manage his secret bank accounts and covert investments.

These— the Generals who have built his Army of the Lord.

"Brothers," he says, "Let me speak now of delusion. Mass delusion.

"Each season, this we know, the Prince of Darkness hands down a new veil to the chattering classes— a new veil to cast over the minds of unbelievers. To obfuscate— to cloud sound judgment.

"And this season— flavor of the hour?"

He looks into the back rows of the assembly; savors the silence.

"Veil of the day?

"Yes—

"War Crimes Tribunals.

"You can't click a remote without hearing it. You can't turn a page without reading it. It dances on the lips of foolish tongues in Washington, London, Brussels, Bonn, and Madrid—

"War Crimes Tribunals.

"The Infidels jump up and down with joy— laugh and punch one another. 'How easily the Crusaders play into our hands,' they say.

"War Crimes Tribunals.

"But what is this? These War Crimes Tribunals?

"September 11, 2001— Remember? How can we forget, my Brothers? Day of infamy. The day the Devil gave Our Lord a black eye.

"They called out our sons and daughters. They called out our sisters and brothers. They called out our mothers and fathers. They called out many in this sacred hall.

"'We must fight this evil,' they said. They sent our sons and daughters, our sisters and brothers, our mothers and fathers to heathen lands.

"I'm talking now to you, esteemed veterans— honored men and women of the intelligence agencies.

"They sent you to the mountains of Afghanistan— the deserts and fetid lanes of Iraq.

"And oh how you performed! How bravely you faced down wickedness. You smote the heathens— sent them like jackals to their caves of darkness.

"You remember that Saddam Hussein? You remember how you found him— the so-called Lion of Baghdad? Anointed in his own filth— that's how you found him. Cowering in his own living grave. Oh how you performed.

"But how are you remembered? How celebrated?

"You? Who remembers you?

"Victory parades? Medals and awards? Invitations to the finest homes? Heroes of books, films, heroic tales for the young leaders of tomorrow?

"No.

"No, sir!

"How are you— heroes of the Global War on Terror— heroes I say—

remembered?

"War Crimes Tribunals.

"They talk of torture. Tsk. Tsk. But what greater torture than the yoke of the secular realm that denies Word of the Lord?

"They talk of secret renditions. Tsk. Tsk. But what of those denied hope of the Lord's rendition on Judgment Day— ensnared in the black propaganda and insidious doctrines of the wicked?

"They talk of political assassination. Tsk. Tsk. But what of those who assassinate His Truth in the name of Dark Powers?

"War Crimes Tribunals.

"Many in this very hall are in their sights— these War Crimes Tribunals.

"Many Godly men, our Brothers, are targeted, smeared, indicted.

"Well now— I have talked with the Lord, my Brothers and Sisters. Of this I have asked, 'Dear Lord, do we submit?'

"'Do we allow our Brothers and Sisters to suffer the lynchings and the firing squads?"

And now there is stirring in the hall.

"'Do we willingly hand over our Brothers— our Sisters— to the agents of Dark Powers?'

"And— do you know what saith the Lord to me?

Now, a pin could drop.

"'Fight!' he said. 'Fight the heathens, apostates, and unbelievers! I have prepared you for this. Fight with all the might I have bestowed upon you. Fight them! Smite them and rid the earth of their putrescence!'"

And now they cheer.

"Fight them! Smite them! Rid the earth—"

The pastor motions for silence.

"Brothers— Sisters— We have a busy weekend before us. Precious time. Sacred. This we have planned for. This we have practiced and rehearsed. We have run the scenarios and the contingencies.

"Well, the time is now upon us. Sacred time. The countdown begins. There will be blood. This we know. But we are undaunted as we gird for battle.

"Friends— Let us give thanks to the Lord for this, our strength and our shield. Then retire to our working groups and committees. Review our reports and plans. Coordinate our last-minute adjustments and changes.

"Then, tomorrow, 4:00 pm precisely, we will elect the Playmaker, the one who will guide us through the final hours— the final hours before— Reunion."

"Come Reunion!" they chant.

"God bless," the Pastor says. "Let us pray."

The General

"LISTEN," Pastor Cecil says.

They hear the susurous of night creatures— the knock of hooves on a distant barn wall.

"Looking to be an early spring."

The General closes his eyes, breathes deeply, feels tension flow into the soft cushions that cradle his slender body between the arms of the wicker rocker.

"Not too cold are you? We could go back inside."

"No— No. I like it here. Out here."

"I can get you a wrap."

"No. I'm fine."

"I see trouble on your face—" the pastor says.

The General is silent. Then, "No. Not so much trouble—"

"Then?"

"It's just—"

The pastor leans forward, looks intently into the General's eyes. Seldom has he seen this forceful man so reflective.

"You know, pastor, I'm just a simple military man—"

"A fine Warrior— The Lord is proud."

"I try. Yes. All my life two pillars of strength have sustained me through every hardship— every mission— every battle—"

"And these pillars?"

"My country and your church. I've dedicated my life— followed faithfully to the best of my ability— first the word of the Lord as you've taught me and— second, my Commander in Chief."

"And now?"

"You've heard. The House just passed that war crimes bill—"

"We knew they would."

"Yes, but somehow I thought—"

"Somehow what? Satan would just up and waltz away— forfeit the prize?"

"I feel—"

"Yes?"

"Uprooted— betrayed."

"Uprooted?"

"My country— this country for which I have taken wounds in battle— for which I proudly bear scars— this country for which I have served as a warrior for forty-one years has turned on me."

"Ah—"

They sit in silence.

"General—"

"Yes, sir?"

"You remember Psalms 27:3?"

"Remind me—"

"Though an army besiege me, my heart will not fear. Though war break out against me, even then I will be confident."

The General is silent.

"General— You are a born warrior— The Lord has called you. The Lord has prepared you."

"I just keep thinking about the fine men with whom I've served— compatriots in arms— the courageous men who've served under me. Now they're branded— war criminals. Disgusting! Weak men who've never faced enemy fire— apostates— take it upon themselves to brand these towering men. War criminals. That's the brush the apostates wield. That's the cudgel they take up to bring down genuine patriots and heroes."

"You know, General— It's not your country that's turned on you."

The General cocks his head.

"It's the unbelievers. The agents of the Prince of Darkness. They see your strength. They fear you. They see you firmly in the Lord's camp and the Dark Powers whisper 'Bring him down. Bring him low!'"

"So how have we come to this?"

"This?"

"Why must I now raise my sword against my own country?"

"So you're ready then?"

"Yes, but—"

"You have doubts still—"

"No— No— it's just— why must we destroy an entire city? A nuclear event— I shudder."

"It was your idea— brilliant."

"A *gedanken* experiment. A what if. Never meant to be."

"And strategically brilliant. That city is a moral cesspit, you know that. Slime seeps out of the gutters— poisons the land."

"But we must face the fact—"

"General— What have I taught you?"

The General is silent.

"Facts are illusion. Faith is truth. Look— We're fourth down on the one yard line. We need just one more shock— One shock to divide and confuse our enemies. One more soul-shaking event to shock the sheep out of lethargy— 9/11 awoke them to vulnerability. Katrina shook their faith in this sham they call government. The crash of 2008— drift and joblessness brought them to the brink. We're prepared to step in. We need now a tipping point— Missionaries have coopted the Tea Parties— shattered that infantile Occupy business. We need now just one more event to herd our blessed followers across the divide. We need a cataclysm."

The men are silent.

"There's anger out there, General," the pastor adds. "And fear. We can fan it. Focus it,"

"But the children— why so many innocents?"

"General, it's the oldest battle on earth— older still in the heavens. The eternal war. Our fathers— their fathers— their fathers' fathers fought it. Fought to the death against the Powers. It's fought on earth as in heaven. The Lord will see to those with pure hearts."

"But why this country that has raised me— nourished me?"

"To save it, man! To return your country to Glory— One nation under the Lord. One world serving the one True Lord— pole-to-pole— girdling every latitude and longitude. None to deny Him!"

The General stares into darkness.

"General— This country has chosen the path of darkness. You've seen it— I've seen it— it's plain to all those with eyes to see. They talk democracy. But democracy is the enemy of the Pure and Sacred Life—spiritual poison. Just look at the fruits of democracy— adultery, abortion, sodomy, rampant materialism, mixing of races. We must cleanse this land— return it to righteousness— mold it— make it again the pristine pride of Our Lord."

Carmichael

THE SOFT tap at the door, faint as a fluttering bug, brings Carmichael up from deep sleep.

He gropes under his pillow, grips his Glock, peels away sweaty sheets.

Carmichael tiptoes to the door, listens, but the only sound is the staccato tick of the fan driving cold air through the air conditioner.

The cool air chills sweat running down his back.

"What is it," he asks, standing well to the side.

"Boswick."

Carmichael cracks the door without removing the chain.

He sees Boswick, fully dressed, and a dark shadow standing behind him, Mrs. Phan.

"Saddle up," Boswick whispers. "Now."

"What's up?" Carmichael asks.

"Later," Boswick says. "Get dressed, grab your passport, money, and weapon. Everything else, leave. Five minutes. We'll be in the car."

Carmichael splashes cold water on his face, touches the angry red slash across his muscular stomach. It throbs now and again, itches often. Bearable, but a bitch.

He dresses quickly, looks around. Not much to leave. Prescription painkillers. Can't forget those.

The wide Phoenix streets are near deserted. Street lights cast cold circles.

"Avery Greene called," Boswick says. "ACTIC is full out Code Red."

"ACTIC?"

"Arizona Counter Terrorism Information Center. Coordinates all federal, state, and local first responders. The Feds are flying in teams from Washington, New York, bunch of other cities."

"What? Some kind of terrorism alert?"

"Yeah. Us."

"Us?"

"Seems we've topped the charts. All the terrorism lists. Domestic terrorist attack on major defense plant. Phoenix SWAT team is gearing up as we speak."

"What, my puny stink bomb? That was a week ago!"

"No. Major sabotage of a classified defense project. Multi-million dollar set-back. They've been keeping it out of the news while they track down leads."

"What are you talking about? What is this?" Carmichael asks.

"My guess— Set up."

"Who? D'Mello and his bunch?"

"No. Supposedly we're one big domestic terrorism cell. All in it together— I've given D'Mello a heads up."

Carmichael is silent. Brooding.

"You OK, Mrs. Phan?" he asks.

"Kim Le," she asks. "How find now?"

"Where we going?" Carmichael asks.

"Avery Greene gave me a meeting place. Says he can help."

"A trap?"

"Don't think so. Why warn us?"

"OK," Carmichael says. "Turn back. Get us over to Phoenix Sky."

"Carmichael!" Boswick says. "We can't just fly out! Phoenix Sky's the first place they'll lock down."

"No. But we need to ditch this vehicle."

"How?" Boswick asks.

"Just do it. Turn back."

They see a towering sign, "Long Term Parking."

"Drive past, pull over," Carmichael says. "We need to work this out before we drive in."

"Work out— what?"

"We need another vehicle."

"What's this? Steal a car? Just drive in— steal some poor sap's ride?"

"Pull over," Carmichael says.

"We can't just up and rip off—"

"In this vehicle we'll be picked up within thirty minutes tops," Carmichael says. "Guaranteed."

"But—"

"Look— No sweat. Done this a million times."

"Steal cars?"

"When I was a kid."

"Milly—" Boswick says.

"No time!" Mrs. Phan says. "Do what Carmichael say."

"Besides," Carmichael says. "Wasn't it just a week ago that you had me breaking into a top-secret defense facility? And you're worried about auto theft?"

Boswick shakes his head.

"Sometimes you have to break the law to save it, isn't that what you preached?"

"OK, OK," Boswick says.

"Case closed," Carmichael says. "The problem now is getting out of that parking lot without a ticket. Ideas?"

"Say we lost our ticket."

"They'll charge us through the nose."

"I can handle it," Boswick says. "Dug under the mattress before we left Boston."

They creep down four rows before Carmichael spots what he wants.

"Stop," He says. This is just going to take a second, Find a parking space for the car— farther away the better— and meet me back here."

"But—"

"Just do it! One more thing. Mrs. Phan— Think you can find a vehicle with out-of-state plates? Big state like California?"

"Think so."

"Start looking then."

Twenty minutes later they're on the road in a white Ford panel van, Carmichael driving.

"Where now?" he asks.

"You couldn't find something more comfortable?" Boswick asks. "A Town Car, maybe?"

"In this heap we're near invisible," Carmichael says. "Millions of 'em on the road. But I need directions here."

"Yeah, yeah— Let me check the map."

It takes another twenty minutes to intersect a way point on Avery Greene's directions.

"Those lights," Boswick says. "In the sky— back toward the motel."

Carmichael cranes his neck.

"Helicopters. Working a pattern. Long-range cameras."

"Looking for us?" Boswick asks.

"No doubt," Carmichael says.

"Yeah. Was afraid of that."

"Be grateful they're over there—" Carmichael says.

"Hope Avery Greene waits," Boswick says. "We've wasted time."

"Had to be done," Carmichael says.

"Maybe so," Boswick says. "Exit on 74, W. Carefree Highway. We'll be taking a right just a mile or two down. There's an entrance road."

They approach the entrance road.

"Look," Carmichael say, "I'll drive past and pull over. You take the wheel. Continue on until you can find a place to pull off without sticking out like a sore thumb."

"And?"

"Don't worry. Just wait. I'll find you."

"Got it," Boswick says.

Boswick drops Carmichael and continues on. He pulls onto a ranch road. Little cover, but he pulls as far as he can into the desert brush without sinking into sand.

He switches off the engine. They sit, engine clicking. Night sounds fill the cab.

"Look at those stars!" Boswick says.

"Boswick," Mrs. Phan asks. "Why they say we terrorists?"

"No idea, Milly," he says. "This is all new to me."

Forty minutes later Carmichael taps on the window, startles Mrs. Phan.

Carmichael opens the side door, picking at his knees, plams, face contorted in pain.

"What?" Boswick asks.

"You try crawling through a cactus patch in the dark!"

"So?" Boswick asks.

"Could use a little sympathy here."

"I mean, what's with Avery Greene?"

"Greene's there. In this modified Jimmie van, motorized wheel chair."

"D'Mello?"

"D'Mello's crew came in while I was tip-toeing through the cactus. School bus."

"School bus?"

"Don't ask."

They back down the ranch road, turn into the entrance road with lights off.

A red laser beam pierces the windshield, jiggles as they close on a looming black structure to their left.

"That's not a laser sight I hope?" Boswick says.

"Laser sight— we'd both be dead."

The red dot dances down the road, beckons them around the large structure.

Avery Greene wheels up, waves. They step out of the van.

"Wha' this place? Mrs. Phan asks.

"Abandoned cement plant," Avery Greene says. "We use it for SWAT training."

Carmichael laughs.

"Nice," he says. "Belly of the Beast."

"No worry," Greene says. "The boys are busy deploying in another part of town."

They step into the corrugated iron structure.

Avery Greene flicks on a flashlight, gray dust coats the galvanized walls, reflects the beam. He leads them to an inside room that's been walled off with two-by-fours and Sheetrock— converted into a classroom.

Inside, a fluorescent camping lantern casts shadows. Charlie D'Mello's team are slumped in steel folding chairs.

"Hey, guys," D'Mello says. "What's going on?"

Avery Greene wheels to the front of the classroom, reaches into a pocket on the side of his chair, slips out a large manila envelope. He lays out photographs like poker cards.

"These photos are now circulating national security wires."

"That's me in my SVS monkey suit!" Carmichael says. "Where'd that come from?"

"My guess, the robot you trashed," Avery Greene says.

"And that's me and Milly, standing in front of the New York Authentic Pizzeria," Boswick says. "Where'd they get those?"

"My guess— the missionaries," Carmichael says.

"They've got my whole damned team here," D'Mello says. "Even the techs. These have been taken over time."

"Knew it!" Duncan Boot says. "Had the feeling. We were goldfish in a bowl."

The techs look up from their Apple PowerBooks. For once they're fully focused.

Mickey Rourke stands, starts walking in circles.

For a moment all are silent.

"So what's going on, man?" Duncan Boot says.

"In a matter of hours these photographs will be on display through every media outlet on the planet. Biggest terrorist hit on U.S. shores since 9/11."

"Boswick here said multi-million dollar attack," Carmichael says. "That must have been one expensive robot."

"More to it," Avery Greene says. "Let me introduce you to my client."

A small figure emerges from the shadows.

Carmichael's breath catches in his throat. Even in the shifty light she's the most beautiful woman he's seen in his life, near albino. He stares.

"Mika?" D'Mello asks.

"Elaine Greene," she says. "Special Agent FBI."

Carmichael looks at Avery Greene.

"Yes," Greene says, "My daughter."

Carmichael

CARMICHAEL can't take his eyes off Elaine Greene. A heart-stopping thing arises from deep within his chest, constricts his breath.

Mrs. Phan nudges him with her elbow.

"You like?"

Carmichael ignores her.

Elaine Greene's manner is crisp, professional.

"Evidence came to the FBI that SVS Aerospace was blackmailing Pentagon officials and legislators to win government contracts," she says.

"Circumstantial— paper thin, really— Strong pressure came down from the top to file it away— bury it. But my boss fought for funds to run me undercover— see what I could dig up.

"I have an MBA— advanced degrees in electrical engineering, and— well— Stone is a known womanizer—"

"*Lo dit* Stone. Snake!" Mrs. Phan says.

"Yes," Elaine Greene says. "Mr. Stone is a snake, for sure. It was easy for me to work myself onto his personal staff."

"Ha!" Mrs. Phan says, "You sleep with snake!"

"Milly, please," Boswick says.

"No," Elaine Greene says. "Not that he didn't try.

"But, to continue— SVS assigned me to the Impaler project. Technical problems— Problems with vendors. As I dug in I realized that there was a lot more going on than we thought. My boss, at the bureau, encouraged me to dig deeper."

"My daughter, Kim Le— You know?" Mrs. Phan asks.

"Kimberly Bolton, yes," Elaine Greene says. "A very brave woman."

"Where now? My daughter? Where?"

"Don't know, Mrs. Phan. I'm sorry."

"Impaler project—" Boswick says. "Shoulder-fired anti-aircraft missiles, am I right?"

"Beyond state of the art. Game changer. It'll completely change the nature of ground warfare."

Duncan Boot looks up.

"How's that?" he asks.

"Later," Avery Greene says. "We're out of time. Let's get on with it."

"Bottom line," Elaine Greene says. "C. Norbert Stone and friends are up to something. Can't tell you what, but it stinks. I tried to report it but— I was shut down."

"Wait," Boswick says. "What makes you think Stone and friends are up to something?"

"Heard them talk— operational stuff— cyber warfare— sabotage of command and control— civil defense networks. Sabotage of the national electrical grid. And the Impaler II surface-to-air missiles— they jumped with joy when they saw the successful test fire. The Impaler II would give them control of the skies."

"And you heard all this where?"

"Stone asked me to demonstrate the Impaler. Out on a boat— Chesapeake Bay."

"So you've seen the Impaler in action," Duncan Boot says.

"Fired it, four times. Totally awesome."

"Your investigation was shut down, why would the FBI shut you down?"

"I reported the conversation between Stone and friends to my boss. A week later my boss was dead. Electrocuted. Freak accident. Supposedly while repairing a light fixture."

"Coincidence?" Boswick says.

"Repairing a lamp? In the bathroom? My boss could barely use a stapler— all thumbs. My new boss told me to turn over all case files."

"And your conclusion?" Boswell asks. "The motive for all this?"

"I just don't know— I just know they've sabotaged a government program for their own ends."

"Take down a country, sounds to me," Boot says.

"But whose? Where?"

"Hate to tell you, kiddies,"Boswick says, "But I fear— ours."

"No way!" D'Mello says.

"I'm with Mr. D'Mello," Mickey Rourke says. "No way these turkeys can take down our government."

"Let the man explain," Duncan Boot says.

"First off," Boswick says, "You've heard the rant, 'government is the problem.' All over the airwaves for years. Someone's been softening up public opinion."

"Maybe government is the problem," D'Mello says.

"Govenment? Our democracy? Or policies carried out by our govenment? But, whatever, we've seen these ideas creep into government itself— they've infiltrated the national security and law enforcement communities."

"What proof?" Duncan Boot asks.

"Not proof, exactly. But Elaine just gave you strong evidence. I've run into it myself— true-blue believers obstructing sensitive investigations."

"But that's still a long way—" D'Mello starts to say.

"Let me continue— more recently we've seen this wave of assassinations around the country— all people in a position to block certain investigations and legislation."

D'Mello is still shaking his head.

"And if the evidence in my shop adds up," Boswick says, "The agenda, whatever it is— whoever's behind it— includes a nuclear event. I fear, somewhere here in the US of A. To say the least, that would provoke a national crisis— make it easy for a well-prepared group to step in."

Now there's silence.

"Reichstag fire—" Avery Greene says.

"These people— these friends of C. Norbert Stone you mentioned," D'Mello says. "Who're we talking about?"

"I've only met two. Serious hombres. High up. One former NSA. The other a retired General. Totally intense man. Totally insane. Scary as hell."

"How so?" Boswick asks.

"Talked like the type who would have happily mixed up the grape-flavored Flavor Aid for Jim Jones down there in Jonestown. Gave me the impression that they're part of some kind of religious cult that's completely infiltrated the government and private defense sectors. I don't know who to trust."

"We being a bit paranoid here?" Duncan Boot says.

"Paranoid?" Elaine Greene says. "Then explain why you're a wanted man?"

Duncan Boot nods.

"I found out something else— The former NSA guy wanted to kill Kimberly Bolton."

"Kim Le?" Mrs. Phan says.

"But Stone was dead set against it."

"Dissension in the ranks?" Boswick asks.

"Stone maybe."

"So the FBI shut you down," Boswick says, "What did you do then?"

"Went to my father."

"Are you still on active duty?"

"Leave of absence. But I've moved off the grid completely. Daddy says they've put a trace on me."

"So we're all fugitives," D'Mello says.

"Wait a minute," Carmichael says. "There's something I don't get. I broke into SVS. Yes. Mrs. Phan phoned in a bomb threat. Yes. I blew off a two dollar stink bomb. But what's this multi-million dollar bullshit?"

Elaine Greene looks at her father. He nods.

"Well, Mr. Carmichael, I'm sorry," she says. "I needed cover."

"Cover?"

"We couldn't let those missiles stand. We used your break-in as cover so I could destroy their stock— more than 450 missiles destined for I don't know what."

"You destroyed 450 missiles?" Boot says.

"Well, all but three."

"And those three— where are they now?"

"Daddy's van."

"You destroyed 450 missiles in a secure facility—" Carmichael says, "Single-handed."

"I had access. Injected a worm into the test software. Fried a few power regulators so they had to retest the whole run. Set a fire in the shipping room."

Carmichael stares at Avery Greene.

"Wait," he says, "If you had your daughter on the inside, why did you need me to break into the SVS computer system?"

"Needed a faint," Avery Greene says.

"That bug on the keyboard, then— what was that about?"

"Poker chip. Double-sided tape."

"A poker chip? I risked my butt for—"

"Yes," Elaine Greene says softly. "You risked your butt to help destroy 450 Impaler missiles destined to blow aircraft out of the sky— for all I knew, Air Force One."

Carmichael stares hard into Elaine Greene's eyes. He sees the heavy fatigue. Hints of age. Worry lines. He can't make out her expression. He wants to hold her head in his hands, rest it against his chest.

It takes him a moment to realize that Elaine Greene's eyes are boring back into his.

She smiles.

"Look, we're running out of time," Avery Greene says. "They're locking down Arizona as we speak. We've got a lot to think about— stuff to do. Can't stay here."

"Where then?" Carmichael asks.

"I've arranged accommodations," Avery Greene says.

On the way to the vehicles Elaine Greene touches Carmichael's arm.

"I'm sorry," she says, "It was the only way."

"Yeah—" he says.

"Forgive me?"

"Maybe—" he says.

They follow Greene: Boswick, Carmichael, and Mrs. Phan in the stolen panel van; the D'Mello crew following in the school bus. They drive South, twenty miles into the mountains, turn onto a ranch road, follow a white wooden fence for a mile.

The eastern sky is just showing red as they pull into a long drive, a large rambling ranch house at the end.

Detective Antonio Martinez greets them.

"Welcome," he says. "*Mi casa es su casa.*"

The General

7:55 A.M. General Lyman R. Baxter, Ret., pulls into the yellow zone in front of Historic Battles.

Books . Maps . Collectibles

Open Mon-Sat 8 am to Midnight.

It's raining.

He sits, tapping his fingers on his steering wheel, watching water rivulets streak down his windshield.

At 7:59 he catches movement behind the glass door.

The General exits his vintage Buick Electra, pulls his jacket tight, locks up, and steps across the wet sidewalk.

"How may I help you, sir," the clerk asks.

"Thermopylae," the General says.

"Ah," the clerk says. "Come with me, please."

They squeeze through a tight maze of bookshelves.

"Thermopylae," the clerk says absently.

They hear a faint click and whine and, with that, a bookshelf rolls back, then rolls to the right on well lubricated tracks.

The General steps into a frigid warehouse, steel racks and narrow aisles run the length.

He shivers.

A muscular man seated behind a dusty CRT looks up, nods.

The General notices an SPAS-15 combat shotgun close at hand.

His eyes pass over racks stacked with wooden boxes marked with large blocky stencils, red and black. He's seen these marks often on invoices and on similar boxes stacked in warehouses around the world—warehouses belonging to leading international arms dealers.

But he takes little notice. Nothing new here.

In a few days, he knows, these racks will be empty, the boxes distributed to safe houses near major military bases around Washington D.C.

He's set up transshipment facilities like this near many cities.

"The men's room," the General says. "Get to my age—"

The man recognizes the code, presses a button.

Now the General opens a plain white door, steps into a well lit, but small, room, scarcely more than a roomy closet.

The door, heavy, hardened steel core, thumps closed behind him.

One wall is black, covered with glass.

The General places his palm against the glass.

The light dims. A pleasant female voice greets him.

"Good morning to you, General Baxter."

"Good morning, Sister," Baxter says.

The room brightens. The wall is silent.

"Shite," General Baxter says.

He has three tries to get it right. Get it wrong, well—

He places his palm against the glass a second time.

The lights dim.

"Good morning to you, General Baxter."

"Top o' the morning to you too, Sister."

Now four Disney cartoon-style icons light up across the top of the glass— a newspaper, a clock, a carpenter's square, and a telephone.

Clowns, the General thinks. The commo team had argued that the cartoon motif aided security.

Bull shit artists, he thinks.

The General touches the newspaper icon and a collage of news items scrolls down the wall.

The 447th, his special regiment, has been attached to Northern Command he sees.

He nods. That one had cost him political capital. But it's done. And it's good.

He notes an item from the Washington Post.

"Full Press Manhunt for SVS Terrorists"

He frowns, reads the story.

"Judas Priest," he mutters. If Stone had kept a firm hand on his hippie-whore daughter this never would have happened. Time to step up the watch on Stone, he thinks.

Now he presses the clock.

A map of the continental United States spreads across the glass.

"R minus one," he says.

Whimsical icons pop up across the map representing U.S. military bases and defense facilities.

The whimsy disgusts him.

He presses one of the icons. A message box lists unit designations, troop strength, and combat readiness.

"D zero," he says.

The icons turn into red circles, the diameter representing defense posture, a function of unit troop strength and combat readiness. The circles are far smaller than one would expect.

The General sighs. Few know as well as he the cost of two long wars in Iraq and Afghanistan on the armed forces.

"I zero—"

Now green pie-shaped segments cut into the red circles. This represents commanders and forces loyal to the Pastor.

He notes more red than green, but key centers of power have been seriously compromised.

"Phase One," he says.

Now he sees a toy ship off the coast of Oregon. A red arrow indicates that it's headed north. He presses the icon. A green legend pops up: "On Critical Path."

Praise the Lord, he thinks.

He glances down, presses a cartoon rocket ship overlaying Phoenix, Arizona. A flashing red legend pops up: "Critical + 21 days."

"Shite," he says. "Phase Two."

The ship disappears. A toy submarine pops up further north. A red arrow indicates that it's headed south.

Microphone icons indicating power grid and mass communication resources pop up across the map. These indicate the beginning of the psywar offensive mounted through the Pastor's media holdings.

Scattered among them, nearly 135,000 purple icons light up. Key routers on the Internet backbone.

Red light bulbs indicate power stations.

Hundreds of tiny ninja icons indicate Missionary teams— sappers and assassination squads.

But, now, many of the red circles are flashing.

"Crit Path," he says.

He counts thirty-six sites ten days or more off the critical path.

So let's play it out, he thinks.

"Phase Three."

The submarine icon disappears, replaced by a mushroom cloud on the designated city.

The purple icons turn yellow, brought down by Stu Graham's cyber team.

Eighty percent of the power grid goes dark.

But— the green pie slices in the red circles slowly start to diminish in size, disappear, as the powerful computers behind the wall work out the complex simulation.

"Cluster fuck!" the General says.

He slams his finger into the telephone icon.

Bugs Bunny lights up the screen— the Playmaker's avatar.

The General wonders what he looks like on the other end.

Clowns, he thinks.

"Three weeks is too long," he yells. "I absolutely require those missiles sooner."

"Or?" the Playmaker asks, his Bugs Bunny voice filling the room.

"We lose."

"What do you mean, lose? Even with the delay your missiles arrive well before Phase Three."

"Not soon enough. We need time to distribute— position— train—"

"Well, that sabotage attack was an unfortunate setback," the Playmaker says. "But we've turned it to our advantage."

"This 'terrorist' nonsense—?"

"Strikes fear in the masses. Ties up Homeland and the Feebies— They'll be running in circles chasing phantoms."

"You hope—"

"It's to our advantage, believe me."

"These 'terrorists' can muck up the works."

"No worry. They're under our thumb. We'll squash them when the time is right."

"I need my missiles! Without them, we lose."

"We can delay Phase Three. Maybe a week."

"But what about the *Marina Quezada*? It can't stay at sea forever."

"Is this something you need to know?"

"Need to know? I've planned this whole damned operation."

"Not to worry. The device will drop on schedule. We'll just program in appropriate course adjustments."

"Isn't that risky?"

"Acceptable risk."

"Maybe— maybe we don't really need the—"

"Need what, General?"

"Maybe we don't need the device— Can you abort?"

"No!" the Playmaker says. "It's crucial. Absolutely."

"It was just pasted on— Not integral to my plan."

"Pastor insists."

"Of course," the General says. "Pastor—"

"We've waited this long," the Playmaker says.

"And now we're in count-down. Eleventh hour— I need my missiles goddamn it! Three weeks is unacceptable. Put a godamned boot up someone's ass!"

"We can delay Phase Three by a week— All I can do. That turn the tide for you?"

"Don't know. Will have to run the simulations."

"Well the vendors are working three shifts to catch up. But I'll see what else can be done."

"Come Reunion," the General says.

"Your mouth to the Lord's ear."

Carmichael

THE GUNSHOT startles the horses.

Carmichael flings the pitchfork, drops to a crouch, listens, then scurries to the barn door.

The noon sun is blinding. Heat ripples off the concrete paddock and into the cool barn.

The Ukrainians are holding D'Mello at gunpoint.

"Whoa! Whoa! Whoa! What's going on?" Carmichael yells.

"They want the key to the school bus," D'Mello responds.

"Why?"

"Want their pay."

"No pay, no work! Bus— We take," Marko yells.

Carmichael sees faces staring out of the ranch house kitchen window.

"The gunshot— What was that?" Carmichael yells.

"Nobody hurt," D'Mello says. "Vitali got a bit excited."

"Guys," he yells. "Put your weapons down. I'm coming out."

Carmichael hears soft steps coming up from behind. He glances back. It's Boswick.

"What's going on?" Boswick whispers.

"Mutiny."

"All we need."

"Look, guys," Carmichael yells, "Can we talk this over?"

"No talk!" Marko yells. "Pay first."

"Mercenaries!" Boswick curses.

"Pay, sure," Carmichael yells. "But first let's talk."

Carmichael sees Mrs. Phan step out of the ranch house.

"Look," he yells, "Let Mrs. Phan hold your weapons. Then we'll talk."

"Is trick! Weapons— We keep."

"We've got things to work out. Pensions, health, unemployment benefits— all that. You want to talk this over, right?"

"Maybe. Yes, sure."

"Then let me get my weapon."

"Why need weapon?"

"How can we talk if one party has weapons?"

Carmichael hears whispers.

"OK. OK." Marko says. "We let madam hold weapons."

Mrs. Phan steps forward, smiles, takes the two pistols.

"I'm too bleepin' old for this!" Boswick says.

Carmichael steps into the splash of sun.

It's then that he notices Duncan Boot and Emmanuel, side-by-side, prone, beside the pump house— rifles aimed at the Ukrainians.

They're sitting in a circle now on bales of hay, exchanging glances. Duncan Boot has pulled the three-wire bales down from the high stack in the hay barn.

Carmichael can't help but glance at Elaine Greene's alabaster knees, muscled calves, delicate ankles. She's wearing shorts, but looks focused, serious.

He wills her to look his way.

She does. Smiles.

"Where's Mickey Rourke?" Boswick asks.

"Back in the hills," Duncan Boot says. "Headed out early. Said he has stuff to think about."

"Great," Boswick says. "Hope he doesn't do anything— stupid—"

"He's my boy," Duncan Boot says.

"OK. Look, We've had our lives turned up-side-down—"

"Oh just the full weight of the United States of America dropped on our heads—" Jeremy French mutters, "If the old uncle can hold out that long."

"Welcome to the dark side," McKenna, the other tech says.

"I'm serious," the first tech says. "This is heavy shit, man. Nightmare."

"I'm sorry, son," Boswick says, "Your name again?"

"Jeremy— Jeremy French."

"You're right, Jeremy. Heavy shit. And not a one of us has had enough sleep to think clearly— think about where go— what to do. But time has come. Time to think about things. Deeply— Think more clearly than ever. Our lives— ours and many others— depend upon what we do here."

"Others? Meaning what? McKenna asks.

"Sorry, you are— Martin?"

"Martin McKenna, sir. Many others you said—"

"I did. I have some data points. Agent Greene here has others. But we don't know the full facts."

Marko, the Ukrainian, jumps up.

"Vitali— Me and Vitali— We don't do anything! We have green card. We work. Why terrorist? Why government call us that?"

"Question of the day, isn't it?" Boswick says.

"Why?"

"Thought we figured that one out last night," Elaine Greene says. "I've been working undercover to keep an eye on C. Norbert Stone, chairman of SVS Aerospace. I can tell you this— C. Norbert Stone is a very powerful man—"

"Cold-blooded killer," D'Mello says.

"But maybe we didn't make it clear," Elaine Greene continues, "All the evidence points to a *coup* in progress— C. Norbert Stone and other powerful men are planning a *coup d'etat*— an armed takeover— of the United States of America. "

"Then THEY terrorist. Why call US terrorist?"

Carmichael studies the two Ukrainians— for the first time notices their youth— despite their muscled bodies, faces tough, blemished with hard action, they're just kids, he realizes— young— and now, scared.

"Well, we are," he says, looking at Elaine Greene. "So far as the authorities know."

"I think there's more to it," Elaine Greene says. "I think we're caught in a power play."

"How so?"

"How is it the authorities know about Sergeant D'Mello and his team? It wouldn't be in Stone's interest for them to know that. But if someone is trying to discredit Stone—"

"Like this NSA guy who wanted to kill his daughter—" Boswick says.

"Dissention in the ranks," Boot says.

"This coup," Jeremy French asks. "Why didn't you report it?"

"She did, bonehead," Martha McKenna says. "Weren't you listening?"

"Yes, I did report it," Elaine Greene says. "And one week later, my boss was dead."

Jeremy blows air through his lips.

"Sounds like the bozos have succeeded."

"Not yet," Elaine Greene says. "But they have more influence— more power— than you can imagine."

"And what's your take, Mr. Boswick—" Charlie D'Mello asks, "If that's your real name."

"Ned Boswick at your service, sir. Slave name, my good man. Proudly handed down from my great great grandfather Ned who died in the cotton fields."

"And?"

"I've been following Stone from another angle— never considered this *coup* angle until Agent Greene filled in a few pieces."

"Angle? What other angle? Where are you coming from?"

"DIA— Defense Intelligence Agency. On special assignment to Homeland Security."

Carmichael looks up.

"I've tracked Stone doing business with some of the nastiest characters on the planet. Agent Greene's ahead of me on this *coup* business. But I know that this C. Norbert Stone spent two years lining up a deal to obtain nuclear material."

"And?"

"He's succeeded. That I know for a fact."

"Jesus," D'Mello says. "And when you reported it?"

"Threats, denials, reports misfiled, budget cuts— basically pushed out into the cold."

Silence.

"And you, Mrs. Phan? Where do you figure in?"

"Daughter. Just want daughter."

Mrs. Phan seems to have aged, Carmichael notes.

"Just as we said—" Boswick says, "We think Mrs. Phan's daughter has information that can bring down this man Stone and his whole house of cards."

"This SVS Aerospace—" Marko says, "Not same SVS as my company? Am I right?"

"Different divisions. Same corporate parent."

"But why my company make me terrorist?"

"My guess," Boswick says, "They need scapegoats."

"Or maybe take us off the board," Carmichael says.

The Ukrainians whisper.

"Like Orange Revolution?" Vasili asks.

"More like Hitler's Beer Hall Putsch. But worse," Boswick says.

"So what do we do now?" Jeremy French asks.

They hear vehicles.

Duncan Boot jumps up, jogs into the shadows behind the barn door, looks out cautiously.

"It's Avery," he says. "And the detective."

They wait until Avery Greene rolls into the barn.

"What's going on?"

"Young Jeremy here was just asking what we're going to do about this pickle we're in—" Boswick says.

"And—?"

"Was just about to say this— We can each go our separate ways. But I'll guarantee that each and every one of us will be in a Homeland Security interrogation cell within twenty-four hours. Maybe even winging our way to some black prison hell-hole in a country that gang bangs women and crushes testicles for national sport. Or—"

"Hold it," Avery Greene interrupts, "My news is that they've activated Northern Command. Brought in combat troops. Road blocks on every road out of Arizona, beefed up patrols along the border, aircraft with thermal imaging running grid patterns above the deserts and mountains. So there's no way you could get out of here half cocked."

"Hang together or hang separately," D'Mello says. "That your news?"

"Ben Franklin," Elaine Greene says.

"Or?" Jeremy asks, looking at Boswick. "You said, 'or—'?"

"We fight," Boswick says.

"So, Emmanuel, my man—" Duncan Boot asks, "What say?"

"Fight. Most definitely, suh."

"Then who pay?" Marko says.

"Look son," D'Mello says with anger. "Just a guess, but the minute your name showed up on the terrorist watch lists, you joined the rolls of the unemployed."

"But need money! Health insurance! Mother sick. What can do?"

"My boy is sick," D'Mello says. "Seven years old. Cancer. I need every paycheck— every dime of health insurance. So you're not alone, my bucko. We're all in the same boat."

"He's right about one thing," Avery Greene says. "We need money— a ton of money."

"I can carry us for a week or two," Boswick says.

"Bought you guys toiletries, clean underwear," Detective Martinez says. "Maxed out my credit card."

"Rob banks?" Martin McKenna says.

"Stone has money," Carmichael says.

"Make me laugh— Just how do we get money out of Stone?"

"Find his daughter, Kim Le."

Mrs. Phan looks up.

"And just how do we do find this Kim Le— Kimberly— Whatever?" Jeremy French asks. "Like— we've been real successful so far."

"She was living with this woman Mattie Flores—"

"Flores," Detective Martinez says. "That's all you've got?"

"More maybe— This young man— gangbanger— was sitting on her front steps when we checked it out. Had the feeling he knew more than he was telling us."

"Wait, Flores— Silvio? Kind of a half-pint Antonio Banderas?"

"Could be— Didn't catch the name."

"Silvio Flores is one of the slickest smugglers in the state— assault rifles and ammo into Mexico— drugs and illegals back out. Has a ranch, fortress some tell me, down near the border. We've yet to make a case against him."

"Assault rifles?" Duncan Boot asks.

"Heard tell his men routinely stroll into Walmart, load their shopping carts with ammo, I'm talking heavy caliber stuff here, clean out the shelves, and lay down four- five- six-thousand green."

"Isn't that illegal?" Jeremy asks.

"Not if you're a U.S. citizen. Thank the NRA. Seems nobody bothers to ask."

"Assault rifles? Interesting—" Duncan Boot says, "Young Jeremy, can you bring up Google Maps?"

Now they hear dogs barking out on the paddock.

It's Mickey Rourke, dripping sweat, carrying a carcass over his shoulders. The ranch dogs are leaping around his feet.

"Man," he says, "That's some kind of good huntin' up in them hills. Got me this wild pig."

"Not a pig," Detective Martinez says. "Around these parts we call 'em javelina."

"Well, whatever, looks like a pig, must taste like a pig. Figured we've got a passel of mouths to feed."

"Ranchers call 'em desert rats."

"Bunch of 'em attacked me," Mickey Rourke says. "Had to beat 'em off with a stick. Shot this bad boy plumb through the eye. Put the fear of God into the rest of them sinners."

"Whoah, what's that stink?" Martin McKenna says.

"Musk glands—" the detective says. Skin out OK, though. Barbecue up right fine. Great tamale meat. So, *muy bueno, Señor Rourke*. But let me show you something—"

Martinez leads them to a small stone structure, stone steps leading down.

"What's with the solar panels," Boswick asks.

"You'll see. This here's the old cool house."

He unlocks an iron door, flips a switch.

Inside they find a cool underground room, walls of concrete block. Steel mesh shelves hold cartons of canned goods, large containers of dried grains, wooden crates filled with MRE's— Meals Ready to Eat.

The floor along one wall is lined with bottled water.

He steps up to a large upright freezer, opens it. Through hazy fog they see two sides of beef.

"I'm sort of a survivalist, you might say," the detective says. "Just a hobby."

"You a survivalist," Carmichael says, "Then you must have weapons."

"Weapons? Why?"

"Right weapons, we can pay a friendly call on this Silvio Flores."

The detective smiles.

"Well now—"

Emmanuel

THE WIND is hot, dry, and gusty.

Not good sniper weather.

Emmanuel is hunkered down in his hide high up on the rock spur. Below he sees the ranch house, two large barns, three small out buildings, and the road in.

Not much different from the Google satellite photo, but more colorful with patches of desert flowers.

To the south he sees purple haze over distant mountains. Mexico. Detective Martinez had run his finger along the border on the PC screen. Now Emmanuel sees it for real. No line, but the land beyond. It gives him a restless feeling.

To the north he sees junipers and pinyon pines. While studying the satellite photo he'd asked about the smudgy sweep of trees and Detective Martinez had named them. This *sahzay* country. So much to learn. He's trying to learn it all— makes his head spin.

Emmanuel fumbles in his rucksack, pulls out the AN/GVS-5 range finder, focuses in on the graveled drive that fronts the ranch house— *"igihumbi ijana mirongo inani--"* he whispers. 1190 meters. He works it out in his head. If he's going to be an American, he needs to learn new units. Not quite three quarters of a— mile.

He ranges each of the barns. A— mile, let's say. And the road in, farthest point— *"rimwe bago kibiri—"* 1.2 miles.

He'd ranged each of these targets much more carefully after settling down into the hide. He'd recorded the numbers in his sniper book, written them down precisely in his school-boy script. And he'd ranged them again just after dawn. Double checked the numbers.

"The AN/GVS-5 is accurate to within 10 meters," Detective Martinez had told him. "Infrared laser— No haze, accurate out to 9,999 meters."

Still, he finds it hard to believe that he gets the same numbers every time.

He slips the range finder back into his rucksack.

"*Yesu ashimwe!*" Praise Jesus!

Never has he been so well equipped. And never so trusted,

Emmanuel pats the receiver of his Barrett 82A1.

Just two days ago he'd hiked into the low hills with Detective Martinez, set up targets, hiked to a bare knoll more than a mile from the targets— nothing but gravel and the prickly husks of dried-up cactus. And gusty wind.

They'd spent the afternoon sighting in the Barrett, test firing. From the first trigger pull Emmanuel knew that he'd found his long lost brother.

"*Rimwe bago kibiri—*" nineteen hundred some meters. Not an easy shot, but the record for the Barrett is 2,500 meters— more than a mile and a half. So, despite the wind, he's confident.

His job is to take out vehicles should the need arise.

"Sure," Detective Martinez had told him, "Just slam it into the engine block— A 50 caliber slug should do the job for sure."

And to put the fear of God into any hostile gangbanger foolish enough to cross his sights.

"Hit a man— what can I tell you?"

It had been a tough climb up the loose scree with his seventy-pound pack, the Barrett accounting for half the weight. One section of his climb was ancient rock, crumbling and near vertical with few hand holds.

Worst part was that it exposed him to the flat plain below.

He'd spent the night on the cold rock scanning through his night-vision goggles, watching the guards move through their lazy rounds, so he is sleepy now, sun hot on his back.

He watches a range cow and calf cross the entrance road, walking slowly. He hears the faint ring of a bell. It reminds him of his home— Umutara, far across a continent and the wide Atlantic.

Emmanuel checks his watch.

It's been thirty minutes since the white pick-up pulling a flat trailer load of tied-down ATVs had pulled out of the largest barn.

"*Vuba,*" he whispers.

Not long now.

He reaches into his rucksack for his canteen.

Carmichael stares into the amber eyes. A bitch coyote and her pup have trotted within a short stone toss of his prone position.

She sniffs, steps forward one step. The pup, frolicking on the trail, stops, tucks in behind her tail. The pup growls. The bitch turns her head then turns back, lowers her head.

The pup is silent— still.

The bitch takes one more cautious step, muzzle down.

Carmichael sees blood stains caked in the white hair around her mouth, fears that he may have to dig into his rucksack— his Glock. But his rucksack is now half buried in sand, pressing into his crotch. No way could he reach it in time.

Carmichael has been crawling slowly around the ranch compound for a day and a night and now into the second day. He'd crossed ATV tracks, bleached cattle bones, moved respectfully around a rattlesnake, held his breath in the night while a scorpion crawled down the bridge of his nose.

He'd noted video cameras, heard loud music and laughter, watched the guards smoke cigarettes in the dark shadows.

Carmichael had smelled the range cattle in the early dawn, heard the bells as they moved in toward the barn for water.

He'd watched the white pick-up with it's load of ATVs pull into the barn at the end of the day yesterday, pull out again just awhile ago.

Silvio Flores owns ATV adventure tour businesses in both Arizona and Mexico, Martinez had told him. Great business for meeting two-legged coyotes and pack mules smuggling in cocaine.

Martinez had verified with certainty that Silvio Flores was kin to Mattie Flores, but so far Carmichael has seen no sign of Kim Le.

The coyote bitch is now still as a statue.

Carmichael's convinced that he's well hidden under his ghillie suit, but he's holding his breath, willing stillness, wondering what the bitch senses.

Something has alerted her. She cocks her ears, sniffs again, turns and trots lightly behind a large saguaro— disappears into the desert brush with an orange swish of tail.

Carmichael listens, but hears only birds and the light rattle of leaves dried black on dessicated branches.

He pulls his rucksack up to chest level, shakes the sand. He digs down for his GPS unit, takes a reading, checks his watch.

Now he fingers again into the rucksack for the Motorola XU2600, clicks the send button three times, hears two sets of three clicks back.

Twenty minutes to reach his weapons cache.

Not long now.

The Motorola in the cradle on the dash clicks three times. Mickey Rourke responds.

Duncan Boot reaches over the front seat and pats Mrs. Phan on the shoulder. He's dressed in full desert camos, face slashed with brown and green.

"You ready, Mother?" he asks.

"Forty-five years— Ready."

"Keep her safe, Mr. Boone," Boot says.

"Locked and loaded, sir."

Mickey Rourke drops off Duncan Boot well before the turn onto the ranch road.

"I'll need twenty minutes to move into position," Boot says.

Mickey Rourke and Mrs. Phan stay parked on the edge of the road. Mickey checks his watch every few minutes, then slowly pulls back onto the black asphalt, hot with morning sun.

A dusty black Jeep Cherokee blocks the entrance to the ranch road.

Mickey Rourke slows down, stops.

Two men climb out of the Cherokee, walk around until they're leaning against the Cherokee's grill. They're both dark from many hours of sun. One is tall and muscular. The short one— all abdomen spilling over his belt.

The tall man has a holstered pistol hanging on his hip. The short one is cradling an AK 47.

"*Buenos dias,*" Mickey Rourke says. He gestures toward the ranch road. "This here the road to Nogales?"

The short man steps forward.

"*Ninguna violación!*" he says formally. "No trespassing."

They hear bells. Birds fly out of a low stand of chorro cactus. Far down the ranch road a brown-and-white cow steps out of the brush, followed by a calf.

Mickey Rourke nods toward the cow.

"This here a real cattle ranch?" he asks.

The two men turn to note the slow-moving cow, then turn back toward Mickey.

Now Mrs. Phan steps out of the passenger side. She walks up to the short man.

"Where my daughter?"

"*Hija?* Daughter?" the short one says. He turns to the tall man, laughs.

"*Esta vaca está buscando a su ternero!*" he says. "This cow is looking for her calf."

He gestures toward the cow on the road.

"*Su hija, quizá,*" he says. "Your daughter, maybe."

But before the fat man can say more he's on the ground, the muzzle of his AK 47 grinding into his ear.

The tall man reaches for his pistol.

"Wouldn't!" Mickey Rourke yells.

The tall man sees the barrel of a Heckler & Koch Mk23 resting on the door sill of the white van, pointing toward his heart.

Mickey Rourke hears a cheerful bird call deep in the brush. Answers with one of his own.

Carmichael sees first the plume of dust above the brush line, then the white van rolling down the entrance road. He follows the van through the Trijicon ACOG three-power scope. He's well positioned now to cover the front of the house and the barns with his M16A4.

He notes the way the dust drifts, breaks up. Worries about the gusty wind.

He shifts the scope toward the ranch house, sees first a guard step down from the porch, disappear behind the high wall surrounding the patio, then cautiously open a high wrought iron gate. The young man he'd seen at the Flores house, Silvio Flores, steps out through the gate.

Carmichael passes the scope over the guard's sculpted brown shoulders bulging out of a kelly green and white sleeveless Boston Celtics tee shirt. Best he can make out the guard is packing an AK 47.

Flores is half hidden behind the guard but Carmichael can make out his jet-black hair plainly enough, his pony tail.

Flores is young, but he moves with the assurance of command.

Can't tell if he's packing.

Through the night Carmichael had spotted three guards around the house.

Where are the other two?

Mrs. Phan had insisted on this plan. Just walk in and ask.

Martinez reminded her that Silvio Flores was a known killer, rumored to have decapitated a rival.

"Don't care," Mrs. Phan had said.

So they'd set it up like this. Not perfect. Much depended upon Emmanuel and Duncan Boot if things went bad.

And himself, of course.

Elaine Greene had objected, reaching out, touching Carmichael on the arm.

What was that about, he wonders.

Carmichael is feeling shaky, his breath harder than it should be. This toy soldier stuff— it's been awhile.

"Just focus, son," he whispers.

The guard steps forward three steps as Mickey Rourke pulls closer, motions him to stop.

"Whoa! Is that a real gun?" Mickey Rourke asks.

"*Ésta no es ninguna violación!*" the guard yells.

Silvio Flores steps forward.

"How is it, *señor*, that you came in past my men— they didn't let me know you are coming?"

"You mean back a piece— those two jokers sleeping in the Jeep Cherokee?" Mickey Rourke says.

Flores gives his guard a look, turns back to Mickey Rourke.

"*Señor*, I suggest you turn around— head back the way you came in."

But now Mrs. Phan is out of the van. As she approaches Flores, the guard steps between them.

She side-steps him. He matches, step-for-step. Damned Texas two-step, Mickey Rourke laughs to himself.

"Where my daughter?" Mrs. Phan asks.

The guard raises his weapon.

Mickey Rourke, framed in the driver-side window of his van, raises his hands.

"Mister, you know your weapons, folks tell me—"

Silvio Flores darkens.

"Weapons? I know nothing of weapons."

Mickey Rourke looks meaningfully at the AK 47 now pointed his way, wavering back toward Mrs. Phan.

"Barrett M107 50 caliber. Familiar with that?"

"Fifty caliber—"

"Mister E. Give the man a demonstration please."

Silence.

Then, 1.4 seconds later, a small explosion bursts at Silvio Flores's feet. Gravel spray hits the guard hard in the legs. The guard yips in pain, nearly drops his weapon. Seconds later, a distant report echos across the desert.

"And the M16—? Mister C, if you please—"

A faint stutter and more gravel skitters across the drive not three feet in front of Silvio Flores.

Now Mickey Rourke is holding the Motorola.

"*Señor*, what is it you want from me?" Silvio Flores says.

"Your man— weapon on the ground please."

Flores nods. The guard stoops, lays his weapon down.

"That's more civilized, ain't it?" Mickey Rourke says.

"Wait a minute—" Silvio Flores says. "You're the terrorists. I saw you on the TV. What is this you want with me?"

"My daughter," Mrs. Phan says.

Silvio Flores looks confused.

Kimberly Bolton steps through the gate.

"Heard gunshots!" She says. "Silvio, who are these people?"

"Kim Le?" Mrs. Phan says.

Kimberly looks confused.

"Your mama," Mickey Rourke says.

"Mama? I have no mother—" Kimberly says.

Now tears are streaming down Mrs. Phan's face. But she stands, paralyzed.

"My mother died—"

"No— No—" Mrs. Phan says. "You Kim Le. Kim Le Stone. Born

Vietnam."

"Stone? How do you know that name?"

"Was husband. Your father. You born Vietnam August 15, 1967."

"There must be some mistake— My father told me—"

"No mistake— Father lied."

Kimberly stares hard at Mrs. Phan.

You have birthmark— here—" Mrs. Phan taps her thigh.

"Oh my God," Kimberly says. Her hands fly to her face.

Now Mattie Flores pokes her head through the gate.

"What you boys shootin' out here?" she asks. "Why is this woman crying? Kimberly, child, you look like you've seen a ghost."

"*Tia*," Silvio Flores says, "Meet the *señora's madre*."

"*Madre?* Mother? You never told me about no mother."

"I never knew," Kimberly says, tears forming in her eyes.

Carmichael

THE CLANG of horseshoes striking iron stakes echoes across the patio. Duncan Boot is huddled with the techs in the shadow of the ranch house, holding them spell-bound with war stories from what Carmichael can overhear.

The Ukrainians are whooping it up across the stakes, jeering and arguing in their native tongue.

Emmanuel is sprawled in a lounge chair near the cactus garden, sound asleep, mouth wide open, Corona bottle in his hand ready to spill.

Boswick nudges Carmichael, nods toward Mrs. Phan.

Mrs. Phan and Kimberly are seated across a nail keg, talking and giggling like school girls.

"Our lady has gone through at least one box of Kleenex by my count," he says.

"Sight to see," Carmichael says. "Had my doubts."

Carmichael is so tired he can barely stand, but hungry too after thirty-six hours of nothing but sand and power bars. The smell of sizzling steak is all that's keeping him on his feet.

Avery Greene rolls across the flagstones in his wheelchair. D'Mello drifts in to listen.

"Outstanding op!" Greene says. "Couldn't have planned it better myself."

"Mrs. Phan deserves the credit," Carmichael says. "Plan was hers."

Greene nods, glances toward the women.

"Quite a gal. Say that for her."

"So," Carmichael says, "What's the news from ANTIC?"

"Same old same old. Jurisdictional disputes. Tony's boss is out

275

struttin' for the national media. Homeland bunch are in a snit."

"Why is the Detective helping us, anyway? His career is on the line."

"Why are you helping Mrs. Phan?"

Carmichael's eyes scan the patio, take in the barn, gaze out toward the mountains.

"No matter— " Greene says, "But you're right. My good friend does indeed have a lot to lose."

"So what about us?"

"What about?"

"ANTIC."

"No worries yet. The feebs are running around like headless chickens. Did get a chance to read your sheet though."

"And?"

"Quite some record you've racked up."

"Bet it is. Way they'd tell it."

"No worry, Boswick has told me about Afghanistan."

Carmichael shifts his weight— stares toward the barn.

"Have I heard this?" D'Mello asks.

"Our kid here was one hell of a soldier— genuine hero."

"Yeah, some stupid kid," Carmichael says.

"No. No. If I've learned one thing in this short and brutal life— Comes a time when a man has to stand up."

"At what price?"

"Damn the price!"

Carmichael looks down at Greene's legs.

"Look— I took a bullet in the spine. Line of duty. Same circumstances? I'd do it all over again."

"Well, here we are then," Carmichael says softly. "Stand tall— see what it gets us."

The three men are silent. Carmichael watches *Señora* Martinez push through the kitchen door, carry a heavy pot of chili across the flag stones to the picnic table.

"It's all water under the bridge now anyway," Greene says quietly. "But one thing worries me—"

"That is?"

"SVS is back to three shifts. Brought in portable trailers to expand their manufacturing space. Elaine thinks they'll be back on schedule in a week or two— these Impalers."

"Why do I think there's a timetable here?" Boswick asks.

"My question exactly. If you guys are right— and these nutzos are moving against the constitutional government of the US of A— and we've got fissile material floating around out there— and a few thousand state-of-the-art shoulder-fired anti-aircraft missiles soon to fall into enemy hands—"

"Yeah, got it," Boswick says.

"You're saying we don't have much time—" D'Mello says.

"Exactly."

"So what next?" D'Mello asks.

Boswick looks to Carmichael for the answer.

Carmichael inhales.

"Bring down Stone. That's all we've got."

Greene looks up. "Easier said than done—"

"Well, we know one thing— it's near impossible for us to travel out-of-state."

"Suicide, I'd say," Greene says.

"Then the mountain must come to Mohammad."

"Lure Stone to Arizona. How do we pull that off?"

"Kimberly," Carmichael says.

"What, dangle Kimberly as bait?"

Carmichael shrugs.

Now there's the sound of a cow bell.

Mickey Rourke is ringing the bell in one hand, waving a long fork over the barbecue grill with the other.

"Come and get it—" he yells, "Or we'll throw it to the dogs!"

"Will you look at that boy," D'Mello says.

A chef's apron is hanging down to Mickey's knees; a chef's hat has added eighteen inches to his height.

The kitchen door slams again. Elaine Greene steps out, carrying a large wooden salad bowl. She glances at Carmichael— smiles. She sets the bowl on the picnic table, walks slowly toward Carmichael, holding his eyes.

"I'm glad you're safe, cowboy," she whispers, standing close, "Way Mrs. Phan tells it you walk on water."

"Mrs. Phan— prone to exaggeration."

Elaine Greene grins, touches his cheek.

"I'd say Mrs. Phan knows you better than you know yourself," she says, moving her fingers to his lips.

A moment later Elaine Greene is serving salad at the picnic table, Carmichael watching. Mrs. Phan edges up.

"Ooh, Ca'michael! Do I see love in you eyes?"

It's still warm in the hay barn when Carmichael climbs up the haystack to his sleeping bag. He's opened a bale and made a nest. The hay has a fresh field smell but makes him sneeze. He hears the swish of a tail, rattle of halter hardware, and hoof stamp on a shaving padded stall floor.

Carmichael thinks he's dreaming.

He feels a soft hand on his forehead, starts to wake, but the hand covers his mouth.

"Shhhh,' the voice says.

He opens his eyes. It's Elaine Greene.

"You—" he says. "What?"

"Mrs. Phan sent me."

"Mrs. Phan—"

"Wants to thank you. Give you a gift."

"A gift?"

"Yes. Me."

Carmichael is too stunned to speak. Elaine Greene is unbuttoning her blouse.

"So you didn't have a say in the matter?"

"Actually, it was my idea. So won't you let me in?"

"Not much room," he says.

"I don't take much."

Now Carmichael is stroking her firm breasts, hard stomach, running his hand over her hip and down her thigh."

"It's been a long time," he says.

"Yes, me too," she says. "Hold me, please. I've been so so scared."

"Yeah, me too," he says.

El Diablo Negro

THE SKY is ablaze with midnight stars as the freighter *Marina Quezada* approaches the designated coordinates.

The sea is black but for white churn of waves sweeping away from the ship through the glow of bow lights.

The tall deck crane is an ink-black shadow sweeping across constellations.

They've worked through the late afternoon and early evening on the countdown, bridging test points with instrument probes, reading scope traces, squirting graphite into mechanical linkages.

Now, out on deck, they stand quiet, shivering, the only sounds the dull throb of the near idling diesel engines, the swish of water off the bow, and the rattle of chains as the deck crane lifts *El Diablo Negro* ever so slowly up out of the black hold.

El Diablo Negro rises to deck level, then higher than the deck railing, sways slightly with the roll of the ship, a bulbous black hole against harsh deck lights.

Sergei Tarasov speaks softly into his communicator.

"Enough," he says. "Now swing it out slowly, slowly."

At first it seems the bulbous black cylinder refuses to respond, then ponderously it swings out over the deck railing, out over the roiling sea.

"Lower slowly now. Slowly. Slowly. Prepare now to— release!"

"It's done," Tarasov says.

The missionary pats Tarasov on the back.

"Well done!" he says. "Let's walk."

The near-arctic air is bracing. They walk toward the stern, strolling slowly.

"So, my friend, the money— what will you do with with the money?"

the missionary asks.

"Money? This I did you think for money?"

"Of course you did."

"Yes, well, money— But only to buy my way home to mother Russia."

"And you think they'll take you back with open arms?"

"A new face— The right papers—"

"But still—"

"A small dacha in the deep forest and a fat young wife to warm my bed. Who should care?"

Now they're standing at the stern, leaning against the railing, watching the dim frothy trail of the ship's wake."

"Cigarette?" the missionary asks.

"Umm," Tarasov nods. The submariner stares morosely into the night, then arches back sharply with a soft "oof" as the thin blade slips between bone and into his heart.

The missionary flips Tarasov over the rail in one fluid motion, knife and all, and the body falls with hardly a splash into the churning foam.

"Go with the Lord," the missionary says.

"Come Reunion."

Kimberly

THE PHONE call goes down just as they'd rehearsed.

"Daddy—?"

"Who— Who is this? How did you get this number?"

"You don't remember my voice?"

"Oh, my goodness— Kimberly? Is this really—"

"Yes, your loving daughter."

"But I thought—"

"What? I was dead?"

"No— Thank goodness, I—"

"Enough. I want you to listen."

"Yes— Yes— But— Are you all right?"

"No. I'm most certainly not all right. And that you know damned well."

"Well, then, where are you now? Maybe I can—"

"That's something you DON'T need to know. Just listen."

"But—"

"Listen! I said. We don't have time for this."

"OK, I'm listening—"

"I need money."

"Money? Well I—"

"Listen! You've destroyed my life. Twice, daddy dear. You owe me."

"I didn't— What you don't know is—"

"I know that the evidence in my hand is enough to destroy you and your cronies—"

"Listen— This is a very dangerous game—"

"No. You listen. This is most definitely not a game."

"OK. OK. I'm listening— How much?"

"Ten million dollars."

"Ten million— what makes you think—?"

"For you, pocket change. For me, a new life. And you owe me that daddy. A new life. Please. I need this money."

"But what you don't understand— Kimberly— What I'm trying to say—"

"Just listen, I said!"

"But what you don't understand is— Others are involved here. Very dangerous men."

"Doesn't matter and you can deal with your slimy friends the way you always do. So just listen. You'll receive instructions—"

"Instructions? For what? From whom?"

"Listen! God damn it! These instructions— You'll have twenty-four hours to comply. Not one minute more."

"But—"

"Twenty-four hours."

"And this— evidence?"

"Twenty-four hours!"

"Yes. Yes. Kimberly?"

Kimberly slams down the phone.

In tears.

Carmichael picks up the phone. Untraceable cell phone. Smashes it under his heel.

"That," Kimberley says, "Was the hardest thing I've ever done in my life."

She collapses into Mrs. Phan's arms.

"Tone perfect," Elaine Greene says. "Just the right note of anger and desperation."

"This houseboy? He's reliable?" Avery Greene asks. "He'll deliver the message?"

"General Vo's man," Carmichael says.

"But how will we know that Stone took the bait?" D'Mello asks.

"When the money hits General Vo's account."

"Can we really trust this General Vo?" Avery Greene asks. "We're talking big money."

"With life—" Mrs. Phan says.

"More to the point," Avery Greene asks, "What makes us think that

Stone will show?"

"The man wants more than the documents," D'Mello says.

"Meaning?"

"Wants Kimberly."

"Why?"

"Keep her safe."

Mrs. Phan looks like she's swallowed something rotten.

"Yeah, he'll show," Carmichael says. "But he'll try something clever."

"Then we'd better stay one step ahead," Greene says.

"Cleva'," Mrs. Phan says.

P. Stewart Graham

P STEWART GRAHAM'S pudgy fingers fumble with the tiny off switch on the digital recorder. Finally he manages it. He stares at the General's craggy face waiting for reaction. But for outside sounds, it's dead quiet now in General Lyman R. Baxter's classic Buick Electra.

Graham watches a range of emotions course over the General's age-bruised complexion and creases, fury first, as always, then calculation. He turns back to watch the Catholic school girls chase a soccer ball down the green field beyond the fence at the end of the parking lot.

My God it's hot, he thinks. Absently he pulls his pipe from his jacket pocket, reaches for his silver pick.

"If you're planning to pollute your lungs," the General says, "Do it elsewhere."

"Don't take it out on me," Graham says. "Stone is your boy. I told you we should have eliminated that woman."

"Drop a memo in the out box. That how you see it? Elimination? Well let me tell you, bucko, elimination is excrement and blood and it's ugly and it's messy."

"But still—"

"But still, I relied on Stone to put a lid on her."

"And I sent Stone a good man to make sure it happened," Graham says.

"The man you sent was an incompetent dipsomaniac. A wild man."

"Says Stone. So what happened to our man?"

"Stone says heart attack."

"And you believe him?"

"No."

"Well then. What about the Missionaries?"

"The Missionaries couldn't find a chicken in a hen house. Over-the-hill cowboys."

Graham is silent. "Like us," he says finally.

"Meaning what?" the General snaps.

"Maybe we're too old for this, Bob. Why are we doing it?"

"You ask me now? Troops mobilizing around the country? Device in countdown?"

"Device. My God, who's idea was that?"

The General's jaw tightens.

"Yours, wasn't it?"

"A straw man— a what if."

"And?"

"Pastor ran with it."

"Pastor. And now there's no way to stop it?"

"No. No, you know Pastor."

"But—"

"We did manage to program in a satellite code— a kill switch."

"So we can stop it?"

"No."

"No, why?"

"Pastor changed the code. Pastor's man, Brother James, discovered the kill switch. Too late to rip it out. Pastor demanded the pass phrase— changed it. Kept it to himself."

Graham wipes perspiration from his eyes. Heat, he thinks. Curse of the fat man. The General would complain of cold in hottest depths of hell.

"Don't you have air conditioning in this crate?" he asks.

"Suck it up," the General says.

Graham watches a young girl move the soccer ball down the field, graceful as a fawn, golden pony tail streaming like a victory flag.

"OK. This thing with Stone— What do you want me to do?"

"The call came in—?"

"Two— two and a half hours ago."

"So Stone could be getting these 'further instructions' at any second."

"Phone, snail mail, e-mail— all covered."

"She won't communicate that way. Too obvious."

"The security guards are on him 24/7. We'll know about physical contact."

"We hope. Any way of sticking him with some kind of tracking device?"

"Not easy. But we could try—"

"Not good enough, dammit! Do it! Stick a tracker on every vehicle within his sight. We lose Stone, we lose the girl. We lose the girl, we lose it all. That simple enough for you?"

"Blood pressure, General," Graham says.

"Damn you, Graham. Aren't you listening? It's imperative! Imperative that we stay one step ahead."

Carmichael

THE WIND tastes of metal, leaves a taste of zinc in Carmichael's mouth. He taps the Motorola XU2600 against his thigh. What have we missed, he wonders.

He scans the line where night shadows rise up from the pit mine. The shadow line is notably higher than when he'd looked moments ago.

He lifts his gaze, scans the opposite ridge line. The ridge is sharply etched against the deep blue of the dying afternoon. He sees nothing but fractured rock.

He presses the Motorola's push-to-talk button to send a single click, hears the responding click, then a second.

Emmanuel is in his hide on the higher ridge. Should have unrestricted line of fire. But about now, Carmichael thinks, the sun must be blinding.

Soon enough, Carmichael thinks.

Soon enough the sun will be below the horizon, exposing the full length of the airstrip to the cross hairs in Emmanuel's passive night vision scope.

Carmichael crosses the airstrip, traces the road where it ribbons up the steep mountain.

The gusting wind buffets his body, kicks up dust. He looks toward the west where sinking sun paints the desert valley in shades of red and gold.

Now he sights down the rock-hard airstrip, blasted and scraped flat along the ridge between natural mountain precipice and far-from-natural deep-gouged amphitheater of played-out ore.

The airstrip had been an executive conceit to save soft bottoms the discomforts of the rough ride up from the valley.

Now it's abandoned, littered with rusting iron. It'd taken the day to clear the runway sufficiently for a small Cessna.

All went without a hitch. But now, the wind.

The wind worries Carmichael. It's strong enough to make his camo shirt sleeves flutter around his hard biceps.

The wind definitely works against Emmanuel. Bad enough. But worse, it's a cross wind, gusty, coming in ninety degrees to the airstrip. Wind picks up a klick and the pilot might scrub the landing on this short and narrow strip.

And then what?

They'd had no time nor resources for Plan B.

Carmichael glances at his watch. Time for his next radio check. He punches the push-to-talk button twice. Two sets of two clicks back tell him that Marko and Vitali are in ambush position, covering the mountain road.

He punches out three clicks. Two sets of three back tell him that Duncan Boot and Mickey Rourke are in position behind the ore cart, ready to take down Stone when he exits the Cessna.

He clicks four times. Two sets of four back tell him that Elaine Greene and D'Mello are in the van, backed up into the pinyon pine grove, three klicks down the back road.

Duncan Boot had discovered the back road, steep and dangerous, but so far as Carmichael could tell, not marked on any map. Ace-in-the-hole Carmichael had said when he and Boot had reconned it.

Mrs. Phan had wanted in on the mission, wanted to run it. Screamed and pouted. But Boswick had said no.

"Ca'michael!" she'd pleaded.

"Sorry," Carmichael had said. "Not this time, Mrs. Phan. You heard the man."

"Why not let her go?" Duncan Boot asked later.

"Precaution," Carmichael had replied, "Lady hates the man— could well kill him before we find out what he knows."

The wind dies down as the sky grows darker.

He listens. Nothing. He's the swing man should Stone choose to do something stupid.

Force of eight and an ace-in-the hole for a simple pick-up.

"Overkill?" D'Mello had asked.

"Maybe," Carmichael had said. "But you never know."

"Maybe we'll catch a break," D'Mello said.

"Maybe," Carmichael replied. "You never know."

Now Carmichael is in position, crouched in the dark diameter of a huge iron pipe placed for what purpose and left for how long to rust he can only wonder.

He steps out again to listen. The Cessna, as instructed, should come in dark, landing lights out.

He checks his watch. It's time. He taps out three clicks followed by one, sees Mickey Rourke step out to light the Sterno cans that mark the narrow strip. It'll give them a twenty minute window.

Two parallel lines of flickering light mark the hard rock landing zone. And now the wait is on again. The sky is ablaze with stars, but Carmichael is too intent on picking up sound to notice.

And now he hears it. Could easily be a mosquito, but for the steady buzz.

The buzz grows louder, coming in low under radar, ever more distinctly an engine sound.

He hears the engine strain to climb then top the ridge. And then he sees it, the Cessna, passing overhead so low that Carmichael feels the prop blast.

The Cessna circles over the dark pit, over the far ridge, then drops low, lower, lining up, and finally touching rock. Carmichael hears the ever so slight screech of brakes and the rush of a feathering prop.

The Cessna is a dark shadow on the rock, Sterno cans flickering out. Carmichael hears a click, senses rather than sees the passenger side door open, a heavy man emerge.

But now he hears a new sound, like the sound of a stuttering sewing machine, the distinctive sound of an M230 chain gun, sees the tracers walk down the airstrip, sparks flying as 30 caliber slugs smash into the hard rock.

Then he hears the distinctive wop wop of a Black Hawk, taking him back years to Afghanistan.

He sees a dark figure sprint across the airstrip, tackle Stone, roll him under the Cessna.

The Cessna revs up. The Black Hawk takes shape, moving fast, passes close over Carmichael.

The Black Hawk pivots, lines up for another pass. Carmichael snaps off three rounds, but his M16 is useless.

The sewing machine starts up again. Weird sounds echo back up from the pit mine.

Carmichael watches helplessly as the snake of 30-caliber slugs slithers down the airstrip and up over the Cessna. He hears a small explosion, sees flashing shadows as a fuel tank spews flame.

But now he hears a loud pop from across the pit mine, and another. The Black Hawk jolts up like a startled horse. Another pop and the Black Hawk tips nose down, new sounds echoing back up from the pit mine as the Black Hawk plunges like a rock, hits rock bottom, throwing up a shower of torn metal and flame.

Carmichael sprints down toward the burning Cessna, nearly collides with Duncan Boot.

"Daniel Boone, you OK?" Boot shouts.

"Can't walk—"

Carmichael hears pain in Mickey Rourke's voice.

Stone starts to rise, but Duncan Boot slams him down on the rock.

"You," he says. "Don't move."

"Ankle," Mickey Rourke says.

Duncan Boot runs his hand down Mickey's shin and over his ankle. He looks Mickey over in the light of the burning Cessna.

"No break, I think," he says.

"The pilot," Mickey says.

The Cessna is nearly too hot to approach, but Carmichael bounces up onto the rear tire, looks into the cockpit, sees splatters of blood in the light of flickering flames.

Carmichael strips off his shirt to protect his hand, tries to open the cabin door, but it's jammed.

Flames spread fast across the high wings of the Cessna.

"Move, man!" Duncan Boot yells.

"The pilot—" Carmichael yells back.

"Toast," Duncan Boot mouths. "You grab Stone."

Carmichael tries again, but the door holds fast, radiating scorching heat.

Carmichael sees Duncan Boot move across the airstrip, Mickey Rourke over his shoulders in a fireman's carry.

Now he sees Stone, crouched, scurrying behind, dragging a bulky briefcase.

Boot pauses, turns.

"Carmichael, move your ass. Av fuel— That thing's gonna blow."

Once again Carmichael feels helpless.

How did they know? Where did they come from?

But Carmichael has no time to reflect. Now he hears Marko's voice through the Motorola.

"They coming! Fast. Three—"

Carmichael shakes his head. One thing they'd tried to slam home was radio silence. But three what?

Now, over the radio, he hears gunfire, M16s then the chatter of assault weapons.

"Vitali! Vitali down!"

"Can you hold 'em?" Carmichael works for a calm voice.

"I kill!"

Carmichael sprints across the airstrip, slides in behind the ore cart.

"You heard," he says.

"What?" Duncan Boot says.

"Marko. Hostiles coming up the mountain road fast. Exchange of fire. Vitali's down, I think. Maybe three vehicles."

Duncan Boot looks at Mickey Rourke. Then turns to Stone.

Fast as a snake Duncan Boot slaps Stone across the face.

"Who are they, scumbag."

Stone's head snaps back, but other than that he hardly reacts.

"Where's Kimberly?" he yells.

"Who are they?" Boot shouts again.

"You—" Stone says. "I recognize you. You work for me."

Boot slaps him again.

"Last time. Who are they?"

Stone shakes his head.

"Don't know."

"So you didn't bring 'em?"

"No—"

Boot moves hard into Stone's space. Leans over him.

"Truth, Mr. Stone!"

"No! I swear."

"Who are they then?"

"Missionaries," he says. "Has to be."

"Your idea?"

"No! No! I followed Kimberly's instructions to the letter."

"Yeah— tell me another," Duncan Boot says.

"Swear to God! I ran a pattern to shake my bodyguards— just like the instructions said."

"Then it's you they're after— You and your daughter," Duncan Boot says. "Because they couldn't have known we were here."

"Kimberly. Where is she?"

"Mr. Stone. I want you to shut the fuck up. We're kind of busy here."

"Give me a weapon. I can fight."

"Shut the fuck up I said!"

Duncan Boot looks at Carmichael.

"Fight or slip away?"

"Fight," Mickey Rourke says.

"We may be outnumbered," Carmichael says.

"But we know the ground," Duncan Boot says.

Carmichael clicks the Motorola once, then breaks radio silence.

"Mr. E," he says. "They'll be cresting up over the mountain road. Can you hold 'em?"

"Yes, suh—" Emmanuel responds.

"OK, Mr. B. You get these two down to the van. Emmanuel and I will do what we can to buy you time."

"No—" Mickey Rourke says.

"We're in deep shit here," Carmichael says. "Best you get Stone out. The rest of us have to exfiltrate best we can."

"You've got hostile forces between you and Marko. Vitali may be dead. We can't leave him to the coyotes."

"Look, Stone's the prize. These guys may have reinforcements. We've got to get Stone out of here and fast."

"I can fight, Mr. Carmichael," Mickey Rourke says.

"No way you can maneuver on that ankle," Duncan Boot says. "Do what Carmichael says or I'll shoot you myself."

Duncan Boot looks at Carmichael.

"You win. I'll deliver the package. But save a few for me— I'll be back."

"Wait. Stone— What's in the briefcase?"

"Money. You said to bring money, right?"

"Right. Look, Mr. B. when you get this bozo back to the van, strip him naked. Dump the money in the van. Ditch the clothes, shoes, briefcase—"

"Tracking device? That what you're thinking?"

"What else."

Just then the Cessna explodes. They feel the rush of hot air, hear debris slam into the ore cart.

"That'll wake 'em up for a hundred miles around," Duncan Boot says. "Forget the missionaries. This mountain will be crawling with authorities before we know it."

"Yeah, now give me your spare magazine."

"Take mine," Mickey says.

Carmichael slips the magazine into his cargo pocket.

"Now, go!" he says.

Marko is still wailing over the Motorola. He's either panicked with his finger stuck on the talk button, or the button is jammed. But the rate of fire is dying down. Then, for a moment, all is silent.

"They slip through," Marko says. "Vitali dead."

Carmichael hears tears in his voice.

"No names. Just hold the road, Mr. M," Carmichael says. "They may be coming back your way soon."

Now Carmichael hears the engines straining up the mountain.

Think fast. The ore cart is good protection, but suicide if surrounded.

Carmichael sprints across the airstrip and in behind the burning Cessna. He slips over the edge, into a rock crevice, aware of the long tumble down the steep mountain slope. He finds firm footing on a ledge of rock, wiggles his belly into the rock, settles into a firm, well protected, firing position.

Now, let 'em come, he thinks.

Hope to God they don't have another chopper.

He hears the first vehicle crest up onto the airstrip, lights out. Then he hears a mighty boom from across the pit mine and a moment later the scream of fast metal on hard. The vehicle, a Jimmie Denalai from what

Carmichael can make out, is dead. But he can't be sure. The Cessna fire is playing havoc with his night vision.

He sees doors start to open, hears another boom, then the sound of shattered glass and screams, tells Carmichael that the crew in the first vehicle is in trouble. Flames and black smoke verify it.

Carmichael sees a figure crawl out of a rear door. He aims carefully, squeezes off a round and the figure slumps, half in and half out of the door. But now a second figure springs over the body and runs.

If three vehicles, where are the other two?

They'll try an assault on foot Carmichael thinks. But they'll be exposed on the flat airstrip.

How many are we up against, Carmichael wonders. Can they bring in reinforcements?

He twists his head, scans for another chopper.

Now he hears Duncan Boot on the Motorola.

"Pull back," he says. "I've got you covered."

"Can you hold 'em, Mr. E?" Carmichael asks.

"Yes, suh."

"Mr. M," Carmichael says, "They may retreat. Let 'em."

"They retreat, I kill!" Marko says.

"No! Dig in. Wait 'em out. We'll bring you in."

"Vitali?"

"Both of you."

"Move now!" Duncan Boot says.

"Out of here," Carmichael responds, slipping back up onto the hard airstrip and sprinting hard toward the back road, keeping the burning Cessna between him and the hostiles.

C. Norbert Stone

THE CEREMONY is simple and solemn.

They gather at dusk, western sky tinged with red.

They walk slowly up the dusty trail to stand together beside the hilltop grave overlooking the Martinez ranch. All remark on the fine wide vista of Arizona desert, purple mountains on the horizon.

Carmichael, Martinez, and D'Mello had dug the grave earlier in the day, handing around the pick and shovel as each tired at the hard, hot work.

No time to build a coffin, so they'd wrapped the body in a fine, soft, lustrous bison-hide robe, handed down through the Martinez family for five generations.

Avery Greene says a few words. He'd argued earlier that he was as responsible as anyone for Vitali's death. Besides, he was the eldest.

"I've known Vitali for a short few days. But he impressed me as a fine young man far from home, a young man who volunteered to fight against a shadowy enemy, a fight he little understood.

"Nor do any of us fully understand. This is an enemy deeply infiltrated into our body politic. This is an enemy that has acquired nuclear materials for purposes we can only guess. This is an enemy implicated in political assassination, an enemy seemingly dedicated to the death of our democracy.

"Who are they? We don't know. What do they want? We don't know. What motivates them? We don't know. But we do know that this is an ancient struggle, an all-out battle for the civic values we cherish.

"I believe Vitali understood this. This young warrior did not die in vain."

D'Mello's words are brief.

"Vitali," he says, "I only wish I'd come to know you better. Go in peace young son."

Boswick sings Swing Low Sweet Chariot. His deep, mellow voice brings tears to all.

They lower the body into the grave. It's a tricky task given the tight confines and the desire to do it with dignity. They lower it stretched across two ropes, Duncan Boot and Mickey Rourke on one side of the grave, Emmanuel and Marko on the other.

They pay out the ropes slowly, hand-over-hand, each release lowering the dark bundle inch-by-inch deeper into the earth.

The women scatter the dark shadows at the bottom of the grave with flowers from the Martinez garden. *Señora* Martinez throws ceremonial herbs.

Marko is dry-eyed throughout, but stiff and silent. He's lost something boyish in the way he moves. He walks like a man with burdens.

Emmanuel volunteers to fill the grave. The techs stay behind to help.

Duncan Boot drops his arm around Marko's shoulders.

"You OK, son?" he asks.

Marko shakes his head, yes, stares off across the desert.

D'Mello approaches.

"I'm so sorry, Marko," he says. "I'm sure Vitali was a fine friend."

Marko nods.

"Best friend. Play together— grow up together— Ukrayina."

"Vitali was supporting his mother—?"

Marko nods.

"Now no one—"

"We've talked it over," D'Mello says. "We've arranged a little fund for Vitali's mother. It's not enough to replace a son, we know. But it's the best we can do under the circumstances."

Marko stands straight. Tears form.

"Come, son," Duncan Boot says. "Let's get us something to dull the edge."

As the three move down the dusty slope, Elaine Greene stops Carmichael, wraps her arms around him. Holds him tight.

"All that gun fire—" she says. "I was so worried."

Carmichael touches her cheek, reaches for her hand to follow the others down the hill, but she holds him back.

"When will it end?" she asks.

"When we win," Carmichael says, pressing her hard against his chest.

"Or we're all dead," she says.

The next morning, three a.m., Elaine Greene and Martinez interrogate C. Norbert Stone.

They'd rehearsed their strategy carefully, Avery Greene offering valuable advice.

Martinez unlocks the tack room, beckons Stone.

"My, my— Mayberry to the rescue—" Stone says, voice groggy. He shields his eyes against the light.

Martinez beckons again.

"You have no right to do this—"

Martinez taps the pistol strapped to his hip.

Stone's face twists into confusion when he sees Elaine Greene.

"Mika?"

"Elaine Greene. Special Agent. FBI."

For a moment, Stone has trouble breathing.

"All— this time?"

Elaine Greene nods.

"I'm— under arrest?"

"Not really—" Elaine Greene says. "Not yet."

Martinez nudges Stone into the hay barn. They've laid out bales for the interrogation, one bale set under lights for Stone.

"Sit," Martinez says.

"And just who are you, hayseed?"

"Sit, I said," Martinez says.

Stone sits, face fixed in a hard stare that shifts from Greene to Martinez and back to Greene.

"Comfortable, Mr. Stone?" Elaine Greene asks.

"Where's Kimberly? My daughter— I want to see her."

"Due course. But first you have things to tell us."

Stone's stare settles on Martinez.

"Who are you? Homeland Security?"

"Does it matter?"

"I have my rights."

"Let me assure you, Norbert—"

"Mr. Stone to you—"

"Norbert— this place you're in— here— now— think of this as Afghanistan. You have no rights."

"But—"

Elaine Greene's voice is soft, but carries an edge.

"Look, Mr. Stone— On your account we just buried a fine young man. We could just as easily bury you beside him."

"Leave his rotting butt for the peccories, ask me," Martinez says.

Stone stares at the interrogators.

"You the bad cop?" he asks Martinez.

"Believe it," Martinez says.

"Well screw you Bad Cop. I have nothing to say."

"Well, we have someone who has something to say to you."

Now Mrs. Phan strides into the barn, walks up until she's inches from Stone's face. She stares into his eyes, then, slaps him hard across the cheek.

"*Dit me may!*" she screams.

Boswick follows her in.

"Enough, Milly," he says.

Stone's narrow eyes are now open wide.

"Milly? Boswick? Milly—"

"How you doin' ol' buddy," Boswick says.

"Boswick— Jesus, man! What's happening here?"

"Your worst nightmare—"

"This can't—" Stone searches dark shadows beyond the light, turns back to Boswick.

"Just who are these people? What happening here?"

"Up to you, Stoneman," Boswick says. "You're not exactly among friends. I'm sure you know that."

"But you're wanted for— You destroyed my—"

"Man follows the news," Boswick says. "Or, maybe he had something to do with setting us up."

Stone slumps.

"Believe me— not my idea."

"Isn't there something you want to say to the good folks?" Boswick asks.

Stone stares at the floor for what seems like many minutes. Finally, he looks up at Mrs. Phan.

"Milly," he says.

"Mei Li Phan!" she shouts. "Mrs. Phan to you."

"Mei Li— Mrs. Phan— that day— that last day— biggest fuckup in my miserable life. I've lived with it. After— whenever I looked at Kimberly, watched her grow, I saw you— your eyes. I just can't— tell you— I— I'm just so so sorry."

Mrs. Phan's body posture softens. She turns, stares into the dark corner of the barn.

"OK," Elaine Greene says. "We've got a lot to talk about and not much time."

"He lies," Mrs. Phan says.

"No. No. I swear to God. My life's been a living hell."

"Well then," Boswick says. "It's come to Jesus time. Wouldn't you say, Conrad ol' buddy?"

"OK. OK," Stone says. "What do you want to know?"

"Take us back some twenty months," Boswick says.

"Twenty months?"

"Belarus."

"Oh, Jesus. You know about that?"

"Tell us."

"I brokered a deal for a tactical nuclear artillery shell."

"For what purpose? And for whom?"

"Purpose? Money, of course."

"For whom?"

"Listen— listen— We're getting into genuinely dangerous ground here."

"For whom?"

"Look, if I tell you this, I'm dead. You're dead. Scorched earth. Anyone within twenty feet of us from this day forward is dead. Do you understand?"

"Conrad— or should I call you C. Norbert Stone now— if you've been following the news you'll know that Milly and I are already as good as dead, along with a few good friends who are in fact actually dead. You, at this point, we don't give a rat's ass about you one way or the other. So give."

"OK," Stone rolls his head to ease tension. "I'm supposed to be this big financial genius, right? Boy wonder of the defense industry, right?"

"So I've read."

"It's all a sham. A front."

"A front! For whom!"

"That's what I'm trying to tell you. These are VEERY serious people."

"Conrad, we're losing patience here."

"Problem is, I don't really know."

"You don't know?"

"They have this tight cell structure."

"So who's in your cell? Who calls the shots?"

"Baxter. General Lyman R. Baxter. Retired now. He's the one who recruited me. Gave me direct orders."

Who else?"

"P. Stewart Graham. Supposedly this boy genius once high up in the NSA. He defers to Baxter."

Elaine Greene nods.

"But you went along with this— this sham. Why? Money?"

"They had me. I'd betrayed my country. Sold arms to the enemy."

"They blackmailed you—"

"Not in so many words. But it was plain enough."

"OK. And who else was in this secret club of yours?"

"That's it," Stone says.

"That's it?" Boswick asks. "There must be others. Who's behind these two fine gentlemen?"

"Don't think I haven't tried to figure that one out?"

"You must have some idea—"

"Some kind of cult thing, I think. Early on Baxter insisted I attend these religious retreats. Prayer breakfasts. Stuff like that. Made a big deal of it. There was this pastor— spooky bastard. But it wasn't for me."

"So who and what do you think is behind it?"

"How much time do we have?"

"All night."

"Going back to the Manhattan Project, right?"

"All night I said. Not all week."

"Right. Manhattan Project. Birth of the A Bomb. We created this secret world— national security at stake— black spot on the map— layers of secrecy, disinformation, and all that. And the idea caught on— black spots have multiplied, divided, mutated, and grown like Topsy ever since. CIA, NSA, DIA, Iran-Contra, alphabet soup agencies, projects, and operations coming and going, some known to Congress and many not. Black spots all over the globe with fine and patriotic men and women doing who knows what."

"Is there a point here?"

"Bear with me. Dick Cheney saw this— thought it was good— and privatized it— outsourced it. Right now, four times as many people as employed in the white side of the federal government live and work in compartmentalized black spots around the world, protected behind a screen of 'national security,' budgets unaccountable to Congress. Many many more in the private sector. More than one million people with Top Secret clearances."

"And a bunch of them work for you."

"Yes, a good number work for me."

"Continue—"

"We're talking big bucks here— big chunk of the economy— *beau coup* lobbyists riding high to keep the party going. Thing is, though, when mamma isn't on the job, little Johnny raids the cookie jar."

"Meaning?"

"We know that after 9/11 some of my friends in the national security crowd, going way high up, got, shall we say, over zealous— broke a bunch of laws—"

"Torture, renditions, domestic eavesdropping—"

"You don't know the half of it. But thing is, some of this stuff went on even before 9/11— Some of it came out after Watergate. More came out during the Iran-Contra business, some say there's a pattern going way back and I'm not one to say they're wrong."

"OK."

"Thing is, the national security zealots could keep the rankest of their dirty linen out of public sight by invoking— well— national security."

"No news there—"

"But then we have this economic melt down— big time. People lose jobs, homes, pensions, retirement savings— Inflation sets in."

"What does this have to do—"

"People have lost faith in the system, Boswick, haven't you noticed? People start hurting. Then they remember. Stuff comes out. They want accountability— Someone to blame— At first the bankers— hedge funds— But then they realize that the rot goes deeper. They lift the covers and find black spots all over their sacred myths, traditions, and history— we hear ever louder talk of investigations, truth commissions, war crimes tribunals. When that talk turned serious, let me tell you, my friends started running scared."

"And you? Scared?

"Of course I'm scared. Who wouldn't be? But there's another dog in the hunt."

"And that is?"

"A certain strain of well-organized religious fundamentalists— self-righteous zealots who have come to believe that liberal democracy is the Devils own brew— time to let God take the reins— create a theocratic state— prepare the way for the second coming."

"A minority, surely."

"But exceedingly powerful. Over the years their influence has spread throughout the far right community. And more, they've infiltrated the national security culture— all the way to the top. Indeed, a cadre of influential national security types have joined cause with certain religious zealots to forge a covert warrior religion marching under the banner of God. And, thanks to the power of the pulpit and modern media, this new religious force comes complete with a fifth column of true believers ready to back any play."

"Such as?"

"Shredding the Constitution itself."

"And you believe this?"

"See their progress every day."

"OK, this warhead you brokered in Belarus— Where is it? What's happened to it?"

"What do you mean, what's happened to it? I brokered the deal. The item was delivered in Afghanistan, Herat."

"To whom?"

"Don't know."

"Then what?"

"Can only guess."

"So guess."

"Two years ago they had me run a line on this cashiered Russian submarine commander down in Columbia. Genius type. Designs mini subs for the drug cartels."

"And?"

"They asked me to find out if he could design a robot sub."

"A robot sub— For what purpose?"

"Well now, let's see— We've got this nuclear warhead and a robot sub. Sounds to me like they'd like to make a big boom. Sound right to you?"

"When? Where?"

"No idea. They never cut me in."

"OK. OK— Mr. Carmichael tells me you mentioned missionaries— thought they were the one's who attacked your plane. Who are they?"

"Hunter killers. Good at what they do. That's all I know."

"You know this how?"

"We had some leaks. Baxter threatened me."

"Kimberly," Boswick says.

"Kimberly. Yes."

"Mr. Stone," Elaine Greene interrupts. "These documents that your daughter allegedly secreted out of SVS. What are they?"

"Have you seen them?"

"I'm asking the questions."

"They were sent to the SVS accounting office by mistake. I can't tell you how Kimberly found the file."

"Can't or won't."

"Can't. Don't know."

"OK, what are they?"

"My guess— They link majority shares of SVS back to the true owners. Plus, even more incriminating stuff."

"And that is?"

"Can't tell you. Haven't seen the documents. My guess? Names. Accounts, maybe. I can tell you that Baxter was rip shit when he found out that Kimberly had those files and that Kimberly was my daughter. Went ballistic."

"So where do we go from here?" Boswick asks.

"Was me," Stone says, "I'd target Graham."

"Why?"

"My guess, he's their top intel and commo guy."

"So, Graham. What can you tell us about this putz?"

"Loves boats."

"What else?"

"Pompous ass. What can I tell you?"

Now Martinez speaks up.

"So, now, Mr. Stone— What should we do with you?"

"Look, look, I hate these guys. I've been dangling from their string long enough. I'll do anything to bring them down. Anything," Stone looks at Mrs. Phan. "For Kimberly. For Mei Li."

"And what about you?"

"Me?"

"Yes, you."

My glory days are done."

"Lies!" Mrs. Phan says.

"Maybe," Martinez says. "But one false step, Norbert baby— and your fat ass is javelina bait."

Carmichael

THE WATER is hot, then cold. Carmichael sprays the hot water over the dust, then runs the cold water from the black hose over his head, shivers as it sluices down his sweaty torso.

The early morning air is still and clear, courses clean and pure through his nose and down into his lungs. He's still heaving from his six-mile run to the top of the far ridge and back.

It's sweltering in the sun, cooler here in the shade of the barn.

Carmichael hears the screech and slam of the ranch house screen door, sees Mrs. Phan.

"Ca'michael! Ca'michael!" she yells across the dusty paddock. "You hear news?"

"What's that, Mrs. Phan?"

"Granddaughter! I have granddaughter!"

"Yes," Carmichael says. "You've told me. It's wonderful."

Carmichael looks into her face. Expects to see joy. Sees pain instead. "What is it?" he asks.

She swerves around him, walks toward the horse corral. He follows. "Tell me," he says.

She's silent, staring.

She turns.

"Elaine Greene. You like?" she says.

"Yes. Yes," he says. "Very much. Thank you."

Elaine Greene is still sleeping in their sleeping bag after her long night of interrogation.

"Marry her, Ca'michael. Elaine Greene."

"Marry her?"

"Give her children. Many many children."

"Mrs. Phan," he says. "What's wrong. Tell me, please."

"You don't understand," she says."

"I try," he says.

"They take—" she starts to say, then stifles it.

He wants to hold her, but knows she'd never allow it.

He sees her tremble. Sees deep emotion trying to break through her essential dignity.

He reaches for her hand, but she pulls away.

"Whole family— They take. Those *ban lon* French—" she says. "kill *me*— *ba*— mama and papa— middle of night. They kill *anh*, brother, rape— murder *chi*, big sister. Broad daylight. I little girl. Now alone. They take my family— all. Leave no one.

"Then, God give me baby, Kim Le. Beautiful baby. Ca'michael, can you see? Can you imagine? I— God give me beautiful daughter. My baby. Then— *lo dit* Stone strike me. Knock me down. Point gun. Take my beautiful Kim Le. Now— Alone— again. I have no one.

"Then— I find Mr. Phan. Good man. Mr. Phan love me. We happy. But gambling— that *con dia* Stanley— cancer— take my Mr. Phan. Mr. Phan— Now, no one.

Tears run down Mrs. Phan's face.

"But now you have Kim Le again," Carmichael says. And me, he wants to say, but is afraid to be so presumptuous.

"Yes! Yes!" she says. "But Ca'michael, you don't una'stand. Kim Le have daughter. My granddaughter! Mine! Maybe beautiful. But I never see. They say terrorist— me. Can't see own granddaughter. Telephone— Can't call. Hear voice. I try, Kim Le say they lock me up fo'eve'. Prison! For what, Ca'michael? Me. Terrorist. Why? I good citizen."

"Your granddaughter," Carmichael asks. "Where is she now?"

"She study. University. Berkeley Kim Le say."

"University of California?"

"Yes, yes. Where is this place, Ca'michael? Berkeley?"

"Berkeley. Near San Francisco."

"How far? This Berkeley?" Mrs. Phan asks. "From here— how far?"

"Not so far," Carmichael says.

"We go," she says.

"No. Not a good idea."

"Don't care! We walk."

"No, Mrs. Phan."

Mrs. Phan stands, watches a bay mare and frisky colt move out of the shadow of their box stall. The horses move their way.

She turns, hits Carmichael hard in the chest with two clenched fists.

"Who are these people, Ca'michael? Terrorist— Why they call me this? Why they do this? Why me? Why can't I see my beautiful grand-daughter?"

Carmichael holds her. Let's her sob.

Now the sun has long set. As he walks from the barn to the house Carmichael hears a lone coyote on a nearby hill and a response across the canyon. They're gathered around the massive stone fireplace in the Martinez family room. Carmichael is last to enter. Elaine Greene pats a spot on the deep leather sofa.

"OK," Boswick says, "What do we know? What can we do about it?"

"We have Stone," D'Mello says.

"And the one hundred twenty seven thousand Stone brought with him," Avery Greene says.

"Where's the rest?" Carmichael asks. "We asked for ten million."

"Moving through off-shore accounts. General Vo promises he'll hold it for us. Deliver cash when we need it."

"So where does that leave us?"

"Stone gave us two names," Elaine Greene says. "Baxter and Graham. And Stone seems to think there's this mysterious cult pulling their strings."

"Al-Qaeda in America," Jeremy the tech says. "Love the irony."

"But we trapped," Marko the Ukrainian says. "We try to leave ranch, we busted!"

"I'm working on that," Duncan Boot says.

"Well, whatever you're doing, son, step it up," Avery Greene says.

"You know something?"

"Feds have been breathing down my neck."

"We knew it would happen," Carmichael says.

"Enlighten us," Boswick says.

"Questions about Elaine, mostly—"

"Mostly?"

"This morning they asked me about Martinez— Our friendship. Why I was making so many calls to the ranch."

"They're tapping your phone?"

"Never doubted It."

"They follow you here?" Boswick asks.

"They tried—"

"And?"

"I showed 'em a thing or two. Will only make 'em more suspicious I'm afraid."

Boswick stares at Carmichael. Carmichael stares out the French doors toward the desert— no longer green— losing it's bloom.

"No worry," Avery Greene says. "We still have a day or two."

There's long silence around the room.

"Tomorrow morning then," Boot says. "Be ready for show and tell at oh seven hundred sharp."

"OK," Boswick says. "What do we know about Baxter and Graham?"

"The boys and I have been burning down the net on that," Avery Greene says, looking toward the techs. "We know a lot, actually. Baxter seems to be a career fuck up, but someone behind the curtain, some mysterious godfather, kept goosing him up the ladder. Only explanation given his record. Retired with two stars.

"Graham, on the other hand, looks to be a clever mutt. Graduated with honors from Rice University. PhD from Carnegie Tech. Computational linguistics, whatever that is. Spent four years in Army signal intelligence, then dropped off the map."

"Dropped off where?" Elaine Greene asks.

"The black halls of NSA, the National Security Agency, ask me," her father says. "Surfaced as Deputy Director. But then, two years ago, there was some kind of scandal. Clearly covered up, but you can still see the dirty smudges if you read between the lines."

"All that's fine," D'Mello says, "but we need to know what these clowns are up to now."

"General Vo," Mrs. Phan says. "General Vo help."

"How's that?"

"He have people— follow this Baxter— this Graham."

"General Vo—" Boswick says. "Can't wait to meet the man. But I'm wondering about this cult thing."

"Good news on that, sir," Jeremy French says. "I think—"

"You think?"

"Well, sir, we found this photo of General Baxter on the web."

"And?"

"Look who's standing beside him."

"Haven't a clue—"

"It's here— in the caption. Rev. Cecil B. Tidwell."

"Tidwell— Where have I heard that name?" Kimberly asks.

"Church of the New Dominion," Avery Greene says. "All over the airwaves. Pulling out every stop to halt the prosecution of torturers."

"Including a *coup*— two to one," D'Mello says.

"Never saw a war that they didn't hail as a religious crusade."

"Wait a minute," Boswick says. "That company that turned up on Kimberly's flash drive— owns all those SVS shares?"

"ND Partners," Jeremy French says. "Blind alley basically. Registered in the British Virgin Islands. Not much on the web."

"ND Partners— Church of the New Dominion," Boswick says.

"Circumstantial. But if anyone has the resources to pull off a *coup*," Avery Greene says, "it would be Tidwell and his bunch. And, from what I hear, they're to the right of Hitler— Taliban in America."

"What else was on Kimberly's flash drive?" Boswick asks.

"Like Mr. Stone said. Names. Lists and lists— financial accounts."

"Interesting—"

"Looked like two kinds of accounts— receivables and disbursements. Notable, too— all transactions involve large sums."

"Like?"

"Low four figures to mid six."

"Did you check out the names associated with the accounts?"

"Only on the disbursements side—"

"Why is that?"

"Nearly half the payees were active military— officers— major and above."

"And the receivables? Did you check that?"

"One better— zip-code analysis of the addresses."

"And—?"

"Average income— more than 1.7 million dollars a year."

"So what do you make of it?"

"Ask me," Avery Greene says, "I think we have the Church of the New Dominion's tithing list."

"And disbursements?"

" Yeah, disbursements—"

"Pay offs?"

"Could be. Or payroll."

"So this ND Partners— you say you couldn't find much?

"Not much. Squeezed the web dry— but they did buy a mountain in North Carolina seventeen years ago."

"Mountain?"

"Abandoned gold mine and all. Filed permits to build a bible camp."

"Gold? North Carolina?" Martinez asks.

"Tranquility Mine— played out back in 1850—"

"Bible camp— seventeen years ago—" Avery Greene says. "Can't see what that has to do with us."

"Idea," Martin McKenna says. "Let's send these files out into the blogosphere."

"So we have a bunch of conspiracy theorists on the job," D'Mello says, "What good will that do?"

"Boy has a point," Greene says. "Bloggers start asking questions— folks on that list— both givers and takers— may not be so happy. Bunch of indie journalists picking over their dirty linen."

Boswick stares at Avery Greene.

"Good point. Couldn't hurt. Go for it, my lad. What else?"

"This ND Partners— if they're on-line— we could break into their network," Jeremy French says. "Maybe plant RATs in their servers."

Avery Greene smiles.

"Rats. Enlighten me," Antonio Martinez says.

"Remote Access Terminals. Take control of their computers over the net. Maybe even turn on the audio— video— hear what's going on in the room."

"You can do that?" D'Mello asks.

"Maybe—"

Avery Greene nods. "Boy after my own heart."

"Carmichael," Boswick says, "What do you think?"

"Ask me," Carmichael says, "put a stake through the heart of the beast."

"Hey! Hey!" Mickey Rourke says.

"Suits me fine," Duncan Boot says.

"Wait a minute," Elaine Greene says. "We can't take the law into our own hands."

The tech, Martin McKenna, usually quiet, snickers.

"Out with it, Mr. McKenna?" Boswick says.

"The law? We're the outlaws now, remember? As I heard it you and Ms. Greene tried the law bit and they put your face up on wanted posters."

"Yeah, point. But still—"

"Look, we know there are still good people out there," Elaine Greene says. "But we just don't know where to turn— who to trust. But we can collect evidence—"

"And we're forgetting one thing, kiddies," Boswick says.

They all turn.

"There's a nuke on the loose."

Silence.

"We're in countdown."

They hear the coyote— call and answer.

"We need to lean on some people," Carmichael says. "Get them talking."

"But we stuck here," Marko says.

"Oh seven hundred folks," Duncan Boot says. "Meanwhile, pack up— Ready to move out on a dime. Feds catch us napping— we're done."

"Yeah," Carmichael says. "Scrub this place down. Leave no trace."

At oh seven hundred Boot opens the shop door for all to enter. Inside they smell paint, find a newly painted school bus, fresh new lettering on the side:

GRENVILLE REVIVAL GOSPEL CHOIR

"Duncan—?" Elaine Greene says.

"Grow your beards, boys," Duncan Boot says, "This puppy— I figure we can tool around the country with ease."

"But what if we can't carry a tune?" Antonio Martinez asks.

"Choir practice at twenty two hundred," Boot says.

"And what about Stone?"
Mrs. Phan spits on the shop floor.
"Shoot," she says. "Feed to pigs."
"Mother!" Kimberly says.

The General

THE SOUR BURN of Campbell's Cream of Tomato soup rises up from General Lyman R. Baxter's unsettled belly, lurches up through his esophagus, and into the back of his throat.

The General has ridden in helicopters plenty of times, but never a stomach-dropping ascent like this.

He glances around the claustrophobic bubble in a slight panic, realizes he'll just have to suck it in, swallow back the hot flood. Wouldn't do to lose it with these young bucks, the hot-shot pilot man-handling the peculiar T-bar cyclic up front and the mouth-breathing slab crowding him on the right.

What is this craft? Robinson R44 Raven I he reads on a safety sticker.

They'd pushed through his front door unexpected and unannounced at precisely 1:02 pm, ignored the remnants of his lunch scattered across the table.

"Pastor's waiting," the mouth-breather had said.

Two words, or three, depending upon enunciation. Totally devoid of military courtesy.

"Who are you and what's this?" the General had started to say, but a look freighted with menace had stolen his command presence.

Pastor's waiting.

He'd heard about these guys. Shaved heads, log-like shoulders rippling under black tees. Missionary Youth Corp. Removed from penniless families at early age. Endless hours of Bible study, military science, weapons training, and physical culture. But he'd taken it as urban myth. He'd heard the murmurs, turned away. Lesser mortals were always trying to tear down great men. But here they were, all grown up, crowding his table, reaching for his arms.

What in the world could Pastor want at this late hour—?

General Baxter takes two deep breaths, wills himself to look out the port-side glazing, sees serpentines of suburban housing, turquoise swimming pools, checkerboards of big box stores and parking lots.

Patterns. Patterns within patterns.

The new battlefield, he thinks. Chaotic up close, but back away and you see the thrust and parry of force and counter force, a dance of dueling patterns, the first to out-step incipient chaos wins.

It had started out so simple. A matter of faith. A return to honor and glory. A cleansing. On paper so pristine— bloodless. Then looked even better as he'd refined it into a detailed battle plan of decisions and contingencies, probabilities and expected values, the simulations taking on ever more comforting weight and validity— a work of genius.

But then they'd introduced the device— a joke at first, a thought experiment. But Pastor loved it, seized on it, moved it under his personal supervision.

The device introduced no end of instabilities in the simulations. Detonate a nuclear device in a major American city and all bets are off— anything can happen. His simulations went to shit.

And then this girl, Stone's hippie spawn, a tiny seed of incipient chaos. Who knows what she has, but she has something, something from Pastor's personal files, something that could bring them down.

He'd never seen Pastor so livid.

And now Stone, off the reservation. Bad enough that, but more— Stone was the spark that ignited the Black Hawk disaster, concerns and recriminations raging up through Northern Command, up to the highest levels of the Pentagon.

And just what happened on that mountain in Arizona? Unexpected vectors of force— compounding unknowns.

Oh, and let's not forget sabotage of 450 Impalers at SVS, the single event that tipped the probability of decisive victory below 50-50.

Incipient chaos. The Second Law of Thermodynamics in action. Butterfly kicks off a storm a world away.

Now General Baxter realizes that they're over mountains. Deep hollows. The Smokies maybe.

"Where are we going," he asks. But the roar of engine, throp of rotating blades, drown him out.

He taps the muscular knee crowding against his leg. The slab turns. Glares.

The General gestures for an ear.

"Where are we going?" he asks.

The slab pulls away, thrusts his lips into the General's ear.

"Classified," the hot breath says.

At first Baxter is offended, the ancient anger, but then he lets it go. He's just so tired, all out really. And so damned cold. Always cold. The Second Law— maybe you just can't beat it.

Indeed, he sees it now. He should have known. Takes infinite energy to maintain infinite order. Who was he to try?

The General pictures the Almighty in his ordered realm.

Who am I? he wonders. Just a man— born of chaos— I've pledged my life to order. Fought with every breath to keep chaos at bay. Chaos— the ultimate evil. But I'm just a man, not a god. Born to fail.

Dear Lord, what have I done to offend thee?

The General opens his eyes, starts to scream. They're headed straight for a cliff. He sees jagged rocks, bare roots, and tufts of clinging vegetation. But the pilot heels back on the cyclic and they start to rise up up until they see trees and a rustic compound, a clearing, and a helipad.

"Welcome to Tranquility," the pilot says, slight sneer.

Now, on the ground, rotor whirling down, the General hears a deep voice counting cadence, sees muscular young men wheeling in perfect formation, close order drill at the end of the clearing.

He hears controlled rifle fire off through the trees.

"General—" a firm hand grabs his upper arm and directs him toward the lodge.

He tenses to shake off the hand, but the grip tightens. The pilot steps up and joins them on the left.

"This place—" he starts to say, but the words catch in his mouth as they propel him up the granite steps, across the rustic porch, through the massive timber doors and into the scent of cedar.

The fellowship lodge is tomb silent, lush with plush divans, oriental rugs, religious iconography.

They steer him across the hushed room and through a service door. The lodge is built against the mountain face, hiding a cold cavernous amphitheater cut from mountain side. Yellow beams of late-day sun

stream over the roof of the lodge. The slab keys in a security code and
a steel blast door wide enough for a Mack truck rolls back revealing
unnatural light. The blast door rolls closed behind them as they step
through, cutting them off from daylight and fresh mountain air. They
wind down a concrete tunnel lit with harsh fluorescents in wired cages,
down through a second blast door to a lower level, passing alert young
men with assault rifles standing at attention.

"Here," the slab says, nudges the General into a small room painted
stark white, motions him to take the single chair set in the center of
the room, arranged as though for meditation. The chair is facing an
enlarged reproduction of a familiar image. It takes a moment for the
General to recognize it. Yes— Albrecht Durer's famous woodcut— Four
Horsemen of the Apocalypse.

The General hears missionary heels click away down the concrete
tunnel, echoes. Then there's silence. Oppressive— as though living rock
is pressing in on the white walls. His back is to the door. The woodcut
fills his field of vision. He studies the wrathful faces, the sword, the
bow, the charging horses. It takes a moment to pick out the scale. But
his eyes finally fall on the mournful eyes of the fallen.

And he waits. And waits.

Finally a soft voice calls him. He turns. A young man, skin soft as
an angel beckons him.

"I'm Simon," the young man says, "Pastor will see you now."

The young man leads the General into Pastor's chamber. Pastor is
standing just inside the door. Pastor's eyes are filled with tears.

Simon turns away, pads back down the concrete corridor.

"Lyman, I have prayed for you," Pastor says, touches the General's
shoulder, leads him across the deep oriental to two facing plush chairs
under an ornate gilded mirror.

"Sit, my son," he says.

"I have tried to intercede," Pastor says, settling into the second chair,
"But the Lord is so angry. Angry. Angry. I have never felt such— such
rage."

"What—" the General starts to say.

"Maybe if we pray together," Pastor says.

"Why—?"

"You know, of all the many the Lord chose you for the vanguard—

You, Lyman! Of all people I would never have expected you to let Him down."

"Me—?"

The General is filled with hurt and confusion. Nothing in his frame of reference has prepared him.

This place, he wonders. Where am I? Why am I here? Why has Pastor never spoken of this?"

"Pastor," he says. "I have served you faithfully. I have served the Lord."

"No!" Pastor says. "This woman— Kimberly Bolton— you promised to bring her in. Where is this woman? Your man Stone— Slipped away in the dead of night. Slipped away, I might add, with millions— twenty million to be precise— twenty million that the Lord entrusted with him under your advisement— twenty million to advance the Lord's plan— stolen."

"Twenty million? The girl asked for ten—"

"Stone slipped away with twenty million and counting from four different special accounts."

The General drops his face into his hands.

"You promised the Lord," Pastor says. "You promised the Lord a seventy three percent chance of success with our mission— Where are we now? Thirty seven percent?"

"That was before—"

"Before nothing! You promised! Lyman— Pledged. Promised the Lord. I know not what to do. The Lord is so angry with you."

"Pastor," the General says, "This place? Where are we?"

"Tranquility," Pastor says. "This is Tranquility, our place of refuge from the sick and evil world."

"Why have you never told me about— this place?"

"Because you have taught me well—"

The General is silent. Waits.

"Containment," Pastor says. "Need to know."

"And you didn't think I need to know?"

"Lyman— we must pray. We must pray. Then you must return. You must track down this woman. No stone unturned. You must recover my files. And you must find your apostate Stone. And you must find these terrorists. You must hunt them down— smite them— send them

to the fiery Hell they deserve. Abominations. Spawn of the Beast—
evil, Lyman.They stand in the Lord's sacred path. The clock is ticking,
Lyman. Seven days— just sevens days. They must be found—"

"Until the device—"

"Yes," Pastor nods.

The General is silent.

"We must stop it," he says finally. "Or postpone. The troops are not
ready."

"Seven days," Pastor says. "Seven days. A world was made and a
world ends. Let us pray."

C. Norbert Stone

STONE stretches his legs to ease the cramps, rubs his fat thighs, licks his bloody knuckles.

Five hours— six at most. Five would be better.

The bruiser, Boot, the gorilla had started the clock ticking.

"Sleep tight, sunshine," gorilla man had said when he'd collected Stone's dinner plate.

"Sun up tomorrow we hit the road."

Sun up.

By sun up he'd be well on his way.

Stone scans the four corners of the small tack room, stares into the dusty shadows between the saddles. He'd done the same when they'd first pulled him from the van, frog-marched him across the yard, shoved him through the weather beaten door, and secured the big iron hasp with a heavy padlock.

It wasn't the first time he'd been locked up— and he'd been locked up in digs far less pleasant than this cozy little tack room with its smell of well-oiled leather, horse sweat, and moldy straw.

Worth a laugh. Here he is, C. Norbert Stone, Chairman of SVS Correctional Systems, largest network of private contract prisons in the world, locked up in a friggin' tack room like a chicken-chasing ranch hound.

Well, this isn't the first time he's engineered a great escape.

Stone works the cramp, stretching his toes, digging his thumbs into his fat thighs. He looks up at the bare 40-watt bulb in the porcelain fixture mounted to the ceiling, yellow to discourage mosquitoes, black spotted with fly specs. Keep burning, he wills. This little project would be near impossible in the dark.

They must think that Mrs. Stone bore stupid children to leave him in this flimsy box— rotten wood siding— western saddles lined up on wooden horses jutting out from the wall; bridles, halters, and lead ropes hanging from wooden pegs; brushes and curry combs lined up on the dusty 4x4 framing, horse liniment, label stained purple.

And— thank the Lord for small favors— he'd spotted it first off, a hoof pick. He'd spotted it and hidden it well the minute gorilla man had first stepped out the door and latched the padlock.

And it had taken him just ten minutes more to find a horseshoe nail, black iron tapering to a wicked point; another ten minutes to gouge off a six-inch leather strap, drill a hole with the nail, shove the nail through the hole, fold the leather back over the nail head. The leather cushioned the head of the nail against his palm. The nail protruded between his middle and ring finger. Within the first half hour in this crappy cell and he had two perfectly deadly weapons— particularly deadly if you knew where to strike and how. And he knew just that.

And that wasn't the end of it. He'd identified ten such simple weapons with which he could kill anyone walking through the door. Even gorilla man. Give him the surprise of his suddenly truncated life.

Or maybe it isn't stupidity. Maybe they have more trust than sense— trust that he wouldn't want to face up to his old partners— the ones who tried to gun him down. Kill his daughter.

Boswick is anything but stupid. And from what he knows about D'Mello and the gorilla, Boot, stupid doesn't play into it. And Milly— Jesus what a shock! Seeing Milly after all these years.Still beautiful. The look on her face. Milly would want him around just to slit his throat. She'd want him trussed up in chains and hung far down a deep well— water rising. Well, fuck knows, he'd deserve it. But no way she'd listen to his craven apologies, understand the regret and pain that has hollowed his heart.

And Kimberly. She'd finally come to visit. Hadn't said a word. Just looked down at him sitting on the camp cot, her stare so fierce he hadn't even thought to stand up. He'd tried to explain, pleaded even, but she'd just turned and locked the wooden door behind her.

Well, there was only one way to make them understand. And to carry that off he had less than six hours to dig out of this ridiculous excuse of a cell.

Stone squats, continues chipping away at the ancient adobe and stone foundation with the sturdy hoof pick.

Boot pushes in through the screen door. Cold pre-dawn air follows him in.

"Stone's flown the coop," he says.

"Told you—" Mrs. Phan says. "Slippery eel."

"Chipped his way through the foundation. Maybe took the buckskin mare. She wasn't in her stall."

"Damn. My favorite trail horse," Detective Martinez says.

"She'll turn up," Boot says.

"Snake," Mrs. Phan says. "I tell you that."

"Ha!" Mickey Rourke laughs. "Bet that was a sight. Fat ol' hog wigglin' through a donut hole."

"Does it matter?" D'Mello asks.

"One less thing to worry about," Boswick says.

"No ID— money. Best buddies ragin' to rip a new asshole," Boot says. "Puke'd been better off stayin' with us. So, we ready to roll?"

Just then Senora Martinez steps into the kitchen.

"What's this?" she asks. "Found it on the floor, just inside the front door."

"Feed receipt," Detective Martinez says. He turns it over, reads the tightly penciled note on the back.

"Will wonders never cease," he says, hands the note to Mrs. Phan.

Mrs. Phan reads it. Her hands start to shake, her eyes fill with tears. She hands it on to Carmichael.

"What say, Ca'michael," she says. "Can't read."

"*Dear Family*," Carmichael reads—

Yes, you are dear. Know you can never forgive my selfish stupidity— heartless mistakes. No excuses. But so so sorry.

Two accounts below— passwords. First for Milly— the other Kimberly and granddaughter I've never seen. One day please say a kind word about this stupid old man who traded ashes for a daugher and a granddaugher's love.

C: Look after Milly and— and thanks for bringing Kimberly in from the cold. Mr. Boot told me all. Owe you sir.

*B: Truly sorry. You were a loyal friend— my only true friend
in Vietnam. But I betrayed you. Betrayed our team. Higher purpose, I thought, but no possible recompense beyond fires of hell.*

*Detective: Thanks for hospitality. Had to liberate your mare.
She doesn't make it back, perhaps Kimberly will reimburse. She
can afford it now.*

Places to do— People to see—

C. N. Stone

Stone had ridden bareback as a kid in South Dakota. But by the
time he reaches the asphalt highway his crotch and inner thighs are
killing him. The sky is turning from black to inky blue. He slides off
the buckskin, removes the bridle, and pats her on the rump, watches as
she fades like a ghost, listens as the clack of her hooves fade down the
narrow road.

"Thanks ol' gal," he says.

He waits, walks a bit, waits some more. At last a pickup approaches,
it's headlights bobbing down the black asphalt. He steps into the road
and waves it over, bridle and reins dangling from his hand.

"Trouble?" the gaunt rancher asks. "That your mare back up a way?"

"Yes, could use a ride—"

"Hop in—" the rancher says. "Want me to help you catch that mare?"

"Thank you kindly, sir." Stone says. "This is your lucky day."

"Lucky how?"

"Take me where I want to go and you get to live."

The rancher's head snaps around.

"Get to live? You jokin'?"

Stone glances down, wiggles his thumb inside his jacket pocket.

"I'm cold, tired, and in a hell of a hurry, sir, but I'm most definitely
not joking. But there's more."

The rancher glances down at the bulge in Stone's jacket pocket.

"More?"

"Take me where I want to go without fuss or muss— you just might
hit the jackpot."

"Jackpot?"

"Let's say generous fee for service."

The rancher sets his jaw.

"Well, Christ on a crutch. Where is it you want to go?"

"Phoenix."

"Phoenix?"

"Wells Fargo Bank, 100 W. Washington St."

"So what's this jackpot you're talkin'?"

"Now, my man— Remember Part One. Let's not get greedy."

They ride in silence. Takes forty-seven minutes.

"Wait here," Stone says.

"You're not going to shoot me—?" the rancher asks.

"No. Nothin' like that. But wait here if you want to see payday."

The young bank officer looks Stone up and down. Barely conceals the contempt for what he sees.

"Mierkat," Stone says. "Cotton in your ears young man?"

"I'm sure Mr. Mierkat is busy—"

"Not too busy for me."

"And who should I say?"

"Just say Conrad."

At last Stone is escorted into Mierkat's office.

"I'm sorry, Mr. Mierkat," the young man starts to say.

"Yes, yes— out—" Mierkat gestures.

"Conrad— You look half a sight!"

"Operational disguise," Stone says.

"Thought you were done with all that."

"Thought so too. Got that package I sent?"

"Yes sir. Been waitin' for you right here."

Mierkat opens the bottom drawer of his desk. Hands over a small package in plain brown wrapper.

"Time for lunch?"

"No, no— Places to go. People to see."

Minutes later, Mierkat checks the lobby, returns to his desk, consults his Rolodex. He picks up the phone and dials.

"General," he says, "Stone was here, just left."

"No— I tried to detain him, but the man was in a hurry."

"No. No idea where he was headed."

"Yes— yes— I know that. We both know damn well he's a dangerous man."

"Yes. Anytime."

The rancher, work-battered pickup out of place among the Mercedes, Audis and BMWs in the bank parking lot, shows total surprise when Stone hands five fresh new one hundred dollar bills through the window.

He stares at the bills, counts them, looks up in gratitude, but Stone is gone.

Avery Greene

THE RANCH DOGS skitter down the drive, chase and bark as Avery Greene's modified van pulls into the roundabout.

Avery Greene is out of the van and rolling toward the school bus before Carmichael can offer help.

"Hi, Daddy," Elaine Greene says.

"Afraid I'd miss you, honey," Avery Greene says. "Started early, but had to shake the feebies without being too obvious about it. They're bringing in the drones."

"We're just loading up."

Greene looks over the school bus, chuckles.

"Greenville Revival Gospel Choir— Just might work at that. But can you sing?"

"Howdy, Mr. Greene," Mickey Rourke says.

Boswick gives a wave, returns to his check-list.

"OK, OK—" he says. "Weapons— Cleaned, oiled, packed in the weapons locker."

"Check, suh," Emmanuel says.

"Ammunition—"

"Check, suh,"

"Provisions— Three meals— snacks. Three days. Twelve people—"

"Thirteen," Detective Martinez says.

"Thirteen?"

"You need another driver—"

"You?"

The detective nods.

"You've got a job, my man— a family— a ranch to run—"

"Kimberly can't handle the whole trip. And the last thing you need—

get stopped with a fugitive behind the wheel."

Boswick looks at *Señora* Martinez.

She's in tears.

"We talked," she nods. "This he must do."

Carmichael stares at the ground, then looks up, nods.

"We're moving across 2,400 miles of hostile territory," Boot says, "don't need to tell you what will happen we get caught. And expect things to get hot. We're up against formidable forces. Odds definitely on the long side.

"So— if anyone wants to bow out, now's the time. No dishonor."

Boot scans the group, engages each one with piercing eyes.

"M'sa Boot," Mrs. Phan says, "We ready."

"Yeah— OK. Here's the thing. We have three objectives— Baxter, Graham, and this Tidwell puke—"

"Four," Boswick says. "The nuke. We've got to stop it."

Boot nods. "Without saying. Now, if we get stopped—"

"We get stopped," Detective Martinez says, "Let me do the talking. My badge should help."

Duncan Boot nods.

"What happens when we get there?" Mickey Rourke asks.

"General Vo has set up a safe house, is arranging new IDs to give us more mobility. Should have our cash. Anything else?"

The group is restless, ready to go.

"Well, then— last chance to do your business."

Boots turns to Carmichael.

"Anything to add, compadre?"

Carmichael nods, no, gestures for Boswick to step outside the group.

"Listen, Boswick, something we should talk about—"

"Sir?"

"Mrs. Phan— that account Stone gave her—"

"And?"

"The techs helped her access. Five mil."

Boswick looks up in surprise.

"Five million? And Kimberly's account?"

"Same— And General Vo tells us Tidwell's goons slapped Not There around. Something about twenty million dollar bank transfer."

"And you're thinking—?"

"My read— boy wonder is cashing out."

"Maybe— But I wouldn't think Stone the type."

"Partners tried to kill him. Took it hard when Kimberly refused to talk to him— nearly spit in his eye."

"Man's got to be worth a whole lot more than twenty mil—"

"Maybe not if he was just a front man."

"Good point. But I can't see him just cut and run. Man's up to something."

"Like?"

"Can't say. But let's talk with Avery. Maybe Mrs. Phan should talk with General Vo as well. The man knows too much about us— big threat running wild."

Kimberly takes the first turn at the wheel, nervous at first with the clutch and floor shift. She cuts a corner too sharp and bounces over a sandy shoulder, but quickly gets the hang of it.

For the first few hours on the road they're jovial, but tension mounts as they approach the state line.

"Hang tough campers," Martinez says. "Road block coming up."

"Smile and sing," Duncan Boot says.

They see the traffic cones.

Troopers have stopped a line of cars in the outside lane.

"Don't like this," Elaine Greene says.

"Keep your head down," Carmichael says.

Kimberly starts to pull over into the line, but a trooper, dark glasses, hat pulled low, glances at the side of the bus, waves her on.

They slowly pass the long line of cars, troopers at the head checking identities.

They pass patrol cars flanking the highway, half-a-dozen unmarked cars.

Kimberly rolls through, picks up speed.

"THAT was a butt pucker," Duncan Boot says. "Who else is up for lunch?"

They eat. Chicken tacos and ice tea. Small talk dwindling. Late Texas sun blazes through the windows. "No air conditioning," Kimberley says.

They ride in silence, too hot to talk. Mickey Rourke tries to rouse them with gospel songs, but soon even he's dozing, head on a pillow fluffed up against the window.

Elaine Greene and Carmichael are seated in the last row, just ahead of the so-called galley. Elaine nudges Carmichael.

"What's on your mind, soldier?"

Carmichael turns from the window, looks at her.

"You're so far away—"

He takes her hand.

"Penny for what was goin' on in that handsome head of yours—"

"Just thinking," he says.

"About us?"

"No— No. Well, maybe."

"Maybe what?"

"Well, for one thing, you're the best thing that's ever happened to me, you know that don't you?"

"But?"

"But what?"

"There's always a but."

"You trying to pick a fight?"

"No. But I want to know."

"I don't know—"

"You can say it."

"Well, for one, I can't see what you see in me."

"Meaning what?"

"Well, look— you're an educated woman— college grad— special agent of the FBI— and I'm—"

"What?"

"You know how I make my living."

"I've seen your file—"

"Yeah. I stare people down. Take their money. Beat 'em up. I'm a thug, Elaine."

"No— you're more than that. Much more."

"Maybe once. But not now."

"No. You listen to me Carmichael. You piss me off."

"What are you saying?"

"So you got a raw deal. Boswick told me. But suck it up. You've been sulking ever since that court marshal. Throwing your life away."

Carmichael starts to react.

"Don't even go there, Carmichael."

Carmichael stares out the window.

"Look, you were a fine soldier. A leader of men. And you did the right thing— screw the Army. And I've seen you in action. You're still a fine soldier. An outstanding leader. So I don't want to hear another word of your 'poor little me' crap!"

Carmichael is silent for a long beat.

"Whoa," he says finally, turning to Elaine. "You're tougher than Mrs. Phan."

"Bet your ass."

"You are."

"We've talked about it. She agrees with me. And I learned it from the best."

"Your father—"

"Yes, my father. H'd say the same thing."

"Think you've got me out-numbered do you? "

"Yes I do."

"Well, I wouldn't have it any other way."

"Well then, kiss me," Elaine Greene says.

Later, sky growing dark, Boswick moves into the row behind Martin McKenna and Jeremy French.

"How you doin', guys?" he asks. "Your asses sore as mine?"

"Twenty-two hours to go," Martin McKenna says. "You know, you fly across this country— don't realize how big it is."

"Never driven across country before?" Boswick asks.

"Before I got this SVS Security gig? Never outside Maryland," McKenna says. "Except a school trip to Washington D.C."

"And you, French?"

"Drove down to Florida with a buddy once— when I was in college."

"Where'd you go to school?"

"Rutgers. You travel much, Mr. Boswick?"

"Vietnam. Army moved me around a bunch— Asia— Europe. Job I got now, they keep me on the move. Mostly in the States."

"So what's your job?"

"Ah, just this government thing."

"Suckin' up taxpayer dollars?"

"Could say that," Boswick says.

"So what's going on, Mr. Boswick?" Martin McKenna asks.

"How so?"

"Is it really as bad as you've been saying?"

"This *coup* thing?"

McKenna nods.

"Why do you think we're on the run?"

"But this is a democracy— I mean—"

"Look, my man," Boswick says, "Democracy is always in danger. Greed, will to power, madness run through history like gray hair through an old man's scalp."

"But this is the United States of America. How can this be happening here?"

"To pose a point— maybe we just forgot—"

"Forgot what?"

"Democracy. Takes work. Teamwork. Know what I mean? People stop listening— start shouting— turn to invective, character assassination, and violence to make their point. How long can a democracy stand under that kind of crap?"

"Like this war crimes thing?"

"What think you, McKenna?"

"War crimes? I mean the people they're talking about putting up on trial were just trying to protect the country—"

"So torture, renditions, all that shit, should be national policy?"

"Well if there's a ticking bomb or something—"

"OK, make torture national policy— how do we contain it? How do we limit it to special circumstances against certain enemies? I mean, way I see it, once you deny your basic humanity you're on a down-hill slope. CIA today— beat cop tomorrow. Know what I'm gettin' at?"

"But war crimes tribunals just stir thing up. Polarize people even more."

"Maybe— maybe not. I say you've got to draw the line somewhere. But that's beside the point— It's war crime tribunals that's got this current bunch riled up. And this group is particularly dangerous— they have people situated throughout the power structure. They've tasted power. Think they're entitled.

"But I could name you a dozen other issues that have got people turning away from respectful democratic debate and due process— turning toward anarchy and violence."

"Like?"

"Abortion, immigration, gun laws, gay marriage, so-called creation science— You name the issue and I can show you preachers pounding the pulpit, so-called media pundits spewing divisive horse pucky— you know, all that scorched earth, take no prisoners talk— my way or the highway? And you know the shame of it?"

"What's that?"

"Half the time the people shouting loudest know better. They figure they stir up enough fear and hate among their blind followers they can get their way—"

"But isn't that just democratic?" Jeremy French asks. "Free speech— vigorous debate?"

"Not when you bring a nuclear device to the table," Boswick says.

"You think it's really true then?" McKenna asks. "This nuke?"

"Wouldn't be here if I didn't," Boswick says.

Carmichael

T HEY'VE been fifty-four hours on the road, truck traffic aggressive and relentless along this stretch. The air is heavy with diesel fumes. Even Mickey Rourke is bone weary, gritty, and cranky.

But they stir when Jeremy French jumps out of his seat and straddles the aisle, holding up his uber-hacked iPhone.

"Hey guys," he says, "You're not going to believe this!"

Now they're listening.

"Mysterious Explosion in Chi Chi Yacht Club. Former National Security Figure Presumed Dead."

Detective Martinez, holding as steady as traffic allows at 45 mph, removes his shades with his left hand, wipes his eyes with the back of his wrist.

Kimberly is curled up in a sweat-scented sleeping bag following her six-hour stint at the wheel, snoring gently.

"Graham?" Boswick asks.

"A near-dawn explosion at the exclusive Harbor Yacht Club, Hampton, Virginia, has taken the life of P. Stewart Graham, former Deputy Director of the National Security Agency yada yada—"

French reads down.

"Authorities suspect defective on-board propane tank. Yacht club president Manfred N. Smith says this tragic accident yada yada"

"Accident my foot," Carmichael says.

"Stone," Mrs. Phan says.

"And two-to-one Baxter's next on his list," Carmichael says.

The crew is now fully alert, up from meditative somnolence.

"How far are we from Baxter's digs?" Boswick asks.

"Checking GPS now," Martin McKenna says, "And, looks like— three hours and twenty minutes."

"How long before our meet with Vo's people?"

"Six tonight," D'Mello says. "Five hours."

"Can you bring up a sat view of Baxter's hooch?" Duncan Boot asks.

They park in a Safeway parking lot six blocks from Baxter's home.

Kimberly has thrown off her sleeping bag and moved back up to the second row to sit with her mother. Boswick has filled her in. But she hasn't taken it well.

"Why do you think it's my dad?" she'd demanded.

Boswick had shrugged.

"You're making a big assumption," she said. "He's not a saint— but, murder?"

The silence had lingered. The tension still does.

"How should we play this?" Carmichael asks Duncan Boot.

"Your play," Boot says.

"Bus sticks out like a sore thumb in this neighborhood," D'Mello says. "Maybe we should wait 'til dark."

"Got the feeling time's of the essence here," Boswick says.

"Look, it's my case," Elaine Greene says. "Easiest thing is just walk up to the front door and knock."

"I don't know—" Detective Martinez says.

"It's my case, Tony," Elaine Greene says, glares.

"OK— OK. Never fight the eagle."

"Where Elaine goes, I go," Carmichael says.

"Wait," Martinez says. He moves down the aisle to the galley, returns with two plastic sandwich bags.

"What's this?" Carmichael asks.

"Case you need 'em. Wear 'em like gloves. You don't want to leave finger prints."

"Check your weapons," Duncan Boot says.

Carmichael ejects the magazine from his Glock 17— checks the load.

"Carmichael—" Kimberly says, voice distraught. "If my daddy's out there— don't hurt him. Please—"

Baxter's street is a quiet working class neighborhood, few cars other than a maroon Ford Taurus pulled up in a driveway at the beginning of the block, a black Jeep Cherokee parked at the curb three houses down from Baxter's door.

Carmichael takes a casual look at the Taurus. Nothing catches his eye. But the Cherokee does, specifically the cracked glass radiating out from the small hole in the center of the driver-side window.

Carmichael looks through the windshield, sees a dark form sprawled across the front seat, young, black tee, muscular shoulders.

"Don't like this," he says.

They walk cautiously toward Baxter's front door, draw their weapons, keep them low and hidden from anyone on the street or in neighboring houses.

Heavy drapes are drawn behind the front windows.

"Approaching entry," Elaine Greene whispers into her communicator.

Two concrete stairs lead up to the concrete porch. Elaine Greene pauses, points. Carmichael leans down, touches a black splotch marring the concrete— brings his finger up to his nose.

"Blood," he whispers, shaking his head.

"Question," she responds, "Was the bleeder going out or coming in?"

She points toward the door. It's slightly ajar.

The tiny concrete porch barely frames a near-new black rubber Welcome mat. Wrought iron railings jut out from the framing around the door.

Carmichael touches Elaine Greene's waist, nudges her onto the grass at the base of the porch.

"Cover me," he whispers.

"He steps up to the door, throws it open, moves in low all in one fluid motion, quickly dodging out of the door frame.

"Clear," he says.

Elaine Greene ducks in, stands by his side. They're at the base of a stairway leading to the second-floor. They note a dining room to the left, living room to the right.

Elaine Greene points out two trails of blood, one up the stairs, the other into the dining room.

Cover the living room, Carmichael gestures.

Carmichael glances again up the stairs, surveys the dining room, holding his Glock in standard two-handed grip. Elaine Greene scans the living room to the right, sweeping left-to-right with her .40 mm Smith & Wesson.

Carmichael points toward the dining room. Elaine Greene nods.

He moves fast and low into the dining room, notes the open archway into the kitchen.

"Christ," he whispers. He'd hated urban warfare drills back in the day. Usually they did this crap with a well-trained team.

He moves slowly, quietly to the archway, ready to duck left out of line of fire from the kitchen.

With one quick sweep he sees a door to the far left, presumably to the garage, a cramped kitchenette, and a door to the back yard. But the motionless body on the floor in front of the refrigerator to his right holds his glance the longest— shaved head, young, black tee, torso of a weight lifter.

The eyes are open, wide in surprise.

The trail of blood leads up to the kitchen sink. The sink is stained with blood. The body is in its own pool of blood. Otherwise, the kitchen is spotless.

I really really don't like this, he thinks.

Beyond the body he sees one other door leading, best guess, into a utility hallway, perhaps looping back into the living room.

Carmichael backs through the way he came, moving slowly on tip toes. Elaine Greene looks at him, eyebrows raised. He sweeps his finger across his throat, points to the floor. One down. Elaine Greene's eyes grow wider.

Carmichael points toward the living room. Cover me again he gestures.

The living room is clear, sofa, floor lamp, coffee table, chair, no carpet. Stark, stark. As he guessed, another door leads into a utility hallway. He tiptoes into the hallway, glances left into the kitchen, glances back. He notes an alcove for washer and dryer at the end of the hall, and one door off the hallway— guest bath?

He crouches low, pulls the door open quickly, ready to fire at hostile movement.

As he'd guessed, it's a guest bathroom and empty. Carmichael shivers. He's struck by the cold, utilitarian, featureless character of the house. Like a house maintained by robots for non-human habitation.

He moves into the kitchen, steps over the body, careful not to step in the trail of blood, checks out the garage. The garage is spotless, but for a classic '87 Buick Electra looking showroom new.

He tiptoes back through the kitchen, the dining room, and into the entrance foyer. He nods.

"First floor clear," Elaine Greene whispers into her communicator.

Carmichael gestures toward the stairway. They both know the hazards of stairways. Elaine Greene gestures, "Me first." Carmichael shakes his head vigorously, "No!" Absolutely not. He starts toward the stairs and moves upward, scanning his Glock around the balustrades above his head, then backs down.

"Eagle to Nest," he whispers into his communicator. "We're feeling kind of exposed here. Can you arrange cover of the street from both ends?"

"Got it," he hears "Give us ten."

"Jitters?" Elaine Greene whispers.

Carmichael shakes his head. Moves back up the stairs.

The upper landing is clear. Hardwood floors, new wax reflects pale light. He sees three doors and a linen closet. Two bedrooms and a bath, he guesses. Given the position of the sink downstairs, he's betting that the bath is the middle door. A trail of blood leads from the door on the left to the center door. Another trail leads from the center door to the top of the stairs.

He chooses the left-most door, ducks low, throws it open, sweeping a bloody wool dressing gown across the floor. Smears of blood. He steps across a rumpled blanket, sees a bedroom set up as an office, nothing but bare necessities, desk computer, printer, rolling office chair tipped on its back, four-drawer file cabinet, round file. The desk and file drawers have been pulled out, papers spilled across the floor. More blood. He notes a bloody letter opener.

He checks the closet. Nothing.

He backs out, ducks low, opens the middle door.

"Jesus!" he whispers.

He steps around the blood, kneels, takes a pulse, feels nothing.

He closes the door, checks the second bedroom. It holds a single bed, army blanket stretched drum-tight military fashion, a bedside table, King James Bible, clock radio.

Man must be some kind of monk, Carmichael thinks.

Elaine Greene climbs the stairs, taking care not to step in blood. One glance at General Baxter's naked body— ravages of torture— and she covers her mouth with her hand.

The General's face is puffy and deformed from hard beating. His body and legs are dimpled with puncture wounds, many bleeding.

Elaine Greene's communicator hisses.

"Eagle— Hunter. Hunter. Patrol car just turned onto your block."

"Wait," Elaine says. "There's stuff written on the mirror here—"

"Elaine—" Carmichael says.

"Give me a pen—"

"Don't have a pen."

"A pencil. Anything."

"Elaine! We've got to move—"

"Then remember this—"

"With my memory?"

"Eagle— Hunter. Hunter. Patrol car has pulled in— your location."

"Elaine, now. We're out of time. Please say you locked the front door."

"'July 4 SF.' Got that?"

"'July 4— Today's July 1. We may be too late."

"Keep focused, Carmichael. Here's the next— 'Sat phone pastor,'"

"What does that mean?"

"Just remember."

"I'm trying—"

"Then 'Joshua 6:21,' like a biblical quotation."

"Joshua— wait, there's a Bible in the bedroom."

"OK— OK. 'Joshua 6:21' then 'Tranquility.'"

"Tranquility!" Carmichael says.

"Yes! That mountain in North Carolina!"

"Eagle— Two officers approaching front door—"

"Elaine, look, if we get caught—"

"Shush up and grab that Bible."

"I don't think—" Carmichael starts to say, but at just that moment they hear a sickening crash from the front of the house.

They share glances, skip down the stairs.

"Back door this way?" Elaine Greene asks.

"Yes— no, wait, you go—" Carmichael says.

He turns, runs back up the stairs and into Baxter's bedroom, grabs the Bible, skips back downstairs, and is gone.

C. Norbert Stone

SHIT oh shit oh shit oh shit—
  Won't stop.

His left hand is wrapped in a dish towel soggy with blood, dripping on the mouse-colored seat and gray vinyl floor mat.

More blood fills his mouth, runs down his pudgy jaw, runs down the fat folds of his neck and under his collar, pools up around his ample belly, soaks through his brand new Jimmy Buffet Hawaiian shirt.

He swallows blood, runs his tongue over the ragged hole inside his cheek, winces, remembers the surprisingly painful clang of hard steel against gold inlay.

But the worst is this thing down between his belly button and his prick. Not much bleeding externally, but Lordy there's something not right inside like he needs to evacuate but can't.

Fuck oh fuck—

Now what?

He's hunkered down in his rented Taurus, watching, waiting, trying to think what and where and how without much success. For all his effort, pain, adrenalin, and incipient shock trump logical thought.

He'd prided himself as a field man.

But that was how many years ago?

How many fingers of single malt? Fat Cuban cigars? Celebrity chef meals with greedy bureaucrats in baggy Hart Shaffner Marx suits?

How many booze, broad, and food-fueled Caribbean cruises with ambitious two- and three-stars angling to pad out their retirement years?

How many five-course country club dinners with humorless corporate titans— short white hair, lifeless eyes and rimless glasses, lips like skinny gray earth worms?

343

Field man, what a joke. Fat fuck. Bleeding duck.

Now what?

Cluster fuck.

He moans, stares at a reflection, single point of light.

Intelligence—

The very word had once filled his heart and soul with purpose, meaning, patriotic self regard.

Intelligence— deceive, suborn, penetrate. Save the free world.

All he'd ever wanted was to be a player at the top of the game. The Answer Man.

But the General had played him.

All he'd ever wanted was to enter the shifting shadows. Dance with ghosts. Return triumphantly with what? Truth?

But he'd sipped from the poisoned chalice. Spent the tainted coin.

Think you're one thing— think it as the years roll by only to discover that your core being has rotted out like water-logged timber.

You've lived your life as an evil clown who's betrayed everything that's ever mattered— country, wife, child.

So, what now stupid cluck? 911?

Right.

Arlington National Cemetery just blocks away.

Fuck oh fuck it hurts.

The Answer Man will never be buried in the Arlington National Cemetery, that's for damned sure.

He draws short sharp breaths to ease the throbbing pain.

He'd believed in the General. Believed the General was a certified genius— crusty, yes, quick to rage without a doubt— but an inspired operator.

Here was a true blue patriot, grievously wounded in action but up fighting from his bed of pain. A deeply religious man.

Who could doubt?

Trade weapons for heroin with the enemy? Sure. What better way to get inside, learn the chain of command, set 'em up for ultimate destruction.

Broker the narcotics through ghetto thugs? No brainer. The money can be put to higher purposes, wider field of play, more aggressive operations.

Burn a few good men? Collateral damage. Goes with the territory. All for the sake of the mission. Got to protect the money trail. The General knows what he's doing.

Abandon a beautiful young wife? Steal her baby? Of course. An agent of the enemy for sure. Should have put a .45 slug between her lying eyes. The General had ordered just that. But he'd clutched up. Fucked up, according to the General, and the General had gone ballistic.

The General had played him.

Then, guns silent, the war contentious history, the General had sought him out.

"A proposal, young Stone—"

General Lyman R. Baxter, Pentagon player, formidable father figure— who could doubt?

Buy this company. Money no problem.

Put these men on your board. Sound men. Heed their counsel.

Leave the tedious details to the money men. Your job is on the front line.

Privatize national security. Efficiency. Buy up, take over, merge, force out, cut the bureaucratic fat. Break the unions. It's all for the greater good.

The years roll on. Became less and less what he had once aspired to be and more and more what he was destined to become— nothing more than a bloated puppet yes man, blinded by ambition and pride, an ultimate agent of evil.

His daughter, Kimberly, had seen the progression early on, rebelled, looked upon him with loathing, removed herself from his life.

And he was too filled with himself to see his true self through her innocent eyes.

Well the Answer Man had set out to make himself right in his daughter's eyes.

The Answer Man had set out to find the ultimate nuggets of truth— save the free world.

And, once again, the Answer Man has fucked up.

Once again the General has played him— outplayed him.

Royally.

He'd certainly fucked up with Graham.

Graham had wanted to terminate his daughter— swat her down like a pesky bug. Took fancy dancing to keep her out of his reach. Graham, spider at the center of the network. Pompous ass. Deserved to die. Not to count the Black Hawk business.

But the Answer Man wanted answers more than retribution— free world at stake.

The Answer Man had tracked down Graham— Found him tinkering inexpertly with a propane heater in his forty-foot yacht. No surprise there.

"Gets damned chilly nights on this tub," Graham had said.

"Surprised to see me?"

"Thought you'd be dead by now," Graham had said.

It was clear that Graham had been drinking. Hitting it hard for days.

"Well, you missed."

"Wasn't me, you know. Nothing personal."

"Whatever this thing, it's got to be stopped."

"Thing?"

"Whatever it is that you and Baxter have cooked up."

"Cooked up?"

"Those missiles."

"Dear man, if you had a neuron in your simple skull you'd realize that it's well past the planning stage. But you always were a dim bulb."

"And there's a nuke involved, am I right?"

"Ah the nuke—" Graham said.

"What's with that?"

"Stop it myself if I could," Graham had said. "But can't. God's will."

"Stop what?" the Answer Man had asked.

"Four days—" Graham had said. "Then you'll know. Four days and I won't give a good goddamn."

"You won't give a damn, why?"

"Poof! Somebody else's problem."

"Poof?"

"Two hundred thousand— maybe half a mil— depends on the winds."

"Good God, man. Where?"

"Well, I'd stay well clear of central California—"

"San Francisco?"

"Target zero."

San Francisco— Berkely— An empty face fills his mind— the granddaughter he's never met!

"Berkeley?"

"Fire storm and ashes."

"Tell me!"

"What do you know about propane?"

"Not much—"

"Three carbon alkane. Heavier than air."

"Why you telling me this?"

"Propane on a boat— have to be careful is all."

"Can we stick to the subject?"

"No worry. Had this tank tested just the other day."

"The subject, Graham."

"Ah, the subject—"

And so they sat in that cramped cabin like old friends, the boat swaying ever so gently, water slapping the hull.

"You know," Graham had said, waving his half-filled glass to an unheard rhythm, "Your daughter has had the key all along."

"Those files?"

"Those files, yes."

"Something to do with Baxter?"

"Not Baxter, no. Baxter. Now there's a donkey's ass for you. Refill?"

"Those files— Why so important you wanted her dead?"

"I'm the one who slipped her the files."

"You? Why?"

"Dropped the files into her back-up server. Remotely crashed her workstation. SVS IT recovers her back-up files and, *viola!* Young Miss is holder of the crown jewels— the secret ledgers."

"But why?"

"The nuke thing had gone too far. The nuke changed the calculus. I wanted out."

"So why Kimberly? The files— whatever they are— why not take them to the proper authorities?"

"Authorities?"

"Someone you trust."

"And that would be who exactly? Besides, my fingerprints— Well let's say I needed some kind of implosion— silent solution."

"But you and Baxter sent men to kill her."

"Don't you see? She had to die. God's will. Case closed."

"Why?"

"Look, I figured if Baxter killed your daughter, you'd take out Baxter. Divide and conquer. That simple."

"Graham, give me one good reason why I shouldn't kill you here and now."

"Do me the favor."

"You sent a man to me. His job was to kill my daughter. Am I right?

"God's will, I tell you."

"And you the instrument of God?"

"No. God is Pastor's portfolio."

"Pastor?"

"You don't know?"

"Enlighten me."

"Reverend Cecil B. Tidwell— Been running us all."

"Tidwell? The nutcase radio preacher?"

"Where do you think the money comes from? All those companies you've been sponging up?"

"Wait, those prayer breakfasts Baxter tried to drag me to? That was Tidwell?"

"Baxter's Tidwell's spiritual butt buddy. Don't you get it? They're on a mission. Wipe out evil. Cleanse the Earth— First Babylon by the Bay. Then our illustrious US of A. Will of God."

"That's crazy! al Qaeda crap."

"Monkey see— Monkey do. What'd you think those missiles were all about?"

"Taiwan. Congressional sneak-around. That's what the General told me. General always had some deal cooking."

"Yes, and you his scullery butt boy— See no evil. Hear no evil."

"So what was in this for you— whatever this is?"

"Know what it's like to be the smartest man in the room?"

"Can't say—"

"Every room you enter?"

"Can't imagine."

"Glorious— Would be."

"Glorious?"

"Glorious if weren't for the pea brains, pencil necks, and beta minuses trying to drag you down to their level of imbecility and mediocrity. Mocking you. Taking credit for your best. Find 'em in every room— world's overflowing."

"And you the smartest man in the room—"

"Always. Thought if I applied myself I'd rise above the mud brains. But the higher I rose the deeper the sheer stupidity."

"So you joined up with this Pastor."

"A horse to ride, yes. Pastor had the money. Pastor had the manpower. Baxter had the plan. I figured with a bit of jiggling I could come out on top."

"On top of what?"

"But it went too far— farther than I could bring myself to go."

"Top of what?"

"What do you think?"

"Some kind of nutball subversion? This what we're talking about?"

"Water under the bridge. Wheels falling off anyway. Refill?"

"Wheels?"

"Baxter lost his nerve. Key commanders running for cover. Sending those files to the bloggers was brilliant. That daughter of yours— smarter than I gave her credit. Now they're scurrying into their hidey-holes— 'Who me? Not me!' All the little chickens. At this point— no future for me. Problem, though, fingerprints—"

"Fingerprints?"

"My fingerprints— Too numerous to wipe away."

"So what was in this for you? Money? Power?"

"Me? Running room. Freedom to try out my very best ideas."

"That's it?"

"A tidy little *coup* I could abide. The people are soft. The government up for highest bidder. But this— horror— that Baxter and Pastor cooked up—"

"A nuclear weapon, man. What were they thinking?"

"A clean slate for God."

"That's crazy—"

"Certifiable."

"But this nuke—"

"Can't be stopped. They'll vaporize their sinners. But imagine the tsunami of rage that will rise up against them. Three days from now.

They haven't a fucking clue."

"Must be some way—"

"To stop the nuke?"

"Must be—"

"Need the phone number— sat phone.

"Tell me!"

"Dial up the device. Enter the password. Disarm the trigger— That's what Baxter tells me."

"So what's the password?"

"Ask Pastor."

"And the sat phone number?"

"Pastor."

"Where's this Pastor?"

"Ask Baxter."

"Look, Graham— I just want to know what's going on here. Details."

"What, evidence? Hard proof?"

"For a start. Something I can bring to the right people."

"What people? Tidwell has people everywhere. Who can you trust? Missionaries will take you down within days. You're already a day late and a dollar short."

"I'll find a way."

"Too late, believe me. But look, old man, we're running out of ice. Least we can share a minor victory—"

"Victory?"

"Be a mensch— Late night liquor store just a block down Atlantic Avenue."

"What?"

"Fetch us ice, dear Stone, and I'll give you all the evidence you need to nail Pastor's ass to the wall. Have it here in a safe place."

And so he'd gone for ice. He'd walked two blocks, had just entered the fluorescent glare of the liquor store when the floor lifted like a trampoline sending bottles arcing off the shelves.

"Holy mother!" the liquor clerk said. "What was that?"

He'd run from the store, seen flames lick the sky.

Holy mother is right.

And what did he have?

Ashes.

And then Baxter.

By now the Answer Man is in a state. He'd tried the buzzer next to Baxter's door. No answer. He'd watched the house, seen the Jeep Cherokee pull up, one ape man exit, check the street both ways, then Baxter exit, a second ape man remaining behind the wheel.

Body guards. That's new.

He'd waited. The first ape had opened the front door, checked the house, gestured for Baxter to enter, closed the door.

Nothing simple.

He'd waited.

He thought about his granddaughter. Four days. Too late for finesse. So he'd popped the bodyguard through the driver-side window, quietly picked the lock on Baxter's front door, entered, heard sounds from the kitchen, tip-toed into the kitchen, and popped the startled bodyguard in front of the kitchen sink.

He'd climbed the stairs, found Baxter at his desk all wrapped in a wool dressing gown with a blanket over his shoulders.

"You!" Baxter had said.

"Bad penny."

"Authorities are looking for you, Mister. Get out. I'll give you a ten minute head start."

"Then what? Call the missionaries?"

"They'll crush you like a bug."

"What do you know about the nuke set to vaporize San Fran in three days?"

General Baxter starts to rise.

"Sit!"

"So what do you want?"

"I want it all Lyman– Your files. This Pastor. Everything you know. The nuke. How do we stop it?"

He could see Baxter's anger rise.

"Stop it? You're a fool!"

His hand snakes out, connects hard with Baxter's cheek, knocking Baxter's glasses across the room.

"You're the fool!"

Baxter lunges for his desk, hand grasping a long chrome-plated letter opener.

The Answer Man is slow, lands on Baxter's back, feels sinewy tendons buck with force, then feels cold steel pierce his hand, recognizes pain but doesn't feel it.

They slide off the desk, pulling papers and file folders off onto the floor, up-ending the desk chair. They land on the floor, Baxter rolling onto his back exposing soft white belly.

It all becomes slow motion. He sees Baxter's red freckled fingers tight around the handle of the slender letter opener. Sees the fist rise. He twists to grab, but too slow, the sharp point now red with blood whips around toward his eyes. He jerks his head, feels steel pierce his cheek, clang with great pain against his teeth. He tastes metal and blood.

Baxter is fast. Before he can react the old man pulls the letter opener free of Stone's cheek, swings it around, low, and buries it deeply into Stone's groin.

Leaves him gasping for breath.

Baxter slips out of his heavy robe, scurries through the door on all fours— into the bathroom.

But The Answer Man is close behind. He jams his shoulder into the bathroom door, forcing it open, and now starts pummeling with his fist, deadly sharp horse shoe nail protruding between his middle and ring finger—

THIS IS FOR BETRAYAL AND THIS IS FOR KIMBERLY AND THIS IS FOR MILLY AND THIS IS

—one blow for every word.

"Stop— stop—" the General had squealed, face contorted in pain. "Joshua 6:21."

"What's that?"

"The code."

"What code—?"

"Tranquility—"

"No tranquility for you. I'll see you in hell."

"No— Pastor's retreat."

"And the nuke?"

"Only Pastor can stop it."

And at this moment The Answer Man feels a heaviness in his body, becomes aware of the blood, his blood and the General's merging on the bathroom floor, co-mingling, spreading out along geometric grout lines.

He pulls himself up, gripping the bathroom sink, blood from his hand running down toward the drain. He stares at the entry wound in his cheek, spits blood, explores the exit wound with his tongue. He stares down at Baxter on the bathroom floor, white hair and liver spots, aging fetus, curled up and sobbing, breathing still.

Out of time, he thinks. He dips his finger in blood. Writes what he knows on the mirror.

Once again Baxter has out-played him.

And now, hunched in his rented Ford Taurus, he opens his eyes, senses movement on the street. He rises in the seat, sees Carmichael and Mika— not Mika— Greene, FBI spy, approach Baxter's house, feels a tinge of hope.

They enter. He waits. But then he hears the patrol car whip around the corner, pull up to the curb in front of Baxter's house.

"Shit," he says. "Shit oh shit. Can't have this."

He gathers strength, starts the Taurus, backs out. Then he lines up on the patrol car and steps on it, nearly peeling rubber, hoping that his air bag will fail.

Brother James

THE STONE fireplace, large enough to roast an ox, throws welcome heat, but many still shiver as they listen to Pastor.

"Brother Kevin, denominate the outers if you please."

"Those who deny, those who turn away, those who defy."

"And what is our duty?"

"Those who deny must be shown the way. Those who turn away must be punished. Those who defy must die."

"Why are those who defy an abomination?"

"Those who defy thwart the Lord."

"And why must they die?"

"They thwart the Lord, his Plan, and his Sacred Works."

Seventy three Missionary Youth recruits and their Missionary Sponsors sprawl tired, hungry, and restless on the vast oriental carpet, black tees still drenched in sweat from their pre-dinner five-mile run. Most are thinking about food, soon to be taken quickly in the mess hall, silently, eyes on the plate. Some are thinking of the long night of Bible study before lights out, the short night of sleep, the grueling tests of flesh and spirit that mark their days.

A few dream of the world, escape this place, if they only knew how and where.

But all eyes are on Pastor as he paces among them, oblivious of the sharp day-end mountain breeze that knifes through the open windows of Fellowship Lodge, wafts isotherms of chill around the room.

Brother Simon closes his eyes, prays silently for Pastor. He knows that Pastor means well, is preparing them for the trials ahead, but these spontaneous catechisms have been coming with ever greater frequency and at ever more disruptive times. It's sparked unrest in the bunkhouses, small acts of rebellion. The Missionary Sponsors have been hard pressed to tamp it down, maintain morale.

Well, let those who will turn away as the hour darkens. They will be punished in due course. But he'll stand four-square behind Pastor. Give his life if need be. Just imagine a world without boundaries, division, or strife, a bounteous world of love and fellowship in communion with the Lord. This is Pastor's promise— planet-wide Dominion— a world worthy of the Lord.

Rumors have been flying. Some say Brother Glenn and Brother Alexander have been promoted to heaven. Ruthlessly murdered by outers. All Simon knows is that Pastor sent the Brothers into the world. And all he knows is that they have yet to return.

Some say Reunion is nigh, but judging by the frantic preparations of recent days— arms, ammunition, medical supplies, packaged food, and water in five-gallon glass bottles carried down into the shafts and stacked against the walls, packed into every corner— well, Simon fears something less joyous.

Simon studies Pastor's face. It's aged over the past week. Pastor's eyes have retreated into dark spaces under his brows. Pastor's white hair lacks the slick sheen that makes him so youthful— So vital— So handsome. Lord he loves Pastor.

Simon knows for a fact that Pastor hasn't been sleeping well.

Then, the other day, Pastor had shown rare anger. He'd asked Simon to make call after call on the secure sat phone, but all Simon could come up with was some variation of "The colonel is in a meeting now. The chief will return your call soon."

And with every call Pastor's face had grown tighter and whiter. His eyes had flashed around his office, alighting on one thing and then another. He'd fished in his desk drawer, pulled out an index card. He'd fingered the card, passing it from one hand to the other. At last he'd written a phrase on the card, stared at it, silently mouthed it, then focused on Simon.

"Brother Simon," he'd said, "Behind the Four Horseman you'll find a touch screen. Simply touch the screen and read aloud the phrase on this card and the computer will tell you what to do."

Simon reached for the card, but Pastor held it back.

"No. Not yet. The time will come. Then you shall have it—"

"But then— what must I do?"

"Carry on."

"But you—"

"You must carry on."

Pastor fall? It was beyond comprehension.

"Why me?" Simon had asked, but Pastor had only looked on, his face slowly softening as anger gave way to sorrow.

Later, Pastor had accosted him.

"Remember, Simon," he'd said, "A great ministry is a work of life-times. I've dedicated my life to this ministry— the great work. Are you prepared to lay down yours?"

"Yes, yes, of course," Simon had said.

"Then remember this— people don't flock to your ministry for enlightenment, Simon. Beckon, but don't expect them to come running."

"What then? Why do they come?"

"Fear, Simon. Fear is the secret hold of every great faith."

"Pastor, please— I don't understand."

"The people wallow in enuii and sloth, Simon. They stumble about in selfish self-preocupation, minds clouded in ignorance, arrogance, greed, social frivolity. But our ministry— Our ministry, Simon, is about power. Power. The night brings terrors. The people tremble. Power is their anodyne. People mass behind power to hold fear at bay. History affirms it. From the early Christians to the Mohammedans. From Hitler to Stalin to Mao. Your ministry, as it marches toward Glory— as it purges darkness— as it wields its sword in the name of Dominion, must embody all-embracing power. A great faith must not turn away from blood."

Simon shivers.

"Remember, Simon. Every great faith has been built on rivers of blood."

Simon knows that something is coming, something less than joyful. He prays for his Pastor.

"Lord please give my Pastor strength to prevail."

Brother James fidgets by long habit. His long legs are too gimped with rheumatism to sprawl on the floor. So he's taken one of the burgundy leather divans. He sits straight, his right knee bouncing up and down. He scratches his head, the back of his neck, under his left arm, can't seem to satisfy every itch, but he too follows Pastor's every move, every expression.

He'd die in fire for Pastor. Likely will. Here's the man who had saved his soul in 'Nam— Pastor had found him naked, writhing in his own sweat and urine, trying to kill himself by banging his head on the slimy steel floor of a converted Conex shipping container— Silver City they called it. The pitiless heart of Long Binh Jail, Camp LBJ. Sixty two days in solitary confinement, day after day temperature 110 degrees or more.

Pastor was the first and the only one to discern his secrets— understand his needs and necessities— his need for blessed relief— the blessed relief of the needle to deaden his rage— quell the voices. His even deeper secret— His compulsive all-consuming drive and necessity to impose his will— his rage— to dominate and slaughter the weak and useless.

They'd taught him how to kill. He relished it— Was good at it— But they'd made senseless distinctions. Gook combatants— fine. Innocent gook civilians— don't ask, don't tell. Ignorant loot bastard who sent his bros to stupid death, no. Black Power bastards who beat him senseless in the shower—

He'd killed the loot bastard. He'd killed the demon blacks. He had a taste for it. Hunger. Monkey on his back. Powerful need. He had a need to kill again and again and would, you watch, he'd told Pastor. A secret craving stronger than his hunger for the needle.

Pastor had counseled him through his stay in the stockade. Testified at his court marshal. Visited him in the federal penitentiary. Fought for his parole.

Pastor had brought him to the Lord. Tutored him. Returned him to his warrior roots.

"Brother James," he'd said, "Your needs are a gift from the Lord. The Lord will provide."

"But," Pastor had said, "You must offer yourself up— submit and obey."

And he had.

Many times since— yes— many times he has killed. Yes— But strictly in the Lord's name. Pastor's bidding.

Fact be told, he's lost his edge for blood.

Sure— those who deny deserve to die, he thinks. And others too— the blood-sucker bureaucraps in Washington with no sense of honor, the shiftless and the lazy sucking off the welfare teat, the world banker Jews, and the colored filling the cities with devil spawn.

But he'd leave the mopping up to others. And mopping up there'd surely be.

But first, the Big Enchilada. He must gird himself— prepare for the Big Enchilada. He's a Missionary Commander— leader of men forged as one into an elite unit. Stone cold ninja killers for the Lord. And he was damned proud of it.

Used to be, anyway.

But still, it's coming— The Big Enchilada. Of that Brother James can say for sure.

He knows about the missing files. He'd found the computer breach.

He knows about the Jezebel, Devil's Whore. He'd pursued her.

He knows about Apostate Stone. He'd set the trap that failed. Lord knows how.

He knows about Brother Baxter and Brother Graham, may they burn in hell fire.

And he knows about the Big Enchilada.

He'd studied the blueprints, helped plot the course, knows how to shut it down. And maybe he should. Doesn't see what good it will do now.

"The outers are massing," Pastor had said.

He, Brother James, had answered, "We'll be ready."

But he has his doubts. Too many snafus. What had once felt like a glide to glory now felt like— what the hell— face it— this ship is going down.

"Top men like you— Rock of my ministry," Pastor used to tell him. But where now— these top men? Hiding under rocks. Pursued by pigmies.

Brother James is head of security. He'd doubled the guard on the road in, mapped lines of fire with his squad leaders, checked and double checked weapons readiness, the mine fields, inventoried and secured supplies— enough for three months at least. And if three months aren't enough, well, he has contingencies for that too.

The sanctuary. He'd set the charges around entrances.

But, still, he can't shake the feeling— ominous— something forgotten— something overlooked. If life has taught him one thing, every power ultimately bows to higher power.

Pastor claims to speak for the highest power of all. But— What— If—?

Brother James tries to pray, but he's never quite found the knack, the very impulse interrupted every time by spiders crawling across his skin— an urgent need to scratch.

Just one day to go.

Mickey Rourke lifts the iron fry pan, swirls hot grease over the sizzling bacon. He glances up, sees Carmichael pushing in through the dense stand of hemlocks.

Boswick is pouring a cup of coffee from the speckled blue pot on the Coleman stove.

"Who's your young friend?" he asks as Carmichael pushes a skinny young boy into the clearing. The boy's wrists are bound. The boy's face is defiant, tears running down through cammo grease.

"Won't tell me his name," Carmichael says. "Tried to kill me up on the mountain."

"Well I'd try to kill you too," Boswick says, "Bind my wrists like that. What's your name, son."

The boy looks away.

"Let me cut you loose there, must hurt something fierce— those wrist ties. Now why'd you go and do that, Carmichael? Bind the boy up like that?"

"Careful—" Carmichael says.

Boswick steps forward. The boy backs into Carmichael.

Elaine Greene steps down from the school bus.

"Who's this?" she asks.

The boy slams an elbow into Carmichael's stomach, tries to twist away.

"Whoa, there," Carmichael says, grabbing the boy's bony shoulder.

"Look, son," Boswick says. "We're friends here. You hungry? Got some grits cookin' up here. Spent the night in the woods did you? Hunting were you?"

The boy spits.

"Well, if you like," Boswick says, "We can tie you to that tree over there while we have our breakfast. Then we can figure out what to do with you. Maybe find your folks. Take you home."

"Let me go," the boy says.

"Well Carmichael here says you tried to kill him."

"Outers!" the boy yells. "Filthy outers! Damn you all to hell!"

"Outers? New one to me. You, Carmichael?"

Elaine Greene steps over, kneels down in front of the boy. The boy shrinks away.

"Hi," she says. "I'm Elaine Greene. You can call me Elaine. What's your name?"

The boy is silent.

"Come on— Won't hurt. You can tell me."

"Brother Jonathan," the boy whispers.

"How old are you, Jonathan?"

The boy shakes his head.

"Won't tell me?"

"Don't know—" the boy whispers.

Elaine Greene looks up at Carmichael.

"When was your last birthday?"

The boy looks at her, vacant.

"Well tell you what, Jonathan," she says, "Suppose I bring you soap and nice warm water. You can clean up and we'll all have a delicious breakfast— hot. Sound good to you?"

The boy looks over at the bacon sizzling in Mickey Rourke's iron fry pan.

"That food tainted?"

"Tainted?"

"Pastor forbids tainted food."

"No, that's bacon," Elaine Greene says, "Perfectly fresh."

"Bacon—" the boy says. "Never heard of it."

"Boy, are you in for a treat!" Mickey Rourke says.

"This your rifle? Carmichael asks, holding up the weapon.

"Yes, sir," the boy says.

"What kind of rifle is this?"

"M16 5.56 caliber, air-cooled, gas-operated, magazine-fed assault rifle."

"You kiddin' me? Must be pretty heavy carrying around in these steep hills."

"Not so bad."

"You a good shot, Johnny?"

"Brother Jonathan!"

"So you a good shot, Brother Jonathan?"

"Fair to middlin'"

"Fair to middlin'? Bet you're damned good. A boy like you."

"Others better."

"Tell you what— See that bole in that tree down there a ways?"

"Bowl, sir?"

"That big knot in the tree down there— Where the branch broke off."

"Which tree? That ol' dead tree?"

"Yes sir."

"Can't see no knot, sir."

Carmichael turns to Boswick.

"Like I figured," Carmichael says, "Boy needs glasses. Reason he missed me. "

"How'd you figure?"

"Squints at everything."

"Your lucky day," Boswick says.

"Had to wonder why he missed," Carmichael says. "Easy shot. Well within pistol range."

"Don't need no damned glasses," the boy says.

"So, boy," Boswick says, "Tell me about your people. Where you from? What you all doing up on that mountain?"

Carmichael

SLEETY RAIN drives wet cold into Carmichael's core. Icy runoff splashes into his face, weakens his grip on the rocky face. Perfect weather for an assault if he can only make it up this damn mountain.

He shivers.

He's well past the 520 foot scramble up scree, well into the 310 feet of fractured granite; not vertical, but close enough to make free climbing a throught-provoking proposition.

"Too dangerous," Elaine Greene had said, running her finger across the crowded contours of the geodetic survey map. "I can't let you do this."

"We can make it," Carmichael had argued.

Never figured on drenching rain, water sluicing into his face, icy finger holds.

He tests his toehold in the rock, takes a step up, but his foot slips on gritty slush. He accelerates down the rocky face, stomach flips as he grabs for a scraggly spruce, tenacious roots entangled deeply into a crevice. He hangs for a second, shuffling for a toe hold.

The cold sends needles of pain through his fingers. Blood pounds in his ears. His breath starts up again, but comes hard. He feels his finger strength wane, lactic acid burn in his bicep.

He pulls himself up, sees Duncan Boot scrambling up behind him. He secures himself in the crevice, reaches down, gives Boot a hand.

"Say one thing," Duncan Boot says, "This sucks big time."

Boot is carrying nearly twice Carmichael's weight— a launcher and an Impaler missile strapped over the top of his already weapon-laden backpack— one of three snatched by Elaine Greene.

"Affirmative," Carmichael says.

"Daniel Boone make it up OK?"

"If not, boy would have whistled on the way down."

"Wouldn't count on it— This wind and rain— wouldn't have heard 'im if he did."

"Then, let's hope."

"Ready?" Boot asks.

"Need a minute—"

"Take your time."

"Need to warm my hands here."

Carmichael has always considered himself a simple man— take what comes and deal with it. But ever since he woke to find Mrs. Phan in his hospital room life has grown ever more— what?

He's had ever more conflicting thoughts, anxious dreams, felt things stirring, unfamiliar longings. Say one thing, life with Stanley was predictable— safe in its way— comfortable even.

What does he owe Mrs. Phan? What does he owe anybody? How did this come to be— hanging by fingers and toes on this fucking mountain in this mother fucking rain?

When did this become his fight?

Well it surely is his fight now. And it surely is personal. That he knows. It's the right goddamn thing to do. Somehow Elaine Greene made it so. Elaine Greene. The future— He'd never given the future much thought. He was a day-to-day man. But somehow Elaine Greene made the future matter. Not only Elaine— Mrs. Phan— Kimberly— the whole damn bunch of them. His country for that matter, whether it wanted him or not. If the future didn't matter— his future— their future— he might as well push off this nasty little crevice— push off into the void.

Maybe he'll die tonight, he thinks. Good chance. But if so, Lord, please, make it matter.

"I'm off," he says to Boot.

Mickey Rourke kneeling on one knee, gives them a hand as they scramble over the rocky lip.

"Man 'o man, don't ask me to do that again," Mickey Rourke says.

"Pussy," Duncan Boot says.

"Maybe. Maybe not," he says, "But I see a tad of white around your ugly gills."

"Lyin' if I denied it."

Fellowship Lodge is dark. Off through the rain they see faint yellow light.

"That's the barracks," Mickey Rourke says. "Most are asleep I think."

"Guards?" Carmichael asks.

"None that I've spotted this side of the compound. But sandbag emplacements on the other side of the parade ground— guards posted— perfect line of fire on the road in."

"And the meadows there? Land mines? Like the kid said?"

"Didn't exactly wander out to test it"

"Well, let's assume. Scope out the generator shed yet?"

"Yes, sir— Yonder. Just beyond the barracks there."

"And the armory?"

"Not sure— Kid's map wasn't exactly scale. But I'm bettin' on that concrete block structure over there."

Carmichael nudges Duncan Boot.

"What think?"

"Call it wrong call— hot time for damn sure."

"Next to the pistol range. Got to be the armory."

"Best to confirm. How long before D'Mello's team sets off the diversion?"

Mickey Rourke presses the button on his watch, lights up the dial.

"Two minutes," he says.

And just now, they hear a soft pop and the whang of a jacketed slug ricocheting off the boulder to their left.

Carmichael slams Mickey Rourke and Duncan Boot down hard, covers them.

A door opens on the near end of the barracks, sending a flood of pale light into the rain.

"What was that, son?" a voice yells. "I hear you firing your weapon again?"

"A light, sir. A light over yonder."

"Nothing over that way but empty space. Sure it wasn't lightning?"

"No, sir. Saw something— a light flash."

"Shooting star? UFO?"

"Sir—"

"You're always seeing something, son. Now straighten up and fly right. Don't fire 'til you see the whites of their eyes."

"Sorry," Mickey Rourke whispers. "Missed that one."

"Hate to say it," Duncan Boot says, "Kid's got to go."

"Let's wait 'til the diversion," Carmichael says. "I'm betting that'll distract him."

"Then what?" Boot asks.

"You call it, Big Guy," Carmichael says. "This is your kind of show."

Duncan Boot lifts his ball cap, runs his hand over his shaved head.

"OK, remember," he says, "We've got to do this one, two three— Carmichael, you and Daniel hit the barracks with tear gas and flash-bangs. I'll take out the armory with the Impaler. Havoc is what we want here, not bloodshed. Daniel Boone, think you can disable the generator without getting yourself killed?"

"Bet on it."

"Well, careful, youngster. We need you for the next movie. "

"What if they panic back this way— get between us and the objective?"

"I'll lay down suppression fire, maybe a taste of tear gas, doubt it'll do much good though— with this rain. Maybe it'll drive them down toward D'Mello."

Now it all happens fast.

Carmichael abandons thought for automatic pilot.

The sky beyond the barracks flashes green and orange as a thousand dollars worth of fireworks detonate at once.

They see lights blink on, hear sustained fire open up on the far side of the barracks.

Carmichael sprints in toward the barracks, zig zagging, knocks the young guard to the ground, likely hurting him, kicks his weapon into the dark, binds his wrists with nylon cable ties.

Mickey Rourke sprints by, shattering glass window after window with flash-bangs and gas grenades.

Carmichael hears a loud whoosh echo off the barracks wall, drops to the ground and buries his head as flash-bangs and missile warhead light up the slashing rain. He forces his cheek into the hard rocky ground as concussions cry havoc into the night.

Carmichael hears screams and harsh voices. The generator kicks on, bringing faint light, then dies. Carmichael hears Duncan Boot's whistle, rises and sprints toward the narrow gap between the Fellowship Lodge and the mountain face. He nearly collides with Mickey Rourke.

"Cover us, Rourke," Carmichael says. He now has a small Maglite in his hand and is moving toward the mine entrance, cone of light bouncing, but suddenly he stops.

"Shit!" he says. "Kid never told us about this."

"What's up?" Duncan Boot whispers.

"Steel door. Solid. Some kind of blast door."

Carmichael's hand is shaky. The bluish-white circle of LED light dances across the steel, settles in on a rusting steel panel with well-worn push buttons.

"What think?" Boot asks.

"We're screwed."

"Wait!" Boot says.

They hear the loud thunk of a relay and a heavy duty motor start to grind.

Carmichael dashes the light, pushes Boot against the rock wall.

The steel door slides open— slowly— man wide, then stops. A dark figure, rifle ready, steps out with caution, but drops as Carmichael slams a rifle butt into the back of his head.

"Geez, just a kid," Boot says.

"Grab the rifle," Carmichael says. He whistles for Mickey Rourke. "Status?"

"Like you said. Havoc. Kids screaming and bawling, rubbing their eyes. Older guys trying to herd 'em."

"Can you hold this position?"

"Bear shit in the woods?"

"Don't get cocky on us now, Boone. They press too hard, lay down tear gas then follow us down the tunnel."

Now Carmichael and Duncan Boot slip through the door.

Buzzing fluorescent lights illuminate a curving tunnel walled with gray concrete. Boxes and kegs and bottled water line the walls.

"Don't like this," Carmichael says.

"Roger that," Boot says. "Stick to the center of the tunnel. Slugs tend to ricochet down the walls. Just keep low."

They make their way down through the tunnel, near silent, pause when a voice echoes up toward them.

"Brother Simon!"

They hear heavy boots jogging fast in their direction.

They drop to the concrete floor.

"Lights!" Duncan Boot whispers

Carmichael takes out the overhead lights with short bursts. As the lights die, sudden black, they see orange streamers; Carmichael's slugs ricocheting down the tunnel.

"Stop! Stop firing!" the voice echoes. "Who's there?"

"Night vision," Duncan Boot whispers, but Carmichael is already ahead of him. The strap behind his head is twisted, but he lets it go.

Now the tunnel jiggles in green.

"Careful," Duncan Boot gestures.

They move forward, hugging the wall, just in time to see a green figure duck through another blast door. They hear a loud relay thunk and a whine and the door starts to slide closed, but Duncan Boot sprays the metal control panel with lead. The door stops, but now they're hit with return fire ricocheting wildly up the tunnel.

Carmichael covers with suppressing fire while Duncan Boot sprints toward the steel door, drops to the floor and slides in under Carmichael's line of fire. He glances quickly into the dim light through the door, then gestures for Carmichael to move in.

They're into fluorescent light again. They remove their night vision, see a dark figure disappear down metal-tread stairs.

They follow, check out a small room to their right, see one chair, a large gloomy painting hanging askew.

They enter a spacious office, wood paneled walls, but back out hacking. The smoke is thick and overwhelming. Carmichael ducks back in, holding his breath, squints at smoke and flame rising out of opened file and desk drawers.

Duncan Boot pushes up from behind.

"Where?" he asks.

Now Carmichael notices smoke swirling away from the base of a large mahogany credenza. Holding breath, they push the credenza aside. A gentle breeze hits them, coming through an opening into black space.

"Careful," Carmichael says. "Tight squeeze."

Duncan Boot stands against the wall, bends for a quick look through the opening, sweeps his Maglite across the dark space beyond.

They wait beside the opening, listening, but now their lungs are convulsing with the acrid bite of burning plastic— stench of burning wool.

Duncan Boot ducks a second time, sweeps the light more slowly across the black.

Carmichael pushes him aside.

"Cover me," he says and dives through the opening.

"Tight squeeze," Duncan Boot says as he follows.

Their Maglites criss cross gray timbers and stone walls.

Carmichael pats cold concrete at his back.

"End of new construction," he says. "But air smells fresh— Coming this way. Feel the breeze? Must be another opening somewhere."

"According to that mine plan Jeremy dug up, this mountain is tunneled out like Swiss cheese."

"Could use that map now," Carmichael says.

Duncan Boot sweeps his light over the timbers shoring up the stone ceiling.

"Rot," he says. "Could give any minute. Sure we want to go further?"

Duncan Boot clicks off his light. Faint glow of orange flame flickers through the opening, casts strange shadows across the dark chamber. They feel the oppressive weight of the mountain, tons of stone over their heads.

"Listen—" Carmichael says.

From far down the tunnel they hear a voice calling— "Pastor—!"

"Night vision," Duncan Boot says.

Carmichael nods.

They move down the tunnel, step by cautious step.

Carmichael stops, takes off his glove, places his palm against the stone wall, sees his fingers dimly green in his night vision. The wall is cold and wet. He kneels, runs his fingers across the floor, realizes that they've been walking in a thin layer of gritty mud.

He stands, reaches up, feels water trickle down his wrist.

"What?" Duncan Boot says.

Carmichael shrugs.

They continue, come to a section where timbers have failed. Stone rubble blocks the tunnel waist high.

"Sure we don't want to give this a re-think—?" Duncan Boot asks.

"Never did like Frisco," Carmichael says. "All that fog."

"Right—" Duncan Boot says. "After you,"

The faint voice, echoing, draws them forward.

"Pastor—! tor—! or—!"

They move toward the voice, boots splashing water.

Now water seeps down the timbered walls, collects into rivulets winding down through the tunnel.

"Wait," Carmichael says. "A side tunnel."

They explore the side tunnel, hit a blank wall.

They move out and on.

More side tunnels.

"This must be the heart of the working mine," Carmichael says.

They continue. Explore more side tunnels.

They come to a Y.

"Which way?" Carmichael asks.

Then they hear the voice again— echoing.

"Pastor—! tor—! or—!"

They follow the voice.

Now they're ankle deep in cold water, a persistent current tugs at their feet.

They hear a loud rumble, hear a scream.

A dense cloud of dust rolls up toward them, engulfs them.

They hurry down through the dust, coughing.

They find a man sprawled face up in the water, pinned under rock and timber.

"Forget me," he says. "Pastor— Down that a way. Took the wrong turn."

They move on. The current feels stronger. Grit and small stones slip out from under Carmichael's soles.

And now they see Tidwell— clinging to a wall timber, water rushing past his knees. Tidwell's face is smeared with mud— old fashioned briefcase clutched in the crook of his arm, a pistol in his fist.

The water is rushing into a vertical shaft, solid stone beyond. The sound of falling water fills the dark tunnel with a hollow roar.

"Who's there?" Tidwell calls.

"Hold on," Carmichael says.

"And you, sir? You are—?"

"Carmichael. Hang on, sir—"

"Give me light—" Carmichael whispers.

Duncan Boot flips up his night vision goggles, clicks on his Maglite.

Tidwell squints. Carmichael knows that Tidwell can't see behind the blinding light, but he still feels Tidwell's piercing eyes.

Tidwell snaps off a shot. Carmichael hears the echoing pop, feels the wind of a passing slug.

Duncan Boots raises his weapon.

"Easy," Carmichael whispers. "We need this nutcase— Alive."

"Pull that again, Tidwell," Carmichael yells, "And you'll join the devil that spawned you."

"Carmichael— I know you, sir. Apostate terrorist."

"You know me?"

"To the depths of your sinful soul, sir. Army washout. Small-time criminal. Terrorist."

"And this you know— how?"

"Make it my point—"

"But how?"

"The Lord provides."

"Let's discuss it. We can pull you out of there—"

"Prefer not."

Carmichael hears another pop, hears a ricochet off the stone wall behind his head. He sends a burst of fire into the water at Tidwell's feet.

"Best you can do?" Tidwell yells. "I'd wagered better."

"Next time— your knees."

Now there's silence.

"Make it easy on yourself Tidwell—"

"We're not so different," Tidwell yells, "You and me—"

"That so—"

"Warriors— To the bone— Least you were once— So they say—"

"So they say—"

Carmichael flicks his light across the rushing water.

"Puke," Duncan Boot says. "Let's take him out."

"Hold back. We've got to talk him out. No other way."

"But there's one big difference," Tidwell yells.

"And that is?"

"I fight for souls— The immortal soul of mankind. I can fight for you. What banner you?"

"Pretty talk."

"I speak for God!"

"That so?"

"Power-mad psycho," Duncan Boot whispers.

"The Lord asks again— What banner you?"

"The innocent."

"None are innocent."

"'Til proven guilty. Law of the land."

"We're all damned. His law— True law."

"And you speak for him."

"That I do, sir. Only He can save us."

"And he says?"

"Offers grace."

"Grace?"

"Come to Him."

"Watch him," Duncan Boot whispers. "He's cookin' up something."

"Join His mighty army."

"And why would I do that?"

"You know well. Save your sinner soul. You're one step from eternal fire—"

"Says you—"

"Come to Him! Save your immortal soul, man. Time is nigh— Eternal grace. Riches beyond imagining."

"I think not—"

"You defy Him!"

"You've perverted him."

"I speak for Him!"

Tidwell's foot slips. He clings to the timber.

"Let us help you—"

"The Lord will smite you— smite you all!"

"Bring him on, little man," Duncan Boot yells.

"He's calling— Hear Him!"

"I hear a pathetic little Osama bin Ladin wanna-be— cowering in a filthy cave."

"You'll roast in Hell's fires, my son."

"What do you think?" Boot whispers.

"I'd say fuck 'im. But then there's Frisco."

"I hear you," Tidwell cries. "Frisco— What do you know?"

"Know it all."

"Too late—"

"How do we stop it?"

"Lord's will!"

Tidwell brings his watch close to his face.

"Seventeen minutes— Less— Sixteen. His will be done."

"Your will— You can stop it."

"Luke 12:49— 'I am come to send fire on the earth.'"

"You twisted fuck!"

"Joshua 6:21— 'And they utterly destroyed all that was in the city, both man and woman, young and old—'"

Tidwell looks triumphant.

"Behold! The Lord at his Sacred Last!"

"You'd let children die?"

"Spawn of iniquity! My Lord judges all!"

Carmichael edges down the tunnel, water tumbling around his calves. He edges toward the wall, reaches out for a supporting timber.

Tidwell's foot slips again.

"Grab him!" Duncan Boot says.

"Oh shit," Carmichael says.

Carmichael reaches, but rushing water sweeps his feet out from under— starts to fall, but Boot grabs, holds tight.

Tidwell's hold fails. They watch him fall, watch in horror as Tidwell and his briefcase tumble through the roiling froth— down into the black maw of the vertical shaft.

"Shit," Carmichael says.

Carmichael stares into Duncan Boot's face, a shadow in the dim reflections of their Maglites.

He sees utter exhaustion.

"What now?"

"Damned if I know," defeat heavy in his voice.

They make their way through the tunnel— back to the man trapped under stone and timber.

They see blood, near black in the bluish white light of their Maglites.

"Pastor dead?" the man whispers.

"Dead," Duncan Boot says.

"Pastor— great man."

"Evil looney."

"Chosen."

"Can you move your toes?"

"'No tea and crumpets—' Pastor said. Work of the Lord."

"We'll get you out of here— hurt bad?"

"Yes— No— hurts, mostly numb— numb and so damned cold."

"Look, I've got paracetamol here. Maybe it'll help."

"No," the man says.

They lift stone and timbers. The man screams as stones shift in configuration, exert new pressures.

"Leave me—" the man whispers.

"Sorry," Duncan Boot says. "Can't do. What's your name, sir?"

"It's all crap. My life is crap."

"Why?"

"Pastor gone—"

"What's your name?"

"James— Brother James."

"I'm Carmichael. This here is Boot— Duncan Boot."

"Yes— the terrorists."

"You know?"

"Everything."

"How?"

"Followed your every move."

"Then you know why we're here."

"The Big Enchilada—"

"The what?"

"*El Diablo Negro.*"

"The nuke, yes. What do you know about it?"

"Everything."

"It must be stopped—"

"No way. Need a sat phone."

"Sat phone?"

"Kill switch— Activated by sat phone."

Carmicheal stares at Boot.

"And you know the number?"

Brother James nods.

"Topside," Carmicheal says, hoisting James up into a fireman carry.

"Let me," Boot says, "Die on us, Brother James, I'll kill you myself."

"Nine minutes," Carmichael says.

"Nine minutes—" Boot grunts, "Go! Go! Go!"

El Diablo Negro

G REEN FOAM swirls over black steel as *El Diablo Negro* parts the two-foot swell, surfaces into low fog for it's final position fix.

Electrons resonate in the stubby antenna at the stern of the hull, flow through black coaxial cable into the GPS receiver embedded in a VLSI IC mounted on a four-by-four-inch circuit board protected from shock by black foam blocks wedged into the tight confines of the black hull.

The receiver demodulates and detects five satellite sources, computes precise coordinates, and locks them into registers in the fist-size navigational computer.

Simultaneously, a modified sat phone dials out, transmits high frequency data packets, a simple query, through its own mini antenna.

The faint 2-gigahertz rf signal travels 22,500 miles into space, is captured by a 60-foot antenna attached to the TerreStar-1 communication satellite parked in synchronous orbit over North America. TerreStar-1 relays the packets back down to an earth station in Las Vegas, Nevada, which, in turn, switches them into the AT&T TCP/IP network.

AT&T routes the TCP/IP packets through a cross-continental backbone cable network to a Comcast router that, in turn, sends them through a local loop to a non-descript glass-faced office building in Arlington, Virginia.

A router in the basement of the building, in turn, activates a tiny black box hidden in the recesses of a seldom used utility closet on the sixth floor.

The black box is no larger than a deck of playing cards.

The tiny box now switches off hook, negotiates a hand-shake response, then sends a simple encoded signal back into cyberspace.

Abort.

Epilogue

"SIGN ON this line here, please," the well-groomed secretary says. "—and here."

They're each handed a copy of the document.

They make room for Avery Greene to roll up to the desk, sign his copy. He rolls back, then they each edge up in turn to sign their own copies. Last to sign is Consuela Martinez.

"You understand that this document pledges you to absolute secrecy over the matters at hand," the secretary says.

Now the smiling secretary ushers them to the white door, opens it.

"Ladies and gentlemen," she says. "The President of the United States."

The President greets them with a winning smile.

"Mr. Carmichael?"

Carmichael nods.

"Our nation owes you an apology— and profound gratitude."

The President extends his hand. Carmichael hesitates. Then accepts.

The President nods with respect, smiles again to take in the whole group.

"You know, the courage and ingenuity of the American people is a constant source of inspiration for me. On behalf of the United States and its citizens I offer you our deepest gratitude. I only wish the world could know your feats of courage and heroism. These medals— well, they're not much, not nearly enough to express our thanks."

He hands out the medals, a personal comment with each.

"Mrs. Bolton—" he bows slightly, holds her hand.

"They tell me that you had a particularly hard time of it. But that list of names you smuggled out— let me tell you, that list turned the tide."

379

"Mr. Boot," he says, "Once again this nation owes you."

They look at Duncan Boot in surprise.

"Oh, yes," the President says, "Mr. Boot has stepped into harms way many times on our behalf. He kept us informed of your challenges and amazing feats at every step of the way. I could trust no one else."

He turns to Mrs. Phan.

"Mrs. Phan, your daughter is one courageous woman. And Mr. Boot tells me that she's a chip off the block."

Mrs. Phan looks puzzled. "Chip off block?"

"Takes after you."

"Best daughter whole world." Mrs. Phan says.

"And this your lovely granddaughter!"

Kimberly's daughter blushes.

The President stops them as they're gathering to depart.

"By the way, Ms. Greene," he says, "I understand that Mr. Carmichael has asked for your hand."

Elaine Greene blushes.

"Well, sir, fact be told— I asked him."

"And?"

"We're thinking about it," Carmichael says.

COMING SOON... A new thriller by Lloyd R. Prentice

El Tiburon

"Abuelo— ¿Dónde está mi papá?"

The man, face of weathered mahogany, sighs, lifts his eyes toward the deep blue sky, fixes on two turkey buzzards gliding on high thermals.

"You know this, *mi chico*. We've talked of this."

The grandson, Enrique, bounces on the man's lap, tugs a pearl snap on the man's Western shirt— the shirt that once fit snugly.

"But where, *Abuelo?* This heaven— Where is it?"

The man's calloused hand wraps around the boy's tiny fingers, lifts them to his lips. So perfect, he thinks, so pure, *inocente*.

The boy pulls his hand free, slaps the man's shoulder.

The man raises his eyebrows, points toward the sky.

"There, *mi chico*," he says. "*Su papá* is with the saints and the angels."

"But I look, *Abuelo*— I see nothing. *Pero no veo nada.* I look so hard. "

"The sun, you see it?"

"Si—"

"The sun burns forever. Maybe this heaven is behind the sun."

"No— No, Abuelo. The sun is just fire."

The man looks at his grandson with surprise.

"You know this how?"

"La televisión— I see this on *la televisión.*"

"And you believe this *televisión*?"

"Si, Abuelo. They say this on *la televisión* . It must be true."

"So maybe you need special eyes to see this heaven— holy eyes."

"Do you have holy eyes, *Abuelo*? Can you see *mi papá* in this heaven?"

The man cannot lie.

"No, *mi chico*, I cannot see this heaven. But this I know— *es verdad! Su papá* is in this heaven. *Su papá* is with the saints. With the angels."

"¡No— No! Abuelo. I don't believe you. I want *mi papá*! I want *mi papá* now!"

The boy pounds the old man's frail chest with his tiny fists.
The man wraps his arms around the boy, holds him tight.

Now the man stares toward the *casa de rancho*—crumbling white
Spanish colonial. They're all there now, gathered like squawking geese
in the *cocina, sala de estar*, shade of the *portico*, leaning back on sturdy
chairs, Negra Modelo and Pacifico bottles dangling from their fat fingers, talking, scheming. He hears the *corridos*, now slow and sad. They're
all there telling their exaggerations and lies. Some, he knows, are stuff-
ing their nostrils with the cursed white powder.

The boy is sobbing. The man kisses the top of his head, smells his
earthy scent. The man shifts his weight on the straw bale, twists to stare
across the once comforting landscape, now a temporary parking lot,
harsh sun glinting off haphazardly parked pick-ups and SUVs, many
new, here and there a battered Volkswagen Beetle, beyond, tied down
on the make-shift airstrip, small aircraft, helicopters, a *jet corporativo*,
corporate jet.

This heaven, what can I know of it the man wonders? I can hope—
pray that *mi hijo*— this *muchacho's papá*— *mi primer nato*— is in this place
now.

But it's a matter of grave doubt.

La Cobra they called him. Outside the family he was ruthless— ruthless, relentless, and cruel. The man had warned him many times— "You
go too far, *mi hijo*," But now— now it's too late to make it right.

So what is it that this man knows for sure?

He knows faint trails through the mountains, how to hide things in
cars, trucks, airplanes, and boats of all sizes. Guns. He knows more
about guns than he ever wanted. And he's had to learn about the *com-
putadoras*— computers, secret codes, and the underground rivers, ebbs
and flow of filthy black *dinero*. Who to pay and how much.

This business the man knows like the back of his gnarled hand—
this business that was started by his own *abuelo*, a man of the earth
driven to desperation by drought and intractable mountain soil. It was
once an easy business— a business of trust among distant cousins and
close friends, *primos y amigos*. But no more. Now it's war— drive-by
assassinations, torture, and decapitations over the raging flow of black
dolares— *dolares* that rot the soul of every *hombre* who sets foot in the

stream.

This hellish business that has taken his first born.

But this heaven, he wonders— what can I know of it?

This I know, he thinks: With the things I've done it's a thing of certainty— it's the other place for me.

Dios, ahorra por favor a este nieto los míos. God, please spare this grandson of mine.

They come in the night. Flashbangs through the windows. Cries and curses. Chatter of guns. He shoves his fat wife off the bed, reaches under his pillow for his pistol but can't find it. They enter his room. Blinding light. He rolls off the bed to cover his wife, Graciela, to protect her, tries to push her under the bed but fails.

They scream beyond understanding, strike him with rifle barrels, kick him. One kick misses. Graciela screams. They drag him across the floor, shackle his hands behind his back with plastic ties, shroud his head. They duck-walk him through the sounds of aggressive confusion, shattering crockery, obscenities and whimpers of surprise and pain.

They load him forcefully into a vehicle, drive fast for hours over unpaved tracks, slamming into ruts and over hard-pan corrugations, bringing pain to his back and kidneys. He wets himself. They stop, drag him from the vehicle. He smells aviation fuel. They lift his hood. It's early dawn. Pink and turquoise sky. He sees the helicopter, rotor turning slowly. He sees the men around the open bay door, sees their blue jackets— DEA. He struggles, fights as best he can. But they're young. Fit. Armed with CAR A4 assault rifles.

A stringy man, face hard under his blue ball cap, pushes forward.

"Hector Javier Godinez, *El Tiburón. Hola mi amigo.* You are one wily SOB, I'll give you that."

Made in the USA
Charleston, SC
23 May 2012